KANSAS WILDFIRE

"What I mean is," Rhiannon continued, "I believe there are things I can do in this town that will really make a difference, Hank. But I have to be mayor to do them."

"And you can't do them if you're married and a mother?"

Rhiannon stroked his forearm and frowned. "This is all very confusing, Hank."

"Why don't you tell me about it, and maybe we can sort it out together."

"Here goes. We can't make love anymore because we're not married, and I don't want to have a baby."

"Okay. We won't."

Rhiannon stared at him blankly. "We won't?"

"No. Not if that's what you want."

She looked at him askance. Was he teasing her? She'd expected a fight, a declaration of love, of marriage, but certainly not simple acquiescence. Did she mean nothing to him? Left with no other choice, she said, "It's what I want."

"There that wasn't so hard, was it?"

She looked at his smiling face for long seconds. "Hank Wolfe, you go to hell!"

Other *Leisure Books* by Cheryl Anne Porter:
JESSIE'S OUTLAW

Kansas Wildfire

CHERYL ANNE PORTER

LEISURE BOOKS NEW YORK CITY

To Paul—always....
To Pauline Warren Deal, my mother,
who is quite possibly more excited by all this than I am.
To Fleetwood Mac, for years of music and inspiration
and for "Rhiannon," a song that inspired a novel.

A LEISURE BOOK®

September 1994

Published by

Dorchester Publishing Co., Inc.
276 Fifth Avenue
New York, NY 10001

Printed in the United States of America.

Kansas Wildfire

Chapter One

Sam Driver—the heavyset, florid-faced mayor of Wolfe, Kansas, up for re-election that year—called the unofficial town meeting to order in the Fancy Lady Saloon. But it wasn't the election of 1889 the men were worried about, not by a long shot. This was a much more serious issue.

"Well, that temperance gal, Carry Nation, just better not come here to Wolfe, I can tell you that right now," the mayor pronounced weightily over the murmuring voices, the scraping chairs, and clinking glasses of the crowded, hot room. Only the overhead fans, barely turning, stirred any breeze on this still July afternoon.

"You tell 'em, Sam," encouraged his friend and chairman of the city council, Ed Hanson. He mopped his thin, lined neck with his handkerchief and put it away in a back pocket. "We don't need no trouble from such as her, comin' here and stirrin' up our own decent womenfolk about our drinkin'."

The murmuring buzz around the room echoed the sentiments of both men. Unnoticed in one corner of the saloon, sitting at a table almost obscured by the old piano next to it, sat Jimmy Pickens, new reporter for *The Wolfe Daily*, the town's only newspaper; he was listening intently and taking notes on everything said. His editor, Mr. Sullivan, had told him to snoop around town and see what he could come up with. Jimmy saw this as a test by Mr. Sullivan to see if he was any good at finding news in such a small town.

Over by the wooden bar, which ran almost the length of the back of the saloon, stood Scarlet Calico and Cat LaFlamme, fancy ladies employed by the saloon and the only women in attendance. They both lounged against the bar, their backs to it and supported by their elbows resting on it. They exchanged amused glances with each other and with Hank Wolfe, who sat off to one side of the gathering, his chair rocked back on two legs, his thumbs hooked in his leather vest pockets, and his booted feet crossed and up on the empty table next to him. The thin cigar clamped between his teeth sent smoky tendrils curling upwards, partially obscuring his face.

Every now and then, one of the men sitting close to him would glance nervously around at him and then quickly look away. But Hank made no comments, offered no advice, and voiced no opinion. Which only made everyone else in the room that much more aware of his presence. Even Mayor Driver seemed unsettled, just knowing Hank Wolfe was there.

"Well, all I got to say is this: If she comes around here and brings all them women and all that trouble with her, she just better watch out. I won't have my business tampered with or destroyed," Big John Savage ranted, slamming a huge, meaty fist down hard on his bar. Cat and Scarlet jumped, along with several of the nearest men, and turned towards the six-foot-five, 300-pound bartender-owner of the saloon. No one said much, but several men shared hard, meaningful glances with each other in silent agreement with Savage.

"And just what do you think you'd do to them, Big John? We're talking about women here," Hank commented. His voice was low and level, almost nonchalant, but the room quieted nonetheless. He raised a dark eyebrow at Savage as he removed his cigar to exhale smoke and tamp the excess ashes onto the already gritty floor. With his other hand, he picked up his glass, downing the whiskey shot.

Big John's tanned face reddened above his full, auburn beard, not in embarrassment but in anger. "Women or not, I guess we'd just have to find out when the time came." He met Hank's level gaze, but he was the first to look away.

Hank shook his head resignedly, brought his long legs and his chair down, crushed out his cigar, and stood up. He wasn't as tall or as big as Savage, but he seemed to have a larger presence. He looked over the assembled men—some he knew, some he didn't, and some he didn't like the looks of—as they turned in their chairs to face him, their backs to the front of the saloon where the mayor sat, staring wide-eyed at Hank.

"Gentlemen," was all Hank said by way of parting, fitting his black Stetson comfortably over his jet-black hair as he exited the smoky, close confines of the saloon. The swinging doors creaked in his wake. Cat and Scarlet sent appreciative stares after his retreating figure, but no one said anything until Hank's footfalls could no longer be heard on the board-walk outside. Reporter Jimmy Pickens wrote away.

Mayor Driver cleared his throat and stood up, regaining the attention of the men, who once more pivoted to face him. "Now, men, there's no need for violence. Mr. Wolfe is right. We're talking about decent women here." He went on to discuss the temperance issue further.

Back at the bar, Cat turned to Scarlet and whispered, "If he says 'decent women' one more time, I'm going to smack him on his fat old face."

"Now, Cat," Scarlet teased in a low voice, mimicking the mayor, "there's no need for violence. We're talking about decent men here."

"Yeah, real decent," Cat snorted. "They're sittin' here in a saloon in the middle of the afternoon, instead of being at their businesses, and talking about beatin' up women. I hope that Carry Nation does come here and turns them all on their ears."

"Cat, you better hope again. If she comes here, there'll be trouble for sure. You heard Big John."

"Yeah, I heard him. He could make things tough, for sure. Oh, now, don't look so scared. Big John wouldn't have no reason to quarrel with us." She pulled her thin satin strap back up onto her fleshy shoulder.

"I s'pose not," Scarlet said, her young, pretty, heavily made-up face reflecting her uncertainty.

Sudden loud guffaws, knee-slapping, and elbow-nudging going on all around the room recaptured Cat and Scarlet's attention. What now? A quick glance at Mayor Driver showed him to be the only one with a discomfitted look; well, the only one besides skinny old Ed Hanson, who looked a little ill, too. Cat and Scarlet listened in, trying to learn what was so funny.

"Now, that's not one damn bit funny, Henry," Mayor Driver was saying. "Just when we need to keep our heads about us, you go and suggest something silly like that."

Henry Hawkins, long, lean, and lanky, unfolded his frame from his chair until he was standing, hooked his thumbs in his suspenders, popped them, looked around at his friends and neighbors, and said, much as if he were Abe Lincoln at Gettysburg, "Why, Mayor, I think it's a right good idea. And so do these men." He made a sweeping gesture over the hooting and jeering crowd. He raised a long, thin, bony hand to quiet them. "Maybe since you and the council are so all-fired afraid of this Carry Nation woman, maybe we should just elect our womenfolk to your offices and let them tear into her." He had trouble finishing his speech, what with the men closest to him pounding him on the back and laughing.

Cat and Scarlet exchanged disbelieving looks back by the bar. Jimmy Pickens kept writing furiously.

"So," Henry continued, struggling to keep a smirk off his face and a laugh out of his voice, "along those lines, I would like to nominate my wife, Joletta, a decent, God-fearin' woman, to run for your position on the city council, Ed. My dear Joletta can wield a rollin' pin with the best of 'em." He put his hat over his heart and raised his eyes reverently to the ceiling, just before he was yanked back down to his seat by his laughing neighbor.

"Now just hold on a minute!" Ed stormed, jumping up out of his seat, but he was hooted down by men who were all caught up in the frivolity and were vying to nominate or second their wives, daughters, and sisters to important positions in the city government.

Mayor Driver gave up trying to restore order and sat down; after all, what difference did this make? The men were just venting some steam. He had nothing to worry about. Women running a city, indeed. Who ever heard of such a thing? Certainly, not here in western Kansas. Thus reassured in his own mind, he playfully joined in, chairing the proceedings, even lending an air of legitimacy to this raucous turn of events by mock-seriously calling the men to order so they could be heard and by having the minutes of this impromptu city meeting duly written down and noted by Tom Haskell, secretary of the city council. Jimmy Pickens duly and seriously noted it, too.

Before it was over, the men had nominated and seconded five women for the city council: Mrs. Joletta Hawkins, a large, bad-tempered woman, best known for her pies—and her rolling pin when Henry came in drunk from the Fancy Lady Saloon; tiny, timid little Miss Susie Johnson, Doc Johnson's bookish daughter who resembled a sparrow; Mrs. Emma Calvert, a stern widow woman who now taught school classes to make her living; Mrs. Freda Gruenwald, the stout, laughing, blond German wife of the dry-goods store owner; and, last but certainly not least in this monumental joke that could never happen, the pièce de résistance, a flabbergasted

11

Miss Cat LaFlamme, saloon hall dancer and fancy lady. Jimmy Pickens got all the names down; he'd check the spelling later.

Now just let that Carry Nation woman come to their town! They'd put their womenfolk up against her anytime! As they all congratulated each other on a great "meeting," and clapped Cat LaFlamme on her back, calling her Councilwoman, Mayor Driver banged his makeshift gavel, a whiskey shot glass, on the scarred-wood table in front of him. "Gentlemen, we are remiss in our civic duties." The room quieted once more. "We have nominations for the city council, but no one for my job. We need a lady mayor!"

That set the men to buzzing—and to drinking and milling about, looking for all the world like Roman senators in the Forum weighing some dire issue. A mayor, a mayor, hmmm. This had to be good. While this was going on, Cat threw back three stiff drinks she was supposed to be selling; Scarlet, looking very solicitous, gently patted her friend's sore back. Had these men all gone crazy? Did they have sunstroke? Jimmy Pickens waited, excited, pen poised over his pad.

"I've got it! I've got it!" Conversation stopped and all heads turned to look at the speaker. It was none other than Ole Jed, town drunk and fixture in the Fancy Lady. No one knew his last name or where he came from. He'd just always been here in Wolfe. Bewhiskered and harmless, Jed pretty much had the run of the place; he seemed to be everyone's and no one's responsibility. Jimmy craned his neck to see Ole Jed.

"Who you got, Ole Jed? You got someone you want to nominate?" Henry Hawkins asked indulgently, winking at a man next to him.

Ole Jed raised his befuddled head another fraction of an inch and pronounced, "Yep, I shore do. I do believe that Miss Rhiannon O'Shea would do this city proud as its mayor." Then, after a pause: "She shore couldn't hurt it none."

If Ole Jed was surprised to see his glass being refilled, he didn't take time to remark on it. He just gulped the burning brew down and put his head back on his table, his work done.

"Well, damned if I don't second that nomination myself," Henry Hawkins whispered in reverent awe in the stunned silence that followed Ole Jed's words. The nomination and the second were duly noted in the minutes by the city council's secretary.

Jimmy Pickens got it, too. He was thinking that it was sure a good thing for all these men that her father, Mr. Edwin O'Shea, the town's banker, wasn't here to hear this. He'd have all their hides nailed to a wall for sure just for mentioning his daughter's name in a saloon, much less for suggesting that she run the town. Not his sainted daughter. But he wasn't here, so it was safe to join the other men in their quiet contemplation of the mayoral candidate.

Nineteen-year-old Rhiannon O'Shea. The town beauty. The untouchable town beauty. Whose wealthy father would gladly shoot you between the eyes for so much as looking at her wrong. Deep chestnut—or was it dark auburn?—hair waving down her back; big ginger-colored eyes framed by thick, black curling lashes; a peaches-and-cream complexion; a figure that was worth getting shot for just to span her waist, just once, with your hands; and a lush, pink mouth that made men's crotches ache, that made men not hear what she was saying, so intent were they on her lips moving. Rhiannon O'Shea. Just back from school back East. She'd been a kid when she left, but now she was all woman. And every red-blooded male over the age of ten was in love with her. Miss Rhiannon O'Shea, Lady Mayor.

Mayor Driver brought the men out of their Rhiannon reverie by banging the table with his shot glass. "Ahem, well, I guess that about concludes this meeting, gentlemen." Titters of laughter were heard around the room. The mayor rested his chubby hands on his considerable paunch. "We'll

13

have our real meeting in a couple weeks to decide on a slate of candidates."

"I thought we just did that," called out Henry Hawkins.

"Now, Henry, that's just about enough out of you. You got this whole thing going in the first place. Now we're all in trouble at home, unless I'm wrong and it's not"—he pulled his watch fob out of his vest pocket and checked it—"five o'clock. Henry's not the only one who's going to get the rolling pin tonight—especially if word of these proceedings gets out to our womenfolk."

Laughing and clapping each other on the back, most of the men gathered up their hats and walked out of the saloon in pairs and groups, most going home to their wives and families and supper. Except for Jimmy Pickens, who pushed his way past several of them and raced toward the newspaper's office. And except for some of the harder-looking men, strangers in town, who moved to huddle at a table by the windows.

In a matter of minutes, only Big John, Ole Jed, Cat and Scarlet, and the knot of hard-looking men were left in the Fancy Lady Saloon. The girls each got a large tray and began the task of picking up glasses and bottles, emptying ashtrays, and straightening tables and chairs. Ole Jed was left where he lay. Big John joined the men, waving the women away from where the men sat speaking in low, threatening tones.

"Cat, that was sure the craziest thing I ever saw," Scarlet remarked. "You being on the city council, and all them other women. Those men were drunk, for sure." She shook her head, loosening even more bedraggled tendrils of dyed red hair from her best imitation of a fancy coiffure. Big John liked his girls to be redheads with fancy coiffures.

"No, they weren't. Not all of them." Cat nodded towards the men by the window, and then continued. "They were just being men. They don't think women could run this city. Hmph, a lot they know. They were just poking fun at all the womenfolk of this city is all, the old coots. I wish Hank

14

Wolfe would've stayed to hear them."

"You do? Why? What could he do?" Scarlet wanted to know, picturing the tall, dark son of the city's founder.

"Why, close their businesses for one," she said, exasperation ringing in her words. Then her voice and her plump, pretty face softened, both going dreamy. "But I meant I wished he'd stayed just so's I could look at him some more."

"Yeah, me too. He's always nice to me, you know. But he don't never go upstairs with me nor you. I wonder why. He ain't married or sweet on nobody, is he?"

"Well, if he is, he sure ain't goin' to discuss it with the likes of us, gal." Cat flipped her bar rag playfully at her friend.

"I guess not," Scarlet remarked absently as she bent over another table to wipe it clean. After a few minutes, she turned to Cat. "Cat, what do you think? Could you work with Miss Rhiannon O'Shea if you was on the city council and she was the mayor?"

Cat's first response was a snort. But then she hefted her loaded tray onto the bar and put a hand on her cocked hip, looking intently at a point just above the mirror behind the bar. Her gaze turned inward for several moments. Finally she turned back to Scarlet and said, "Not that it's ever goin' to happen, mind you. But if it did, I tell you what, missy, I'd sure give it one hell of a try."

Chapter Two

A few streets and another world away, Rhiannon O'Shea was listening to her father chastise her. Her eyes sparked fire, and her chin rose a fraction of an inch, but she held her tongue—by biting it.

"Rhiannon O'Shea, me girl, you're not a little one no more. You're a woman, and you don't go traipsing around the countryside astride a horse like a man. You take the buggy like a lady. And you take someone with you—you have three brothers. There're all sorts of strangers on the streets of Wolfe these days. Things have changed since you were away at school back East." His slight Irish brogue, which he worked so hard to tame, became more pronounced when he was upset.

"Your father's right, my love. Three years have brought many changes, and not all of them good."

Rhiannon shifted her gaze to her mother, a tiny bundle of Irish energy, but very proper and very prim, and very aware of her status as a leading lady in Wolfe, Kansas, society. Rhiannon knew her mother was more concerned that someone from the Ladies Aid Society might have seen her daughter on horseback than she was about the very unlikely probability of a strange man accosting her in daylight in town.

But just to prove to her parents that they had not wasted their money by sending their rebellious eldest child back east to Miss Constance's Finishing School for Young Ladies in Baltimore, Rhiannon assumed an apologetic demeanor and even managed to look down repentantly. To her amazement, the lightning flashing from her eyes didn't send her shoes up in smoke. But all she said was, "Yes, Papa. Yes, Mama. You're absolutely right, of course. I had no right to scare you or to endanger myself like that. I'll be more careful next time." Not to get caught, she added to herself.

Rhiannon looked up to gauge her parents' reaction. Their momentary shock at her submissiveness, in place of what three years ago would have been open war, became exchanged looks of relieved satisfaction, which seemed to Rhiannon to say Miss Constance had certainly earned her high fees and no wonder she came so highly recommended. Rhiannon pressed her lips together firmly. Let them think what they would.

"Well, Mother," Edwin O'Shea said to his wife, "that was simple enough. It seems our Rhiannon is now a lady, wouldn't you say?" He tucked his thumbs into his vest pockets and rocked back and forth on his heels. His obvious relief in not having to fight his daughter tooth and nail brought a mischievous grin to Rhiannon's face, one she hid with a quickly raised hand.

"I believe so, Father," Patience O'Shea affirmed, patting her elaborate coiffure. She let out the breath she'd been holding since Rhiannon turned 13. "I'd say she's very presentable now."

Very marriageable was what they really meant, Rhiannon thought, but again she bit her tongue. She had to choose her battles carefully, and the evening of her official welcome-home dinner party was not the time to rile her parents. "May I be excused now, Father, Mother? I must dress for this evening. I wish to be . . . presentable."

Patience O'Shea narrowed her eyes at her firstborn, but Rhiannon schooled her features into absolute innocence. She turned her eyes, purposely widened like a child's, on her parents. After a second or two of scrutiny, Mrs. O'Shea seemed to be satisfied and dismissed Rhiannon to her room.

Rhiannon very nearly bolted out of the parlor, but caught herself just in time. She proceeded with great decorum, literally gliding from the room, her hands held demurely at her waist (Miss Constance would have been apoplectic; Rhiannon would never do it for *her*). She continued her charade even as she very elegantly and very correctly ascended the carved, polished stairs. She noted the silence—astounded silence, she was sure—from the parlor that marked her retreat. Never in the 16 years prior to her going to Baltimore three years ago, practically bound and gagged, had she ever left a room or gone up the stairs in anything but a tomboyish gallop.

Once she was in her room, Rhiannon let out her own relieved breath and flopped onto her bed, stomach-first. Being a lady, or pretending to be one, was going to make her pop one day, she was sure. She turned on her side, crooking her elbow and supporting her head in her hand. She picked at imaginary threads in her quilted bedcover. For heaven's sake, all this fuss over one little horseback ride—astride like a man, Rhiannon thought as she giggled.

But then she sobered. Home only two days and already called into the parlor before both parents. They were going to have to decide if she were truly the grown-up they kept telling her she was—or not. One did not call grown-up children onto the carpet, so to speak. In a snit, Rhiannon caught a real thread and yanked it, causing a considerable portion of the quilt design to gather unattractively. "Oh, for—" she exclaimed, and quickly sat up to smooth out the pattern. She bent over and bit off the thread with her teeth.

Just in time, too, because the door to her room opened. She jerked around guiltily, but it was only her baby brother,

John, or Johnny-Cake, as the O'Shea siblings had dubbed him. Of her three brothers, he'd changed the most in the past three years, but at six, he still had his baby fat and his baby adorableness. And his red hair and big brown eyes.

"Wha' cha doin'?" he asked, clambering up onto her four-poster bed, heedless of his dirty play clothes.

Rhiannon gathered him up into her arms and planted wet, sisterly kisses over his flushed little face. "I was waiting for a little Johnny-Cake to come to my room, so I could eat him all up," she growled into his dusty, grimy baby neck.

John shrieked and chortled, fighting to be loose from her grip. "Don't, Rhi-Rhi, don't! You're tickling me! Stop! I'll wet my pants!"

Rhiannon let him up instantly. She knew that was no empty threat, as her hapless brothers had found out in the past. It was his ultimate defense against older brothers who could so easily overpower him.

Rhiannon sat cross-legged in the middle of her bed, and John mimicked her. She reached out to ruffle his hair, and he did the same thing right back to her. "Oh, a little toughie, huh?" she teased, laughing at this little urchin brother of hers.

"Yep. I'm all growed up since you left. I even had a fight at school." His narrow chest puffed out proudly.

"My goodness. Did you win?" Rhiannon struggled to be just as serious as John was, even puckering her forehead to match his.

John snorted in six-year-old indignation. "You betcha. I even had to stand in the corner. Widow Calvert said I was a bad boy."

"You're not a bad boy, John. You were just defending yourself."

"No, I wasn't. I started it."

"Why, you little toad! You deserve to stand in the corner. Now, tell me, who is Widow Calvert?"

"She's the teacher. Her husband died while you was gone to Baltibore."

"Baltimore," Rhiannon corrected laughingly. She'd never heard of the Calverts. Things were changing in her hometown. "Who're the Calverts, John?"

Before he could answer, his older brother, Patrick, a dark-headed 11-year-old, spoke from the doorway, drawing Rhiannon's and John's attention. "They were passing through Wolfe last spring on their way to Oklahoma. But the mister took sick and died. Miz Calvert couldn't farm by herself, so she stayed here. And now she's the teacher."

Rhiannon nodded soberly, absorbing this, thinking of the devastating soil erosion in Kansas that was forcing thousands of farmers off their land and pushing them south to Oklahoma's newly opened territory.

"She gots a big nose, and she's mean, Rhi-Rhi," John interjected, clearly looking for an ally.

Rhiannon glanced briefly at Paddy, as everyone called Patrick, and then back to John. "Who is, Johnny-Cake? Mrs. Calvert?"

"No, she isn't, John." It was Paddy again. Of the four O'Shea children, Paddy was the serious one, the one who loved books and school and learning. His dark hair and eyes made him a miniature of their father, even though he was not his father's namesake. That was 15-year-old Edwin Junior, Eddie to his sister and brothers. Eddie was sandy-haired and blue-eyed, unlike either of his parents. "You just don't like her because she gets onto you when you don't behave."

John took the bait. Standing up on Rhiannon's bed, shoes and all, he pulled himself to his full six-year-old height and put his pudgy fists to his waist. "I don't never behave," he mistated angrily. At his older brother and sister's strangled outburst of laughter, he frowned and went on, unnecessarily loud, "I mean I don't never be bad. And you better hush up right now, Paddy-Batty."

With that horrible insult, he launched himself at Patrick, who caught him handily, positioned him kicking and squealing under his arm, and hauled him off down the hall like a sack of potatoes. "Come on, Johnny-Cake, Mother says you're to have a bath."

Renewed shrieking and howling protests accompanied the two boys down the hall. Rhiannon chuckled and shook her head; she leaned back against the many fluffy pillows at the head of her bed. Her mood turned thoughtful. She had missed her brothers terribly while she was in Baltibore, as Johnny-Cake had pronounced it. And yes, she had missed her parents. For even though they tried hard to be so cultured and civil and fashionable, they were indulgent and loving parents, wanting only the best for their four children.

Though, to Rhiannon's way of thinking, they mistakenly believed that the best for Rhiannon was for her to be a L-A-D-Y. She spelled it out in her mind, using capital letters. She had to admit that it hurt some to think they hadn't liked her as she'd been at 16—scrappy, loud, fun-loving, and disheveled all the time, something of a tomboy. How will you ever attract a husband, Rhiannon, she could hear her mother saying all those years ago; she'd even clucked her tongue disapprovingly at the sight her daughter made.

A husband. Married. Rhiannon thought of the many nights in the past three years when she and some of her bolder classmates had slipped out of the dormitory to meet boys from the nearby university. Innocent trysts, but ones that included introductions to liquor and even to smoking. She wrinkled her nose; she hadn't liked either, no more than she had the bumbling, wet kisses of the young men. A lifetime of those? Rhiannon shuddered. No, she didn't see marriage in her immediate future. She wanted to live, really live, whatever that meant, before she gave up her freedom to some . . . some man. Marriage would just have to wait.

So there, she said adamantly to herself, as if she were agreeing with some unseen person in her room. Feeling better about things, she scooted off her bed, pulled the curtains together, and crossed the room to close her door. Then, turning to her armoire, she opened it, stared wordlessly at the bulging contents, and engaged in the purely feminine lament that she had absolutely nothing to wear.

"Dammit, MacGregor, this seems like an awful lot of fuss to go through for one meal," Hank Wolfe fumed as MacGregor fussily straightened the finely tailored black gabardine coat over Hank's broad shoulders.

"I know, sir, and I'm ever so sorry. But one's social position makes certain demands upon one," answered the patient, slightly stooped, but starchily formal valet. He was as much of an inheritance from Hank's lately deceased father, Ezra Wolfe, as was the huge house, the land, all the money, and his mother's two maiden aunts, Penelope and Tillie. "There, sir, I believe you are presentable now." A final imaginary piece of lint was picked off the sleeve.

"Well, I sure as hell hope so. And quit calling me sir. Hell, you've known me since I was born. Why don't you call me Hank? You're the one who hung that moniker on me," Hank muttered, picking up a thin cigar and quickly lighting it himself before MacGregor could perform this small personal service. Damned if having MacGregor do the things for him he'd watched him do for his father all his life didn't make him feel like . . . his father.

Besides, he liked to do things for himself; West Point training and years of military service had taught him that much. And the solitary life had suited him well, much more so than the tight fit of this new suit or his inheritance of barely six months ago. His inheritance—a whole damned town, he thought wryly. Realizing MacGregor had not answered him, Hank looked up. The butler's face very plainly showed that he'd sooner drop through the floor than call him Hank.

"That will be all, MacGregor," Hank said on a sigh. He half expected the old man to bow before he left.

"Very well, sir, if you're sure. Shall I wait up for you?" MacGregor neither bowed nor left.

Hank snorted. "I don't think there'll be any waiting up to it. I'm eating, doing my social duty, and leaving."

MacGregor raised his eyebrows, but said nothing. Hank felt his temper come close to the surface. Now why did MacGregor always make him feel like less than a gentleman somehow? Or like an obstinate little boy?

Out of his mouth came the cigar; he used it to gesture at the unflappable MacGregor and sent ashes everywhere. "Look, it's just some welcome-home affair for Edwin O'Shea's daughter, some skinny little kid with red hair, from what I remember," he ranted. "And don't look at me like that. You've known I didn't want to go since you handed me that damned invitation and practically insisted I go, using that cursed social-position argument for the hundredth time. It's not like this is Boston or Newport, for God's sake. It's Wolfe, Kansas," Hank went on, in essence arguing with himself since MacGregor remained stiff-lipped and quiet.

"I mean, what's the point? She's been home two days, so most likely everyone but me has already seen her. Hell, they've known her all their lives. Why don't they just say hello, welcome home, and save me all this torture?" MacGregor's face told him he was not gaining an ally. Hank looked away and worked his mouth, trying to regain his temper. "All right, if it'll make you happy, wait up for me." He poked the cigar back into his mouth and turned to leave the room.

"If you wish, sir."

Hank was halfway out of the room, but stopped short. Without turning around, he took his cigar out of his mouth, and said, "No, I don't wish. I didn't wish this house"— his free hand gestured wildly, indicating the house, as he went on out of the room and into the hallway—"this wheat-filled land, this damn money, and all these . . . these parties and people . . ." His voice trailed after him as he went down the carved, curved stairway of what was really a mansion, a total incongruity on the outskirts of a tiny Western town.

"So you say, sir," MacGregor commented into the quiet as the front door slammed. He sincerely hoped that his master's loud exit hadn't disturbed the Misses Penland, Hank's maiden great-aunts on his mother's side.

Deciding to check on them in a few minutes, MacGregor straightened the huge master bedroom. A sigh escaped him as he thought of Hank's father. He often talked to Ezra's memory when he was alone. His soft Scottish burr stirred the otherwise empty room. "You know, Mr. Wolfe, I was with you for over forty years, and I practically helped raise young Master Henry 'Hank' Penland Wolfe when his angel mother, Sara Penland, died. The lad wasn't even hardly seven years then. Twenty-five years ago. And now I'm to keep my promise made to you on your deathbed to make a great gentleman out of him before I return to me beloved Scotland and me own retirement." MacGregor sighed and looked up to the ceiling. "And I suppose you'll require me to stay until the lad has produced an heir, too."

MacGregor paused, not as if he expected an answer; after all, he wasn't dotty. He just felt that Ezra was in heaven with God, and if one could talk to God, then one could talk to the souls up there with Him. He held Hank's discarded shirt up in his hand, as if it proved his next point. "You know he always chafed at civilized trappings, even as a wee lad, so you shouldna ha' been shocked when our young Major Hank Wolfe preferred the rough-and-tumble military life he led all those years over what ye could offer him right here in Kansas. And don't think I don't know about the strings ye pulled in Washington to get him back home."

MacGregor pursed his thin lips together at the memories. The lad's military career had distanced him from his father in more than one way. He'd rarely come home since he was 18 and had won an appointment to West Point, something he'd coveted since he was a wee lad. MacGregor knew that part of Hank's present surliness was resentment for having to resign his commission in order to take control of the vast

Wolfe holdings, too vast to merely sell off for the money, as determined as the lad was to do just that.

"You were right, Mr. Ezra Wolfe," MacGregor went on, pushing in a drawer. "Saddling your only child, the last male Wolfe, with all the trappings and investments and social obligations of your wealth—his, now—would get him out of the military saddle and home where he belonged. I only wish you didn't have to die to prove it. After all, owning most all of this city you built—and a lot of what lies between here and the cold Atlantic—couldn't keep you alive a minute longer than the Good Lord intended. Not at all. But still, I'm glad you came here, and me tagging along, to look over your cattle and wheat and farms and such."

MacGregor closed the armoire doors and shook a bony finger skyward. "And do you remember the first time you saw Sara Penland? A proper little farm lass and raring beauty she was, that one." MacGregor shook his head. "Has ever a man loved a woman like you loved that one? I think not, Ezra—you built this mansion and this town around her. You told her to pick wherever in the world she wanted to live, and if she married you, you'd build her mansion right there. And weren't you properly shocked when the lass said right here? She said you could be just as happy here, in Kansas no less, as you could back East with all the noise, hurry, and dirt. She was a bonny lass, that one."

And all that just before the War Between the States. It'd been hell, MacGregor reflected, keeping the family and fortune together. But Ezra had done it, and added admirably to the Wolfe wealth. And Ezra had gambled that Hank was enough like him (and didn't the boy bristle at that idea) that he too would draw his last breath doing his damnedest to keep it all together. Wolfes did not admit or accept defeat. Aye, the lad might chafe at the tremendous burden of his wealth now, but he'd not let it go through his fingers. Pride was a damnable master.

MacGregor looked around him. The room was in order, except for cigar ashes on the carpet. He turned to go, but turned back and fancied he could see Ezra and Sara themselves in here, laughing and loving. He shook his old gray head. If only the lad could find his Sara. The quicker the better, so he, Ian MacGregor, could take the more-than-generous stipend left him by Ezra and return to his beloved Scotland. And hadn't he given his word to the dying man that he'd stay until the young heir was properly married? MacGregor determined that he would do his Scottish best to see the lad married—and soon.

Chapter Three

Damn, Hank thought admiringly. Suddenly the evening held great promise. He mentally thanked MacGregor for browbeating him (if one raised eyebrow could be called browbeating) into attending this affair. Taking a sip of his wine, Hank made eye contact across the laden oak table with the evening's honoree, Miss Rhiannon O'Shea. This was no skinny kid with red hair—not anymore. He grinned when she turned the same color pink as her low-cut gown, looked down quickly, and used her fork to stab at her food. So, she'd been staring and didn't like being caught.

Feeling devilish, Hank decided to call her on it. "Tell me, Miss O'Shea," he began, but paused, noticing that whenever he said anything—anything at all—everyone at the table stopped talking and paid deferential, if not overeager attention to him, as if he were some damned king.

"Yes, Mr. Wolfe?" she asked, looking around her at the quiet and staring guests, some with forks poised halfway to their open mouths.

She looked downright confused by their behavior, Hank realized. Finally, maybe there was someone in this town of his father's who wouldn't kowtow to the name of Wolfe. Abandoning his earlier notion to tease her, he cast about quickly for some innocuous comment, keeping in mind that her mother was seated just to his right at this end of the massive table. And that 14 other people, all prominent people in the town of Wolfe, including her father at the opposite end of the table, were beginning to lean forward, the better to hear his latest royal proclamation. Only Miss O'Shea sat bolt upright, eyes slightly widened.

"Tell me," he began again, and 14 heads inched in closer. Why in the living hell don't you all mind your own damnable business and quit hanging on every silly syllable I utter, he railed in his head. But aloud he said, "After your three-year absence, what do you think of Wolfe now?"

All heads pivoted to Rhiannon.

"Do you mean your town or yourself, Mr. Wolfe? Certainly you're not the same Mr. Wolfe who was reigning when I left. Unless, of course, the Wolfe family also owns a fountain of youth." Rhiannon's father's frantic clearing of his throat did not stop her. She didn't even spare him a glance. "And as for the town, as my parents told me only hours ago, many things in and of Wolfe have changed—and not all of them good."

Mrs. Patience O'Shea's sudden and violent choking fit cut off any rejoinder Hank might have made. In fact, the gasping seemed to be making the rounds of the assembled guests, all except for Hank and Rhiannon, who stared levelly at each other. Hank couldn't be sure, but he thought he detected the slightest smirk on Miss O'Shea's lovely face. Certainly, one fine eyebrow arched in a dare.

Once the choking epidemic began to subside, leaving only one or two women needing to be patted solicitously on their backs by their husbands, Hank, who'd never taken his eyes off Rhiannon, said, "Which changes don't you like, Miss O'Shea? And I mean in the town, not the man."

"Well, I think—"

"Mr. Wolfe, would you like more potatoes? Or some more fried squash, maybe?" Mrs. O'Shea asked, a trifle shrilly, desperately reaching for any dish within her grasp. She heaped his plate full without waiting for an answer. Then, reaching for the bread basket, she added, "Or how about a nice biscuit? You know, our Ella—that's our cook—makes the best biscuits around, doesn't she, Edwin? Edwin?!"

Edwin blinked twice and seemed to come to himself. He put down his goblet of wine and then immediately picked it up again. "Harumphh..uh, yes, Mother, that she does, that she does. Ahem, may I have your attention, please?" He paused, but completely unnecessarily as every eye in the room was already on him, grateful for the distraction. "I would like to propose a toast to my . . . uhm, lovely daughter, Rhiannon Pauline O'Shea, newly returned from her schooling back East, where she learned to be a great . . . ahem, lady. We—Mrs. O'Shea and meself—are greatly pleased to have her home."

Expressions such as "Here, here" went around the table, along with the soft clinking of crystal touching. Hank reached across the table to touch Rhiannon's goblet. She again arched a fine brown eyebrow at him before smiling and nodding her acknowledgment of her father's words.

But her father wasn't through. "And now, if only all my money could be paid back by her getting for herself a great gentleman to be her husband," he teased good-naturedly.

In the ensuing laughter and commentary making the rounds of the table, only Hank and Patience O'Shea saw Rhiannon jerk and spill her wine. While her face turned the prettiest shade of deep red, Hank raised his goblet high and added his "Here, here" to the chorus. But being the great gentleman that he was, he then offered his cloth napkin to Mrs. O'Shea to sop up the spilled wine that stained the linen tablecloth in front of Rhiannon.

"Miss O'Shea, I do believe you'll sustain a nasty cut if you squeeze that fine goblet any tighter. Are you perhaps pretending it's someone's neck?" Hank whispered, leaning towards her.

"Yes, I am," she hissed, leaning towards him, exposing an enticing amount of bosom, and dodging her mother's daubing attempts to clean up the spill. "Someone very close, as a matter of fact."

"My neck or your father's, Miss O'Shea?"

"Your choice, Mr. Wolfe," she came right back, ignoring her mother's gasp and heavy collapse onto her chair with the wine-soddened napkin clutched to her bosom. Rhiannon then sat back and proceeded to ignore the son of the town's founding father, much to his wry amusement.

"Touché, Miss O'Shea." Yes, a very interesting evening, indeed, Hank decided, eyeing the decidedly beautiful young woman across from him. He'd seen and known many other beautiful women, but none as sassy and as captivating as Miss Rhiannon Pauline O'Shea. And she seemed totally unimpressed by him. Imagine that.

Hank remained in this thoughtful vein until after dinner when the other guests, all friends of the older O'Sheas, were in the spacious and tastefully decorated parlor. The children, including Rhiannon's brothers, had been excused from their table in the kitchen and sent upstairs to the large bedroom shared by Paddy and John to visit and to play. To Edwin Junior's consternation, he was given charge of watching the younger ones for the remainder of the evening.

Hank joined the men, who, typically, were standing to one side of the parlor, away from their wives. The conversation inevitably turned to business and then to the impending arrival of Mrs. Carry Nation. Hank half listened, made brief comments, nodded every now and then, and generally passed for someone who was paying attention. But what really captivated his attention was Miss O'Shea across the room.

She sat prettily on a small pink damask settee in front of the bay window, her hands demurely clasped in her pink satin lap. From where Hank was standing, she appeared to be enjoying the limelight and the conversation of the older women who either sat or stood around her, the guest of honor. She looked very ladylike, nodding, smiling, commenting. Hank figured she was probably being grilled by her mother's friends about the latest fashions and dances and such from back East, something every woman loved to hear about.

As he watched her, the vaguest and most illogical sense of disappointment overtook him that Miss O'Shea—oh, hell, Rhiannon—would find those exclusively female, and completely inane, topics interesting. What more had he expected of her? After all, her upswept hair, which exposed a slim, kissable neck, was done in what he recognized from recent trips back East as the latest style, as was her dress.

Then she looked up; Hank caught the bored look on her face and nearly laughed out loud. Why, she was as big a fake as he was!

As her gaze lit on him, and she realized she'd been caught again by him, she narrowed her big eyes at him. What color were they? Brown? No, more like cinnamon or ginger. Yes, spices suited her—ginger eyes. Hank winked, trying to convey that he knew how she felt, that the conversation of the men was as boring to him as the conversation of the women was to her. But she refused to be mollified or to share anything with him. With haughty disdain, so characteristic of a great lady, or of someone pretending to be one, she raised her head regally and turned away, showing him an absolutely elegant profile.

Hank was truly amused. He couldn't decide if he wanted to kiss her or put her over his knee. Either prospect tantalized him, he thought jadedly. Then, instantly he became as predatory as a real wolf when he saw her arise and leave the room. She turned to her left as she exited the parlor; that route would take her outside, he realized. Hank suddenly felt the need for fresh air himself. He excused himself from the group of men, nodded to the ladies as he passed them, and turned left out of the parlor, stalking her as surely as his namesakes stalked their dinner.

Outside, the twilight was lit by the bright white cast of a full July moon. It splashed light and dark over the veranda, which fronted two sides of the large, white, mint-green-trimmed, two-story Victorian home. Hank didn't see Rhiannon right off, so he took out a thin cheroot and lit it, feeling as obvious as any schoolboy. At least this gave him an adult excuse to be out here. He leaned a shoulder against one of the many white columns that sprang from the floor of the veranda to support the overhanging roof; he looked out uninterestedly over the front lawn and put the cigar to his lips, inhaling deeply.

"Mind if I have one?"

Hank whirled around, nearly inhaling the whole cigar instead of just the smoke. He snatched it out of his mouth as he choked and coughed; spying Rhiannon, he handed it to her and strangled out, "Here. Take mine."

Almost lost in the shadows right behind him, she was sitting in one of the two long wooden gliding chairs that sat to either side of a double window. "Thanks," she said, sitting forward to take the cigar; she appeared totally oblivious to what could have been her guest's last dying gasps. Instead, she took a deep drag on the tobacco, looking very sophisticated while doing so. Within a second, though, she had joined Hank in his whooping and choking. She jumped up and bent over at the waist, one hand at her throat, the other clutching the errant cigar out in front of her.

Hank was recovered enough to pound on her bare back above her gown. "Stop it!" she gasped out finally, straightening up and clutching at his lapel for support. Hank, eyes watering, nose running, put an arm around her and took the cigar, tossing it down and crushing the fire with his boot.

"That damned thing nearly killed me."

Her comment brought Hank up short—with amusement. He gripped her upper arms and held her away from him.

32

Looking down into her red and sweating face, with escaped curls clinging limply to her cheeks, he teased, "My word, Miss O'Shea. In one evening, I've observed you insult your guests, embarrass your parents, drink, smoke, and curse, and none of it very well. Tell me again, what finishing school for ladies was it that you attended? I do believe that I'll have to recommend to your father that you return immediately for further instruction. Either that, or he should demand his money back."

"I have an idea," she retorted. "Why don't you pack your bags and go back with me to learn how to be a gentleman? A *real* gentleman wouldn't point out a lady's shortcomings to her."

It took about one second for her words to hit him. Forgetting he had a hold on her arms, Hank reared back his head and practically screamed his laughter. The girl didn't care who she insulted, and she treated him as if he were just anybody, and not a Somebody. He loved it. It was only when she wriggled in his grasp that he sobered. But he didn't let go of her just yet. He was afraid she'd stomp back into the house and thus end the most fun he'd had in . . . how long had it been? Forever?

"Touché again, Miss O'Shea. You're absolutely right, of course. I apologize." Knowing he couldn't hold onto her all night, although that prospect was tempting, he risked letting go of her to wipe his eyes and sketch a fancy bow. "You are truly a great lady."

"As you are a gentleman," she intoned seriously, curtsying so low she nearly sat down on the wooden floor. She held this position and looked up at him.

An indulgent grin still on his lips, Hank straightened up to tower over her. Looking into her eyes, right now hard ginger-colored diamonds, Hank was somewhat taken aback to realize there was a shininess to her eyes, as reflected by the moon, that looked suspiciously like tears. His grin faded, but he dismissed the thought, attributing the tears, if they

33

existed, to her choking on the cigar. At any rate, she didn't begin to cry, but she did look away for a moment and sniff suspiciously.

Remembering his manners and wondering what he'd said to upset her, Hank very formally extended his hand to her as she arose from her curtsy. He led her to the gliding chair she'd been sitting in moments ago. Her hand felt small and soft and warm, like a baby bird. She sat in the middle of the rocker and artfully arranged her full skirt around her. Then, she turned on him the brightest, most unbeguiling smile he'd ever seen. The tears must have been his imagination, because here she was smiling. She may not be the great lady she pretends so hard to be, but she's a consummate actress, he decided.

Hank felt very intrigued by this beautiful, complicated woman of inconsistencies in front of him. But right now he was most intrigued by the fact that she obviously did not intend for him to sit by her, judging by how spread out her skirts were around her. Deciding this was one battle of wills that he was not going to lose, Hank pushed the yards of material that made up her skirt to one side and prepared to sit down.

He forced her to move over or be sat on. She moved all the way over to the armrest. The gliding swing was long enough to comfortably sit three adults, but Hank settled himself comfortably enough right up against Rhiannon's side. He sat with his legs apart, one arm draped negligently along the back of the glider and around Rhiannon's shoulder. When she made a move to stand up, his fingers curled tightly around her arm, effectively holding her in place. She sat back and glared at him. He smiled affably at her and then turned his head to breathe in the night air, which seemed to be charged with electricity—or was it anticipation?

Myriad crickets chirped, a dog barked somewhere in town, a door slammed close by, the tinkling notes of the piano in the Fancy Lady Saloon carried on the wind, and an owl hooted forlornly. But the only sound on the veranda was the creaking of the glider as they wordlessly rocked it.

Hank looked over at Rhiannon. She was staring straight ahead. He'd expected her to be flirtatious and full of peppery talk, so her quiet surprised him. And her rigidity, she looked like she was holding her breath, like she'd never had a man's arm around her before. Suddenly, Hank felt awkward with her, but he shrugged that feeling off. Hell, she was way past the age for her first kiss. And she sure didn't talk like she was afraid of men. Hank inhaled deeply, somewhat disconcerted, taking in her rosy scent and her warm nearness. The velvet night demanded he kiss her.

Without thinking further about what he was doing, or the possible consequences, Hank turned in the seat and pulled her to him. Before she had time to react, he bent his head, aiming for the tender spot where her neck met her shoulder. He heard her sharp intake of breath and felt her stiffen, but he was too lost in her rosy scent to pay her reaction much heed. He felt her shudder when his lips met the very soft, very tender, very naked spot he'd wanted to kiss all evening. But what surprised him was the tremor that went through him, and the way his lips tingled when they touched her flesh. It was that, and not her reaction, that brought his head up abruptly.

He let go of her as if she were hot, too hot, and stood up, facing away from her. He walked to the edge of the veranda and ran a hand through his hair. Letting out a slow, heavy breath, he turned back to her. She hadn't moved. She sat looking down at her hands, which were folded in her lap.

For once in his adult life, Hank didn't know what to say to a woman. Suddenly she looked more like a girl, which was probably a lot closer to the truth, he decided. Damn, he could be a bastard. The quiet between them gave rise to other night noises, ones Hank was just barely aware of. The muted sounds of laughter and conversation coming from inside the house, the soft nicker of a horse tethered at the front gate, the low mewling of a cat that strolled across the veranda, and the beating of his own heart. And boyish snickering coming from around the corner. Hank stiffened. Snickering? What the hell?

Apparently Rhiannon heard it at the same moment he did, because she raised her head and looked wide-eyed at him, as if she thought he was snickering.

"It came from around there," he said in a low voice, pointing to his left.

A sudden scuffling and snorting commotion from the side of the house preceded the two of them hurrying towards the noise. Just as they rounded the corner, Rhiannon right behind Hank, two little boys managed to untangle their limbs from each other's and were a step away from full flight when Hank's arms snaked out and grabbed them by their collars, one in each hand. "Not so fast, pardners. Miss O'Shea, do you recognize either of these varmints?"

"I certainly do, Mr. Wolfe. This one is my brother, John, and that's Mayor Driver's son, Charlie."

"Evening, boys," Hank drawled.

"We wasn't spyin' on you! Honest!" six-year-old John confessed, squirming for all he was worth.

"Yeah, Rhiannon. We didn't see you smoking, nor him kissing you. Promise!" Charlie said, trying to help out, crossing his heart. His feet barely touched the bare wood floor.

John gave his smaller friend a disbelieving look and poked him in the arm with his pudgy fist. "Stupid! Now she knows!"

Charlie yelped and looked like he was going to cry.

"Well, Miss O'Shea, I believe this one is your call. What should we do with them?"

"I'm not sure, Mr. Wolfe. I do believe that hanging's too good for them, don't you?"

A sudden intaking of breath came from the culprits.

"Oh, indubitably," Hank agreed. "Something more creative is called for here, I do believe. After all, spying on an older sister is a pretty serious crime."

"Not half as serious as reporting what you've seen, which is the other half of a spy's job, isn't it, boys?"

The boys suddenly became very still in Hank's grasp. They exchanged uneasy glances. Feeling pretty certain they wouldn't run off now, Hank let go of them. He gave Rhiannon a grin and a wink over the boys' heads.

She raised her eyebrows slightly at him and bit off a return grin. She then turned a stern glare to her brother and his friend. With her arms crossed under her bosom and her foot tapping the wooden floor, she narrowed her eyes at the two boys. "Well, I'm waiting."

Apparently John knew when he was defeated, and Charlie did whatever John told him, because when John heaved a leaden sigh, so did Charlie. When John hung his head, so did Charlie. When John poked Charlie in his side with his elbow, they both raised their heads and said at the same time, "Sorry."

"That's a good start. Now, let's hear the rest of it."

"Rhi-ann-on!" John protested, but seeing her unflinching expression, he gave in. "All right, blast it. We won't tell no one, will we, Charlie?"

"No, sirree, ma'am," Charlie said, as serious as a choirboy, shaking his head for emphasis. "My pa'd kill me for sure if I went tattlin'."

"They sound sincere to me, Miss O'Shea; what do you think?" Hank asked her. He now had a hand on each boy's shoulder, as if he were their lawyer pleading their case.

Two pairs of very wide, very hopeful, very begging eyes stared up at her.

"Oh, I think we can safely turn them loose, Mr. Wolfe. I think they've learned their lesson."

"Whoopee!" the boys yelled, and propelled by Hank's encouraging push on their backs, they took off around the back of the house. It wasn't five seconds later that Hank and Rhiannon heard the back door open and slam against the house. They exchanged very superior, very adult smiles that proved also to be very premature.

John's breathless voice could be heard over his running feet as he galloped down the hallway towards the parlor. "Ma, Pa, guess what Rhiannon and Mr. Wolfe was doing out on the veranda!"

And Charlie chimed in. "Yeah, we seen everything!"

Chapter Four

Early the next morning, Rhiannon jerked awake instantly to the sound of Ella, the cook, self-appointed nanny, and undisputed boss of the O'Shea family, admonishing her to get up. Rhiannon would have sworn she'd not slept all night. But she must have fallen asleep at some point in her tossing and turning, because here was Ella bent over "her favorite child" and shaking her shoulder.

"Rhiannon Pauline O'Shea, you get yourself up this very minute. Your daddy wants a word wit' you, missy. Come on now; he ain't in no mood for laziness, gal. You better git up for me, 'cause you don't want your momma up here. The only thing patient 'bout her is her name. She's down there now all yelling about a scandal. Says cain't nobody in this house hold they head up now. Must be your doin's."

Rhiannon turned over reluctantly and blinkingly faced Ella's dark and censuring face. Ella stood next to Rhiannon's bed with her slim, black arms folded under her bosom. She managed to look imperious, even with her apron dusted in the flour of this morning's biscuits. Her lips were pursed. Not a good sign.

Rhiannon sighed and pushed up on her elbows. She tossed her head slightly to get her hair out of her eyes. A glance out her bedroom window showed the early morning sun to be framed in it. Rhiannon wanted to roll her eyes with weariness but didn't dare.

"I'm up, Ella. I'll be right down." Sleep—not repentance—made her voice low and husky. After all, what had she done wrong?

Ella hesitated, looking from Rhiannon to the open bedroom door. In the moment's silence, Rhiannon heard what was making her old and beloved nanny so anxious: her father's voice berating one of her brothers. Probably poor Edwin Junior for letting John and Charlie out of his sight last night. Rhiannon knew that Ella could not stand for any one of the O'Shea children, each of them her professed "favorite," to be punished—whether or not they deserved it. "Go on, Ella. I'll be down. I promise."

Ella nodded and left, closing the door behind her. Rhiannon looked at the door in silence and then flung herself backwards onto the warm nest her pillows made. This was utterly and absolutely ridiculous, she fumed. Three years away from home, three years older, three years wiser, three years more refined, and she was still being treated like a child. When would her parents start treating her like an adult, for heaven's sake?

When you start acting like one, her conscience berated her. When you stop insulting dinner guests—important dinner guests. When you quit doing childish things like sneaking out of the house to ride a horse astride like a man. When you quit letting strange men kiss you in the dark on your own front porch. When you start acting like the lady they sent you away to become. When you get married.

"Oh, be quiet," Rhiannon grumped, feeling the least bit chastised. All right, so they had reason to be angry. Well, it wasn't as if she'd started any of it with Mr. Wolfe, or had even invited his kiss. Rhiannon shuddered and tingled all over deliciously, feeling his warm lips on her skin right now just as surely as if he were right here in her bed. . . .

"Good heavens!" She tossed her covers back and jumped out of bed, looking back at it as if she fully expected to see Mr. Wolfe lying there, stretched out and . . . and naked.

"Good heavens," she said again, putting her hands to her cheeks; they felt very, very warm. Rhiannon reached for her silk wrapper, tugged it on, and tied it around her waist. She then raked her fingers through the tangled mass of her hair, and went to the closed door of her room. Just before she turned the crystal knob, she looked back once more at her bed. No, he wasn't there. Right then, she couldn't have said if she was relieved or disappointed.

With a careless shrug of her shoulder, she turned the knob and left her room. On the landing at the head of the stairs, she paused. Silence greeted her ears. So, her father was done with Eddie. Rhiannon took a deep breath and began her descent, feeling all her childhood tummy nervousness come rushing back at the prospect of a dressing down by her father. She made up her mind that she would not stand there demurely as she'd done yesterday. Today, her parents would see the real Rhiannon, who was not the blasted lady they so desperately wanted their daughter to be. Her bottom lip poked out the tiniest, stubbornest fraction.

Just as Rhiannon stepped off the bottom stair, someone knocked on the front door just to her left, drawing her gaze. She looked to her right down the long hall which led to the dining room. Ella wasn't coming to answer it; but then again, she never did. Rhiannon grimaced and turned back to answer the door, a welcome delaying tactic before confronting her parents.

The oval window set in the door sported a stained-glass red rose; looking through the petals, she saw two short, distorted figures. Probably Paddy's friends, she decided, since they were roughly his size. Wondering what brought these two to the O'Shea front door so early, she opened the door.

"Yes?" she asked by way of a greeting. Two young boys of about 11 or 12 stood before her silently, adoringly, eyes widened. One clutched a newspaper in his hands, and the other one held a bunch of fancy envelopes. But neither one said anything. They just fidgeted and stared with mouths slightly open.

Bemused, Rhiannon looked from the brown-headed, freckle-faced boy with the newspaper to the blond, blue-eyed boy with the envelopes. When they still didn't speak, she took a deep breath, which nearly caused the boys to pass out, and combed her hair back with her hand. They followed every move she made with worshipful expressions on their faces.

"Is it Paddy you want?" she asked, recognizing the boys from town. She turned away slightly to call for her brother.

"No, ma'am. It ain't Paddy we want. We want you," the blond boy blurted out, and then sucked in a sharp breath. His friend looked as if he'd just been mortally wounded.

Rhiannon looked at them, dipping her chin slightly to one side and raising her eyebrows. "Oh?"

The darker, taller boy poked his companion in the ribs angrily. He started to speak, his voice broke, and he turned red, but he finally stammered out, "What Joe means, Miss O'Shea, is that our business is with you." His knuckles were white as he gripped the newspaper as tightly as if it were a lifeline.

"Your business?" Intrigued, Rhiannon leaned a shoulder against the doorjamb and folded her arms together under her bosom, her confrontation with her father momentarily forgotten. "With me?"

"Yes'em, miss," Joe stammered out, swallowing hard. "Mr. Wolfe sent us—me—around . . . with this." He shoved a cream-colored envelope toward Rhiannon. He still had a handful of like-colored and -sized envelopes clutched to his chest. "It's a invite to a party—for you—at Mr. Wolfe's. He ain't never had a party before."

Eyes narrowed slightly at this bit of news, Rhiannon straightened up and took the envelope warily, much as if it were a trap that would snap over her hand. Joe tried to smile, but didn't quite succeed. Deciding not to kill the messenger, Rhiannon thanked him and put the envelope, unopened, in the deep pocket of her silk wrapper. It felt heavy against her hip, as if it carried a weighted message.

But Joe wasn't finished. He fished through his stash and came up with another envelope. "And . . . and this one's for your ma and pa. They're invited, too. So's the whole town; leastwise, the growed-up folks is."

Rhiannon took this envelope too and again thanked Joe. She held it in one hand and tapped it absently against her other palm. "Is that all?" she asked, now intensely curious about the invitation to a party in her honor given by Mr. Wolfe. She wanted to be alone to open hers.

But apparently the boys' mission was not concluded. Joe, giddy from talking to the girl of his dreams and of every other boy's in town, except for her brothers, adopted a swaggering stance and attitude toward the other boy. "Go on, Tom, she ain't goin' ta bite you. Tell the lady what you got ta say." He pushed the taller boy, Tom, forward.

Tom turned a bright red again and ran a finger around his shirt collar. He smiled and opened his mouth to speak, but nothing came out.

"Did Mr. Wolfe send you, too?" Rhiannon prompted, flattered and amused at the obvious puppy love these two displayed for her.

Tom shook his head no.

"Is that newspaper for me?"

Tom shook his head yes.

"May I have it then, please?"

Tom shook his head yes again, but he didn't offer the paper to her. When Rhiannon held her hand out, Tom stared at it so adoringly that Rhiannon was half afraid he was going to take it and kiss it. Joe jumped in to end the obvious stalemate.

43

He pried the paper out of Tom's frozen fingers and offered it, with a slight manly bow.

Rhiannon took the newspaper, wondering why a copy was sent specifically to her and by whom. Then, remembering her manners, she made a small curtsy in answer to Joe's bow. "Thank you, kind sirs," she said, playing along, "and now if you'll excuse me . . ."

Joe took her cue, grabbing a handful of Tom's shirt sleeve and pulling him back off the veranda with him. "Yes, ma'am, Rhian—uh, Miss O'Shea." He looked behind him for the two gray steps. Finding them, he hauled the silent, transfixed Tom down them with him, and continued to back out of the O'Shea yard.

Rhiannon chuckled, shook her head, and stepped back to close the front door. Inside now, she looked at the handwriting on the envelope. The penmanship was superb, but a bit fussier than she would have thought for a man of Mr. Wolfe's size and personality. Well, of course, what was she thinking? A man of his stature wouldn't address his own invitations. But then, who had? A woman? To her surprise, Rhiannon found she didn't like the idea of a woman performing that personal service for . . . Mr. Wolfe. And she didn't like thinking of him as Mr. Wolfe. She'd been barely five years old when he'd left for West Point, but all her life she'd heard talk of Hank Wolfe, the only son of the town's founder. She felt like she knew him, even if she really didn't.

Well, she certainly knew his father—hadn't he always had a kind word and a pat on the head for her when she was little? And hadn't he always been the kindest gentleman when she'd met him in town or at her father's bank? She'd always thought that the older Mr. Wolfe looked a trifle sad, for all his wealth, after his wife, the town's own Sara Penland, had died, and especially after his son had left for West Point. He'd hardly ever come into town after that. Suddenly Rhiannon felt very sorry for the old gentleman, living in that mansion with only his valet, MacGregor, and Mrs. Wolfe's two old spinster aunts, Miss Tillie and Miss Penelope, for company.

Of course, Rhiannon thought, remembering the two old women. A smile came to her lips. They must still be alive, and they must have addressed these envelopes. She felt an instant lifting of her spirits. Only to have them dashed again by the question of why in the world was Mr. Wolfe—Hank— giving her a party. And without having asked her in the first place if he could. Who did he think he was?

"Rhiannon Pauline O'Shea, where in the world are—why, there you are, girl. What in the world's keeping you? Your father will not—what's that you have there?"

Rhiannon looked up at the sound of her mother's voice. She was coming from the kitchen at the back of the house at a pace that clearly said she was not pleased by her daughter's delay. "Mother, are the Misses Penland still alive?"

That stopped her mother. "Now why in the world are you asking me that? What's that got to do—"

"Mother, are they?"

"Why, certainly, the old dears are still around and just as spry as ever. Now, will you tell me what—"

"Here," Rhiannon said, holding out her parents' invitation to her mother as she walked to her. "I believe it's from the Wolfe mansion."

Mrs. O'Shea took the envelope, gazed at it a moment, and gasped in delight. "Why, I'd almost forgotten. The old dears. They told me they wanted to have a party . . . but I didn't know they were serious—or would even remember saying it. I never thought about it again." She opened the envelope, quickly scanned the contents, put a hand to her throat, and looked wide-eyed at her daughter. "There hasn't been a party at the mansion since poor Sara passed on. And now, there's to be one . . . for you . . . with dancing."

Rhiannon knew she should be excited and honored, but in truth, all she felt was keen if unreasonable disappointment. The party for her wasn't Hank's idea. It had been

45

planned long before she'd even come home, and by his aunts. Long before he'd seen her all grown up . . . and a lady. That brought a scoff to her lips, one she barely swallowed. After all, why should she care?

Rhiannon watched as her mother continued to look at her, but she could tell she didn't really see her daughter. Her mother looked as if she were in a trance. Rhiannon knew exactly what she was thinking: This party would overshadow the scandal of last night. It would put Rhiannon and her family back in the center of attention, but in a positive way.

Patience O'Shea snapped out of her reverie at the sound of her husband's bellow. "For the love of Pete, Mother, where is that girl? I've got a business to run. I can't be shilly-shallying around here all day." His last words brought him around the corner and into the hall.

"Edwin, come here. The most wonderful thing has happened and all because of Rhiannon." She motioned excitedly for her husband to join them.

"Well, now," he gruffed as he came up the hall, "that'd be a definite switch."

Rhiannon pursed her lips in a fair imitation of her mother, but didn't say anything. She tucked the folded newspaper under one arm and moved closer to her mother so she could read over her shoulder. Her father looked over his wife's other shoulder. Huddled there in the hallway, last night's transgression obviously forgotten, if only for the moment, the three O'Sheas read the invitation silently. The engraved silver words requested the honor of their presence at a formal soiree to be given in honor of Miss Rhiannon O'Shea's homecoming. The date was set for the following weekend. Finished reading, the three looked up and at each other. A reverent silence filled the hallway for a second or two before Patience twittered into action.

"A week away? For heaven's sake, what will I wear? Oh, my, there's so much to do!" She smoothed her hair back from her face, and did the same thing to Rhiannon. She then turned to her husband and straightened his already straight lapels. She then corrected the angle of a picture hanging on the wall to her side. Still clutching the precious invitation in her hand and clucking her tongue, she hurried off to the kitchen, as if overseeing Ella, their combined cook, housekeeper, nanny, and family boss, was vital to her attending this fete for her daughter. She could be heard hurrying the boys to finish their breakfast and to scat outside. She didn't need a gang of boys underfoot.

Rhiannon looked askance at her father. He merely sighed. Then, spying the newspaper under Rhiannon's arm, he reached out for it. "Why, there's the paper. What in the world are you doing with it, girl?" His smile told her he wasn't going to berate her for last night if her mother didn't demand it. He rarely did, left to himself.

"I have no idea why I have it. It was delivered to me personally just now, along with the invitations—I mean, invitation—to the mansion." She handed the newspaper over to him.

"Well, that's exceeding strange, now isn't it? Who would do such a thing, do you suppose?" Edwin O'Shea was unfolding *The Wolfe Daily* as he spoke.

"I'm sure I don't know, Father. Now, if you'll excuse me, I must get dressed and . . . and help Mother." Help her do what, she had no idea, knowing that Ella would actually do all the work with Patience O'Shea only getting in her way. What Rhiannon really wanted was to be alone to read her own invitation. And she was counting on her father to be sufficiently distracted that he wouldn't question her.

To her relief, her father's frowning attention was focused on the twisted-up pages of the paper, for he murmured, "Of course, darlin', of course. Go ahead. Now why in the world is the paper all knotted up like this? It looks as if someone has been wringing it out like a wet rag." He gave up trying to straighten the pages and called out to his wife as he went back to the kitchen. "Patience, will you just look at this paper?

47

I must have a word with Mr. Sullivan. That boy Tom has nearly destroyed this until it's practically unreadable. . . ." His voice trailed off as he went back around the corner.

Rhiannon heaved a sigh of relief and turned to make a running dash up the stairs. She had the envelope out of her pocket almost before she closed the door to her room. With her back pressed against the door, she tore it open and pulled the invitation out. Her heart stopped. She'd just known it. Scrawled across the silver letters was a bold handwriting— and it was his. Not stopping to ask herself why she was so excited and so weak-kneed, especially since she didn't care about men and getting married, she held the small elegant square in both hands and brought it close to her face. She took a deep breath, inhaling to see if his scent, the way he'd smelled last night, was on the paper. She fancied it was.

"Miss O'Shea," she read aloud, "I will call for you at ten this morning. My aunts, Miss Tillie and Miss Penelope Penland, desire a visit with you in order to renew your acquaintanceship before the party in your honor. Hank."

Rhiannon tried to mask her pure excitement at seeing Hank again so soon by huffing about the tone of his note. It was a command, actually. Not a request. Not a "May I call for you," but an "I will call for you." Like some royal decree. Well, she humphed, perhaps she just wouldn't be available when he called. But she knew darn well she would be. Even now her feet were moving her to her armoire, and the feminine part of her brain was sorting through appropriate outfits.

But that was as far as she got before a roaring bellow from downstairs froze her in her tracks and then whirled her around to face her closed door. What now? The muffled sounds of her mother's raised voice and her father's continued bellowing filtered up to Rhiannon. Within a few seconds, the house shook again, but this time with the sounds of desperate, pounding feet, more than one set, flying up the stairs. The stampeding herd continued past her room and down the hall. Two doors slammed, and then all was quiet.

Rhiannon laughed and relaxed. Whatever Eddie, Patrick, and John had done, they were now safe in their rooms. For once, Rhiannon thought, whatever was wrong, it wasn't her doing.

Dismissing the ruckus, she placed Hank's note on her vanity and opened the doors to her armoire. She let the giddiness she was trying so hard to deny wash over her while she gazed sightlessly at her clothes. Almost of their own volition, her fingers found the spot on her neck that Hank had kissed last night. She closed her eyes, savoring the velvet moment in her mind. She swore she could feel his lips on her even now. In her mind's eye, she saw the scene they must have made, sitting there on the veranda, in the moonlight, kissing—

"Rhiannon!"

Her mother's shrill voice, sounding like she was calling up from the foot of the stairs, shattered Rhiannon's romantic vision. And piqued her temper. Was there never to be any peace in this house? And how was she supposed to get dressed when these constant summons kept detaining her?

"Rhiannon! I say, girl, come here now and tell me what the meaning of all this is! Why, the very idea! Rhiannon!" It must be serious. That was Father. He never called up to the children. Being the bailiff, presenting the accused, was always Mother's responsibility.

Rhiannon strode purposefully toward her door, jerked it open with more force than necessary, and hurried to the landing. "I'm coming, Father, for heaven's sake. What is all the fuss? I have to get dressed—"

"Look! Just look at this! How do you explain this? Not home more than a few days and already—!"

Rhiannon could see he held up the front page of the newspaper, but she couldn't make out the headlines or what they had to do with her. Surely her riding astride a horse like a man, even while dressed like a man, hadn't made the front page. This town couldn't be that desperate for news stories.

But it was the only outrageous thing she'd done since she'd been home . . . if she didn't count insulting Hank Wolfe last night at dinner and then getting caught letting him kiss her.

"Explain what, Father? I haven't done anything. I—"

"Haven't done anything? Do you hear that, Mother? The girl says she hasn't done anything."

Rhiannon looked from her father to her mother, who sadly clucked her tongue and wrung her hands, and back again. A large knot began to form in her stomach as she quickly skipped down the polished stairs and anxiously cast about in her mind for some recent but forgotten breach of ladyhood on her part. Nothing presented itself.

And nothing could have prepared her for the stomach-punch of the newspaper's headlines, held up so accusingly in her father's shaking hands. "MISS RHIANNON O'SHEA TO RUN FOR MAYOR OF WOLFE."

No one had to tell Rhiannon her eyes were bulging. With a gasp of disbelief, she snatched the paper from her father and read the sub-headline: "All-Woman Slate for City Council Also Nominated."

"I swear," she gasped out, her own hands shaking now, "I had nothing to do with this. Why, it's absolutely preposterous—even for me."

"Let me see that." Her father took the paper and began to read snippets of the story aloud. Rhiannon and her mother looked over his shoulders. "It says here, according to Jimmy Pickens, the reporter, that a meeting was called to order in the Fancy Lady Saloon yesterday afternoon by Mayor Driver. Why, the blasted man was in my own home last night, eating my food."

"Oh, Edwin, do go on with the story!"

"For the purpose of discussing the upcoming visit of Mrs. Carry A. Nation and her Temperance League. He goes on to say that the voting citizenry came up with this female slate. Imagine those men daring to mention my sainted daughter in a saloon. By God, I'll—"

"Edwin! Either tell me what it says or give me that newspaper!"

"To combat the prohibitionist women of the League." He read the rest of the story in a rambling murmur and then synopsized it for his wife and daughter. "It turns out that the meeting was perfectly legal, and the women were duly nominated. So, if they decide to run, they can. This is outrageous! Why, the scandal must be all over town by now! But that's not all. Our own Rhiannon was nominated by Old Jed—the town drunk! And she's on a slate with Widow Calvert, Mrs. Freda Gruenwald, Miss Susie Johnson, Mrs. Joletta Hawkins, and . . . and one Cat LaFlamme."

Cat LaFlamme? Rhiannon knew the other women, but not her. Things were changing in Wolfe. Patience O'Shea suddenly needed to sit down; the bottom stair served. "Cat LaFlamme? Edwin, what is a Cat LaFlamme?"

"Ahem . . . well, my dear . . . it's a who, not a what. Or actually a she. She's a . . . she's a fancy lady at the Fancy Lady Saloon."

"Father!"

"Now, Rhiannon. I know that from talk in town. It's not like I frequent the place or anything."

"Edwin, I think I need to sit down."

"You are sitting down, dear."

"Oh. Good."

"Does that mean she's a whore, Father?"

All heads snapped around at the sound of six-year-old John's voice. He and Patrick were sitting at the top of the stairs. Apparently, they'd been there a while . . . at least, long enough. Rhiannon's snort of laughter was drowned out by her father's strangled bellow. The boys jumped up and fled.

Edwin O'Shea crushed the newspaper in his hands, much as if it were someone's neck, and headed towards the door. "Rhiannon, see to your mother. I'm going down to that newspaper office to confront that blasted editor, Mr. Sullivan. Why, the scandal of it all. The absolute besmirching of your good name! I only pray that Mr. Wolfe hasn't seen this edition yet. I'll be ruined. We'll all be ruined! That editor will retract this story with a public apology, or there will be a public hanging, by God!"

Rhiannon tore her worried gaze from her mother, who appeared to be in a trance, and grabbed her father's coat sleeve. "Father, you can't do that! You can't storm in there and accost Mr. Sullivan. You need to calm down, or you'll only make things worse. Of course this story is all a joke; don't you see that?"

Edwin O'Shea covered his daughter's hand on his sleeve with his own. The gesture was tender, but his words weren't. "Of course it's a joke. Women running a town. Whoever heard of such a thing? Everyone knows women aren't capable of governing anything but a home. The very idea."

"I beg your pardon!" Rhiannon removed her hand from her father's grip and pulled herself up to her full, offended height. "And why couldn't women run a city government? They certainly couldn't do any worse than you men."

"Rhiannon Pauline O'Shea, that will be quite enough. You keep a civil tongue in your head. Now, see to your mother, like I asked, and . . . and get dressed."

Rhiannon had a stinging retort on the tip of her tongue, but she never got to use it, because her father turned away and jerked open the front door. Hank Wolfe nearly hit him on his forehead with his fist, which he had poised to knock on the O'Shea front door.

The O'Sheas, Rhiannon just slightly behind her father, stood speechless in front of Hank Wolfe. When no one greeted him, he silently brought his hand down to his side and stared back at them. "Is something wrong? Did you get my message? I'm here for Miss O'Shea." He looked around Edwin O'Shea to Rhiannon, still clad in her silk morning wrapper. His gaze raked her up and down. "I commend you on an interesting choice, Miss O'Shea, but it's hardly a riding habit."

Rhiannon gaped at him momentarily until his meaning sunk in. She looked down at herself, squeaked out a tiny "oh!" slammed the front door shut in Hank's face, and nearly knocked her mother over as she brushed by her on the stairs. "Honestly, Father, why didn't you tell me it's ten o'clock?" she cried accusingly.

Hank brazenly opened the door and leaned in to watch Rhiannon's bottom bounce up the stairs. He smiled appreciatively. She was ready all right—for bed.

Edwin O'Shea finally recovered. "Ten o'clock? What the devil does ten o'clock have to do with anything?" he called up the stairwell after his oldest child. Then he remembered that Mr. Wolfe was still standing in the doorway. And that his wife was sitting on the bottom step. He looked from Hank to his wife, clearly undecided as to whom he should deal with first. Hank very graciously waved his hand towards Mrs. O'Shea. Thus absolved, Edwin bent over his wife and put his hand on her shoulder.

"Patience, dear, try to pull yourself together. We have company," he said very quietly. With awkward tenderness, he tugged at the crossed panels of her morning coat, trying to make her more presentable. Then, with a large, gruff hand he smoothed the loose hair away from her face and helped her to her feet. "Now, dear, why don't you go upstairs to dress? I'll take care of everything."

Finally, Patience's eyes cleared. She looked at her husband and then at Hank, still standing in the doorway. Her eyes widened considerably. "Edwin, Mr. Wolfe is here. Do invite him in. If you'll excuse me, I believe I will go get dressed."

"Yes, Mother, that would be nice." Edwin watched his wife slowly ascend the stairs, as if making sure she took no unexpected detours. He then turned to Hank, waving him inside and closing the door behind him. "Why don't we sit in the parlor? I'm sorry you found us in such a state of domestic upheaval, Mr. Wolfe," Edwin commented, clearly embarrassed. "But you know how family is."

53

"Yes," Hank commented absently, but he really didn't know how family was; there'd always only been his father, MacGregor, and himself. He sat gingerly on the edge of a delicate-looking chair, not at all sure it could support his weight.

The brief but awkward silence between the two men, one that existed between Hank and everyone else in this town because of the accident of his birth, was broken by the noisy entrance of Paddy and John into the room. They gave a sidelong glance at Hank and went directly up to their father.

"Eddie says Rhiannon is going to kill Momma one day. Papa, I don't want Momma to die," John blurted out, his little chin quavering. A muffled snort was heard from the general direction of Hank's chair.

Patrick shook his 11-year-old head. "I tried to tell him, Papa. But he won't listen to me. He didn't really mean it like that, Johnny-Cake."

Before Mr. O'Shea could respond, John had another question. "If Rhiannon is the mayor, does that make me her grandpa?"

Edwin nearly came off his seat. "Your sister most certainly will not be the mayor! And you'll be no one's grandpa for years to come—and neither will I, at this rate. Now, go on, the two of you, see what's keeping your sister." He then looked at Hank. "You did say you were here for Rhiannon?"

"Yes, I did."

"Are you going to kiss her again?"

John's bald but innocent question did lift Mr. O'Shea off his seat. Patrick very wisely grabbed his younger brother and hauled him out of the room and out of his father's reach.

Hank coughed behind his hand and resettled himself in his seat. He gave Mr. O'Shea a moment to compose himself on the settee before he commented, "Obviously Miss O'Shea did not inform you that I would be calling this morning."

"My daughter very rarely informs me of anything, Mr. Wolfe. But if this is about that ridiculous story in *The Wolfe Daily,* let me assure you that I fully intend to have Mr Sullivan retract it this very day. In fact, I was on my way to his office when you arrived. I can't imagine what the man was thinking about, except increasing that rag's circulation." He stopped short, as if he'd just remembered that Hank owned the newspaper—and the bank, from which Mr. O'Shea was very absent this morning. "But perhaps I'd best be on my way to work. It is after ten o'clock."

Hank smiled and stood when he did, content to let Mr. O'Shea draw his own conclusions about what he wanted with his daughter and what he thought of the front page of *The Wolfe Daily.* Actually, he'd had to change his pants after spilling his coffee all over his lap when he opened the paper this morning at breakfast. His own thoughts had echoed those of Mr. O'Shea—what indeed was Sullivan, the editor, thinking?

"Well, then, I'll be going, Mr. Wolfe." Mr. O'Shea reached out a hand, which Hank clasped. "I'm sure my daughter will be right down." But he didn't look sure to Hank, as his gaze kept darting to the empty stairwell.

After Mr. O'Shea left, Hank sat back down to wait for Rhiannon. An unusual name for an unusual lady, he thought. She'd been back in Wolfe for only a few days, and already she had the entire town on its ear. A chuckling snort escaped Hank as he ran a hand over his jaw in an absent manner. The town? Hell, him too. After all, because of her, here he was all gussied up and sitting in a tiny parlor chair on a weekday morning when he should be out attending to the business of the Wolfe holdings.

The Wolfe holdings, he mused, a purely predatory turn of mind overcoming him. The only holding this Wolfe was interested in was a redheaded young lady upstairs. And she certainly didn't need to be dressed for what he had in mind.

Chapter Five

She should be comfortable. After all, the well-sprung surrey made light of any ruts on the road that ran from the town of Wolfe to the mansion itself. Since they were now away from the gazes, which ranged from curious to shocked, of the townspeople and were in the open country, she should be relaxed. The seat under her was well padded; the July morning was young and warm; the earth smelled fresh; and the company was incredibly handsome.

And incredibly big and taking up almost the entire seat. Indeed, she was pressed right up against the man's side from her shoulder to her knee. It was a most unsettling feeling, not unpleasant—just unsettling.

"Would you mind moving over, Mr. Wolfe? You're taking up the entire seat. It's much too hot to be pressed up against another human being like this."

Now what had she said that was so vastly amusing?

"Do you really think so, Miss O'Shea?"

"Do I really think what, Mr. Wolfe?"

"That it's too hot to be pressed up against another human being. How disappointing."

Finally getting the import he'd given her innocent comment, Rhiannon felt her face flush warmly, but she did manage a retort. "Wipe that silly smirk off your face. You know what I mean."

"I seriously doubt, Miss O'Shea, that I've ever had a silly smirk on my face in my entire life. But if it will make you happy, I'll stop the surrey and you can get in the backseat."

"That's ridiculous. Of course I'll do no such thing." She turned her face away from his gleaming black eyes and laughing mouth, and raised her chin an elegant notch.

"Then, perhaps you'd like the reins and for me to get in the backseat."

She turned back to him, eyes narrowed, lips pressed together. "Never mind," she said with glaring finality.

"If you say so." He stretched back, shifted the reins to one hand, and put his arm around Rhiannon's shoulders. His muscled weight sent the seat rocking precariously, but Rhiannon refused to acknowledge her very real fear that she was going to end up in the dirt. Besides, his mocking grin dared her to protest his forwardness.

Acutely aware of the virile man seated to her left, she felt her heart thudding in time with the horse's clopping gait. She cast about for a safe topic. "It's a very nice thing your aunts are doing, hostessing this party for me. It was a pleasant surprise."

"For me as well."

Rhiannon had only to turn her head a fraction of an inch to look into his eyes. They were that close. "What do you mean? Didn't you know about the party before now?"

"Certainly, I did. But you . . . you're the pleasant surprise in all this, Rhiannon."

Rhiannon looked into his eyes, which had just warmed dangerously. She found she had to look down at her hands, and was surprised to see they were knotted together in her lap. She decided not to comment on his calling her by her given name. "Well, Mr Wolfe, I'm used to being a surprise to people. But hardly ever a pleasant one."

There must have been some quality to her voice or in her words of which she was unaware, because he gave her a sharp look, sat up straighter, and brought the gleaming bay to a halt. He turned to her and looked into her eyes, holding her gaze for all eternity if he so willed it. She wasn't aware of him raising his hand until his fingers, lean and strong, stroked her cheek and fondled a loose curl.

She just knew he was going to kiss her; and she just knew she was going to let him. But instead, he held her chin with his thumb and forefinger and spoke softly. "Rhiannon, anyone who is not pleasantly surprised by you is a fool. Don't ever let anyone tell you any differently."

She was afraid she was going to cry. His tenderness was more unnerving than his teasing. And then he did kiss her, just a feather-soft touching of lips brushing across one another. Her gooseflesh belied the July heat. She took a shuddering breath and said, "Thank you," on the exhalation.

"That's more like it," he teased, breaking the spell and setting them on their way again. "Now, tell me all about how it feels to be a candidate for mayor."

That did it. Rhiannon regained her balance admirably with that dig. She sat up very straight, very prim, with her folded hands in her lap; she'd show him she could jest with the best of them. "I'm afraid I can't do that at this time. You see, I haven't as yet officially accepted the town's nomination."

Had he just smirked again, or just chuckled, or anything but what he actually did, which was laugh out loud like a braying ass, she might have let the story and her jest die right there. But his laugh implied too much—about her and about women in general. Men. They were all alike.

A knot of resolution that she hadn't even known until this moment existed tightened within her. She'd show him and all of them. Women were as fully capable of governing a town as were any men. Let them laugh.

"I take it by your laughter that you don't agree with the majority of the town's men that I would make a good mayor."

Her words, or maybe it was the conviction in her voice, must have sunk in. Hank sobered and looked over at her. "You can't be serious. Those men certainly weren't. They were drunk, Rhiannon; they were just joking."

"I'll thank you to call me Miss O'Shea, Mr. Wolfe. And joke or no, I'm going to run. The paper—*your* paper—said the nominations were all legal. I assume *your* editor would not print anything that was not true."

"Oh, boy."

"Oh, boy? That's all you can think to say? Quite succinct, Mr. Wolfe."

"Look, Rhian—Miss O'Shea, I did not mean to offend you just now. You have to see that you can't do this; you can't run for mayor." His next words came out in a measured clip, each one its own sentence. "You. Can't."

"Excuse me, Mr. Wolfe, but I don't see any wedding band on my hand or yours that says you have any right to tell me what I can or cannot do. *Not* that being married would stop me, either. You have no claim on me, sir."

"Claim? I don't have to have any claim on you to know you can't run for mayor."

"You needn't shout. And why can't I run? I was nominated. I saw it for myself in *your* newspaper. Ole Jed nominated me and Mayor Driver himself seconded it."

"Well, there's a recommendation—Ole Jed. And now you're the one shouting. I'm telling you for the last time that you are not to campaign for the office of mayor of Wolfe, Kansas. Goddammit, it's *my* town."

"*Your* town?! Why, you pompous, braying ass. And I thought you were different."

"Different? Different has nothing to do with it. I'm talking about trouble. I'm trying to protect you."

"Protect me from whom?"

"Where should I start? The townspeople, for one. That joke of a story will have them all riled up by now. The last thing we need is for you to declare your intention to actually run. If you do that, then the other women will fall in behind you. Then there'd be trouble between the men and women of Wolfe. And God knows there'll be enough of that with Carry Nation coming to town this summer. Which will bring every sort of vigilante and otherwise twisted individual west of the Mississippi to Wolfe. Do you want to face all that and deal with it, Rhiannon? Do you?"

Rhiannon faced forward for a moment. She hadn't thought about all that. But it sounded very exciting, much more so than the summer of socials and teas and benefits and the like her mother had planned for them. She was now ready to turn back to Hank.

"Yes, I believe I do want to face all that and deal with it. After all, wasn't that exactly why the men nominated us women—to deal with everything you just mentioned, because they don't want to? And another thing, Mr. Wolfe. You wouldn't be this angry if you didn't think we had a chance of winning. So you see, I can't let down my hometown in its hour of need. I must do my civic duty."

Hank looked in serious danger of losing his temper, his health, and a vein or two in his head. Indeed, his face was almost purple. Rhiannon pulled back in alarm. When he spoke, it was through gritted teeth. "Its hour of need, Rhiannon? Civic duty?" He took her arm and pulled her slightly toward him. Angry heat radiated from him. "Get this through that beautiful head of yours, young lady: The story was a joke. Do you hear me? A joke. Neither you nor any other woman is going to run for office in Wolfe."

Rhiannon freed her arm, ignoring his comment about her beauty. "I see, Hank." She made a specific point of using his first name. "But Hank, how do you propose to stop me?"

Black, angry, glistening eyes bored into hers. But she'd be hanged if she'd be the first one to look away—or even blink. His face looked like a thundercloud. And here came the lightning. Hank exploded out of the surrey, tossing the reins to the floorboard with an angry gesture. He strode away five or six measured paces before he stopped suddenly, much as if he'd hit an invisible brick wall, and slowly looked to his left, and then to his right.

Watching him, Rhiannon suddenly realized for herself what was wrong. She sat up straight with all the grace of a prairie dog popping up out of its hole. It was her turn to look slowly around her. Great merciful heavens, the horse had simply continued on its way home while they'd argued. And it had deposited them right in front of the Wolfe mansion. They hadn't even noticed, so heated had been their argument. But that wasn't the worst of it. Rhiannon gasped. Their fuss had an audience other than the bay gelding . . . and other than the wide-eyed stable boy who held the bridle.

Only several yards away, certainly within hearing distance, stood two tiny, elegantly dressed older women, the sisters Penland, Hank's great-aunts. They shared the wide, sweeping front steps of the mansion with an elderly gentleman, who appeared to be all starch and polish. The two women were clutching each other's hands in dismay, if the looks on their faces were to be believed. The man had no expression whatsoever, but one eyebrow was raised almost to his hairline. With a sinking feeling, Rhiannon recognized MacGregor, the Wolfe valet for two generations, and the western Kansas arbiter of proper dress—and behavior.

Hank very slowly turned back around, regaining Rhiannon's attention. She didn't know what to expect, but certainly in a million years she would not have expected the mirthful outburst that shook Hank's large frame. He laughed his way back to her side of the surrey, the side furthest away from the mansion, and put his hands up to her to help her down.

Her first instinct was to bat his hands away; he might find this highly amusing, but she certainly didn't. And she was perfectly capable of getting out of a surrey by herself. She did not need a man's help. Apparently, her thoughts were written on her face, because Hank quirked an eyebrow, a fair imitation of his valet, reached into the surrey, and took hold of her waist.

Shocked at his forwardness with her person, and left with no other option but to allow him to help her down or add a physical struggle to this already public scene, Rhiannon gave in—after a fashion. She behaved for all the world as if she were the Queen of England being helped out of the royal carriage by a faithful servant. But Hank's bemused chuckle told her he saw through her haughty demeanor.

In fact, he saw her challenge and gave her one of his own: He didn't just hand her down; he inched her down . . . down, very intimately, right down his front, so that Rhiannon got a breathtaking view of every one of Hank's features from the top of his head to the middle of his chest, which was at her eye level with her feet on the ground. At least, she thought her feet were on the ground.

And apparently they were, because she found herself whirled around briskly, before she could recover her equilibrium, and herded trippingly toward the trio on the wide semicircular front steps of the mansion. If Hank's huge hand had not been holding onto her elbow, she would have fallen over her tangled peach-colored skirt. The rotten scoundrel hadn't given her a moment to straighten her clothing after he'd rubbed her all over him.

Hauled up short in front of the two sisters, MacGregor having distanced himself from his employers to hold open one side of the double front doors, Rhiannon found herself grateful, for the first time, for three years of constant drilling by Miss Constance at her blasted finishing school. Despite being so disconcerted, so bulldog-angry at her host, she made it through the greetings with a fair semblance of elegant manners.

Ushered inside by Hank, after allowing his aunts to precede them, Rhiannon put up a valiant but futile struggle to free her elbow from Hank's grasp. And that huge toad appeared not even to be aware of her jerking motions as they crossed the black-and-white tiled entryway and turned right into a richly turned-out and sunny room. But the disdainful sniff from somewhere behind them, in the general direction of the front door, which MacGregor had held open for them and had just now closed, gave eloquent witness to the silent scene.

"Here. Sit here. We'll have tea," Miss Tillie ordered with no preamble. With a tiny, frail, blue-veined hand, she pointed to a lovely damask-covered parlor chair.

Rhiannon sat, or she would have had Hank not plopped her down on the delicate piece. As best she could, she arranged her clothing and her face to give a pleasant picture. While she smiled congenially at her hostesses as they sat together on a beautiful maroon horsehair sofa and prepared to pour tea from an ornate silver service, Rhiannon's mind raced to catalogue various tortures to which she could subject her still-hovering host.

"Dear Henry, do sit down. You're going to smother our guest, I fear." Aunt Penelope handed Rhiannon an almost transparent bone-china teacup and saucer while she spoke to her great-nephew. Her hand shook slightly from old-age palsy.

"Yes, Henry, do sit down," Rhiannon echoed, giving complete and unnecessary emphasis to Hank's formal name. She liked it; it made him sound . . . small. Perhaps she'd call him that from now on.

Or perhaps she wouldn't. Henry Hank Wolfe startled the elegant assemblage by dragging an upholstered Queen Anne wing-back chair from its proper place by the huge marbled fireplace to arrange it right next to Rhiannon's seat. Eyebrows were raised all around, but no one commented.

Shocked at his outrageous behavior, which was quickly becoming the norm, Rhiannon cut her eyes over at the sisters. She caught them exchanging a glance that could only be called conspiratorial. She would have expected disdain, outrage, anger, anything but the tiniest of smirks that she witnessed. Not knowing what to think, Rhiannon took another sip of her tea.

Hank chose that moment to reach over to the low coffee table, pick up an ornately carved humidor, and flip open the lid. He held it out to Rhiannon. "Cigar?" he asked.

Rhiannon choked, and the sisters gasped. Penelope handed her guest a linen napkin and turned to her nephew. "Henry, how could you? You've caused the dear girl to choke. Of course, she doesn't want a cigar. It's much too early in the day. Now, see to her." She waved her lace-covered hand in Rhiannon's direction.

"Remember your manners, dear," Aunt Tillie offered, a slightly dotty smile on her tiny, wrinkled face.

"Oh, what could I have been thinking?" Hank intoned, thumping the humidor back down on the table. He took the cup and saucer from Rhiannon with one hand and pounded the life out of her with his other one. "There, see? She's fine now. Aren't you, Miss O'Shea?"

Hank should have died right there on the spot. That he didn't was proof positive that looks could not kill. At least not someone of his size and strength. Lucky for the frail sisters Penland, though, Rhiannon's malignant visage was blocked from killing them by Hank's face being right in front of hers. They were almost nose-to-nose as he bent over her in an attitude of solicitous care. Otherwise, there would have been an immediate need for the undertaker to bring two small coffins to the Wolfe mansion.

"I'm fine," Rhiannon gargled out, covering her coughing with her white linen napkin. She narrowed her eyes at Hank.

"See? I told you. No harm done." Hank smiled at his aunts and straightened up. He put the china down on the silver tray and retook his seat, negligently crossing one ankle over the opposite knee. His fingers drummed the armrests restlessly.

"Perhaps you'd like a cake, Miss O'Shea?" Aunt Tillie held out a serving plate of delicately frosted little squares.

Rhiannon shook her head, not yet trusting herself to speak, much less swallow food. She dabbed at her eyes with her napkin and watched Hank, a picture of leashed energy. He gave every appearance of soon bolting from the room. Was he still this angry with her for her determination to run for mayor? Or was it something else?

"Well, then," Aunt Tillie pronounced, "perhaps I shall." She then heaped six squares onto her dessert plate, drawing all eyes to her.

"Tillie," her sister warned, taking the serving plate away from her. Tillie pretended not to notice as she very delicately stuffed a square into her mouth.

Despite herself, Rhiannon was forced to bite back a bark of laughter. Hank wasn't so lucky; his snorting guffaw tore through the formal room.

"She does so love her sweets," Penelope felt compelled to comment. Tillie licked her fingers and reached for another square, ignoring her sister. "I'm afraid that if you continue on like this, Tillie, I shall be forced to tell Dr. Johnson that you're not staying with your diet regimen."

Tillie's thin, pale eyebrows waggled defiantly. Only her full mouth kept her from commenting.

Rhiannon took it upon herself to save the morning. Ignoring Hank's black-eyed gaze that bored into her from his chair, she smiled sweetly and kept her eyes on Penelope. "It's very kind of you and your sister to hostess a fete in my honor. I can't tell you how pleased I am, as is my family."

Penelope latched onto her comment, apparently grateful for any noise other than Tillie's smacking. "Why, the honor is all ours; isn't it, sister?"

Tillie nodded and smiled, her full cheeks making her look for all the world like an elegantly dressed chipmunk.

Penelope went on, revealing much more than Hank would have wanted, Rhiannon realized. Indeed, the more she prattled on, the more rigidly he sat up. "Your homecoming has been just the thing for all of us. We've all been so mournful since our dear Ezra's passing six months ago. And Henry has been the worst. He stalks around here like some sort of caged, exotic animal. I'm afraid that Tillie and I aren't the sort of diversions he needs. We're much too old and gloomy, I fear. Our nephew needs young people and fun and laughter, don't you think, Miss O'Shea? And that's where you come in, dear."

Now it was Rhiannon's turn to be uncomfortable and to sit up rigidly. Dear God . . .

"I'm forced to admit that Tillie and I shamelessly used you and your advantageous return home to pester Henry into opening this huge old house to the townspeople. Now, don't get me wrong, we've always thought you were the dearest child. Why, our own dear Ezra, Henry's departed father, used to delight in telling some tale or other of your childish pranks in town when he'd come home. So, we know he would approve of this fete, too. And we truly do want to welcome you home. In fact, in your honor, we've put aside our black bombazine. This day is our first one out of mourning. And it's all because of you, Miss O'Shea." She punctuated her cheerful trilling by delicately holding up handfuls of her lavender skirt as proof.

Rhiannon hoped she was smiling. She thought she was. She prayed she was. "How . . . nice," she managed to squeak.

"Oh, good," Penelope warbled, clapping her hands together and clasping them to her thin chest. "Then, perhaps you'd care for a tour of the house and grounds, so we can have your valuable input into the arrangements? The soiree is less than a week away, you know."

How could she refuse? She wondered what Hank would be doing while she allowed the sisters to escort her on this grand tour. "Of course. I believe that is just the thing we need to do."

"Lovely," Penelope pronounced, her pale eyes fairly dancing. She turned to her taciturn nephew. "Henry, do be sure to include the gardens out back."

"The what?" He'd been about to light one of the now-infamous cigars, a considerable breach of etiquette in front of the ladies. The flaming match he held burned down, forgotten for the moment—by him. Rhiannon, though, watched it steadily, ticking off the seconds before it burned his fingers.

"The gardens, Hank. Penelope wants you to show our guest the gardens." It was Tillie; she was obviously feeling out of sorts with her sister.

Penelope pulled herself up short. "His name is Henry, sister. Not Hank."

"Oh, pooh, Penelope. You're the only one who calls him that. The boy hates it; don't you?"

The boy yelped when the fire stung his fingers. He vigorously shook the match to extinguish the flame. Rhiannon sat back in her chair, a self-satisfied smirk on her face, as if she'd somehow been responsible for his pain. She actually crossed her legs at the knees and swung one foot.

Hank tossed the cigar and the match onto the table and leaned forward towards his aunts. "Let me get this straight. You want me to show her around?"

"Of course she does, Hank. Catch on, boy. I thought we were the ones who were old and dotty."

Penelope wisely decided to ignore her sister. "Is there some reason why you can't, Henry?"

What could he say with all three women staring at him? "Why, no, Aunt Penelope. I have nothing better to do this morning. I'd love to show our esteemed guest of honor around the place."

If he'd hoped to insult Rhiannon with his less than gracious acceptance of this task, he'd failed. She loved the further discomfort this would so obviously cause him. It served him right for being such a boor. But the prospect of being alone with him for the considerable length of time it would take to show her the mansion and grounds sent a thrill racing across her nerve endings. Alone with him. Being pressed up against him in the surrey had been torture. What would walking through romantic gardens do to her?

"Well, good then," Penelope pronounced, standing and hauling Tillie up by the elbow. "We'll leave you young people to your stroll. Remember, Henry, to make note of any of Miss O'Shea's opinions for the soiree. Come, Tillie; we must go find MacGregor to tell him we believe we've found the answer to his problem."

Chapter Six

Rhiannon stood as the sisters left. Hank escorted them tenderly to the door, suffered a kiss on the cheek from each of them, and then closed the door behind them. He turned to face his guest. Rhiannon didn't like the look on his face— it was blank; purposely so, she suspected. If he was trying to frighten her, he was doing an admirable job of it.

But the painful tightening in her chest was nothing compared to what her teeth were doing to the inside of her cheek. She'd never been alone like this with a man before. Alone with boys, yes; but not a man. Not one like this one. What would he say? Or worse yet, what would he do?

It was only through an act of sheer will that Rhiannon did not flee out through the open French doors to her left when Wolfe began to advance steadily toward her. He appeared every bit as cunning and as powerful as the animal whose name he bore. In truth, had he grown long, pointed ears and sharp fangs, she could not have been more frightened than she was at this moment. His look alone was enough to shred her nerves; what then could his hands do to her?

He stopped not ten feet from her. Only the delicate parlor chair Rhiannon had just vacated separated them. Not much protection. His eyes, black and fathomless, came to rest on her neck. Rhiannon latched onto her full skirt to keep from bringing her hands up to cover her neck; she'd heard that if you didn't show fear—

"This, Miss O'Shea," he said, sweeping the room with his hand, "is the morning room. You've seen the entry."

Rhiannon nearly fainted into the chair, but instead she put a steadying hand on its back. Thank God, it didn't—*he* didn't intend to make a meal of her. Feeling weak and silly for letting her imagination carry her away like that, and playing for time to recover her equilibrium, she took her cue and let her gaze roam slowly over the room.

"Very nice," she commented. She'd been about to add "Mr. Wolfe," but found she wasn't comfortable calling up that particular animal and its vision again just yet.

Then, from out of nowhere, being afraid made her angry; more at herself than at him, but who else did she have to take it out on? "Look, you don't have to give me a tour of your home. It's really not necessary, and you obviously don't want to act as guide. I'm sure that whatever your aunts have planned will be just fine. Perhaps you could have someone see me home?"

She moved out from the dubious protection of the delicate chair, intending to head for the door he'd just closed after his aunts. She never made it past him. His hand snaked out to hold her arm; her heart thumped at his warm, strong grip. She was forced to look up into his eyes if she hoped to gauge his intent. His intent was not gaugeable.

"Next, I'll show you the library."

"Of course," she quickly agreed. Not that it mattered; his hand took possession of her elbow, and they were off. She could barely keep up with his masculine stride, and indeed she would have lagged far behind had he not held onto her. Outside his home, she had fought off his grip. But now, in his home, his territory, she felt somewhat off balance, as if she weren't allowed to protest. Perhaps it was because this mansion was such a tangible symbol of who he was and of the power he held in this town—his town, just as he'd declared earlier.

Once they were in the entryway, his black, polished boots clicked on the marble tiles. Rhiannon looked quickly around. Neither MacGregor nor anybody else was visible. Not even a maid with a feather duster or a butler to open and close doors. She felt this was decidedly strange in a house—nay, mansion—this size. The bustle of weekday duties should have made the staff very visible. But they weren't.

She could spare the absent staff no more of her thoughts when, directly across the entryway from the morning room, Hank slid open a ten-foot-high carved wooden door, which disappeared into the wall, and revealed the library. Her breath caught at the sheer number of volumes in the room.

"Are all these yours?" Of course, it was a stupid question; whose else would they be? But she couldn't help asking. She was completely mesmerized by shelf after shelf of precious volumes, which extended all the way to the ceiling along one whole wall; by the long tables scattered about the room, all of them with several matching chairs pulled up to them; by the reading nooks tucked into the window seats; by the lingering scent of furniture polish; but most of all, by the tantalizing smell of the leather that bound the volumes and the faint smell of cigar smoke.

So captivated was she by this room, which was easily larger than the entire first floor of her parents' home, that it was only when she turned to hear his reply that she realized she was no longer attached to Hank by the elbow.

Instead, she found him still standing at the doorway, a shoulder leaned against the jamb, his arms crossed over his broad chest. "I take it you like to read?"

Finally, he was smiling; and its immediate effect was to cause her to babble. "Oh, yes. Our mandatory reading hour

71

each day was the only time during my three years away that I didn't find myself at odds with Miss Constance. She was quite adamant that her charges be well read. Quite radical, even for Baltimore, don't you think? She said that gentlemen soon tire of a pretty face and a pleasing manner. That they wanted something to be underneath all that."

"Astute lady, our Miss Constance. Speaking as a gentleman, despite my recent behavior, I can assure you that it is precisely all that . . . underneath business that gentlemen most desire."

Rhiannon stared at him momentarily, then gasped and turned away. She latched onto the nearest book that lay on the nearest table and thumbed through it with a vengeance. Tears of embarrassment threatened to fall onto the pages.

Before she could recover, she felt herself being turned around by the shoulders and the book being removed from her hands. Then, to her astonishment, she was taken into the strongest, warmest, most tender arms she'd ever felt. Her head was held gently to his hard but comfortable chest; his other arm cradled her back. Almost of their own volition, her arms encircled his waist. He rested his chin on her head.

"Sweet, sweet Rhiannon," he sighed. "What am I to do with you?" His voice rumbled through his chest and vibrated pleasantly against her ear. "One minute you're cussing and smoking, or wearing men's clothing so you can ride your horse through town; the next you're the belle of the dinner party for the town's social elite; then, you're calling me out for doubting that you could run an entire town and face down Carry Nation and vigilantes; then I find out you are an accomplished women who is well read; and yet I can bring you to tears by alluding to your . . . underneath." A chuckling laugh escaped him.

Rhiannon smiled into his chest. She wasn't about to pull away from him; indeed, she settled herself further into his embrace and waited to hear more about herself from him.

She rather liked this intriguing female he was describing.

But he ruined it all by pulling slightly away from her and looking down at her. "Is it any wonder that I'm on my worst behavior with you? I swear I forget how very young, how innocent you really are."

"You're forgiven."

He laughed aloud. "I wasn't apologizing."

"You weren't? Well, you would have, had you kept on in that vein."

"Oh, would I, now?" With a shake of his head and an earth-shattering grin, he looked down at her . . . at her mouth. Then suddenly, he sobered. Watching his whole demeanor change, watching his eyes become hooded and his mouth open slightly, Rhiannon tensed, as did her nipples against his chest, not to mention her . . . underneath.

What did this mean? What was happening to her body? Whatever it was, she loved it. Feeling absolutely wanton, as only the absolutely innocent can, not knowing what fires they can ignite, she raised up slightly on her toes in anticipation of the crushing feel of his lips on hers.

But that crushing kiss never came. Almost brusquely, she was set away from him. Startled and disappointed, and not knowing what to do, what to say, how to act, she took her cues from him.

But he was no help. He distanced himself from her, even going to a window seat across the room. He stood with his back to her for long moments, gazing out across his front lawn, not saying anything. Rhiannon could only guess what the matter was. All she could do was appreciate his broad back, tapering hips, and long, muscular legs. But why was he taking several deep breaths, one after the other? What had happened to him? Had she done something wrong?

When whatever was wrong with him passed; he turned to face her. She hadn't moved from where he'd left her. Again, another shake of his head and that enigmatic smile; somehow Rhiannon knew that the emotion behind that expression was directed at himself, and not at her. She accepted it at that for now; what choice did she have?

"Come on, I'll show you the rest of the monstrosity." He held a hand out to her, more of a gesture for her to precede him than for her to take it.

Glad for his friendly tone, but with her curiosity piqued by his choice of words to describe his home, she felt compelled to ask, as he escorted her, with a hand at her back, out of the library and back into the foyer, "Why do you call this very elegant home a monstrosity?"

He made a sound which could only be called a snort. "Very elegant in Boston or Newport or even Baltimore, perhaps, but in Kansas? Surely, growing up in Wolfe as you did, and having traveled back East, you of all people can appreciate how out of place, to put it mildly, my father's folly is."

He directed her back across the black-and-white-tiled floor, skirting the round oak table with the huge bouquet of fresh flowers that stood right in the middle of the room.

"Folly? I don't see it that way at all, Mr. Wolfe. I think it's all very romantic that your father built it right here for the woman he loved."

He laughed, and it sounded suspiciously to Rhiannon like the indulgent laugh adults reserve for children who've just said something very naive and very amusing. "Yes, I suppose you would see it like that."

That did it; she rounded on him—so quickly that he almost bumped into her. "Just what does that mean—you suppose I would see it like that?"

"I mean, you're a romantic young girl, just like my mother was when she met my father."

"And?" Her hands went to her waist, a gesture of hers that always seemed to make her bottom lip poke out slightly.

"*And* you would think that a place like this, a monstrosity in its given setting, was wonderful."

"And you don't? This is your home, the one your father built for your mother out of love; the one in which you were raised. Are you going to tell me that I and every other child in Wolfe—your town, as you so delighted in telling me— have spent our lives being jealous of you and this house for no reason, that you hate it?"

Several emotions played over his face as the silent seconds ticked by. Rhiannon knew she'd gone too far, been too familiar, when his face closed, putting him as distant from her as he had been moments ago in the library. "Hate it? I used to. Maybe I still do. Now, if you'd like to see the dining room . . ."

Rhiannon nodded a little too vigorously and turned abruptly, her face warm. The dining room, on the same side of the house as the morning room and just down a short hall from it, was no less breathtaking than the other rooms she'd viewed. Everywhere was polished and gleaming wood, with furniture she recognized as the best that could be bought, a table that could easily seat 50 guests, a carpet that had to be imported, pictures that should have hung in galleries, crystal and china that could have graced any royal court, and huge bouquets of fresh flowers that enhanced the air and the atmosphere of tremendous wealth.

"Of course, the buffet dinner will be set up in here, and the guests can seat themselves however they wish in the library. At least, that's what I'm told by my aunts. Does all this meet with your approval so far?"

Rhiannon looked up sharply. He was being mock-serious. Still, she felt compelled to say, "If my hostesses decided to serve us in the stables, I daresay that I would be gracious. I am, after all, the guest of honor. My only obligation is to show up and to be gracious. I assure you I have no intention of changing any arrangement in any way whatsoever. I did learn that much from Miss Constance.

"Furthermore, I have no more idea than you do why your aunts insisted on this—this . . . practically public tour of your home. You don't owe me anything; in fact, we can stop it right here if you'd like. I'm sure a man of your stature has more to do than show me around your home."

"What? And have you off rallying the women and gaining public support for your campaign? Never, Miss O'Shea."

With another gesture, he indicated the overwhelming sweep of the centrally located, highly polished, curved stairway. "Shall we? There's nothing down that hall behind the library except my office and the kitchen and pantry—the guts of the place, if you will."

Rhiannon gave up, nodded grimly, much to his delight, and held her skirt up slightly so as not to trip up the stairs. She would see this tour to its natural end. She also would have loved to have seen his office, that most private of rooms to men, but she didn't dare ask. In fact, with his warm hand burning a hole in the small of her back, she couldn't right now ask anything—of anybody.

At the top of the stairs, ones she could already picture herself ascending in all her finery, her breath was absolutely taken away by the fairy-tale ballroom. It was directly above the library, and was as huge. The wall to her immediate right was completely covered in mirrors, and the two end walls sported wainscoting and rich, red wallpaper. The opposite wall was not really a wall, but was a series of French doors, through which Rhiannon could see private balconies outside each door. She stepped into the room as if she were stepping into a dream. The wooden floor gleamed like glass. She did a slow turn, letting the room soak into her. The raised dais to the left of the double-wide doorway begged for musicians.

She turned back to Hank, her hands clasped to her bosom. "This is the most beautiful room I believe I have ever seen."

He looked around him, a frown on his face. "Do you really think so? I hadn't noticed." Then, his gaze came to rest on her. "Perhaps it's you that makes it beautiful."

Rhiannon just stared at him, and then she lowered her eyes. Biting at her bottom lip, she willed her heart to stop thudding and to start beating normally. It wouldn't cooperate.

"Come on, we're almost done," he said, "unless you want to see all the bedrooms on the third floor. There are quite a few of them. I'm sure we could find one to our liking—"

"I hardly think so, Mr. Wolfe." There, that had done it—restored the friendly bantering between them and put her heart to rights.

"Well, you can't blame me for trying. Let me show you the private rooms we've set up for the ladies, and then we can quit the house and take in the garden. And if you're nice, I'll show you the stables and the coach house and the pigsty and—"

"You don't have a pigsty," Rhiannon said with a laugh.

"Thank God. That's one thing we can leave out."

The private rooms were everything they should be, replete as they were with every feminine necessity, including delicate vanities and boudoir chairs and mirrors. Rhiannon nodded politely, anxious to see the gardens—and to get fresh air to help her keep her wits about her. Being alone with Hank was proving to be most disconcerting. In the 30 minutes or so it had taken him to show her around, she'd already been put through almost every emotion she owned. She needed to sit down.

Coming back down the sweep of the stairs, they were met by Aunt Penelope. She stood at the bottom stair, staring up at them. Her brow was puckered slightly, and she held her hands at her waist. "Oh, dear, that didn't take long at all."

Hank, his hand again at Rhiannon's elbow, commented, "Aunt, if I didn't know better, I'd say you were conspiring to keep me and our guest closeted together."

Miss Penelope Penland drew herself up. "I'm doing no such thing. I—"

"Yes, she is. She just won't admit it." It was Aunt Tillie; she came shuffling out of the morning room. In her hands was the dessert platter with the remaining cakes. At her sister's stern glare, she defended herself. "I'm taking them to the birds."

"We don't have any birds, Aunt Tillie," Hank teased gently. Rhiannon loved this soft side of him, the indulgent way he treated the two old ladies.

Tillie gave him a malignant glare. "Well, we will soon enough when I throw these cakes out on the lawn."

Penelope gasped. "You'll do no such thing!"

"Oh, no? Humphh. Guess I better take them up to my room, then. Wouldn't want them to go to waste."

"You'll do no such thing!" Penelope repeated. Crossing her arms, she turned her back to her sister.

Tillie, her little bird-like mouth working furiously, stared at her sister's back. "You want me to just stand here and hold them, then?"

At the obvious stalemate, Hank stepped in. The ease with which he did so told Rhiannon that he was the usual arbiter between the two sisters. Giving her elbow a gentle squeeze, he left Rhiannon on the third step up. He descended the remaining stairs with all the elegant grace of the king of the jungle to stand between the warring women.

"Here, Aunt Tillie, dear, why don't you give me the plate, and I'll have one of the kitchen girls come for it. And Aunt Penelope can help you up the stairs. I do believe it's time for your nap before lunch."

He took the plate from Tillie, who smiled and reached up a frail little hand to pat his cheek. Rhiannon was positioned so that she could see Hank pluck two or three cake squares off the plate and put them in Tillie's wide pocket. She almost bit her lower lip in two to keep from laughing. He then turned to the taller and the younger of the sisters.

"Aunt Penelope, your sister needs you." Those apparently were the magic words.

Penelope instantly softened and turned around, putting her arms out to her sister, who looked the slightest bit confused as to her surroundings. "Come, sister. I must see you upstairs. You know how easily you tire."

"I do?" Tillie questioned, as if surprised to hear it.

Rhiannon, all but forgotten by them, stepped aside to let them pass. She met Hank at the bottom of the stairs. He shook his head at the retreating figures and put the plate on the round table with the flowers.

"They are absolutely precious," Rhiannon remarked.

"Yes, they are," Hank said, his eyes soft and somehow not so black. "They're really all the family I've ever had since my mother's death when I was seven."

Rhiannon turned her head sharply to look at him. What a strange remark—his father had died only six months ago. Hadn't he been "family" up until then?

When his aunts disappeared from view, Hank turned to his guest, his manner pleasant but all business. "Now, where were we off to? Oh, yes, the gardens. Shall we?" He offered her his crooked elbow; she took it, matching him mood for mood, and felt a thrill of happiness when he pulled her hand firmly onto his lower arm and crossed the foyer.

"Thank you, Watson, my good man," Hank intoned starchily to the spit-and-polish butler who saw them through the door. Rhiannon eyed the man curiously, and looked up questioningly at Hank. "I brought Watson here with me. He's worked for us for years—back East. He hates it here, too." All Rhiannon could do was nod as if she understood.

Once outside, Hank turned them onto a flagstone path that jutted out from the wide circular driveway and trailed off around the side of the imposing structure that was the mansion. It was still well before noon, so the temperature was still well below 100; hot, but not unbearably so. No cloud marred the blue canvas of the sky, and no breeze fluttered the blooms of the many cultivated bushes to either side of the path.

"Will this path take us to the gardens?"

"Eventually. Why? Are you in a hurry?"

Rhiannon's chin came up a notch. "Certainly not. My time is yours."

"Then that will just have to be enough for now."

Rhiannon looked up at him, the tiniest smile on her lips. She liked it that he felt inclined to banter with her, and even to leer the slightest bit. His attention was all very flattering to her young, female heart. If not somewhat frightening. She felt as if she were toying with some wild creature that was merely trained to be civil, but not yet tamed. An instinct warned her that this Wolfe could become wild and uncontrollable in a moment's notice.

"Here we are," he said, turning them onto yet another short path that led to an ornately carved, almost totally secluded gazebo somewhere toward the back of the mansion. A profusion of blooming vines overgrew its wooden sides and trailed fragrantly into the octagonal interior. When Rhiannon stepped inside it, she felt as if she had entered a fairy kingdom and was standing inside a flower.

"I've never seen anything so magical," she breathed, turning slowly around, much like she had in the ballroom.

"Or so unexpected in Kansas?"

She turned to look at him. He stood with a booted foot up on the bench that ran the circumference of the gazebo's interior. His forearms were resting on his bent knee. He looked at her from under suddenly hooded eyes. She felt her mouth go dry, but she commented lightly, "This would be unexpected anywhere, Mr. Wolfe."

"Will you please quit calling me that." It was a statement.

"Should I call you Henry?" she teased.

He straightened up and put his hands at his trim waist, stretching his finely tailored white shirt tightly across the muscled expanse of his chest. An eyebrow arched in mock threat. "Not if you like living. Why can't you just call me Hank? Every time you say 'Mr. Wolfe,' I have to stop myself from turning around to see if my father's standing behind me."

"Would that be so terrible?" She said it softly, but she'd meant for it to sound teasing.

"Terrible? It'd be downright frightening. He's been dead for six months."

It should have been funny, but it wasn't. He sounded so . . . angry. Rhiannon should have stopped there, but she was infamous for not knowing when to quit. So she took her life into her own hands and asked, "Was he so awful, then?"

"My father?" Hank asked, somewhat sharply. When she didn't answer, but continued to stare at him, he turned away, filling the opening of the gazebo. "No, he wasn't awful. At least, I guess he wasn't. I never saw very much of him. He had an empire to build, you know."

It was all there: the resentment, the loneliness, the hurt. Rhiannon ached to take him in her arms, and fervently wished she'd never brought up the subject of his father. Indeed, the memory of the man seemed to be a hovering presence, one that clouded the morning . . . and his son's face.

"I remember him as being very kind, Hank."

Perhaps it was just hearing her say his name, or perhaps it was her words, but something turned him around to look at her. His face, at once closed and disbelieving, still held a hint of wanting to hear more.

Encouraged, Rhiannon rushed on. "Yes, he built an empire out here in the middle of nowhere. And I know that took him away from you, probably when you needed him the most. But all you have to do is look around you, Hank, to see how much he loved your mother—and you. To me, everything he did held a promise of heaven. I mean, he built Wolfe, the town and the name, into something special, something unique, a place where everyone wants to be. Just look how much Wolfe has grown."

She stopped to draw a nervous breath. Had she angered him? After all, this was really none of her business—and now was his chance to tell her so. But to her surprise, Hank moved to sit down; he stretched one arm out along the side wall and ran his other hand through his hair. "Go on," he said, the look on his face plainly telling her he was not yet convinced.

Rhiannon paced back and forth in front of him, gathering her thoughts, looking for all the world like a defense attorney defending Ezra Wolfe to his son. She had no idea where her effrontery came from to even be broaching so intimate a subject with a man she hardly knew, despite their having grown up in the same town. For truly, until now, their worlds had been completely separate.

As if she'd just thought of another important point in her case, she stopped her pacing and held up a finger, wagging it at him. "Of course! You were already gone to West Point, so you might not know about this. Your father paid off mortgages for any farmers around here who were in danger of losing their land in the drought. And he paid for the new school to be built and helped Widow Calvert get a start here after her husband died. My father told me all that. And that's not all. His regular contributions to the church, which I know you're continuing, have made it possible for Reverend Philpott to concentrate on saving souls instead of raising money."

Hank just looked at her. "I never said he wasn't civic-minded, Rhiannon. Remember, he had a vested interest in all this. But heaven?"

Rhiannon rushed to sit by his side in her eagerness to make her point. Before she knew it, she had her hand on his chest. "But Hank, don't you see? He didn't have to do any of those things. Not one of them. He could have walked away after your mother died. But he didn't. He had you to care for— and about."

Hank slanted her a look; his hand came off the side wall to toy with a strand of her ginger-colored hair. "Are you sure about that?" He spoke softly, almost teasingly, but as if he wanted to believe it.

Rhiannon pressed on, eager to make her point. "Of course I am. He loved you. He just had to, Hank. Think about it:

His problem was the same as yours is now."

He rubbed her silky tress between his thumb and fore-finger, and wouldn't look at her. "And what's my problem, Rhiannon?"

She couldn't get the words out fast enough. "Knowing who to love. You were *his*—his own son, his only child. You, of all people, loved him simply for who he was—and not what he was, or for what he could do for you. How hard it must have been for him, just as it must be for you, to know who truly loved him for himself, and not his money and power. Don't you think that's why he fell so deeply in love with your mother, a simple farm girl who could have had the world at her feet for the asking, but who chose to stay here, on the outer edge of nowhere, in total obscurity, and build a life based on love and not the artificiality of money?"

There. She'd said it all. And it had exhausted her. She leaned back, right into the crook of his arm. His embrace tightened around her, but she didn't protest. It felt very right, very natural for him to do so. His masculine scent mingled with the flowery scent that perfumed the still air. Rhiannon closed her eyes, content with the world—and with his nearness.

His quiet words a few moments later opened her eyes. "I think perhaps our tour lasted too long."

She looked up at him questioningly. She couldn't have said which was brighter—his eyes or his smile. But both took her breath away and made her heart do funny things.

"I mean," he went on, "when did you get so old and wise? I started out escorting a sheltered young debutante, but ended up with an intelligent, insightful woman. Where was I when all these changes were happening?"

Did that mean he'd been thinking about what she said? And had he believed her? She had no way of knowing, so she pretended to think about his question for a moment. "Where were you? Oh, now I know. I believe you were stuffing cakes in Aunt Tillie's pocket."

A strangled guffaw greeted her words. "Why, you little minx! You saw that, did you?"

"Yes, I did. And I thought it was very sweet."

"Sweet? Please don't let that get out. I do have my reputation to consider."

"Not to worry, kind sir. Your reputation is safe with me."

"Is it now? And what about yours? Is your reputation safe with me?"

She slapped at his arm playfully to hide the unsettling feeling his last words left with her. It was one thing to recline in the most friendly of embraces, but quite another to find one's self lying against such a warm and powerful masculine chest that sent tingling feelings up and down her nerve endings. She was amazed that she could, after so short a time, talk intimately with him as if they were the best of friends, almost as if they were unaware of each other in an . . . intimate way. And yet, the slightest little gesture or look or word that held even one jot of desire could make her fiercely aware of him as a man. Like right now . . . when his grip was tightening around her, drawing her closer to him. Would this be the kiss she'd been waiting for all morning?

But instead of following through with his embrace, he once again surprised and disappointed her by sitting up straighter and setting her away from him. Turning her to face him, he kept his hands on her arms and said, "Rhiannon, you may be very right in what you said about my father, about him . . . caring about me and building all this for me. But I feel I have to tell you that this place is not for me. It's not what I want. Can you understand that?"

No, she couldn't, not at all . . . not at first. Not until a pulse of foreboding rippled through her, one that tried to warn her, though she couldn't grasp its meaning. Shaking it off, and after a moment or two of silent reasoning, she offered, "Well, when I think that what everyone around me, meaning my parents, wants—no, expects—from me is to be a well-behaved lady and to settle sedately into marriage and motherhood, no matter how much I try to convince them that is not what I want, at least not now, when I think that, yes, I . . . I understand."

"No, Rhiannon, I don't think you do. Because ultimately marriage is a choice, not an inheritance thrust upon you. But I have to agree with you, marriage is not something I think favorably of either, despite the best efforts of the town's mothers. On that one point we do agree and can form a friendship." He let go of her and got up to pace the tiny open-air interior of the gazebo.

Rhiannon watched him for a moment, fascinated in a purely physical way by the untamed grace of her friend's body. His powerful legs carried him to and fro in the gazebo's confines in only a few steps. Her tongue tipped out to run over her suddenly dry lips, but she kept quiet, afraid to interrupt his thoughts, because she wasn't the least bit sure she wanted to hear his thoughts. A moment later, when his physical presence threatened to overwhelm her, she allowed herself to be distracted by an inquisitive butterfly that flittered around Hank. It seemed to be seeking the source of the disturbance on this otherwise tranquil July morning.

When Hank stopped and spoke, the butterfly floated away, as did Rhiannon's stomach. "You of all people should understand."

She felt the frown form on her face; she didn't care in the least for the accusatory tone of his voice—or for the fact that she had no idea what he meant. "Please explain that. Why me of all people?"

"Because we both want the same thing, don't you see?"

Rhiannon's hands fluttered up and out in an eloquent gesture that bespoke her confusion.

"Dammit," Hank spat out. "I had no idea this morning would be so . . ." His words, cut off though they were, carried him to the opposite side of the gazebo, where he sat down in a sprawled attitude of carelessness. But his face belied his pose. His eyes, reflective black chips of coal, bore into Rhiannon.

"What we both want, my dear Rhiannon, is our freedom. I want to be free of the strictures placed on me by my . . . heaven, as you call it. And you, if I heard you correctly on the ride out here and again just now, yearn to be free of the strictures placed on you by the conventions of . . . what? Society? Your being female?"

Rhiannon stared at her hands folded in her lap and thought about this . . . seriously thought about this. He was absolutely right. She looked up at him, slanting her head to one side. "Then I suppose we're both trapped, aren't we?"

Her words hung in the air while Hank stared at her . . . seriously stared at her, much as if he were seeing her for the first time. He narrowed his eyes at her slightly, crinkling the skin at the corners. For once, he wasn't staring at her like a predator. It was more like he was . . . assessing her for something. When he finally spoke, Rhiannon gave a start, so thick was the air of expectancy surrounding them and this conversation.

"Rhiannon, do you know what a wolf does when its foot is caught in a trap?"

Rhiannon's heartbeat pulsed in her throat, trapping her breath. All she could do was nod by way of an answer.

Still, he had to say the words. "It chews its own foot off." He sat up and leaned forward. "That's how much it wants to be free."

Tears stung her eyes. Why was he doing this? What did he want from her? Looking at him, she came very near to hating him. He was trying to pull more from her than she could give, or even understand. The morning had been so warm, so full of promise. But now, the fragrant vines were cloying and the heat overwhelming. She had to think straight; she had the distinct impression that this was probably the most important conversation of her life.

She thought about the wolf limping away, bleeding and broken. "How free is that wolf, Hank, without its foot? What are its chances of survival? Can it ever hope to run again, to

86

lead the pack, to be whole? No. He's more likely to crawl off somewhere and die.

"Even though he's trapped, he's still alive—and whole. And the trapper just might surprise him by setting him free; maybe the wolf isn't his prey. So maybe we shouldn't look at our own situations as traps, Hank. Maybe we should wait and see what develops. After all, we just might be cutting our hearts out, instead of chewing our feet off."

He clearly hadn't thought about that. Rhiannon was gratified to see him literally sit up and take notice of her . . . and her words. "Well, I'll be damned."

Was that admiration and maybe even respect in his voice? He was certainly grinning at her as if she'd just done some wonderful, even miraculous, stunt.

"By God, Miss Rhiannon O'Shea, I'm beginning to think you can run this town. In fact, I'm beginning to think you can do just about anything you set your mind to. I feel sorry for Wolfe, Kansas, and Carry Nation if they should decide to cross you." He stood up and extended his hand to her. "May I, as a newfound friend and admirer, have the honor of being the first to shake the hand of the first female candidate for mayor of Wolfe?"

Chapter Seven

Rhiannon looked from his hand to his face. He appeared to be serious, despite his grin. He really thought she could run a town. Well, why shouldn't he? She knew she could. He'd said he admired her and thought of her as a friend. Wasn't that exactly what she wanted? To be treated as an equal? Well, here was her chance, despite the small stab of disappointment that they were to be "friends."

Still, it was with delight that she stood and took his hand with a firm but feminine grip. What could be more wonderful than to be taken seriously, despite one's gender; and what could be better than to have such a powerful friend?

In a matter of seconds, she had her answer. Hank brought her hand up to his lips . . . so warm and firm against her skin. His drawing her arm up pulled her even closer to him. And the closer she got to him, the more her heart beat like a scared rabbit's. But still the moment hung suspended on the edge of time, and pressed itself into Rhiannon's memory. She looked helplessly into his face, entranced by black-fringed ebony eyes that bore into her and blinked oh . . . so . . . slowly. Rhiannon managed to swallow just once before her throat seemed to close; then her knees really buckled.

Hank's other arm snaked out to catch her and encircle her waist. He may have saved her from an impending physical fall, but pulling her full-length against the granite wall that was his chest plunged her even further into her emotional abyss. Despite her fear at these new awakenings in her body, crushed as it was to his, she could only be aware of his mouth as it tipped ever closer to hers, offering her the only breath she dare inhale.

And then, his mouth covered hers. Rhiannon was ablaze in his arms. A heat that could only be coming from him coursed through her, threatening to consume her. It ran amok just under her skin and finally settled in her secret female place, a pulsing flame of desire.

But it was nothing compared to what his tongue was doing to the tender skin just inside her lips as he rubbed the tip of his tongue back and forth and then plunged with exquisite gentleness into the depth of her mouth, only to withdraw again to suck at her petal-delicate lips.

Rhiannon had never . . . ever been kissed like this before, but her girlish innocence had apparently vanished, leaving in its stead a woman who desperately wanted this man and who knew exactly what to do to communicate that need. Somehow, sometime, he'd let go of her hand, for his other arm now rested under her hair against her neck, which his fingers massaged sensuously. And Rhiannon, who now stood on tiptoe, offering herself up to him, slowly became aware that her fingers were enmeshed in the thickness of his hair; that she gripped him with the same unbridled longing he'd awakened in her.

With awareness came withdrawal, came the distancing that this intense closeness of two near-strangers almost made mandatory. Rhiannon could not have said who pulled away first, so gradual was the end of the kiss and the parting. But finally, they were standing apart . . . maybe only a few feet apart, but it might as well have been a million miles.

No one had to tell this previously untried girl that Hank was just as aroused, and just as shaken, as she was. His breathing was as labored as hers, even now as he ran his own hand through his hair and looked at her as if he didn't have an explanation for what had just happened; and too, hadn't she felt his desire pressed hard against her? And hadn't her own flame wanted to lick out against it?

Shocked at her own wantonness, both in thought and deed, she withdrew even further, straightening her peach-colored lawn skirt. She hastily tucked her frothy blouse back into her waistband, and smoothed a hand through her hair, which hung in thick, gleaming curls to her waist. Miss Constance hadn't covered the aftermath of this eventuality in any finishing-school lesson that Rhiannon could remember. Just how was she supposed to bank the pulsing flame that still raged under her skirt?

"Rhiannon." His voice was like silk and honey, sweet and husky.

The small hairs raised at the nape of her neck. Her heart flopped around in her chest.

"Rhiannon, are you all right? Do you understand what just happened here?" He was reaching out to her again.

"Yes. Do you?" she answered, hearing her voice as if from afar.

A slight chuckle came from him. "Oh, yes, I understand—all too well. But I'm not sure you do."

"You kissed me." It was hard to talk with his hand rubbing her arm. And with his . . . nearness again.

"And you kissed me."

"Yes." She hadn't noticed the pearlish buttons on his shirt before. Had he always had this brocade vest on this morning? Was it still morning? Of the same day?

"Come on, Lady Mayor, I'll take you home."

Rhiannon had plenty of time in the next few days to contemplate her first real kiss. And she was beginning to think that Hank Wolfe, the black-eyed devil, had purposely stayed away from her in order to force her to do just that. Was she supposed to be ashamed of kissing her . . . friend? Well, she decided, a toss of her head and a tipping upward of her chin punctuating her renegade emotion, she wasn't. Not in the least. In fact, she'd liked it, thank you very much. And why shouldn't a woman be able to enjoy a man? Was that so horrible?

Yes. Yes, it was. Her shoulders slumped dejectedly. Only bad women, like the ones in the Fancy Lady Saloon, were supposed to like it. She'd heard that all her life. Now, as she walked past that very establishment, she let her gaze cut over to peer inside the saloon. Was she, Rhiannon Pauline O'Shea, a bad woman because she'd liked—loved Hank's kiss?

Was he in there even now, enjoying one of those women and laughing with them about her behavior? The sudden burning Rhiannon felt in her cheeks had nothing to do with passion. But she couldn't say if her anger was caused by the thought of him laughing at her, or by the thought of Hank Wolfe with another woman.

Once she realized she'd completely stopped and was standing, in broad daylight, looking right into the dim, dusty interior of the saloon, drawing curious stares from both refined passersby and from the questionable sorts inside the saloon, she jerked around and stepped off the boardwalk, intending to cross the street and head in the direction of the dry-goods store.

As she strode purposefully across the broad dirt street, she was glad she'd let Paddy and Johnny-Cake, her two younger brothers, run on ahead to the store. Heaven knows they would have been bursting with the story of her looking into the saloon. She rolled her eyes. As if merely looking into that establishment could give her some sort of disease. Still, she had to be about her business and pick her brothers up if she hoped to forestall any questions from her mother about what had taken her so long on her errands. Errands, indeed.

She was on her way to talk with Mrs. Freda Gruenwald, the jovial wife of the dry-goods store's owner. At least, Rhiannon assumed he owned it. The Gruenwald name was on the sign, but just like every other thing for miles around, it sat on Wolfe land.

But that issue was neither here nor there. What was at stake was the upcoming mayoral race. Rhiannon intended to sound out the other women nominees the newspaper had mentioned before she made her final decision. And Mrs. Gruenwald was one of them. Thinking of the blond, stout, laughing German woman she was off to see made her shake her head. She had to hand it to the men; they'd picked the most unlikely women in town, herself included.

But that didn't mean they couldn't run—or win. Strangers things had happened before. But not much stranger, she snorted. Still, she certainly didn't intend to make a serious attempt to win the office if everyone in town thought of this as a joke except for her. After all, she couldn't manage it alone, despite what Hank had said in his gazebo and despite his handshake and the offer of his vote. Surely he had been teasing her.

"Miss O'Shea."

Hearing her name called out by a feminine voice, Rhiannon turned around. At first she didn't see who it could have been. Her gaze swept the boardwalk and the people nearby. No woman waved to her or greeted her; there were certainly plenty of people about on this fine morning, but no one was looking her way. Except for the young woman in the thin, loose wrapper standing in the doorway of the Fancy Lady Saloon.

She stood partially in shadows, but Rhiannon could see that her hair was disheveled and her feet bare. She was plump and pretty, and a redhead. Rhiannon looked past her once, even twice—after all, it couldn't have been her—before her gaze finally settled on the woman, who held her wrapper closed with one hand and held open the swinging door with her other one. She had a tentative, if faint, smile on her face. She let go of her wrapper to make a halfhearted gesture of greeting to Rhiannon.

Astounded, Rhiannon took a step or two closer to the board steps which led up to the corner saloon. But she didn't know what else to do . . . or to say. Had anyone else heard this person call out to her? Instantly, Rhiannon flushed with guilt. Who was she to judge anyone, especially given her own behavior only a few days ago with Hank Wolfe? And too, when had she ever cared what people thought of her? She would speak with whomever she chose.

"Did you call out to me?" she asked, holding her gray wrap-around overskirt up with her hands as she came back up the two steps. Rhiannon caught her breath when she stepped into the shadow of the overhanging roof. The woman was really not much more than a girl; she couldn't have been more than a few years older than Rhiannon herself. And her face was bruised. Rhiannon forced herself not to stare at the purplish-black mark on the other woman's cheekbone. A sudden welling up of incredible anger that a man would use a defenseless woman thus stung Rhiannon.

"Yes, I did, ma'am. I wasn't sure it was you at first. I mean, I seen you from a distance before, an' you been gone an' all. But I thought it was you. I . . . well, I hope you don't mind talkin' to the likes of me like this, but I—I need to talk to you, Miss O'Shea." She fingered her wrapper; this close, Rhiannon could see that it was old and thin, but clean.

Rhiannon's heart went out to this unfortunate creature. What kind of life must she have had to force her into this degradation? "I don't mind at all, Miss . . . ?"

"Well, you see, my professional name, the one Big John had me to take, is Cat LaFlamme." She looked down, embarrassment and apology rife in her face and gestures.

Rhiannon couldn't help the slight upward tilt in her eyebrows. The name was as outlandish as the girl's obviously dyed hair; nature had not produced this brassy color.

"Oh," Rhiannon commented, nodding her head as if she understood.

Cat looked back over her shoulder and turned back to Rhiannon. "I can't talk long. Big John don't like it when we . . . girls bring ourselves to the notice of the decent townfolk."

"Please don't say things like that."

The girl was genuinely perplexed. "Like what?"

"Like you're not decent and . . . acceptable. You make yourself sound so . . . so—"

Cat pulled herself up and cocked her head to one side. "Well, I am all them things you're thinkin', Miss O'Shea. That's just the way it is. You can't tell me you was particularly thrilled to step up here to talk with me just now. I seen your face."

Rhiannon felt the red-hot flush spread over her cheeks. How could she deny it?

"An' I don't blame you none, mind you. I'm used to it. It's just that I have to ask you somethin' real important to me." She stopped and took a deep breath, as if she were gathering her courage. "Are you goin' to run for mayor?"

The question was so unexpected that all Rhiannon could do for a moment or two was stand there and blink at the prostitute. Prostitute! It was then, and only then, that Rhiannon made the connection. This was the fancy lady that the men had nominated to run for city council. This was Cat LaFlamme in the flesh. Rhiannon wanted to cry for her; the exotic name and the brassy hair could not hide the scared and beaten girl underneath.

"Why do you want to know? Why is it so important to you . . . Cat?"

Cat must have noticed Rhiannon's hesitancy with her name, for she said, "Cat's short for Catherine, you know. It don't mean no four-legged cat or all such as that."

"I'm sorry, Cat. I didn't mean—"

"I know. Nobody ever does. But, see, if you run for mayor, like you should just to show these here men that a woman can be tough, then I'd . . . why, I'd be right proud to stand with you and run for the city council myself. I couldn't take no stand on my own, just like some of them other women that reporter named in the paper, but with the likes of you takin' the lead an' all, why, I do believe we women could win. An' I got some money put aside that Big John don't know about. I could use it for a real campaign an' all. I wouldn't be no burden to you . . . if you'd have me, that is."

The merest gust of wind could have blown Rhiannon over. But in the end, the silent pleading in Cat's eyes did the job. Clearly, she was looking to this campaign as a way out of her present life; how could Rhiannon dash that hope? Especially when that hope was also her own.

And darned if she didn't want to encourage the spark that was lighting up this battered girl's eyes. Her face might be beaten, but her spirit wasn't. If Rhiannon had been uncertain of her intent before, she no longer was. She put her gloved hand out to Cat. "Miss LaFlamme, I'd be very proud to have you run on the same slate with me."

Cat looked at Rhiannon's hand blankly and then up at Rhiannon. Her voice was low and hushed when she spoke. "Do you mean it? Are we going to do it, ma'am?"

"Yes, we are, Miss LaFlamme."

Cat hastily wiped her hand on her wrapper and put it in Rhiannon's grip. Just then, someone bellowed Cat's name from inside the saloon. Rhiannon recognized Big John's voice. Cat jerked and tried to pull her hand from Rhiannon's, but Rhiannon held on. Cat looked at her, her face a mixture of surprise, fear, and curiosity.

"Did he do that to you?" Rhiannon asked point-blank, indicating the bruise on the other girl's cheek.

Cat's free hand went to her cheek. "I almost forgot about that. Don't worry none—it's happened before. I lived through it plenty of times. Now I got to go before he gives me a matchin' mark."

Distraught, Rhiannon let go of Cat's hand and patted her shoulder. Cat turned to go back inside, but Big John was right behind her and was blocking her way. Both women gasped in fear. Big John grabbed Cat's arm and practically threw her further into the saloon. Horrified, Rhiannon watched as Cat crashed into a table and chairs and went sprawling over them. Then, fear melting into anger, Rhiannon took one purposeful step which would have taken her inside the saloon. But Big John blocked the swinging doors from within.

All she could do was stand there helplessly and watch Cat pull herself up and scurry away in the direction of the stairs. Assured that the girl was relatively safe, at least for the moment, Rhiannon turned her venom on the large man who was looking at her with a mixture of insolence and, God forbid, lust.

"How could you do it? How could you beat on an innocent girl—"

"Innocent? Cat LaFlamme? You're wasting your sympathy on that one. Why, she's been had by every man within—"

"And what choice did she have in the matter? The day will come when you'll be very sorry you ever laid a hand on her."

His piggish eyes narrowed in his sweating face. "Are you threatening me, Miss O'Shea?"

"You call it what you want, Mr. Savage. You call it what you want."

Some time later, Hank was signing papers that Edwin O'Shea, President of the First Bank of Wolfe on Main Street, put in front of him. Hank chafed to be done with this tedious business, so he could seek out this man's daughter. She was making a spectacle of herself traipsing all over town trying to talk the other women into running for the city council. At every turn, Hank was being met by another outraged citizen who felt compelled to apprise him of Miss O'Shea's activities. He had to find her and talk some sense into her.

"Well, there we are, Mr. Wolfe. All done, I do believe. That should take care of the account for another six months." Edwin O'Shea picked up the papers and took the pen from Hank, replacing it in its well.

"Good." Hank had the uneasy feeling that he was going to be extremely busy in the next six months and might not have time to attend to mundane things like running his . . . heaven, he believed Rhiannon had called it. He stood up, dwarfing the other man and the orderly, polished office. Through the open office door behind him, the everyday sounds of banking business murmured in the background. Then, one voice, louder than the others caught his—and Edwin's—attention.

"I tell you, I know what I saw, Susie Johnson. She hasn't changed a bit. Three years in Baltimore were wasted on that girl."

Hank met Edwin's widened eyes. There was only one girl in Wolfe who'd been in Baltimore for three years. Hank felt sorry for Edwin O'Shea; he liked the man. He was a respected banker, a solid family man, and overall a pillar of the community. And he could be totally undone by the antics of one 19-year-old girl. Hank knew just how he felt.

Before either man could say a word, the woman went on. "Now, I know how you always like everyone and think everyone is just so sweet and all. But I tell you, Susie, you'd best stay clear of Rhiannon O'Shea. I just this day saw her talking to and petting on one of those saloon girls at the Fancy Lady. Why, the scandal of it all will put her poor mother six feet under."

"I like Rhiannon, Effie. I'm sure she has a good reason for talking to one of those poor creatures. Rhiannon has a kind heart. We should follow her lead, instead of condemning her so."

Good for you, Susie Johnson, Hank thought, all the while watching the color drain from Edwin's rapidly aging face.

"Oh, pooh, Susie. You like everyone. Just wait until Hank Wolfe finds out that she intends to run for mayor. Then we'll just see how far a kind heart gets her."

"Why are you being so mean, Effie? I thought she was your friend, too. We all grew up right here in Wolfe."

"Now, don't you tell me you intend to take that silly story in the paper seriously. Has she gotten to you, too? What will your father say when you tell him you've thrown in with Rhiannon O'Shea?"

Hank turned slightly to look out the doorway toward the two women who stood together on the other side of the tellers' bays. Effie, the town gossip, was a passably pretty girl, already married and pregnant. Susie, however, was a tiny, timid little brown sparrow of a woman, the bookish, spinster daughter of the town's doctor. And Hank liked her. There was a certain amount of steel under all that timidity. He waited to hear her answer. And so did Edwin, if his going all tense could be a sign of waiting.

"Why, my father already knows, Effie Parsons. And he says it's about time I asserted my independence and used my mind on something important." Her little bird-like head actually rose a notch or two.

Hank wanted to leap the tellers' bays and thump Susie heartily on her back as she watched Effie Parsons stomp her way out of the bank. But he knew she would have died right there on the spot if he made any gesture so physical . . . and so male. And speaking of dying on the spot, Edwin O'Shea didn't look too well right now.

Thinking the bank's president might like to be alone, Hank picked up his Stetson and drawled, "If you'll excuse me, Mr. O'Shea, I believe I'll just drop by the Fancy Lady Saloon."

"What? . . . oh . . . yes. The Fancy Lady. Yes, do that, Mr. Wolfe. Please." Even distraught as he was, Edwin O'Shea did not forget his manners or his position. He stood and shook Hank's hand and escorted him to the door of his office.

Crossing the lobby took Hank past Miss Susie Johnson. He was still feeling kindly towards her for her staunch defense of Rhiannon against Effie Parson's snide remarks, so when the spinster turned from the teller's window, her business complete, Hank caught her eye . . . and winked. Her thin hand flew to her narrow chest, and her startled gasp followed Hank out of the building.

Thinking of Susie and seeing her in a different light, just as he now did when he met the other women from town on the mock-slate for office, Hank was beginning to think he'd created a monster when he'd encouraged one ginger-eyed Irish graduate of a finishing school to run for office in his town. His town. He'd been calling it that more and more lately, he'd noticed. It was almost as if he intended to stay. Well, he had to admit, he had nothing better to do than stay here and watch the coming fireworks. And they were indeed coming.

And here came the fire that would light them, Hank thought, pulling up short and putting his hands to his waist. He couldn't hide the grin that welled up from inside him at the sight of her. But beyond that, he was glad to see that she wasn't actually inside the Fancy Lady Saloon. That was one fight he could postpone. And too, the lovely Miss Rhiannon O'Shea was kicking up a fair cloud of dust as she stomped toward him. Hank sighed; thousands of dollars spent on a finishing school and she still stomped around, oblivious to the many curious and catty glances she was drawing. She was certainly a challenge—one he was more than willing to accept. He was just glad that the age of dueling had passed; he felt sure he would have had to defend her honor, or pull her off some hapless creature, at least once a day a few years back. That thought stopped him; when had he made himself her champion?

Just then, she drew abreast of him right in the middle of Main Street, right in the middle of the day, right in the middle of traffic. She began her tirade with no preamble. "There you are, Mr. Wolfe. Just the man I want to see."

"I find I don't quite know how to respond to that, Miss O'Shea. A hundred retorts come to mind."

Ignoring his comment, she burst out, "I want you to kill Mr. Savage."

"Come again?"

"I said, I want you to kill Big John Savage. But not until he's been ridden out of town on a rail after we've drawn and quartered him and cut his head off with a guillotine and gutted him and closed down his saloon and beat him to a pulp and dragged him behind horses and put him in jail and hung him and . . . and—"

"Whoa, whoa, Rhiannon!" Hank threw his hands up, truly alarmed. He took hold of her and led her off the street. Hank seriously believed that he was going to be forced to trot to keep up with her anger-propelled gait. Once they were safely onto a side street, he turned her to face him. "Now tell me exactly what Big John said."

"It's not what he said. It's what he did."

"John Savage did something to you?" Hank felt a gorge of dangerous smoldering anger begin to build in his chest. He'd kill the big son of a bitch with his bare hands if he'd so much as touched a hair on this girl's head.

"Ouch, Hank, you're hurting my arms. And you're scaring me."

Her words brought Hank to himself. He looked down into Rhiannon's glimmering eyes, the eyes of a frightened doe. He knew he could look fierce when he was aroused; how many men had he backed down with a single look? But not this girl—never did he want to frighten her. He relaxed his grip on her, fearful that she would bear his marks on her arms tomorrow, but he still held onto his anger. "Tell me what he did, Rhiannon. Tell me everything."

"Oh, Hank, it's so awful." Her chin quivered, and it was nearly Hank's undoing. He'd seen her be brave, reckless, alluring, shocking, tempting, amusing . . . but never defeated.

Suddenly, all the things that she wanted him to do to John Savage began to seem possible, if the coiling in his gut was any indication.

"For God's sake, Rhiannon, tell me."

Her huge ginger-colored eyes were brimming with tears. Hank wanted to crush her to him, to protect her from the whole world of hurt that waited out there for someone so young and tender and brave. But he knew he couldn't do that. She wouldn't have allowed it.

"Hank, do you know that he beats those girls?" The agony in her soul twisted her face.

Hank was momentarily stymied. "What girls, Rhiannon? Are you saying he didn't do anything to you?"

"No, he didn't do anything to me. But I did threaten him."

"You threatened him?" Hank almost barked out his relieved laughter, but the look on her face warned him that this was far from over. "Why did you threaten him? Because he wouldn't let you inside for a drink?" He was serious; he could see her challenging that convention.

"No. Because he wouldn't let me inside to help Cat LaFlamme. After he'd bruised her cheek and thrown her against a table and some chairs. Then she ran upstairs, and he wouldn't let me see to her. Oh, Hank, it was so awful. I felt so helpless. But there was nothing I could do."

She stood in front of him, a picture of dejected defeat, her arms hanging limply at her sides. Her gay little outfit with its little confection of a hat, the stylish gloves, and jaunty reticule looked completely incongruous, given her present state of mind.

Hank took in a slow, deep breath and let it out the same way. He still held her arms; he didn't seem to want to turn her loose. "And did you think I was just the man to see to do something about him?"

Rhiannon looked up at him, her brow furrowed. "Well, aren't you?"

101

"What did you want me to do?"

"I want you to close down the Fancy Lady Saloon. I want Cat LaFlamme and all those other girls to be safe."

"What makes you think I can close down the saloon? Have you taken sides with Carry Nation and the Temperance League?"

"This has nothing to do with drinking, Hank Wolfe. It has to do with treating people like . . . people."

"I understand that, Rhiannon. But you can't help people who don't want to be helped."

She blinked several times while absorbing that. Hank hated like hell to be the one to educate her in the ways of the world. "Are you telling me that Cat LaFlamme and the rest of those women like being beat? And that you knew about this?"

Hank finally let go of her arms. He did a half-turn away from her, ran a hand through his hair, and shook his head. "Dammit, Rhiannon, I've only been home for six months. And contrary to what you might think or hear, I don't frequent the Fancy Lady on a regular basis—for drinks or women. I've heard rumors about Big John being rough on his girls, but I've never heard of one of them leaving or wanting out."

"That just can't be. Why would they want to stay?" Her voice rose on a plaintive note.

"For too many reasons, Rhiannon. Maybe they like the money; some of them just like to drink, like Ole Jed; some of them don't think they deserve anything better—maybe they've never known anything better. And some of them just don't have anyplace else to go."

Rhiannon looked at him. Or more accurately at the middle of his chest, which was at her eye level. Then, she covered her face with her hands. Hank put a hand out to her, but let it fall without touching her. There was nothing he could do to soften the punch of reality.

"Rhiannon, look at me, sweetheart."

She did. He'd thought she was crying, but she was dry-eyed—and anguished.

"If I or you or the current mayor or the citizens or the church—or anybody were to close down the Fancy Lady, another place, maybe worse than that one, would open right back up again within a few weeks. And the same women would go there to work.

"And I can't close Big John down. The Fancy Lady is about the only piece of property that doesn't belong to my father—to me, I mean. Big John owns it outright, lock, stock, and barrel. That's how profitable his business is."

"Then, there's nothing we can do?" She took a step forward, placing her gloved hand on his leather vest. Hank had hooked his thumbs into the front pockets of his denims as he'd talked, but now he raised his hands to lightly hold her arms, as moved by her use of "we," indicating that she wasn't completely disillusioned with him, as he was by her touching him.

He smiled. "Do you mean to tell me that you're going to give up that easily?" Hank knew he shouldn't tease her at this moment, but he was hoping to lighten her burden some. After all, she'd already swallowed a huge dose of the darker side of life this morning.

She rose to the bait, but not in any way Hank had expected—which was pretty normal for her, he already knew. "Give up? Not hardly. All those women need is someplace else to go. Someplace where they'll be told they are worth something. You said so yourself."

Hank looked down into her piquant little face. What in the world was going around in that beautiful, intelligent head? "And just what do you intend to do?"

She pulled away from him and started toward Main Street. Over her shoulder, she said, "I don't exactly know yet, Mr. Wolfe, but if I were you I'd stick around for the fireworks."

Hank watched her bustling little bottom sashay off. "I think I have met my match," he said to no one in particular.

Chapter Eight

The soft caress of the summer twilight was enticing. Rhiannon, her color heightened, hugged herself, breathing in deeply of the intoxicating air of expectancy as she rode along in the stylish carriage Hank Wolfe had sent, along with a driver, for her and her parents to use tonight. So the guest of honor would travel and arrive in style, the note had said. A shiver of anticipation rippled through her. In only moments she would be face-to-face with Hank Wolfe— and the entire town. At a party given in her honor. For once in her life, she was determined to be on her best behavior.

She looked across the open carriage at her parents sitting so elegantly together in all their finery on the seat opposite her. They smiled at their only daughter, but didn't say anything. They really were handsome people, Rhiannon thought. She felt a welling up of love toward her parents that was of a special nature, that of the grown-up child for her parents when she first realizes she really does like them as people, that she would admire and respect them even if they were only neighbors. For the first time, Rhiannon saw herself as separate from her family, and her parents as people other than her parents.

Her father was the first to break the companionable silence. "Might I say that I feel I have the distinct honor of escorting the two most beautiful women in all of Kansas to this evening's festivities?"

"Why, thank you, Father." Rhiannon smiled, demurely lowering her eyes as Miss Constance had taught her to do upon receiving compliments from gentlemen. She desperately wanted to play this sweet game of manners with her parents. She fully intended to be on her best behavior this evening, to prove to them that their money had not been wasted and that their daughter truly was a great lady. She vowed that no one and nothing would make her misbehave. She would be perfect—for her parents.

"Why in Kansas only, Edwin? Not the whole world? Surely that's what you meant," Patience O'Shea added, teasing and flirting with her husband in a way that Rhiannon had never witnessed before. To her surprise, it embarrassed her.

"Sure and you're right, Mother. What could I have been thinking?"

As she laughed with her parents, Rhiannon watched her father draw her mother's hand more firmly through the crook of his arm and pat it as it rested on his forearm. Seeing their closeness, she was very happy for them . . . but she also felt very alone on her side of the carriage. Startled that she of all women would feel that way, she quickly pushed that emotion aside; was that all she wanted out of life—a husband and children? What about living to the fullest? What about her freedom?

That word—freedom—brought back to her mind her conversation with Hank last week in his gazebo. All that talk about freedom and traps and wolves. She hadn't really understood it all beyond realizing that somehow he had ended up agreeing with her and perhaps even respecting her. And then he'd kissed her. Rhiannon shivered, despite the warm,

Cheryl Anne Porter

windless night air. She pulled her mint-green lace shawl up around her bare shoulders anyway, as if that act could brush away the memory of Hank's hands on her. Wasn't it enough that he'd left faint purple bruises on her arms where he'd gripped her so hard the other day in town?

And then the carriage arrived at the Wolfe mansion. Rhiannon's breath caught in her throat when she saw the beautiful building lit up so wondrously in her honor. The scene was like Christmas in July. People were dressed in their best; thanks to the Wolfe largesse in the development of this part of the state, many of the citizens of Wolfe were wealthy, and so able to afford the finest in clothing and conveyances. Carriages of every description were in a single-file line in the wide circular driveway, waiting to unload their gaily chattering occupants. Wolfe servants scurried hither and thither holding bridles, assisting ladies out of the carriages, and just generally being useful.

Apparently, one young servant in particular had drawn the job of watching for the Wolfe carriage to pull up. For when the driver circumvented the other waiting carriages, maneuvered his horse—the same bay that had pulled the surrey on the day Hank'd brought Rhiannon out to visit his aunts, and pulled to a stop at the head of the lane, the boy ran over to them and looked at each one of them in turn, as if assuring himself it was indeed the O'Sheas. With a big grin, he took off for the opened double doors of the mansion, taking the elegant steps two at a time.

Rhiannon exchanged an indulgent look with her parents that said a mouthful about exuberant youth, for once feeling herself far removed from that sort of childish display. Not waiting to fathom what the boy's possible errand or purpose could be, Edwin got out of the carriage first and held his hand up to his wife. Patience batted her eyes at his gallantry— Rhiannon rolled hers, but she loved it.

Patience, aware of the staring eyes and whispered comments to the effect that the O'Sheas were here, raised her head at a haughty angle, causing her to misstep as she descended. Had it not been for Edwin grabbing her arm and Rhiannon grabbing her waist, Mrs. Edwin O'Shea would have arrived at the Event of the Year, as she'd been calling it all week, in a tangled heap of finery on the ground.

Rhiannon almost cackled out loud, but that was most definitely not allowed in such rarified circumstances. She settled for firmly clamping her lips together as her mother, as fussily as any wet hen, rearranged her satin gown and cream-colored lace shawl. Rhiannon decided her father was even more comical in his efforts not to laugh, for he was making an even greater scene with his loud coughing and guffaws to cover his wife's faux pas. Once he had his wife's dignity and person restored, Edwin turned to his daughter and raised his hand to aid her.

"Allow me," said a deep and cultured voice, one that raised the hairs at the nape of Rhiannon's neck. She swallowed hard, imagining that she could feel the caress of that voice on the bare skin of her neck.

Edwin O'Shea jumped and turned around. "Why and it's Mr. Wolfe, it is. Rhiannon, girl, be gettin' yourself out of the carriage." His Irish was as thick as stew when he was nervous; and right now, Rhiannon could have cut it with a knife.

Well, now she knew what the boy's errand had been—to alert Hank Wolfe to the O'Sheas' arrival. If Hank's breaking with etiquette—leaving the receiving line to come out here personally to escort her in—didn't start the town tongues to wagging, then nothing would.

"May I, Miss O'Shea?" Hank asked, being the gallant gentleman, his hand held up and out for her to take. For a moment, all Rhiannon could do was sit and stare at him.

He slowly raised a dark brow at her, as if not sure she was going to take his hand. But she couldn't help herself. He was absolutely breathtaking in his black, finely tailored evening clothes. But it wasn't his clothes that held her spellbound in her seat. It was him, pure and simple. He was overwhelming in his male physical beauty. Clothes on this man were an afterthought, a mere sop to the conventions of society. And his handsome face above his snowy shirt collar, so strong of jaw, so wide of brow, so rife with clean angles and planes, convinced Rhiannon that she was looking at a come-to-life statue that had been meant as a standard for male perfection.

"Uh, Miss O'Shea?"

"Rhiannon, girl, what's the matter?"

"Oh, Edwin, do something."

They'd all spoken at once—Hank, her father, and her mother. Rhiannon broke her reverie, actually shaking her head once to clear it, and put her hand in Hank's. The contact was startling in the thrill it sent racing through her. It also sent her gaze to lock with his, as if she sought an explanation for what this feeling was. His hooded eyes and full, devilishly smiling lips gave her the answer. A coiling warmth low in her abdomen punctuated Hank's message.

"Well, now, and will we be standing out here all evening, or will we be joining in the festivities? Are you going to sit yourself out here all night, girl? 'Cause if you are, me and your mother will be going in ourselves." With that, Edwin O'Shea took his wife's plumply rounded arm, bowed slightly to his host, and swept Mrs. O'Shea off toward the lights, the laughter, the music, and the awaiting glory this night would bring them.

Hank watched them leave. He then turned back to Rhiannon and looked the slightest bit amused to see his hand still holding hers. "Well, what will it be, Miss O'Shea? I'm perfectly content to stay out here all night if you are. But may I point out that your father's accent is thick enough to turn him into a leprechaun at midnight? And in my experiences with him, that means he's in a high state of upset. Am I right, madam?"

Rhiannon smiled, the tension broken. "You are most definitely right, sir." She stood up, using Hank's hand and strength as leverage to make a smooth, cultured exit from the carriage. The driver gave a cluck to the bay, and the carriage moved away.

Hank offered Rhiannon his arm, and she took it, reveling in the rock-hardness of the muscles that bunched under her touch. Absurdly, she found she was proud of his physique, as if he'd been formed as he was just for her pleasure. But she knew that was an illusion, a dangerous one. The man who walked beside her, his heels crunching on the driveway, his legs swishing her skirts, was not an appendage to or for anyone. He was just like his name—a wolf, a skilled hunter, a powerful creature that could only live free, a lone wolf who lived by his own rules. But, a secret little voice whispered, once a wolf mates—it's for life.

Rhiannon darted a glance at her escort. His dark hair curled low on his neck, brushing his collar. She was glad he wasn't looking down at her at this moment; she wasn't so sure she could have stood up under the power of his gaze. That, and the fact that she was busily picturing herself mated to Hank for life. An audible breath escaped her.

"Nervous?" Hank asked, placing his other hand on top of hers. She looked up into the dazzling sexuality of his smile. That lazy grin of his would be her undoing one day, if she weren't careful.

And despite images of forever and mating and . . . thoughts such as that, she fully intended to be careful. Hank didn't intend to stay in town, much less take a mate; and she didn't intend to marry. At least, not right away. So there; their goals were stated, and each one knew the other's. And that was what made them friends: They both wanted their freedom. But good Lord, she'd never had another friend make her legs weak like this and make her heart beat a tattoo in her chest like this.

Once they'd reached the front door, the townspeople having moved aside deferentially at their approach, Rhiannon was surprised and amused to see only Miss Penelope standing in the entryway greeting guests. Apparently, Hank was feeling the same way, because his comment echoed her own thoughts.

"Aunt Pene, dear, did Miss Tillie abandon you for the delights of the table?"

Miss Penelope, tall, slender, elegant, cutting quite a figure in her high-necked, long-sleeved, striped mauve gown, and surrounded by entering and milling guests, grabbed at Hank's other sleeve when he spoke and drew her attention. "Thank heavens, there you are, Henry. Oh, good evening, Miss O'Shea. You're more beautiful every time I see you."

"Then I must stop bringing her out, Aunt. A few more trips and we'll all be blinded by her radiance."

Rhiannon dug her elbow into his side at such an outlandish compliment. He looked over and down at her, a teasing grin showing white, even teeth and laugh lines to either side of his firm mouth.

"Now, Henry, you'll absolutely turn the girl's head with that tongue of yours."

The coughing snort from Hank earned him another surreptitious dig in his side. It was the only sign she gave that she was thinking about what he was—the scene at the gazebo, where he'd definitely turned her head with his tongue in one long, hot kiss on one long, hot day not so long ago.

Aunt Penelope went on. "Now, stay here and greet the guests—oh, hello, Mr. and Mrs. Haskell; so glad you could come—while Miss O'Shea and I go salvage the buffet before Tillie has her pockets absolutely stuffed full. I swear, I don't know how she manages to get that food past me and into her pockets."

Hank moved away from Rhiannon with lightning speed. Now how did he know another pointed elbow was headed for his ribs? Taking his great-aunt's place, he greeted the next guests, the Hansons, with an exuberance far and beyond anything anyone in Wolfe, Kansas, had ever seen him display. Rhiannon narrowed her eyes at him in shared amusement. He looked over at her and winked conspiratorially. She raised her chin and turned away with great haughtiness. But he knew his secret, and Tillie's, was safe with her, darn him.

"Come, dear," Aunt Penelope said to her, "Let me introduce you around, though I suppose that isn't really necessary since you grew up here. But still, you are our guest of honor, so if you'll allow me, I'll play hostess and see you safely entrenched in the festivities. Then I'll deal with my sister."

As she talked, Penelope Penland deftly maneuvered Rhiannon through the crush of the laughing, drinking, and eating throng. Rhiannon realized that they were headed generally in the direction of the dining room, where she knew from her visit that the buffet was set up. Miss Penelope proved to be a very gracious hostess, indeed; she greeted everyone within touching distance, inquired as to their well-being, made sure they had plenty of everything, and that no one stood alone, neglected and ignored. This was a side of the older woman that Rhiannon had never seen. She certainly wasn't the dottering old woman that the townspeople would have outsiders believe.

Rhiannon did her share of greeting, too. She nodded and spoke to the older guests, assured them she was delighted to be home, and allowed them to gush over how she'd grown and how beautiful she was. That was the easy part. Not so easy were the snickers that followed in her wake when she moved from one group to the next with Miss Penelope, whose attention was honed on finding her sister and rescuing the food.

Rhiannon could hear them; perhaps they meant her to. She could catch only snatches of conversations, but that was enough.

". . . running for mayor . . ."

". . . saw her talking to that whore . . ."

". . . walked right into the Fancy Lady Saloon, she did . . ."

". . . Mayor Driver's boy, Charlie, says he saw her smoking and kissing Hank Wolfe . . ."

111

"... I'd like to get my hands on her..."

"... got all the women thinking they're really going to run for office. Not my wife, by God..."

"... all we need with Carry Nation coming to town..."

Rhiannon did her best to pretend she didn't hear them. Let them talk. That was all it was, anyway. What did she care what they thought? She blinked rapidly against a sudden moisture in her eyes. She hated the fact that she cried when she was angry. Surely, it would be different when she found her own friends; after all, they were young, they still had dreams. Oh, good, there was Effie Parsons; they'd shared their dreams as girls. She'd understand.

"Excuse me, Miss Penland," Rhiannon called out, touching the older woman's slender arm. Penelope turned from moving toward the dining room to look questioningly at her guest of honor. "I see one of my friends over there. Do you mind if I go greet her?"

"Why, of course not, dear. That's what this whole affair is about—greeting old friends. You go ahead. I can handle Tillie."

Rhiannon smiled at that; she wasn't so sure anyone could handle Tillie, the little dickens. But all she said was, "Thank you," as she took the other woman's hand in a slight squeeze.

Turning, she veered off to her left to seek out Effie. Her stomach knotted in excited anticipation at seeing a childhood friend. But she found her way blocked by the short, wiry, but determined body of James Sullivan, editor-in-chief of the *The Wolfe Daily*. He stepped whichever way Rhiannon did, a grin on his bespectacled middle-aged face.

Rhiannon gave up trying to get around him and away from him. Even though she'd always liked him, she was still somewhat angry at him for printing the story that seemed to be changing her life. "Good evening, Mr. Sullivan. How nice to see you."

"You don't mean that."

"No."

He laughed. "That's what I like in a woman—honesty."

"I daresay."

"Did you get your copy of *The Wolfe Daily?*"

"And which one would that be? We get a copy every day."

"Now don't be coy with me, young lady. I've known you since you were in pigtails and used to hang out at my office begging to help me run the printer."

Rhiannon sighed and looked past him. Effie was gone. With a huff, she looked back at Mr. Sullivan.

"Don't worry. Hank Wolfe didn't get away," he said.

"I beg your pardon?"

"That look and that huff. Weren't they meant for Mr. Wolfe?"

Stung at thinking she was that transparent, and feeling self-righteous because he really was off the mark—at least this time—Rhiannon frowned at him. He was most definitely exceeding the boundaries of the casual relationship they'd had when she was a child. He needed to know that he was dealing with a woman and a lady now. "How dare you, Mr. Sullivan. If you're looking for another ridiculous story to print about me, why don't you at least be honest enough to get out your pad and take notes?"

"Ridiculous? I think that story was one of the best things— and one of the best ideas from our esteemed mayor and city council—I ever heard."

Rhiannon re-assessed him. Was he serious? "Are you serious?"

"As serious as the drought and the current state of affairs."

Rhiannon began to get excited. "Then, you didn't print it as a joke? You weren't making fun of the notion of women running a city?"

"Rhiannon, you've been away for a while. In your absence we've had rapid expansion in Wolfe, on top of a drought and bad elements moving in, and now Carry Nation is on her way. And there's unchecked growth, and widows and orphans practically on the streets; why, you name it. And are they being dealt with, what with Old Man Wolfe dead and the young Mr. Wolfe not even sure he's staying here? These men don't know what to do without a Wolfe leading the pack—pardon my expression. We need someone young and fresh and totally independent to shake things up and get these people moving independently, someone not beholden to the Wolfe name. And that, darlin', is where you come in. So I ask you, how in the hell could you and the other women do any worse?"

Rhiannon blinked in surprise to hear her very own thoughts spoken aloud, and by a respected, if not feared, man of the town. He would make a powerful ally. She dared not stop to think about the part about being beholden to the Wolfe name, beyond the thought that she wasn't . . . not really . . . not directly.

The churning wheels in her brain must have made themselves known on her face, because James Sullivan burst out laughing and practically bellowed, "By God, I knew I knew my man—woman! You're going to do it, aren't you?"

Rhiannon's eyes narrowed in determination. She ignored the startled glances of nearby guests that his outburst had sent their way. "Yes, Mr. Sullivan, I am going to do it. And you're going to help me."

James Sullivan threw his head back again and laughed. His drink sloshed threateningly in its crystal goblet. He took a huge gulp of the wine and extended his hand to Rhiannon. "Miss O'Shea, may I have the honor of being the first to shake the hand of the new candidate for mayor?"

Rhiannon hated to tease a newspaperman, but the opening was too perfect. Let him wonder. She took his hand and, thinking of Hank and Cat LaFlamme, said, "I'm afraid you're the third, Mr. Sullivan."

Rhiannon shook his hand and left him laughing again. She smiled very prettily for anyone close enough to glance their way. Looking back towards the door, she spotted Hank still greeting the steady flow of guests. He was never hard to spot in a crowd; he usually stood head and shoulders above everyone else. Rhiannon was unwilling to put a name to the emotion that just the mere sight of him exploded in her, but she did grab a goblet of champagne off the tray of a passing servant and drank a good portion of it.

To her, he looked like a veritable prince or head of state standing there, bestowing that bone-melting grin on undeserving women. As she watched him, she noticed two things. One, it was hard to miss the respectful deference with which men treated him. And two, it was even harder to miss the open longing with which women, young and old, looked at him. She didn't really blame the men or the women; he elicited all those things—and much more—in her. But still, the next woman who touched him like that or simpered next to him, so casually allowing a breast or two to rub against him, was going to have her hair snatched out and—

"My word, Rhiannon O'Shea, I never realized your eyes were so green."

Startled by the sound of Effie Parson's voice so close to her, Rhiannon jumped guiltily. But she recovered quickly and, careful of her goblet, hugged her old friend to her—as best she could, anyway, what with Effie being so pregnant. "Why, Effie Parsons—Momma wrote to tell me about your marriage to Jack—what do you mean, my green eyes? You know very well my eyes aren't green."

Effie smiled, but there was a quality to it that Rhiannon remembered from their girlhood days—slightly mean, maybe even cunning. It made Rhiannon very uneasy now, just as it had back then. "They most certainly are," Effie said, "at least, they are when you're looking at Mr. Hank Wolfe being surrounded by a gaggle of females."

She was caught; what could she say? Thank God, again, for Miss Constance, who'd taught her that when a lady was confronted with a delicate or troublesome subject, she simply changed the topic. "My, Effie, you look wonderful. It's easy to see that marriage agrees with you. When is your baby due?"

"Not for a while. Three months or so, according to Doc Johnson. My husband, Jack"—Rhiannon noted that she said "husband" as if Rhiannon's lack of one somehow made her wanting as a woman—"he's the sheriff, you know—is really excited. He dotes on me, and gives me everything I want."

Rhiannon could barely stand the girl's smugness. She decided she really didn't like Effie Parsons. Perhaps she never had. "And I'm sure you take complete advantage of that, don't you, Effie?"

Perhaps it was Rhiannon's sweet and pure smile that threw Effie off. She appeared not to know quite how to respond to that. Rhiannon silently savored her triumph, but at the same time she felt a sting of sorrow that this was probably the way it would always be between her and Effie. It was hard to give up the things of childhood, especially friendships.

Rhiannon decided to give Effie another chance. "I'm very glad to be home. I've missed all of you."

"Well, it was certainly quiet here what with you gone. But it didn't take you long to stir things up, did it?"

Even as she answered, Rhiannon knew, with a sinking feeling, what she meant. "I'm not aware of anything I've done to stir anything or anybody up, Effie. I haven't been home very long."

"Long enough! Are you going to run for mayor? Some of these silly old women here, who were in that story in the paper—and don't think I don't know why each one of them was named—seem to think you are. They say you've even talked to some of them about running. And I saw you myself talking to that . . . that fancy lady, that Cat LaFlamme person. You better be careful, Rhiannon. You'll get yourself run out of town."

Rhiannon's temper burst behind her eyes and around her heart. She longed to throw her drink in Effie's puffed-up, pasty face—and that was just to begin with. But she'd made a vow to herself that she would do nothing to upset this evening for her parents. With tremendous restraint and tight lips, she rasped out, "If you'll excuse me . . ."

She turned to make a hasty retreat—and nearly bumped right into Hank. He grabbed her arms to steady her. She was off balance and blinded by angry tears, and all she could do was stare dumbly up into his face. A detached part of her brain noted that his face was a mask of cold fury; her tears dried instantly. His look raised the hair on her arms, and she was very thankful that it wasn't directed at her. She knew that because his black eyes bore into Effie.

"Perhaps you'd best not stay for long, Mrs. Parsons, given your . . . delicate condition. I understand one tires easily being with child. Please find your husband and inform him that I will not be offended if you wish to leave."

Rhiannon's eyes widened at his words. He'd heard everything! She stole a quick look at Effie and saw that she was as pale as a plucked chicken. She almost felt sorry for Effie—almost. Effie took her cue and turned abruptly away, melting into the crowd.

Rhiannon, allowing herself the tiniest twinge of triumph, looked back up at Hank. "You didn't have to do that."

He smiled down at her warmly, warmly enough to heat Rhiannon's blood. She took another huge gulp of her champagne and emptied her slender goblet. Hank took it from her, placed it on the tray held out to them by a servant who had magically appeared, took another full one for himself, and handed Rhiannon a replacement. "Yes, I did. She had it coming. And you're too much of a lady to come down to her level."

Rhiannon slanted him a glance. Had he just complimented her, or had he just reminded her to be on her best behavior?

She decided she didn't care which it was. Hank was here by her side, and she suddenly felt beautiful. She took a rather delicate sip, delicate considering her swigging of the first glass of champagne, and giggled prettily as the bubbles tickled her nose.

Hank smiled down at her and turned into Price Charming. He took her free hand and held her out from him at arm's length. He turned her in a slow pirouette, giving a low, appreciative whistle. "I do believe I haven't told my esteemed guest of honor just how beautiful she looks tonight. Would I be too forward if I told you that your frock is stunning?"

Rhiannon giggled again. What was wrong with her? She never, ever giggled. And she hated women who did. But not right now. "What, this old thing?" she minced, trying to remember she had a full glass of champagne in her hand. Oh, yes, the champagne. She took another sip.

She watched Hank raise an eyebrow as he sipped his own champagne. "This old thing? The eternal female lament. Now, I'm not really good at this sort of thing, but let me see if I can do it justice. Hmmm." He turned her this way and that; the room began to go this way and that, too, for Rhiannon. "Let me see. Ah, yes. If I had to describe this lovely concoction I would say it was low-cut, off the shoulder, somewhat pinkish and cream in color. Oh, yes, watered-silk with tiny, delicate—what are those?" He peered closer at Rhiannon's bosom. She gurgled in her throat, as if bubbles were caught there. "Now I see—they're tea roses and they're embroidered on your dress. Why, my dear, they're all over your dress."

"I thought you said you weren't good at this."

He was fairly leering at her now, but in a comical fashion. Rhiannon knew he was trying to get her over the hurt and insults that Effie had dealt out, but she loved him for it anyway. He was a good friend, and he would never say the sorts of things Effie had.

"Well, apparently I am, if you're satisfied with it. I'll add describing female fashion to my rather long list of accomplishments."

That did it. His manner was so droll and foppish, so outlandish on someone of his physique and demeanor, that Rhiannon laughed out loud. And it wasn't the pleasant tinkling laughter that Miss Constance had actually had her charges practice, bless her hide. No, this was a loud, raucous laugh, and God help her, she was dangerously close to snorting.

Hank saved her again by drawing her up close to him, and in the process huffing the excess air out of her. Rhiannon saw the hundred or so pairs of eyes that were staring; she heard the whispering and the exchanging of comments. But Hank didn't seem to care. Why should he? He owned the whole damned town. And they could just leave if they didn't like it. Hadn't Effie Parsons found that out?

Rhiannon, her nose pressed firmly against Hank's chest, found a lucid moment to wonder just where in the hell— oops, she always cursed when she drank—where in the heck these drunken thoughts were coming from. Luckily for her, the close scents of Hank, the mingling of male musk, starched clothing, bay rum, and alcohol, cleared her head some. She pulled away from him and said, "I think I'd better eat something."

"I think you're right. This way, my sweet. We'll get you a plate, providing Aunt Tillie left anything, and then we'll go up to the ballroom."

"That's my favorite room in your house," Rhiannon said. She thought her voice sounded childish. She hoped it was her imagination.

Hank's mouth twisted in a failed attempt to suppress a grin. "Damn. I was hoping my bedroom would be your favorite room in my house."

"I've never been in your bedroom, so how would I know?"

"Good point. Perhaps we can remedy that."

Rhiannon rolled her eyes. He was still teasing her. Couldn't he see she was cheered up?

They were in the dining room now. Hank took her goblet from her and placed both of theirs on a silver tray on the sideboard. He took her lace shawl from around her shoulders and handed it to a servant, giving him instructions to deposit it in a private room upstairs. He then turned to the heavily laden table, picked up a beautifully patterned china plate from the tall stack at one end, and plopped it into her hands. She held it in both hands while Hank worked his way down the table beside her, chatting with the other guests and filling the plate in earnest. When he turned towards her, Rhiannon took the opportunity to raise her eyebrows, looking from him to the mound of food on the plate, and back.

"We'll share it."

"Oh." Somehow, the thought of sharing a plate of food with him was titillating. Because even though her mouth was watering, it wasn't just from the mingled scents of the delicious Western fare. She wasn't that hungry, at least not for food. She hadn't consciously realized where her thoughts had led her eyes until Hank turned around again and caught her looking at his posterior. Only now, with him turned around, it wasn't his . . . posterior.

"Dessert?" he asked, that drollness back in his voice.

Rhiannon blinked. "What?" Then she focused, and saw he held up a piece of apple pie. "Oh, of course."

"Good," Hank said in an approving but strident voice. "I would have been insulted had you said no."

"What?" Rhiannon knew she couldn't continue to keep saying "What?" It wasn't exactly a sparkling rejoinder, but she had the distinct impression that there were undercurrents to this conversation that she wasn't quite clear-headed enough to pick up on.

"Never mind, beautiful Rhiannon, my friend. Come on. We'll seek out a quiet corner and empty our plate."

"And if we don't, we can always stick the food in our pockets."

Hank stopped short. "I'm never going to live that down, am I? You're going to torture me with that one act of kindness even when I'm an old man, aren't you?"

Rhiannon's laugh had nothing to do with drink or undertones of any kind. It was a genuine friend-to-friend teasing. "Afraid so."

"All right, then. I'll have to catch you at some furtive good deed to throw back in your face when you're ninety or so. Then we'll see how you like it."

"I would like it very much." She spoke almost in a whisper, her heart in her eyes in this unguarded moment.

Now it was Hank's turn to speak sparkling rejoinders. "What?"

"To still be around you when I'm ninety. I would love that very much."

Hank's smile faded. So did Rhiannon's. The milling, laughing, noisy, jostling crowd faded. Rhiannon forgot that she was holding a plate of food; oh, it remained firmly in her hands, but she just wasn't aware of it. Her awareness was trained solely, and soulfully, on Hank Wolfe. Whose eyes were so black that she couldn't read them, couldn't see beyond their glittering surface. In fact, looking at him watching her as if he were memorizing her face, she couldn't quite remember what she'd said to put that look on his face.

"Rhiannon, don't ever say anything like that again. And don't ever look at me like this again. Because if you do, our friendship will be over."

Chapter Nine

"Dammit," was all Hank could think or say. He wished he could get rip-roaring drunk, but his obligations as host would not allow it. One more good reason why he wished he were out west with his Army unit. If you weren't on duty, you were free. No demands on your time, your person, or your heart.

"Dammit," he said again. The swirling dancers with their happy faces and bright colors annoyed him deeply, as if they were being cheerful just to spite him. Especially spiteful was one couple which consisted of Rhiannon and some bald-headed old idiot.

Hank set down his whiskey glass with a hard clink on the small table that rested against the wall at the doors of the ballroom. He'd switched from champagne to whiskey right after he'd walked away from Rhiannon and that ridiculously full plate a couple of hours ago. Why in hell had she looked at him with puppy-dog love in her eyes and said she wanted to still be around him when she was ninety? Didn't she know what that meant—that in order to do that they would have to be married, dammit?

"Dammit."

He straightened up from his leaning stance in the doorway. That lecherous son of a bitch was holding her entirely too close. And she looked like she didn't like it. She better not, by God. Hank wasn't quite drunk enough or angry enough to move in on the dancing couple. Taking a closer look, though, Hank saw the man dancing with Rhiannon was Sam Driver, the mayor. Now he was mad enough.

And he didn't give a damn, dammit, if he'd simply walked off and left her standing there a couple hours ago with that stupid plate full of food. She, by God, would dance with him now and quit ignoring him. He'd had his fill of trying to get close to her, once he'd gotten over the initial shock of seeing just how deeply she was beginning to feel for him. No matter where she'd been, he'd tried to get her attention, to talk to her, to explain. But she'd been very elusive, slipping away in the crowd each time.

But no more. And he didn't care if he had to chase her all over the mansion. His black mood, just like all his other moods, was plainly visible on his face; he knew that, and he didn't care. The crowd watching the dancers parted for him as if at some silent command. Apparently, no one felt the need to question him or greet him. Still, Hank could see that they kept darting their gazes from him to Rhiannon.

The sober, sane part of Hank's brain kept trying to tell him that he was thinking and behaving irrationally. But it did no good; he wouldn't listen. All he knew was that he was going to hold Rhiannon in his arms, whether she liked it or not. Another sober part of his brain, the totally male part, told him she would like it—if he didn't behave like a belligerent, drunken ass.

That halted Hank's steps long enough for him to consider his intentions. If they weren't totally honorable, totally social and innocent, then he could very well find himself in that confining state of matrimony he wanted to avoid. He needed to think about this.

123

But then, all of a sudden, it was as if he would die if he didn't hold her. Consequences, social conventions, honorable or dishonorable intentions be damned, dammit. He needed to feel her luscious female body in his arms. He needed to hear the sound of her voice, the sound of her laughter. He needed . . . her.

The fire in Hank moved his feet forward. He shouldered his way among the swirling couples, not even hearing the music and the conversations, intent only on his prey. He didn't even pause when he brushed by the older O'Sheas, who danced by and gave him a smile-turned-startled-look. It wasn't them he wanted. It was their daughter.

His large hand clamped on the mayor's chubby, sloping shoulder, effectively stopping the older man in his tracks. Hank didn't waste a look on him; his eyes were on Rhiannon as he said, "May I cut in?" It really wasn't a question.

"Uh, oh, of course. By all means." The mayor looked from Hank to Rhiannon momentarily, and then blazed a trail of retreat off the dance floor. But he could have stood there all night and Hank wouldn't have known—or cared.

Hank reached out and scooped Rhiannon into his arms. And knew instantly that this dance was a mistake. Never would he be content to end the evening with the subtle closeness of a waltz being the only contact they had. Too many people, too many clothes. But as he looked wordlessly into her face, trying not to notice her wide-eyed perplexity, he knew he was lost. She was the end of his freedom; or was she the beginning? Interesting question. Devastating question.

"I think we're supposed to move our feet when we waltz," Rhiannon whispered, darting her gaze from his face to the other couples around them, who were desperately trying to maintain their dance rhythm and not to run into their stationary host and the guest of honor in his arms.

"This dance be damned," Hank pronounced, much as if he'd just said, "Throw the Christians to the lions." He then took Rhiannon's hand and pulled her after him and off the dance floor. He felt her tugging resistance, but held on anyway. He had to be with her, and he had to understand just exactly why that was. He was tired of thinking, breathing, dreaming, and living Rhiannon. He wanted her out of his system.

When he practically hauled her around in front of him on one of the many balconies off the second-floor ballroom, and closed the French doors behind them, he didn't blame Rhiannon for her hissing response. "Just what do you think you're doing, Hank Wolfe? How dare you embarrass me like that by hauling me off like I'm some child who's misbehaved. And right in front of my parents, your aunts, and the other guests! What must they be thinking? No—what are you thinking?"

"I'm thinking I'm damned tired of you ignoring me. I am your host, after all." He kept his voice down, too, mindful of other guests taking in the night air on the four other balconies that ran the length of the ballroom.

She blinked at him. "Pardon me if I'm wrong, but who left whom standing with a full plate about two hours ago and said we can no longer be friends? Did you expect me to cry and follow around after you?"

Just as he'd feared. She was even more beautiful when aroused like this. Her ginger eyes fairly snapped, as her stubborn little chin poked its way up toward his face and her burnished copper curls fell over her shoulder. She was about to come out of her dress as she strained toward him. This vision did nothing to help Hank clear his mind; quite the contrary was happening. Still, he took her anger seriously; she was totally justified.

"You're right," he declared, giving in to her.

She put her balled up fists to her waist, narrowed her eyes as if ready for a fight, and said, "What?"

"I just apologized. I said you're right."

Apparently, she was still too angry to understand the fuss was over before it began, because neither her stance nor her voice softened. She was still arguing her side in a low, strident voice. "Oh, I am, huh?" Then she stopped, as if his last words had just sunk in. She cocked her head to a side and slanted him a questioning look. "About what?"

Finally, Hank wanted to laugh. But he didn't dare. He had the distinct impression that she would sock him right in the jaw and send him crashing over the balcony railing if he did. "About me being a boor and a rude host, and a not-very-good friend."

He was content to watch the play of changing emotions, the switching of mental gears, move over her face. She didn't trust him yet, he could tell. She still looked wary of his intentions, as well she should be, Hank knew. As if to confirm this impression, she swished her full skirt back and took a step away from him. "What do you want from me, Hank Wolfe?"

Hank nearly exploded in a kaleidoscope of jumbled doubts and misgivings. "Goddammit, girl, if I knew the answer to that one, this scene wouldn't be necessary."

His agitation and her nearness propelled him toward the edge of the narrow balcony. As he looked out into the velvet night, his hands at his waist, a strong urge to jump over the railing and take off running, just to rid himself of this excess physical energy, took him by surprise.

Before he could act on such a foolhardy whim, he felt her hand, small and warm, on his sleeve. His body jerked at the electric jolt that ran through him. Fighting for control, he turned to look at her. "You really shouldn't be out here with me."

"Oh?" she asked, cocking her head to one side. "Then I suppose I shouldn't have dragged you out here."

"Touché." He looked at her hard. There was enough light filtering out through the thinly curtained French doors to allow him to see every facet of her jewel-like face. "You're not the least bit afraid of me, are you?"

That surprised her. She took her hand off his arm and stepped away from him, going to her side of the balcony and trailing her hand over the railing. Hank's gaze followed her. She didn't turn to him when she spoke. "Do you want me to be?"

"No. But it would be so much the better for you if you were."

"For me? Or for you?"

Hank gave in further. "Yes. For me, too."

Rhiannon did a slow turn, stopping when she faced him. Hank held his breath, hoping and fearing she was feeling the same things he was. He couldn't help but notice the way her full breasts moved above her low-cut bodice whenever she breathed. He wanted to reach out and . . .

When she spoke, it was in such a soft, kitten's-paws, whispery voice that Hank felt it pad over his flesh. "Hank, we can't do this. We can't. It's not what either of us wants."

"I know," he managed, swallowing hard. Never in his entire life had he ever felt so helpless, not when his mother died, not when his father was always absent, not even when his father died. But this loss was much worse, because he'd never really had her. With a sudden jerking motion, he moved toward the French doors and opened them to the light and the music. "Go. You're free to go. You always were."

His words hung in the air between them. Hank died a thousand times waiting for her response. And he had no idea in hell what he hoped it would be. An undying declaration of love? Her begging him to let her stay? But in the end, it was neither of those.

After a brief but piercing look into his eyes, she gathered up her silk skirt and swept by him, head held at a regal angle. Her wake trailed a flowery perfume that swirled around Hank and embedded itself in his senses. He had to close his eyes for a moment or two to compose himself.

For almost the remainder of the evening, Hank could do nothing but watch Rhiannon from afar as she pretended a gaiety he refused to believe she felt. But perhaps she was unaffected after their balcony scene, as he was beginning to think of it; certainly, theirs had had a decidedly different ending than the one in Shakespeare's *Romeo and Juliet.* Those two had ended up in bed . . . eventually.

As the evening wore on, becoming more pale and cloying as the hours crawled by, Hank played the gracious host to all the guests, as much for his aunts' sakes as anyone's. Left to himself, he would have thrown everybody out and gotten drunk. As Rhiannon apparently was doing, he thought, catching a glimpse of her across the black-and-white tiled entryway as she took yet another slender crystal goblet off a servant's silver tray.

She hadn't danced anymore after he'd cut in on her and the mayor. Perhaps the men were afraid to ask her, thinking Hank would do the same thing or worse to them. Good, let them think that, he decided. She had visited with her childhood friends some, and then had come downstairs. But she certainly hadn't eaten anything that he had seen; and he would know, because everywhere she went, he was there. To make sure, as her host, that no one took advantage of her in her slightly inebriated state, he told himself.

Hank turned from his conversation with a local woman, who was pressing her pretty enough but overeager buxom daughter on him in what she believed was a coy manner, to realize that Rhiannon was nowhere in sight. Where could she have gone to in such a short time? Extricating himself from the two women, Hank went in search of Rhiannon. She was nowhere downstairs in any of the rooms that were open to the party. She couldn't have gone upstairs—he had been facing them the entire time. If some young buck had taken her outside . . .

No, the butler, Watson, told him. No one had left. Hank very nearly scratched his head trying to think where she could be. Perhaps she was just sitting down somewhere, and he couldn't see her right off. But he knew that wasn't it; she'd been flitting like a butterfly all night. There was no reason to think she'd stopped now. A search of the other rooms on

this floor was in order, then. Starting down the long, narrow
hall that was to the other side of the grand central stairway,
Hank got no further than the door of his private office. It was
slightly ajar, and low moans where issuing from the interior
of the room.

What the hell? Hank pushed open the door and peered
inside, letting his eyes adjust to the dimness of the room.
At first, what with most of the light streaming in from
behind him, he didn't see anyone. Just when he decided
he'd imagined the moans and was turning away to close
the door, he heard them again. They were coming from the
imported French sofa that faced the fireplace. Hank walked
slowly into the room, purposely allowing his heels to ring
on the polished wood floor. It was in his mind that he might
be interrupting a lovers' tryst. But no guilty heads popped
up. Intrigued now, he walked to the back of the sofa and
peered over.

He'd found his prey. Rhiannon was lying full out on the
horsehair sofa, one hand over her stomach, the other over
her eyes. Hank shook his head and grinned as he leaned
over, crooking one knee and resting his crossed forearms
on the sofa's back. He watched her for a moment, and
then reached down to touch her hair, which lay across her
exposed upper bosom. The curl, seemingly of its own volition, sprang up and coiled itself around Hank's finger. The
symbolism wasn't wasted on Hank, but he didn't take time
to analyze it.

Straightening up, he went back to the door and closed it,
blocking out most of the light. Familiar with the room, he
unerringly made his way to the long windows across from
the door and down from the fireplace. He drew the heavy
curtains open and let in the moonlight. Another moan from
the sofa drew him back to Rhiannon's side. Squatting beside
her, he moved her hand slightly and felt her forehead—
cool and clammy. This was a sick little girl. But not on
his expensive sofa, thank you.

"Come on, Rhiannon," he crooned as he sat her up, despite her mumbled protests. Holding her arms, he peered—cautiously—into her face, trying to see around her tangled hair. "Rhiannon, can you hear me?"

"I'm going to die."

He laughed. "No, you're not. You just feel like you're going to die."

"I want to die."

Another guffaw escaped Hank. "I've felt it also, little one. You're going to hate yourself in the morning."

"I already do."

"Yeah, me too."

She looked up—pale, befuddled, clammy, red-eyed. "You hate me, too?"

Well, here comes the maudlin, sentimental stage of drunkenness. "No, sweetheart, I don't hate you. I hate me for letting you get like this."

"You did this to me?"

Hank grinned. "I think so."

Silence for a moment. "Well, then I hate you, too."

Hank laughed. "Good. You remember that. You're going to need it come tomorrow."

Silence again.

"Hank."

"Yes?"

"I need something else right now."

"Let me guess."

"I think I'm going to be sick."

"I thought so." He whisked her up into his arms as delicately and as quickly as he dared and headed for the closed door, wondering just how in the hell he was going to get it open while he held Rhiannon. Time was of the essence, what with her threatened eruption.

His dilemma was solved for him when the door to the study suddenly opened just as he reached it. MacGregor, his valet, stood there. With the light behind the older man, Hank couldn't see his face clearly, but he didn't have to. And he didn't have time for the man's fussing.

"She's sick, MacGregor. I wasn't taking advantage of her."

"I beg your pardon, sir. I never thought to—"

"Just get out of the way and see if anyone else is in this hallway. I'd like to keep this our little secret if I can. Miss O'Shea doesn't need further headlines at this point."

"Miss O'Shea?" MacGregor fairly squeaked. Still, he moved back out of the room, looked both ways, and then signaled for his master to come out. "Now we have a fine mess. I was just sent by your aunts to look for her. They're retiring and want to tell her good night."

Hank cursed roundly and moved past MacGregor. He turned left out of the room and went back toward the kitchen. MacGregor followed on his heels, trying to help and awaiting his orders about the Misses Penland. Just before Hank got to the noise and bustle that was the kitchen, he turned left again into a small alcove. "Open that door before we all three get baptized."

MacGregor squeezed past Hank and the bundle in his arms to open the door. The night air, decidedly and blessedly cooler than earlier, hit them. MacGregor backed out into the tiny, private garden ahead of Hank and his moaning bundle. Hank sat Rhiannon down on a small marble bench, using his hip and thigh as leverage to keep her upright. She put her arms around his thigh and rested her head against his hip. Hank rolled his eyes at her drunken familiarity.

With his hand firmly on her shoulder, Hank turned to MacGregor. "Tell my aunts that you couldn't find Miss O'Shea, and that I'll personally take them into town tomorrow to visit her. That should do it."

"Yes, I do believe you're right. They do love to go to town," MacGregor commented, sounding for all the world as if this were some sort of conspiracy they were planning. Hank thought about that; he supposed it was a conspiracy.

"And what should I tell the other guests, Mr. Wolfe?"

"The other guests? What about them?"

"Well, sir, it is well after one o'clock and some of them are starting to leave."

"I'm going to be sick."

Hank looked down at Rhiannon and patted her shoulder. "Not just yet, darling. Hold on."

"All right," she agreed amiably.

Hank and MacGregor both looked at her for a moment or two, and then resumed their conversation, much as if she hadn't interrupted. "All right," Hank said, "I'll be there as soon as I can. Take my aunts up first and then bring me some wet cloths. I believe I'm going to need them. Then, you can stay with her while I say good night to everyone."

"Yes, sir. But there's one more thing."

"Yes, dammit?"

"Her parents, sir. What about the O'Sheas?"

Hank ran his free hand over his mouth and jaw. Somehow, he didn't think the Battle of Bull Run had required this much logistics and planning. A string of solid epithets escaped him while he thought. "I'll talk to them, too. I'll think of something. Just get my aunts to bed and bring me those wet cloths."

Sudden retching sounds from Rhiannon caught both their attentions. They both jumped back, and Hank managed to turn her around to face the flowerbeds and the high bower wall.

"Oh, sir, the rose bushes."

"Yes, I know. It appears she's going to feed them."

"Indeed, sir." MacGregor remained rooted to the spot in horrid fascination as rumblings, but nothing else, emitted from Rhiannon.

"Uh, MacGregor, do you think you could possibly go get the cloths now? I believe I can manage here."

MacGregor jumped and came to himself, a hand to his chest. "Of course, sir." He then beat a hasty retreat as the first eruption from Rhiannon issued forth.

Hank talked and soothed her through it. He held her hair out of her way and leaned over her, holding her arm and steadying her. When the worst of it was over, she started to cry.

"It's all right, sweetheart. You should be glad you got rid of all that champagne in your stomach."

"Shut up," she strangled out miserably.

"No, I mean it. You won't feel so badly in the morning now."

"I hate champagne."

"That's only natural."

"I feel sick again."

"Here we go."

Within moments, it was all over. "I hate champagne."

"I know, sweetheart."

"And don't call me that. I'm not anybody's sweetheart." She began to cry again.

Hank rolled his eyes and patted her back gently. There wasn't much else he could do until MacGregor returned. As if on cue, MacGregor opened the door and came into the garden carrying a glass of water and an enamel basin that proved to be full of wet cloths.

"Good thinking, MacGregor." Hank took off his jacket and tossed it aside onto the flagstone walk. He then rolled up his shirtsleeves, and wrung out a cloth, using it to wipe Rhiannon's sullen little face. She tried to bat his hand away, but she didn't have the strength. "Here now, don't fight me, I'm trying to help," he said. He took the glass from MacGregor and put it to her lips. She turned her head away. He forced it back. "It's just water—for you to wash your mouth out with. That's better; there's a good girl."

Hank stood up while Rhiannon rolled the cool water around in her mouth. When she spat it onto the already violated rose bushes, Hank turned to his valet. "Attractive, isn't she?"

MacGregor barely suppressed a guffaw as he took the glass from Hank.

Then Rhiannon surprised them both by silently wilting backwards in a dead faint. "Great—" was all Hank got out before he caught her. With her safely in his arms, her unconscious body a slight but unwieldy weight, Hank said, "Now let's see if we can get her back into my office undetected. Get my coat; leave the other things here."

Hank said a silent prayer of thanks when they quietly closed his office door behind them. No one had seen them since this room was a good ways from the front of the mansion and was down a long, dim hallway. Hank laid his precious bundle back on the same sofa, slightly sorry that he had to put her down. Drunk and sick or not, she felt good and right.

"Now, you stay here with her," he said to MacGregor. "I'm pretty sure the worst is over. I'll go take care of her parents and the guests. Did my aunts give you any trouble?"

"Oh, no, sir. They're very excited about their trip to town. They're being very secretive, saying they have need of certain ingredients for some secret project of theirs."

Hank wasn't really paying attention to the gist of MacGregor's words as he rolled his sleeves back down and retrieved his coat, so he just commented, "Good. I'll be back as soon as I can."

As he shrugged back into his black evening coat, he took another look at Rhiannon. There was no way she was going home tonight in a carriage. She was too sick; she would just have to spend the night here. He stilled his movements for a moment as he continued to stare at Rhiannon and absorb that thought. Then, with a wink and a smile at his quizzical valet, Hank left his office, his step almost jaunty.

Chapter Ten

Hank was grateful that most of the guests, as if at some silent cue or stroke of the clock, had all decided to leave within a few minutes of each other. Still, it took a while to get that many people out the double-wide front doors. Leaving Watson, his impassive butler, to bow the guests out, Hank went in search of the O'Sheas. And found them hunting the rooms for their daughter.

"There you are," Hank said by way of a greeting when he entered the library. Already the tired maids were cleaning and straightening the room. The O'Sheas too looked tired, he noted. And something else.

"Well, Mr. Wolfe, an' it's me own daughter Rhiannon we're not able to find. Have you seen her?"

Ahh. The Irish brogue. He was a little angry, too.

"Now, Father. I'm sure there's a good reason for her disappearance," Patience O'Shea put in, cutting her eyes from her husband to Hank and back.

"And of course you're absolutely right, Mrs. O'Shea. There is a very good reason. She's . . . fallen ill."

The color drained from both their faces as they clutched

hands with one another and stared at Hank blankly. Patience recovered first. "Where is she?"

Edwin O'Shea chimed in. "Great Mother of God, me own girl lying sick and me out dancin'."

"Now, wait a minute. Hold on," Hank soothed, putting a hand on Mr. O'Shea's arm. He looked around the O'Sheas to see the maids staring curiously. With a nod of his head, he dismissed them. When they were alone, Hank explained. "She's not sick in that sense. Not like you think. She . . . uh . . . got drunk on champagne and—"

"Great Mother of God!"

"Edwin, don't say that. It's blasphemous."

Hank bit back a grin. "She's perfectly all right—now. But she passed out after she threw up, and—"

"Great Mother of God."

"Patience!"

"—and now she's asleep in my office. I assure you that the only ones who know about this are me, you, and my valet, MacGregor. So there is no scandal involved. I believe you should leave her here overnight to sleep it off."

They gasped in unison; Patience's hand flew to her throat. Edwin turned a bright shade of red.

"I assure you that she will be well chaperoned here with my aunts, my valet, and all my servants in attendance. Surely you don't object?" Hank didn't give them a chance to object. In fact, he began herding them towards the front door as he talked. "Good. Then that's settled. I'll bring her home when I bring my aunts into Wolfe tomorrow, or more accurately, later today. I'm sure you must be very tired, so I'll leave you to your ride home. Good night, and thank you so much for coming." Hank shooed them out the front door and closed it after them, but not quite in their faces.

Blowing air out through his puffed up cheeks, he exchanged glances with Watson, who merely raised his eyebrows. "Have everyone go on to bed, Watson. The mess can wait until morning."

"Very good, sir." He bowed and walked off toward the kitchen, his bearing almost military in its stiffness.

Hank shook his head as always at the incongruities of this mansion and all these formal servants in western Kansas. Hell, they didn't even have hoedowns and barn dances here. No, they had fancy-dress balls where the female candidate for mayor got drunk and threw up in your rose bushes.

Hank smiled. So maybe it was all worth it after all. It sure wasn't as boring as he thought it'd be around here; at least, it hadn't been since one Miss Rhiannon O'Shea had returned from finishing school not quite finished. Hell, he hoped she never did quite become the great lady she thought she had to be; that aspiration certainly went against her exuberant, outspoken grain.

And now, to relieve MacGregor.

Hank almost laughed out loud when he reentered his office. He certainly couldn't fault MacGregor for following orders. He'd been told to watch her, and watch her he was. He'd pulled Hank's desk chair right up to the sofa, had seated himself rigidly, and was keeping guard with an intense frown and a basin held right under the sleeping girl's face.

"Good job, MacGregor," Hank teased.

"Thank you, sir. One never knows about . . . erupting volcanoes."

"No, one certainly doesn't," Hank answered in an offhand manner, since his attention was riveted on the picture Rhiannon made there on his sofa. He wasn't sure he'd ever look at it again without seeing her there, his Sleeping Beauty. "Well, come on, MacGregor. It's time we turned in."

MacGregor stood up, the basin still in his hands. "Yes, sir, but what shall we do with Miss O'Shea?"

"Why, put her to bed, of course." Hank bent over to scoop Rhiannon's sleeping form into his arms.

"Of course, sir. But where?"

Hank straightened up. Rhiannon still lay prone on the sofa. "In a bed, MacGregor. You don't think I'm just going to leave her here, do you? We have several empty bedrooms, if memory serves." He bent over again to scoop her up.

"Indeed, sir. But that's just it."

Hank straightened up, again without Rhiannon. His hands went to his waist, and his face clouded up. "My God, man, make your point."

"The beds, sir. They're not prepared for guests."

"Well, have one prepared."

MacGregor pulled himself up to his full outraged height. A long silence stretched out between the two men as they stared at each other. Personal valets did not deal with maids. "Dammit."

"Indeed, sir."

"Well, we can't have the valet doing a maid's job, now can we? So, I guess there's no help for it except to deposit the young lady in my bed. I assume it is made?"

"Of course, sir. But I hardly think—"

"Neither do I at this hour, MacGregor. But let me assure you I am completely capable of throwing some sheets on the bed in the room adjoining my own. I know you hate to think it, but I was entirely self-sufficient when serving as a cavalry officer."

"If you say so, sir."

Hank chewed up and swallowed the biting retort that was on the tip of his tongue. He then, with great determination—and a pointed stare at MacGregor—bent over for the third time to pick up Rhiannon. The third time proved to be the charm. He stood back up smoothly, his arms full of the guest of honor. He shifted her slightly, resettling her weight and her voluminous skirts. Why in the hell did women wear all this frippery anyway, he fumed. All it did was get in the way.

"If I may, sir," MacGregor offered, leading the way for Hank, turning down lights and closing doors as they went. The winding stairs proved to be interesting when Rhiannon stirred and threw her arms tightly around Hank's neck, effectively strangling him and blocking his vision. Had it not been for MacGregor's steadying hand on his back, he and his bundle would have been a heap at the bottom of the stairway.

Hank had to admit silently that he had indeed pictured himself carrying Rhiannon up these very same stairs, but not like this, and not for the purpose of innocently putting her to bed. He stopped at his closed bedroom door and waited momentarily for MacGregor to open it. That done, he strode purposefully in and gently lay Rhiannon on the bed. MacGregor gave him a hand in unwinding her arms from around Hank's neck and then went to light a lamp. She made a soft purring sound and turned over on her side, facing them.

The two men looked down at her in silence.

"I say, sir, she is quite a lovely thing, isn't she?"

Hank cut his eyes over at his valet. "Yes, she is. And now to undress her."

MacGregor's hair stood straight up, or at least Hank could have sworn it did, such was the look on the older man's face. "I beg your pardon, sir? I thought I heard you say—"

"—that I am going to undress her?"

"Yes, sir."

"Well, your hearing is just fine. I'd wager she's hardly able to breath in that tight bodice, much less turn over in all those yards of material. She looks most uncomfortable, don't you think?"

MacGregor cut his eyes from his master to the girl on the bed. "I try not to think in situations such as this, sir."

"Indeed. That probably explains why you're still holding that cursed basin." Hank bent over Rhiannon and began undoing the back of her gown. A solid thunk told him the basin had been laid down on the stand next to the bed. Without looking up and while his hands, with very practiced motions, undid the laces of Rhiannon's bodice, Hank said, "That will be all, MacGregor. I believe I can manage this alone."

"Another area of self-sufficiency, sir?"

Hank nearly jumped. Never before had MacGregor lingered after being dismissed, much less made a comment bordering on sarcasm, even insolence. Hank fought for control, trying to remember that MacGregor was really much more than a valet in this household; in truth, he had been much more of a father to Hank than his real father had been.

But Hank was tired, plain and simple. "MacGregor, for God's sake, I'm not going to ravish an innocent young girl. In fact, I wouldn't ravish an experienced old woman, either. I'm not an animal, despite my being a Wolfe. Now, if you don't mind, I'd like to get her to bed, so I can do the same thing—in the other room."

MacGregor stood his ground and assessed his young master, apparently searching for sincerity of purpose and manner before he left. He must have seen it, for he bowed, smiled slightly to himself—more strange behavior for him—and left the room, closing the door behind him.

Hank shook his head, for about the hundredth time that evening. Damn, but nothing was simple anymore. He turned his attention back to the woman in his bed.

"And it's all your fault, young lady," he said aloud to Rhiannon. She chose that moment to murmur something in her sleep and turn over again. Her loosened bodice came away, revealing her tight corset underneath . . . and her bosom, which strained to be free of the confining garment. Hank straightened up as if he'd touched something hot. All he could do was stare at the exposed femininity under his hands. Rhiannon's arms were flung out wide on the pillows; her russet hair fanned out around her head. So she gave every appearance of inviting him into her open arms. Only she was totally unconscious.

Hank couldn't remember the last time he'd needed help in undressing a beautiful woman who was already in his bed, but he was seriously considering getting a maid up right now to do just that. A sudden image of the probable reaction of one of his little maids awakening to find her master leaning over her in her bedroom squelched that idea in its infancy. Well, there was no help for it. He'd just have to approach this task with all the detachment he felt when unsaddling his horse.

Right. Taking a deep breath and ignoring the slight shake of his hands, Hank plunged into the fray again. His fingers fairly flew as he loosened the corset stays and turned Rhiannon over to remove the garment. He felt it best for all concerned if he left her on her stomach for now. But apparently she didn't, for back over she flipped. Hank nearly bit his tongue off in his shock at being faced, literally, with a vision he had spent many sleepless nights imagining. Her breasts, exposed through the very thin fabric of her camisole, were everything he'd imagined—full, firm, luscious, rosy-tipped. They ached to be touched. . . .

Hank swallowed hard, tearing his eyes away and allowing his innate sense of decency to take over. He felt almost ashamed for seeing his friend, this beautiful woman he cared deeply about, in this unguarded state. She deserved better than that. Hank's mind and heart knew that, but his body felt differently. Her corset hadn't been the only thing that was tight and confining; now the crotch of his pants was, too.

Cursing himself for a sick dog, Hank fought to ignore his rigidness and the raging fire in his blood as he slipped Rhiannon's dress and series of crinolines off over her hips and her heart-shaped little bottom, leaving only her summer pantalets in place. This was pure torture. Hank was sure he'd died and gone to Hell, and this was his punishment. He would spend all of eternity undressing Rhiannon without ever being able to touch her.

Tossing her clothes aside on the floor, Hank cursed his own erection. The damn thing was hard enough to cut diamonds, and was making it very hard for him to think clearly. In desperation, he took her slippers off her slender feet and dropped them onto the pile of her clothes. There, he was done. He stepped away from his bed and the temptation that lay on it, and allowed himself a heavy sigh of relief. But it ended on a telling groan of agony.

Rhiannon, in her relaxed and alcohol-induced sleep, was doing nothing to make this any easier for him to walk away. She mewled something under her breath, and curled herself up into a little ball, pulling one of Hank's pillows into her arms. Hank was nearly undone. Her little-girl pose of innocence was as appealing and as adorable as was her state of near-nakedness. Not trusting himself to approach her from the side of his bed she slept on, Hank went around to the other side of the huge four-poster and loosened the bedding. He was able to free one sheet enough to throw it over her. He wasn't sure she needed to be covered half as much as he was sure he needed her to be covered.

As it was, his hand lingered on her shoulder, lightly caressing it and begging to be allowed to roam the soft woman curves of her body. With every bit of willpower he had left, Hank moved his hand up, instead of down, and caressed her cheek. With that, he pushed away from his bed, turned down the lamp, and forced himself to walk straight over to the door that connected the two bedrooms meant to be occupied by the master and mistress. Not daring to look back even in the darkness, he opened the door silently and went through it, closing it firmly behind him. No one had to tell him that the July heat would not be responsible for the burning torture he'd have to endure tonight before he slept— if he slept.

Rhiannon didn't know how long her eyes had been open before she realized she was indeed awake. At first, she lay perfectly still on her stomach, moving only her eyes, allowing them to adjust . . . to total darkness. Her chest tightened, causing her limbs to feel heavy. Where was she? She felt pretty safe in assuming she wasn't in her own bed. But why she wasn't just wouldn't come to her. She tried to think, but the effort was too painful. Her head revolted at even having to move her eyes, much less at forming coherent thoughts. Gradually, as she lay there, the dimness in the room began to take on gray forms and shadowy features. This was a huge room, and this was a huge bed she was lying in.

For the life of her, she couldn't think why she was here . . . and undressed, she realized upon taking a mental and sensory inventory of herself. She started to suck in a great breath of surprise at that discovery, but her head warned her that it would splinter if she did. And this head . . . was she ill? Oh, God, she hoped so; she'd hate to feel like this and not be ill. Surely some strange malady explained the war that raged between her head and her stomach at being attached to one another.

But apparently, whatever the nature of the illness was, it had not yet impaired her bodily systems. Fully awake now, she realized there was a tremendous pressure making itself known against her abdomen; and it didn't like in the least being pressed into the mattress. With a sinking feeling, Rhiannon realized she was going to have to get up. If only she could remember in which direction was "up."

Slowly, cautiously, she turned over, allowing her head all the time it needed to adjust to the change in position. When she tried to sit up, she realized it was totally out of the question. Well, what then? Was she just to slither off the side of the bed like some slimy serpent or reptile? Apparently so. Because the need for a chamber pot was quickly taking on the proportions and the earnestness of the search for the Holy Grail. Fortunately, her head didn't seem to mind if she moved her legs and hung them off the side of the bed, for it sent out little warning pulses only if she moved it.

Rhiannon allowed gravity to take over; her legs sought the floor, pulling the rest of her after them until her entire panting, desperate being was sitting in a pathetic heap on the blessedly cool floor. Never mind that her damp face was pressed against her hand, which in turn grasped the covers that hung over the bedside. She was off the bed, and that was progress, despite the repeated attempts of her head and stomach to meet in her throat.

With her hand that wasn't supporting her head, she felt along under the bed until she hit something cold and round. To Rhiannon, this was proof-positive that there was a God—for the shape her groping hand revealed confirmed that this was the chamber pot. She pulled it out, nosily scraping it on the polished wood floor. Pulling herself up to her knees, she pulled down her pantalets and sat, with the greatest sense of relief and achievement, on the cold unmentionable.

For the first time since waking up, she thought she just might live. That is, until her will to live completely abandoned her when a door directly in front of her suddenly swung open, sending a widening shaft of light along the floor to finally illuminate her in all her glory. Shocked, but too feeble and in too delicate a position to help herself, Rhiannon could do nothing but sit and stare, openmouthed, at the large man silhouetted in the doorway by the light from the room behind him.

"Rhiannon, you're alive."

Relief flooded her. It was Hank. But still, she couldn't help but be testy; her head was killing her. "Well, of course I'm alive. Why? Was there some discussion to the contrary?"

A snorting laugh came from the man in the doorway. Rhiannon hoped her malevolent glare was visible to him. "At one point—yes, I'm afraid. In fact, I believe it was you who said you wanted to die."

"Well, we don't always get our way, do we?" Her pounding head must be making her tongue this sharp, she decided. Well, it was hard to be pleasant when one was half nude and sitting on a chamber pot . . . her eyes popped open wide. "Get out! Get out! How dare you come into my room unannounced? You cad—you cur—you dog—you—"

"You're repeating yourself. I believe a cur and a dog are the same thing. And cousins of mine, I might add." The man had the audacity to stay in her . . . presence and actually lean a shoulder against the doorjamb, all very amiably, all very neighbors-talking-over-the-back-fence. And the worst of it was, he had on only his pants, like they were on a most intimate basis. She concentrated on his bare feet; they were much safer than his bare chest to stare at. Stare at?

"Get out! Get out! Get out!"

"I wouldn't yell like that, if I were you. It'll only make your head hurt worse. Whoops. Never mind. I see you found that out for yourself."

"I hate you, Hank Wolfe." Resting her elbows on her bent knees, she miserably clutched her head in her hands. "Now, please get out of my room."

"Okay, but just so you know, it's my room I'm getting out of. This is my house you're in. I undressed you. You drank too much, got sick—literally, and passed out." He straightened up, took hold of the doorknob, and started to swing it shut.

"Wait!" Rhiannon cried, but it was too late. The door closed . . . with him on the other side of it.

She sat in the darkness and stared blankly at the thin band of light that seeped under the door Hank had just closed. She'd gotten sick and passed out? And her parents had left her here? And Hank had undressed her? Was that all he'd done? Her hand came up to cover her mouth. The scandal of it all. She was ruined. All her plans and promises to herself to be on her best behavior? Ruined. All her determination to prove to her parents and the town that she was a lady? Ruined. Unless . . .

Rhiannon finished her business and got up, testing her equilibrium and hoping there wasn't a permanent red ring around her bottom from the lip of the chamber pot since she'd sat on it so long. Well, she'd found "up" easily enough, because here she was standing. And the room wasn't even spinning—and it was no longer as dark. She used her foot to slide the chamber pot back under the bed. Making her way cautiously across the room, she found the curtain pull and gave it a tug.

The drapes, of a heavy fabric and a maroon color, parted effortlessly, allowing in a modicum of light. That was enough, her head warned her. She glimpsed outside and determined that it was early morning. The picture outside Hank's bedroom window was really very lovely, since it overlooked the gardens and the sun was just peeking over the horizon, lending a pinkish tinge to the white stone walls of the mansion, but . . . she'd appreciate it later. Right now, she needed some answers, and some clothes—other than her own that lay in a hopeless heap at the foot of the bed. She just didn't have the strength for all those tiny buttons and that tight bodice.

Spying a polished cherrywood washstand that cradled a bowl and ewer, she padded over to it and, grateful that it held water, splashed her face, neck, chest, and arms. She next rinsed her mouth out several times and ran a finger over her teeth, much as she would have a toothbrush. Then, using the thick towel that hung from the rack attached to the washstand, she dried herself off. Peering into the oval full-length mirror, also framed in cherry, that reposed next to the washstand, she pronounced herself a fright. Looking around her, she spied a man's brush amongst the masculine bric-a-brac on the cherry dresser. She dragged it through her hair, unsnarling the tangles as she went. Finished with the brush, she replaced it, and turned to the wardrobe. After staring at its closed doors for a second or two, she decided she just didn't have the courage to rummage through Hank's clothes to find something suitable for her to wear. As if there'd be anything in there suitable for this occasion.

So, gathering her courage and her underclothes about her, she approached the adjoining door that Hank had opened and closed only minutes ago. The light was still coming from under the door, so he must still be in there. Taking a deep breath, she grasped the crystal knob and turned it; the door opened inward, so Rhiannon was a step or two inside the other bedroom before she realized what she was witnessing. It was her turn to see Hank in a compromising position. But if he were the one who was compromised, why was she the one with the hot cheeks?

Because he was the one standing in profile to her and taking his pants off, and she was the one playing the voyeur. When she'd opened the door, he'd obviously frozen like he was, with his pants almost off his hips . . . his bare hips. Her gaze locked with his; she watched as his eyes took on that lazy, hooded look that issued a bedroom challenge. She could only swallow as he straightened up, hitched his pants back up and fastened them . . . partially. He then turned full front to her, still holding her breathless gaze. The moment was so intense that Rhiannon would have sworn later that even the hands on the clock didn't move.

Rapt with the vision of masculine power and virility that stood before her, she forgot to be mortified; she forgot to let go of the doorknob; she forgot to leave . . . she forgot to breathe. It wasn't until he took a step toward her, with his hand out, that she woke up, strangled out an apology, and quickly closed the door. She stood on her side of the door, hands to her flaming cheeks. Within seconds, the door opened again, and Hank filled the frame. He was within arm's reach of her, but he kept his muscled arms at his sides.

And all Rhiannon could do was stand there and stare at the wonderfully crisp and curling black hair that covered his broad, muscular chest and narrowed to a thin line down the middle of his washboard stomach, only to disappear into his waistband. The bulge just below there made it necessary for her to wet her lips.

"Rhiannon, I—"

Rhiannon reached out in her fascination with this so alien and so beautiful male form, and raked her fingers in an unconsciously seductive manner right down his chest and over the steel ridges of his stomach, effectively silencing him. The feel of him was like nothing she'd ever felt before. He felt like a warm statue of Adonis, a smooth, satiny warm rock-hard statue that made secret parts of her soften and harden all in the same moment.

Her eyes full of wonder at the effect his body had on hers, she looked up at him. He took her hand in his and held it to his chest, the slightest smile turning up the corners of his mouth. For a long moment, neither of them moved.

Then, Rhiannon became aware that she was being pulled towards him, ever so slowly. She didn't resist, for the quality of the air was dreamlike, was fluid, was mystical. Finally, she was in his arms, crushed to him, her breasts separated from his skin only by the thin material of her camisole. Without hesitation, she turned her face up to him and parted her lips, breathless with wonder, not needing any explanations . . . or declarations.

Hank looked into her eyes, night looking into autumn, apparently saw her consent, and then captured her mouth with a kiss that she felt to her toes, a kiss that invaded her mouth in the same way that her body begged for his total invasion.

Rhiannon was raging wildfire in his arms, responding to him with total abandon; she enjoyed him as much as he enjoyed her. She couldn't get enough of the feel of him, returning him caress for caress as their kiss took on a hungering urgency that exploded Rhiannon's buried bud into a full, open flowering. She moaned under the onslaught of his lips and tongue, wordlessly begging him to teach her what it was that a man and a woman did together. And Hank was more than willing to oblige.

Breaking off their kiss and holding her by her upper arms, Hank rained kisses on her neck and shoulders, sending shuddering thrills through Rhiannon's body. His hands smoothed her camisole off her shoulders, down her arms, to her waist. Holding her steady, he trailed nipping, sucking kisses down her collarbone . . . finally taking her breast. When his hot, moist mouth settled over a sensitive tender peak, Rhiannon went rigid, but then could barely stand up, so wonderfully stabbing was the pleasure. She begged for release, grabbing handfuls of his thick, curling hair; but when he gave up her nipple, she urged him onto the other one. The throbbing pulsation at the vee of her thighs became a living entity, itself crying out for attention.

When her legs began to buckle from her building desire, Hank wordlessly lifted her into his arms and carried her to his bed. Laying her down gently, he peeled her underthings off her, leaving her naked before his eyes. In an instant, his pants joined her clothes on the floor, and he joined her on the bed. If Rhiannon were going to change her mind and call a halt to this act, now was the moment. . . . It passed unchallenged. It seemed so right to be here with him, doing these things, that she never stopped to question her behavior or her responses to him.

She wanted only to feel, not to think, not to moralize. She wanted to use her heart and her body and her senses. She didn't need words of passion or love or longing to know that this was right. To know that this was inevitable from the moment he'd sat across from her at her parents' dinner party a week ago. So she didn't try to stop the inevitable now, not when he lay half on her, gathering her in his arms to take up where he'd left off in his kissing quest for the secrets of her body.

Not when he slipped lower and lower down her abdomen, his hands and his mouth driving her to a fever pitch that tossed her head from side to side and lifted her hips off the bed. All she could do was grab handfuls of the bedclothes and ride the wave of fiery passion Hank was building.

She merely gasped in aquiescence, too far gone to be shocked or prudish, when he slipped between her thighs, bent her knees and parted them, cupped her buttocks, and raised her most tender, most secret bud to his mouth. With

149

his tongue, he stroked and probed the velvet-soft lips that nestled under her thatch of curling hair until he found the bud itself. And then he was merciless; he kissed it in the same way he had her mouth, driving Rhiannon absolutely out of her mind, driving her toward the inevitable climax of such an act of passion.

The tightening coil in her belly sent out warning tremors of the impending explosion, but Rhiannon did not, could not stop them. Indeed, she welcomed them, reveled in them, arched her back to press herself more firmly to Hank, made guttural, animal sounds at the back of her throat . . . until she had no more to give. Or so she thought. With a bursting blaze of color behind her closed eyes, Rhiannon felt the hot ripples of undulating spasms tear out from her center, sending blazing tendrils of hot liquid through her veins. The pleasure was so intense that it bordered on pain, but still Rhiannon rode Hank's mouth until there was not a sensation, not a ripple, not a breath left in her.

As she lay gasping in blinding release, she felt Hank slide up her body and take her mouth again. He smelled of her musk, a scent she'd never known before, but one that fired her senses anew. When the kiss ended, she pushed on Hank's shoulder, letting him know that she wanted to explore, she wanted to make him respond to her, she wanted to learn his man's body. Hank rolled onto his back, taking her with him, laying her full length on top of him. Rhiannon scooted down until she rested in the saddle of his thighs, pressed against the satiny hardness of his erection, and began a kissing quest of her own.

She was thrilled to discover that his nipples were as sensitive as hers . . . if what she felt against her abdomen were any barometer. She found out that the hair on his chest tickled her nose when she moved her lips over his chest. She renewed her fingertips' acquaintance with the ridge of muscle on his abdomen. She reveled in the sounds coming from his throat at her touch, and an ancient smile of feminine knowledge and triumph rode her lips. He was hers as much as she was his. When she slipped lower, intent on his erect manhood, Hank gasped out, raised up, caught her hand, and pulled her to him.

Taking her with him, he rolled again; this time, he was on top of her, weighing her down and yet somehow lifting her higher. Rhiannon knew that what her body cried out for, what she couldn't name, was about to happen. And she couldn't wait. She felt as if her entire life had been lived to achieve this moment.

When Hank positioned himself between her thighs and ran his gaze from her face to her vee, Rhiannon gave him his signal by raising her hips. "Please," she uttered.

"Rhiannon," Hank breathed.

Bracing himself off her with his arms, he began his probing invasion into the tight folds of her virginity. Rhiannon opened her eyes, somehow afraid, somehow hesitant after all, to find him watching her face.

"I don't want to hurt you, Rhiannon. Do you understand what's about to happen?" His voice was at once tender and ragged. He rained soothing kisses on her face and smoothed her hair out of her face, as if waiting for her response.

His tenderness and concern for her tore at her heart. Just as his desire for her spurred her own. Nothing could be more right than what they were about to do, no matter the consequences to their lives later. She needed to, had to give herself to this man. Later would be the time to reflect, to rejoice, or to repent.

"Please," she cried, no longer hesitant, taking hold of his tensed buttocks, urging him onward.

Hank lay more fully on her and took her mouth when he took her virginity. He seemed to want to take her cry of pain into him, to somehow lessen it for her. Fully sheathed, he stilled again, kissing the tears that escaped her eyes. "I'll stop if you want me to, but God, Rhiannon, don't want me to."

"No, Hank, love me, please love me," she breathed.

"I do, Rhiannon, I do." He said it in all level seriousness and then began the thrusting rhythm of life and love.

Rhiannon knew instinctively what to do. She wrapped her legs around his waist, her arms around his neck, and rocked with him, matching him in thrusts and building intensity. She cried out when the pulsing tremors began again, when they overtook her in startling intensity. She was astounded by how her body, seemingly of its own volition, clutched and puckered around Hank, as if begging him for the seed he had to give, as if milking his body for the response she now had thrilling through her until she was slick with loving perspiration.

And still the driving thrusts continued, glazing Rhiannon's world with the scent, the feel, the power of Hank Wolfe. When she was sure she would pass out from the sheer energy of his lovemaking and of her climax, he gave one last powerful thrust and went rigid over her, holding them both in a vacuum of time, while he poured his milky seed into her woman's body, while they both blazed in the passionate wildfire that made them one. . . .

And then it was over. Hank collapsed on top of her, but held his full weight off her by resting his elbows to either side of her head. His head hung in the crook of her neck and shoulder. His ragged breathing heated her skin. Rhiannon realized she was still clutching his back, and her legs were still wrapped around him. She should have been uncomfortable, but she wasn't. She was satisfied. In fact, the world could end right now as far as she was concerned; she would be content to die while her nostrils were full of the scent of Hank, who smelled of her. There was no longer any separation between the two. They were still one, in body and in shared experience of one another. It was enough.

Until the master-bedroom door to the hallway suddenly opened without preamble, startling the lovers. Hank's head came up off Rhiannon's neck like a shot; as one, they looked toward the doorway and took only one second to untangle and dive under the covers.

"Good morning, dear. MacGregor told us you stayed overnight. I do hope you're awake," Penelope trilled as she approached the bed in the semi-darkness of the room. Apparently the roiling bedcovers did not make an impression on her.

"Well, where is she, Penelope? I'm hungry."

A snorting guffaw—or two—was heard from under the covers.

"She's not even awake, Penelope. Can't you hear her snoring?" There was a moment's silence. "She makes a pretty big lump for such a small thing, don't you think?"

"Oh, dear, Tillie. Do you suppose we could have misunderstood MacGregor about her sleeping in here? Perhaps Hank is in his bed after all."

A shuffling of feet was heard going around to the other side of the bed. "I think all your calling the boy Henry has made him funny, Penelope. According to this pile of clothes, the boy wears women's underthings—here they are with his pants."

That did it. The occupants of the bed sat up as one, clutching covers to their bare bodies as best they could and laughing for all they were worth. Screams of hilarity punctuated their helplessness as they clung to each other.

The looks on the sisters' faces did nothing toward sobering the lovers. The two old women could not have looked more shocked if the nude ghost of George Washington had sat up in the bed. Penelope clutched a hand to her chest in abject terror, while Tillie reeled backwards a step or two.

Tillie recovered first. "I told you we should have eaten breakfast first. Then, none of this would have happened."

That logic was apparently lost on Penelope, who came around the bed, grabbed her sister's hand, and dragged her out of the room, nearly knocking MacGregor over and the tray out of his hands as he rounded the corner into the bedroom. Tillie plucked a roll off the tray as she sailed by in her sister's clutches.

MacGregor, seemingly not quite comprehending the nature of the disturbance yet, couldn't decide who to look at first, so he divided his attention between the fleeing figures and the people in the bed for several turns of his head. Then, his head stilled and he looked straight ahead, clearly stunned at the dawning realization of what he was seeing. With awesome intensity, he swung his gaze slowly to the occupants of the bed. His eyes widened dangerously; a fraction of an inch more and they would have touched the floor.

"Great good heavens and all the saints, Ezra. I'll be seein' Scotland afore ye know it."

Chapter Eleven

Rhiannon could stand no more scrutiny this morning. She did a dying-swan version of sinking back under the covers.

Still, MacGregor's stunned and stupefied voice could be clearly heard to say, "I've brought breakfast . . . less one roll . . . sir, miss—uh, sir."

Hank's voice, so near, so rumbling, came clearly to Rhiannon as she pretended she would be invisible if only her eyes were closed. "Put the tray down and close the door after you, MacGregor." Hank spoke very evenly, very slowly, as if to a slightly demented child.

"Yes, sir."

There was a long silence. Rhiannon held her breath.

"Then do it."

"Oh. Yes, sir. Will that be all, sir?"

"Yes. That will be all."

"Yes, sir."

"MacGregor, if you're not out of this room in five seconds, there will be bloodshed."

Rhiannon, shaking with suppressed laughter, heard very definite sounds, that of the tray being hastily set down, which set the dishes to rattling, and of the door being hastily and firmly closed. Then, Hank let out a long breath and shifted his position in the bed. Rhiannon did not have to have her eyes open to know he'd turned to her, for his muscled thigh was now draped over her legs, and his arm was around her, cupping a breast and pulling her back against him. He kissed the shell of her ear and whispered, "Don't cry, Rhiannon. I couldn't stand it if you were crying."

Rhiannon turned over in his embrace, a huge grin on her face. She laughed when his eyebrows arched in surprise. He laughed right back at her. "Why, you little hellion! You're not the least bit tearful, are you?"

"No. Only when I'm mad." She put her arms around his neck, totally content in the warm nest of Hank's arms and his bed. But still, she sobered some. "I suppose I should be, though, shouldn't I?" Then, she lowered her eyes, embarrassment finally coming once she was faced with him in the aftermath of what had happened. His eyes had the power to shame her, unlike the discovery of their tryst by his aunts and his valet. "Why aren't I, Hank? Why aren't I ashamed or tearful? Is . . . is there something wrong with me?"

"Wrong?" Hank's voice was full of incredulity. "My darling, there's nothing wrong with you. In fact, everything is right." He shook his head and sighed. "You've been told all your precious life that to enjoy the pleasures of the bed is wrong, haven't you?"

With her eyes downcast, Rhiannon nodded. Still, she allowed him to raise her chin until she was looking into his eyes. She could barely stand the intensity of his emotion.

"Listen to me, Rhiannon. There is nothing wrong with you, or with what we just did. It doesn't make you bad. It won't ruin your reputation, or show on your face, or make you look any differently."

"But what about your aunts . . . and MacGregor? They certainly won't think this is right. They'll look at me differently. I'm not sure I can face them again, Hank."

Hank placed a nipping kiss on the end of her nose. "No matter what MacGregor thinks, he won't say anything, Rhiannon. Neither will my aunts. They think very highly of you, just as I do. You've done nothing to diminish my or their respect for you in any way. They probably expected no less from me, though. I do believe they half-suspect I am a defiler of young, innocent women . . . and by all appearances"—his eyes raked her up and down meaningfully—"they're right."

Rhiannon grinned, feeling heartened by his teasing words and his acceptance of the rightness of her in his bed. Feeling suddenly impish, she scrunched up against Hank. "Did you see MacGregor's face when he came in? I thought his eyes would pop right out of his head! What was he talking about— Ezra and seeing Scotland?"

"Who knows?" Hank began kissing her neck. He then raised his head, as if at another thought. "Do you suppose Aunt Tillie got her breakfast?"

Rhiannon smirked. "I don't know, but she did get mine."

Hank leered at her. "Well here then, let me make that up to you." His hold on her tightened, just as his manhood did against her belly.

Rhiannon tensed momentarily. "Hank, do you think we should? They might come back."

Hank gave her a quizzical look. "Are you serious? After what they just witnessed, none of them may ever open that door again. But, if you don't want to . . ."

"No! I mean yes! Yes, I want to."

"Wanton," Hank teased, rolling over on top of her.

Soaking in the warm water, Rhiannon closed her eyes and laid the back of her head against the cold, hard rim of the porcelain tub at home, allowing cold, hard thoughts to bob to the surface of her mind.

The tiny red stain on his sheets. Blood. Her blood. The pointed look she and Hank had exchanged from opposite sides of his bed upon spying it at the same time. The quiet that had settled over them both after that. Their subdued ride back into Wolfe with the Misses Penland. The something-more-than-curious stares of the townspeople they'd driven past on their way to her home. The picture she must have made riding next to Hank in broad daylight in the same gown the entire town had seen her in last night. The looks on her family's faces when she'd opened the front door about an hour ago. Usually exuberant in their greetings, they'd all been . . .

Ashamed? Rhiannon hated to think it, usually defied it, most often ignored it. But not today. That was because she was feeling it, too. No matter what Hank had said earlier about her not having done anything wrong and about how much he liked and admired her, what they'd done was wrong, pure and simple. They weren't married; therefore, they'd had no right to indulge in the pleasures of the marital bed.

But especially hard to take when she'd come home had been the look on Eddie's face. Being 15 and closest in age to her, he was more apt to hear rumors and gossip about his older sister than was anyone else in her family. Certainly, her outrageous behavior over the years had gotten him into more fights than anything he'd ever done on his own.

Rhiannon sighed, half tempted to soak her head under the water for longer than was prudent. Being a woman, which Hank said she'd just become, was hard. With it came the attendant responsibilities and regrets for one's actions. Rhiannon knew, as surely as her water was cooling, that the carefree days of blithely going her own way, and to hell with the consequences, were over. She'd done what she'd done, she'd loved it—and quite possibly loved Hank, but now she had to move forward. What other choice was there? She had to face what she'd done and what that act meant to everyone around her. So this was what being grown-up was like.

Opening her eyes and sitting up in the tub, her arms resting on its sides, she mentally ticked off her course of action. One, she would make up this, her latest breach, somehow to Eddie.

Two, she would hold her head up high in town—that wasn't hard; she always had before. Three, she wouldn't wear this guilt or remorse or shame, call it what you would, around her neck like a stone. And four, she would . . . what? Tell Hank it could never happen again? Tell him she didn't want to see him anymore? Tell him she was shocked at herself for wanting to cry, even though she wasn't angry, because he hadn't told her he loved her and would marry her to make an honest woman out of her? Tell him that she would have turned him down if he had proposed? Tell him that she was angry with him for not at least making the attempt? Tell him that he'd had her heart long before he'd had her virginity?

Enough. Rhiannon stood up in the tub, letting the water cascade down her body in caressing sheets. She reached for her towel and caught her reflection in the mirror mounted on the back of the door. Hank was right, she thought, looking herself up and down. Her body was no different. It was still the youthful, pink, fit body she was accustomed to. Her inner turmoil was not reflected in any outward change in her body.

But her face, her eyes. That was a different story. A woman's soul looked back at her from the depths of the black-fringed ginger eyes in the mirror. With a surprise, she realized there was a sparkle in those eyes; they weren't dull and lifeless. On the contrary, they sparked fire and challenge. Feeling the least bit silly, Rhiannon nevertheless tried a tentative smile at the face in the mirror. The reflection smiled back, encouraging her. Rhiannon liked the light in those eyes. It told her everything was going to be all right. Because she was going to make it right.

When she was dressed in a simple cotton skirt and loose blouse, and feeling much better about the past night's—and that morning's—events, she went downstairs to seek out food and Eddie. No wonder the house had seemed quiet to her. No one but her and Ella, the cook and self-appointed nanny and head of the household, were home. Rhiannon smiled to herself. She was such a ninny. She'd imagined the house to be unusually quiet, as if everyone in it felt the pall of her indiscretion. But nothing could be further from the truth, apparently. It was just another day in the O'Shea house. Sweet relief washed over her.

"Good morning, Ella. Where is everyone?" she said, coming into the neat yet cozy room and seating herself at the small, round oak table that served as the official center of Ella's command. Ella told anyone who'd listen that she'd raised the O'Shea young'uns right here at this table.

"Good afternoon, you mean. Your daddy's at the bank; your momma's at some ladies meetin' where they talk about helpin' the poor folks. It don't seem like they do much but talk about it, but ain't nobody asked me what I think. And your brothers? I shooed them out a hour ago, I expect. All except Eddie. He's off moonin' after some girl on the other side of town. So, missy, everybody but you done gone off about their business and left me to mine," she scolded, her hands skillfully kneading yeasty dough. She then looked at her favorite child. "You hungry?"

"Have you ever seen me when I wasn't?" Rhiannon bantered, hiding both her surprise that she'd missed lunch and her disappointment that she'd missed Eddie.

Ella's friendly black face lit up. "Not in all the years I've been here, missy. I swear I don't know how you keep that figure of yours. I know worry don't keep the weight off, 'cause you one child that don't think nothing 'bout what you do. You just does it. Now, git that plate over there I saved you and eat that food."

Ella had been scolding Rhiannon like this since Rhiannon could remember. And always before she'd had some saucy retort or a wrinkling of her nose as an answer for Ella. But not today. Too much was different. Wordlessly, she got up, retrieved the plate off the back of the stove, and sat back down. Removing the cheesecloth, she picked up the crispy-fried chicken breast, tore off a strip of juicy meat, and poked it in her mouth.

Feeling Ella's keen eyes on her, she looked up. "What?"

"What you done now?"

Rhiannon swallowed before answering. "What makes you think I've done something?"

"The fact that you ain't done tole me to mind my own business, for one thing."

Rhiannon broke a biscuit in half and bit into it. Ella wiped her hands on her apron and poured Rhiannon a glass of milk, which she set in front of her. "Here, drink that. It'll make you feel better."

Rhiannon smiled at that; Ella was a firm believer that food and milk made you feel better, no matter the cause of the problem. Still, she drank about half the glass, surprising herself at how thirsty she was.

"Well? You gone tell me or not?"

"There's nothing to tell, Ella. I swear."

"You'd best not be swearin' on nothing sacred, missy. 'Cause you done somethin'. I knows it as sure as I knows what we havin' for supper tonight."

Rhiannon sighed and finished her meal in silence. She'd never kept anything from Ella before, and it made her feel bad that she couldn't share this with her. After all, how many times during her life had she hugged Ella's legs for comfort as a child when her parents were incensed or just plain angry with her? Still, childish pranks and injuries were one thing . . . this morning was another.

Ella had just finished with the dough, which she was shaping into loaves, when a knock was heard at the front door. Rhiannon looked up at her expectantly.

"Well, what you waitin' for, missy? The door ain't gone to answer itself."

With a huff, Rhiannon wiped her hands off and pushed her chair back. Nothing had changed while she was in Baltimore. Everyone in this family still worked for Ella. She smiled at that when she was sure Ella couldn't see her as she went down the hall.

When she came abreast of the front rooms, she also smiled at how the sun shining in through the many windows dappled the rooms and the furniture in a quiet glow. And at how the soft breeze riffled the light curtains inward into the rooms. Now, where had these thoughts come from? She'd never noticed rooms and furniture before; they were just something for her to rush by on the way to her next adventure.

What was happening to her? She was so very distracted . . . and calm, two things she'd never been before. Trying to puzzle that out, and looking more in the direction of the parlor than the door, she put her hand on the knob. She hoped whoever was here could tell her why everyday things and ordinary objects seemed to warrant a second look today.

She took yet another second look when she opened the door. Hank Wolfe was standing there. And a huge paint stallion was tied at the fence. He'd ridden in just to see her. The big, dumb, freshly shaven, beautiful man, with his black Stetson in his hand, wearing boots, denims, a cotton shirt, and a fringed buckskin vest, made her cry. She burst into tears at the sight of him.

He stepped into the tiny foyer and wrapped her in his arms, obviously not caring if anyone else were at home to see them. "How'd I know?" he asked into her hair.

"Now thass just what I said to myself not more'n a minute ago. I knowed it all along. Missy done gone and got herself a man. And will you jist look at who it is."

Rhiannon heard Ella at the other end of the hall, but couldn't bring herself to raise her head from the comfort of Hank's embrace. She did, however, manage to look up into his handsome, chiseled, tender face to see his reaction to Ella's words.

"Hello, Ella. I guess you found us out." He smiled down at Rhiannon and held her even more closely.

Encouraged but a little confused—was he going to tell Ella everything that had happened? Surely not—Rhiannon turned her head and looked through tears down the narrow hallway.

Tall, slim, regal Ella stood there, shaking her gray head and wiping her hands on her apron. "Ain't nothin' to be found out, Mr. Wolfe. Leastwise, there'd best not be. Ain't none of my business, thass for sure. Ain't none at all. But things goin' to get mighty ex-citin' aroun' here now. Course, they always have been with that child around." Her mutterings carried her back around the corner into the kitchen.

Rhiannon hated that Hank would see a helpless, crying female when he looked back down into her face, but there was nothing she could do but bask in his nearness.

"I think Ella's in love with me," he teased, using the back of his thumb to wipe her tears away.

Rhiannon almost blurted out that that made two of them, but she was able to swallow the words and breathe out in little hiccupping sobs instead. She could never tell him that. He wanted his freedom, just like she did. A declaration of love would send him packing quicker than anything else— just as it would her if he said it. So in the end she just said, "Why are you here?"

"Because I knew you'd had enough time alone. We need to talk, Rhiannon. And I'd prefer not to do it here."

Rhiannon pulled free of him. He sounded so serious that it scared her. Was he indeed going to tell her he didn't want to see her anymore? That would be impossible in a town the size of Wolfe. One of them would have to leave—one of them already wanted to do just that. Maybe he was coming here to tell her just that—that he was leaving. The words were out almost before she knew it. "Are you leaving Wolfe?"

He looked at her blankly for a moment, as if he'd forgotten that he'd said he didn't want to stay in Kansas. "No. I'm not leaving Wolfe. Not now."

Then later? She couldn't ask; she didn't want to know. "No one's here but me and Ella."

"No, not here. I've tried to have a moment alone with you here before with disastrous results, if you'll remember."

163

How could she forget? She could still hear Johnny-Cake and Charlie Driver running through the house to tell everyone that Hank had kissed her neck. And any one of her brothers could come running through at any minute. "You're right. Then where?"

Rhiannon watched his face, memorizing every stirring feature, as he cast about for a solution. "Well, hell, there's not any place too private in a town named Wolfe when your name is Wolfe, is there? Come on, let's walk to the stores. I need to take care of some business in town anyway. We can talk on the way. I learned in the army that there's no better way to hide something or someone than to place it right out in the open. So, we'll have our private talk right out in public. That ought to keep the town tongues quiet."

Rhiannon doubted that, but she didn't say it aloud. Still, his concern for her reputation and honor in town, tarnished as they were, was touching. After an initial panic at the thought of going into town again with Hank so soon after having ridden though it this morning in last night's gown, Rhiannon warmed to the idea. No matter what else might be wrong between them, she always felt better when she was with him. And what he had to talk to her about must not be all that dire if he was willing to talk about it in public. "Just let me tell Ella I'm leaving. I'll see if she needs anything."

Once outside the house and in the sunshine, and best of all, on Hank's arm, Rhiannon felt much better. To be with him was intoxicating. Had the sun always been this bright? Had her step always been this lively? She didn't know; she didn't care, if the huge smile spreading over her face was any indication. She wanted to sing and dance—just for now, just for this moment.

Later she would be a grown-up woman; later she would do something about running for mayor—that seemed like such a distant prospect right now, for some reason; later she would concern herself with how to help Cat LaFlamme and all those other women that Big John abused; later she would deal with her brother Eddie's 15-year-old feelings. Later. Right now was for her . . . and Hank.

"What do you look so happy about all of a sudden?" he teased. "Are you the same girl who was crying all over my shirt a few minutes ago?"

Rhiannon looked up into his face, and then shyly looked down. He chuckled and looked straight ahead. It seemed that every time she looked at him, she found something else new to love. Right now, she loved how he'd slowed his swaggering, long-stepped stride so she could keep up with him. She loved the look of his clean-shaven cheek, and almost shivered at the memory of that same beard-roughened cheek against her thigh earlier today.

Had that really been today? It seemed like forever ago. And here she was dreaming about him again already. She was truly a wanton, just as he'd called her earlier . . . today. It just wasn't possible. Rhiannon was sure she'd been taken by the wind, so light was her step. She didn't even care now what it was Hank wanted to talk to her about. It didn't matter. Nothing could ruin this euphoric feeling that just being with him produced in her.

Their companionable silence carried them into the heart of Wolfe. As always, Hank's presence in town drew deferential greetings from the men and simpering poses from the women. He didn't seem to notice either response, Rhiannon realized, looking up at him for the hundredth time. Oh, he replied readily enough and was cordial, but beyond that, he kept moving, clearly communicating his desire not to be embroiled in long-winded conversations with the men or inane ones with the women. And the women were the worst—they acted as if Rhiannon weren't even with him. She'd bitten her tongue so many times, she was afraid to open her mouth for fear blood would gush out.

True to his word, Hank did have business in town. But certainly not on any scale Rhiannon had imagined. She'd thought they would make the rounds of local little shops and stores. She hadn't been prepared for his "business." And she didn't know what to think when he stopped in front of a new brick building that sported a large brass plaque proclaiming this to be the headquarters of "Wolfe Enterprises International."

Rhiannon could only stare. When she'd left for Baltimore three years ago, this lot at the other end of town, to which she hadn't yet ventured in the week or so she'd been home, had been a horse stable. She supposed that she hadn't heard about it from anyone because they were used to it being here by now and just considered it one of many changes going on in Wolfe, not very newsworthy any longer. But she could hardly believe that a red brick building at the other end of Wolfe that housed an international operation would not be news to relay to someone who'd been away for three years. What were people thinking about? Oh, yes—her running for mayor, the other women running for city council, and Carry A. Nation with her Temperance League. It seemed the townspeople of Wolfe had women on their minds.

When Hank escorted her inside into the richly appointed lobby, done all in muted greens, beiges, and deep reds, Rhiannon had the distinct impression that she'd just been transported back East to some fancy big-city office. She was sure that if she turned around to look outside, she would see Boston or New York. But the physical surroundings of Hank's office were nothing compared to his physical presence in the room. He could have been President McKinley, such was the scurrying and murmuring amongst the men inside upon seeing their boss walk in on a Saturday afternoon.

After introducing her around, he seated her behind a desk in a comfortable leather chair while he conducted an impromptu meeting. Rhiannon couldn't help but feel all the male eyes on her, appreciative and speculative. She did her best not to look anywhere or at anyone in particular for too long. She felt as out of place here as . . . as a rose would be in a cactus garden.

So she concentrated on watching and listening to Hank. This was a side of him she'd never seen—or even realized. As she listened to him talking with his vice president, a Mr. Gaines, and the staff, she began to get a new sense of just how rich and powerful he was. Why, the man's influence and interests were global, which explained "International" on the plaque outside. Her head was spinning after only a few minutes of talk of mining, cattle, shipping, exporting, banking, railroading, commercial building—the list went on and on. How did he keep it all straight?

Shaking her head, she took another look around the office. Her heart almost stopped. There were packing crates scattered about. With a sinking feeling, she realized she had no reason to be surprised and no claim to be upset. Hank had never made any bones about staying here in Wolfe. And earlier at her house, when she'd asked him if he was leaving, he'd said not now—which could mean later, just as she'd thought. Apparently, it wouldn't be too much later, because at that moment she saw a man putting heavy files into one of the crates. Rhiannon looked away. She couldn't bear to watch the evidence of Hank's leave-taking.

A few minutes later, Hank returned to Rhiannon. She must have had a telling expression on her face, because he gave her a quizzical look, as if to ask her if she were okay. She smiled and shrugged away his concern, hoping to forestall any questions he might have about something being wrong with her. To her surprise, and apparently to the men's, too, judging by their reactions, Hank instructed them all to take the rest of the day off.

As the men put down their work, gathered up their belongings, and filed out, they each cast a glance of one sort or another in her direction. If her cheeks were as pink as they were warm under this scrutiny, the men could have warmed their hands on them in winter. She tried at first to look haughty and disdainful, but couldn't quite manage it, so she settled for what she hoped wasn't a sickly smile.

When the last of the men had filed out, Hank closed and locked the door. He then turned to Rhiannon; the look on his face sucked the breath out of her, so scorching was it in its intensity and its implied intention. She had that same feeling, watching him stalking over to her, she'd had last week in his morning room after his aunts had left on the occasion of her first visit to the Wolfe mansion.

Her eyes widened and her breath finally came back to her, but in short, quick breaths. Almost roughly, she was pulled up out of the chair by her arms and pulled into his embrace for a crushing, bruising kiss. It seemed to last forever, and it fired Rhiannon's senses beyond reasoning. His tongue was doing to her mouth what it had done to her . . . self this morning. Instantly came the moistness between her legs, and the heavy opening of her body, at once ready to receive him, as she gave free rein to his hands to explore her curves under her clothes.

It was all she could do to get moaning gasps past her lips, so intense was his onslaught. When she was sure she going to have to tear his clothes off him to get on with the deed, he tore his mouth from hers and took a great, gulping breath. "I've wanted to do that all day," he said in a husky whisper.

Rhiannon thought to tell him that he had done that all day—or morning, but the words just wouldn't form.

As surprised as she was at his taking her into his arms, it did not compare to her surprise when he set her away from him. And that didn't even belong in the same world as the level of surprise that his next words moved her to.

"Rhiannon, wait a minute. Wait a minute. There's something I have to say. I've thought about this since I took you home this morning." He took another deep breath. "After everything's that's happened today . . . we have no choice—we have to get married."

Chapter Twelve

Rhiannon could not have been more shocked if Hank had just said that one of his huge cargo ships was pulling into mooring right now out in the sandy street outside. But that spectacle made more sense than his farfetched . . . proposal. He wanted to marry her? No, that wasn't what he'd said—he'd said they had to get married.

His grip on her arms was fierce, as fierce as his expression. Rhiannon could do nothing for several seconds but catalogue his features as she searched his face. As always his fiery black eyes held her gaze, and as always, she couldn't interpret the glittering in their depths. She was forced to speak. "I . . . I don't understand. Why do we have to get married? You said yourself that no one would ever know but us, MacGregor, and your aunts."

"And that's what I thought, too, Rhiannon. But I had another thought—and another and another—after I took you home, right through town and in the same clothes you had on last night."

The shame of that memory caused Rhiannon to lower her eyes from his face. She looked down at the carpeted floor at

169

their feet. Hank cursed under his breath and pulled her again into his embrace. She felt his light kiss in her hair. "What was I thinking to subject you to that?" he said.

Rhiannon found herself making excuses for him. "Well, there is only one road into town, and we did have your aunts with us. You couldn't hardly bump them around roughly on back roads."

"That doesn't make me feel any better. Or you, either. That whole scene for the town to see was my fault. I couldn't expect you to know better, but I sure as hell do. But that's past now. We have other problems to consider."

Rhiannon broke their embrace; she couldn't think clearly while breathing in his intoxicating male scent. She moved to perch against Mr. Gaines's huge oak desk. "Like what?"

Hank looked at her pose for a moment, as if assessing the distance between them. Rhiannon felt it, too. The actual distance was minimal; the emotional distance was becoming a gulf. "Like this morning will not be the only time we make love. It's going to happen again and again."

He stopped, as if waiting for her to deny it. She kept silent. Apparently satisfied with her silence, he went on. "And eventually, you'll be carrying my child."

Rhiannon jerked up from the desk, mouth agape. She'd never thought about that.

"Just as I suspected. You hadn't thought about that. Well, neither did I at the moment, and I should have more than you. Again, that's my fault. But wait, there's more. You could already be carrying my child."

Rhiannon's hands went reflexively to cover her womb. She couldn't seem to close her mouth.

"Exactly. I hate to keep shocking you like this, piling concern on top of concern, but there're still more consequences to our . . . passion."

"I don't think I want to hear them, Hank," Rhiannon said with a moan. She felt ill all over again, and this had nothing to do with champagne.

"I'm sorry, but we have to deal with all this now, Rhiannon." His voice was brusque, business-like, much the same way he'd spoken to the men in this office earlier. She could almost hear the wheels turning in that keen mind of his. "There are important decisions to be made, and they must be made today."

"Why today? I don't understand."

He looked at her, his face a mixture of indulgence and impatience. No one had to tell her that he was used to making decisions and having them carried out on the spot. After all, he'd been a cavalry officer, and he was a Wolfe. Obviously, he didn't care for having to explain himself. But this concerned the rest of her life, and he would therefore explain.

"Why today? Well, let me tell you." He counted off the reasons on his fingers as he paced in front of her. "One, if you're carrying my child, time is of the essence. I will have no scandal attached to the birth of my heir. Two, I have two sweet, dotty aunts who may have told everything they know this morning when they were in town. Oh, and by the way, they're already planning our wedding. Three, you are setting in motion some potentially dangerous events by insisting on running for mayor, for God's sake. You're stirring up an entire town that's already stirred up enough by the prospect of Carry Nation coming. And four, you're—"

Rhiannon had heard enough. "And four, I'll do as I damn well please, Henry Penland Wolfe, Mr. Owner of Wolfe Enterprises International."

It was Hank's turn to gape openmouthed at her. He froze in his pacing, one finger still poised to count off reason number four on his other hand.

Rhiannon's anger threatened to ooze out of every outraged pore. She took a step towards him, her hands at her waist digging fiercely into her hipbones. Her chin jutted toward him like an exclamation point to her words. "Do you hear yourself, Hank? Do you? I don't think you do. It's all my fault and your fault; there's no we, no us, no our fault.

Like I'm some child who doesn't know better, who has to be protected from her own silly whims.

"Well, that's where you and everyone else are wrong, Hank. Because I do know. I do. I may not have thought through all the consequences of what we did just yet, like you have, but I would have. I am not a child. I am a woman. And that's not only because of your actions, Hank. I was in that bed, too."

"Rhiannon—" Hank cut in, putting a hand out to her. In her anger, Rhiannon slapped it away.

A corner of her mind noted the dangerous feral gleam that came into his eyes and hardened his jaw, but she wasn't through yet. "And if I am carrying your child? You'd best remember it is my child, too." She poked her finger at her chest to emphasize her words. "Our baby would not only be your heir, Hank; it would be mine, too. I may not have an empire to leave it, but that doesn't mean it won't carry my bloodlines, too. And don't think that I'm so naive or so unfeeling as to bring a bastard into the world. If I'm with child—if, Hank, if—then I'll agree to marry you. For the sake of the child."

"You're damned right you will."

"Don't you tell me what to do. And another thing, I won't listen to you insult your aunts by calling them dotty and thinking they have no honor or conscience. They would do or say nothing to hurt you—or me—in any way. Granted, Tillie is getting forgetful, but Penelope isn't, not by a long shot. I do believe those two still have a surprise or two for everyone up their sleeves—"

"My aunts," Hank bellowed, "are planning our wedding!"

"Well . . . let them! There may be a need for one, just like you said. I suppose MacGregor is helping?"

"You're going too far, Rhiannon," he said in a low growl. The wolf, predator, dangerous and cunning, emerged.

"I went too far this morning! And I don't blame you. I wanted you too, you know. In fact, I do believe I initiated this morning. And for that I am proud. Just as I am proud of my intentions to run for mayor. And you, you hypocrite, shook my hand not more than a week ago, congratulating me on my decision to run. Explain that." She put the period to her challenge by poking her index finger at him.

"I was applauding your spirit, Rhiannon Pauline O'Shea. It was a symbolic gesture. One I'm beginning to regret, I might add." He crossed his arms over his massive chest and stood there, glaring at her.

"Well, I don't regret it. Not at all."

"Goddammit, Rhiannon, don't you see why you're so intent on running for mayor? You want to do it just because everyone says you can't. You're acting like the spoiled, willful child that you're so afraid you still are. And another thing, you can stop going around shouting about how you're a woman and a lady. That's already obvious to everyone . . . but you. You're the only one who still doesn't believe it."

That stung. That stung hard, like a million bees. And maybe hit a little too close to home, which only made Rhiannon angrier. But instead of shouting, she spoke quietly, herself a dangerous she-wolf. "Are you finished? It's obvious that you don't have much respect for me. Why in the world would you ever consider marrying me?"

He looked at her, the hard glittering coal of his eyes boring into her. But he didn't say anything.

Despite her heightened anger, she felt the tendrils of deep disappointment. He had no words of caring for her at all? But would she have listened if he had said them? Wouldn't she have just flung them back at him, like his hand a moment ago when he'd reached out to her, before all these horrible words between them? And before she'd continued to add to those horrible words?

"And I have one more thing to say before I go home. My reasons for running for mayor, even given all the dangers involved in that venture, which you've been so kind to enumerate for me, could not be any further from the motives you ascribe to me than your horse could be to a chicken."

Hank frowned quizzically at that one, as if trying to pin down her allusion. Or as if trying to remember exactly where his horse was. She really had no way of knowing, and couldn't have cared less, actually.

"I'll admit that my first impulse was to wage a campaign to throw the joke right back in the faces of the men in this town, to show them that women are intelligent, capable beings who can run more than a house."

And here, something else occurred to her, getting her off track. She'd meant to tell him that she now wanted to be mayor so she could really make a difference in this town, just like Mr. Sullivan, the editor of the newspaper, had said. She wanted to bring the town's problems to the forefront, instead of just accepting things the way they were. She wanted to help the women at the Fancy Lady; she wanted to help the poor widows and children, and not just talk about it, like Ella accused the other women of doing. She wanted to do that and much more.

But she said none of those things. Instead, very smugly, she said, "And that brings me to another point, Mr. Wolfe. You men would do well to remember that you were raised by women, which probably accounts for your much-vaunted capabilities."

"Not me. My aunts didn't come to live with my father until after I left for West Point. So I was raised by men."

"And I can tell." It was his superior tone that made her say that. She didn't even know what she meant.

"Explain that."

"You know how to take, but not how to give." It was the first thing that came to her mind. She knew it was unfair, indeed even untrue, when she said it, but it was too late. She'd already blurted it out.

He looked at her in silence, the wounded soul of the lonely child staring back at her. "I'll try to remember that," he said evenly, after interminable seconds had ticked away and a thousand emotions had flickered across his face.

Rhiannon wanted to sink into the carpet. She had never thought to hurt him or to be responsible for ever wounding such a proud and fierce man. Indeed, she was stunned that she had the power to touch him that deeply. And with that thought came the sudden and blinding intuition that she was probably the only person in the entire world, outside of MacGregor and his aunts, who could touch him, who could wound him mortally. And probably they couldn't even score the killing blow that the woman he entrusted with his heart could. She, Rhiannon O'Shea, was the chink in this man's armor. He'd let her in, and she had slapped him away.

Would he ever let her in again? How stupid could she be? He'd brought her here today to give her much more than his name for a child who might not even exist yet. In fact, he'd been willing to marry her now, not even knowing if she carried his child. He'd brought her here today and had tried, in his dictatorial, coolly logical, very male way, using the only words and the only way he knew how, to give her his heart.

And she'd slapped him away and raged at him and insulted him . . . and behaved like the spoiled, willful child he'd said she was. What had she done? What had she done?

Chapter Thirteen

Hank, a thin cigar in his mouth and a shot of whiskey in his hand, followed Cat LaFlamme up to the second floor of the Fancy Lady Saloon. The gravelly voice of the piano player raised in a bawdy song, the scraping of chairs, the raucous calls and laughter of the drinking and carousing patrons, none of it could hide the fact that most, if not all, of the people below were marking his progress up the less-than-sturdy stairs, his first time to go upstairs with one of the whores.

Hank's booted foot nearly went through the loose planking of one of the steps. Big John certainly didn't spend his money on keeping the place up. And he certainly didn't spend it on making sure his whores were provided for, if the condition of the skimpy, tawdry outfit of the girl in front of him on the stairs was any indication. Hank pressed his lips together in anger. It would have been hard to miss the smattering of bruises on her back, some old, some new.

Hank had talked with Cat enough downstairs on various occasions to know she was outspoken and no coward. He just imagined that as a result, she bore the brunt of Big John's anger and blows for her own transgressions—ironic term, Hank thought—as well as those of the other girls.

Well, hell, he'd paid for her time, and he intended to use it wisely. Hank followed Cat into a small, unadorned room that smelled of stale cigar smoke, liquor, body odor, and sex. He closed and locked the door behind him, his nose wrinkling almost involuntarily at the commingling of the noxious odors in the trapped, close air of the room. The feeble light in the room, coming from a kerosene lamp, struggled to emerge from the smudged globe that covered it.

Hank made a visual sweep of the room, noting all the details. This habit of his was a holdover from his days in the cavalry: Know your terrain. The only furnishings were the rumpled, dirty bed, covered in dun-colored, greasy sheets, a rickety wood chair, and a dusty table on which sat a washbasin, which apparently nobody ever used.

He decided on the chair, sitting on it gingerly, testing it to see if it would hold his weight. Once settled, he looked up in mild surprise to see Cat undressing. He took the cigar out of his mouth.

"That's all right, sweetheart. You don't have to do that."

Her fingers quit moving on the catches at the back of her short, satiny dress. She gave him a pointed look. "You goin' to do it for me?"

"No."

"Then, you want me to stay dressed while we . . ."

"No. We're not going to . . ." He made the same motion with his head, indicating the bed, that she had made.

She put her hands to her waist. "What'd you pay twice the money for, then? I never figured you for one of them men who like to watch the girl on the bed while she—"

"You figured right. We're just going to talk."

"I never figured you for the talking type, neither."

Hank laughed and threw back the shot of whiskey. "It appears, Miss LaFlamme, that you spend quite a bit of time figuring about me."

Cheryl Anne Porter

He couldn't believe it—maybe it was just a trick of the light—but he'd be damned if she wasn't blushing.

"A girl's got to think of something when men are pawing on her," she said, all brass and daring, and vulnerability.

Hank's heart did a funny flop, thinking about this girl dreaming about him while other men used her body. He was flattered and saddened at the same time. How many whores had he sowed his wild oats on in his younger days without even thinking twice, or even once, about them as people? He knew he had one Rhiannon O'Shea to thank, if that was the right word, for this new insight.

"Sit down, Cat. I want to talk to you. And not about sex."

As if to punctuate his words, moans and cries came from the next room, accompanied by the thump-thump-thumping of a headboard against the wall. Cat looked at the wall and then back at Hank. "That might be a tad hard to do."

Hank laughed again. He liked this girl. She was a survivor. Cat sat down on the end of the bed and self-consciously tugged a thin strap back up onto her shoulder. She then wrapped her arms around her plump abdomen and waited. Hank looked closely at her; there was a yellowish bruise on her jaw. His hands formed into fists in his lap.

"Cat, does Big John beat you?"

Her hand followed his gaze to her jaw. She then rubbed her knuckles across her mouth. "It don't hurt none now."

Every instinct in Hank urged him to find the huge bartender and give him a dose of his own medicine. Instead, he asked softly, "But it hurt then, didn't it?"

She looked down at her lap and picked at the uneven hem of her dress. If not for the outfit, which included torn black hose and high-heeled shoes, she would have looked like the virtual child she actually was. "Yeah, it did. But I couldn't let him beat no more on Scarlet. She's just a little thing. He'd of killed her for sure. But not me. I can take it."

178

Hank kept his gaze and his voice level, but inside he was smoldering. "Why do you think you have to take it?"

She looked up at him, much as if she'd never thought about that before. "I been beat on all my life. First, it was my pa, until I run away. And now Big John. I guess I just make men mad. My pa always told me I was a bad one. I suppose I am." She stopped and looked over at him, alarm widening her eyes. "You ain't goin' to make no trouble, are you, 'cause I told you about Big John? Why, he'd kill me for sure then. And even if he didn't, he'd kick me out. And I ain't got nowheres else to go. The Fancy Lady's the only home I've ever had."

Hank's gut tightened. He'd said much the same things about this type of woman to Rhiannon not so many days ago. Words were one thing; evidence was another. "No, Cat, I won't make any trouble for you." But he'd sure as hell make a mountain of trouble for Big John the first chance he got, and in such a way that Cat and Scarlet would not be around to bear the brunt of the big man's anger. "Where's Scarlet? Is she okay now?"

"Okay enough, I guess. That's her room," she said, jerking her thumb toward the wall where the moans and groans, not all of them masculine, were winding down. Cat looked at Hank for a moment and then added, "She thinks about you, too."

"I'm flattered," Hank said, ducking his head in a courtly manner and smiling.

Cat smiled back at him, pretty under all the makeup and the dyed red hair. That red hair . . .

The sudden image of another redhead he knew prompted him to ask, "Why'd you dye your hair that color, Cat?"

She put a self-conscious hand to her twisted-up hair. "Oh, that's Big John's doin's. If you're goin' to work for him, you're goin' to have red hair. My hair's more like yellow on its own. But he likes redheads, even if he does beat on 'em."

Again, Rhiannon's redheaded image came into Hank's mind, along with her recent squabble with Big John. Hank knew he was going to do his damnedest to keep Rhiannon away from this place, even despite the way they'd left off this afternoon. Even despite the ache in his heart for her refusal to marry him, or even to have anything to do with him, actually. Still, if that big son of a bitch ever laid a hand on her, he'd kill him—if he didn't anyway for what he'd done to Cat and Scarlet.

Hank looked over at Cat and caught her quizzical expression. "You're wondering exactly what I'm doing up here with you, aren't you?"

She shrugged a shoulder, sending her strap down her arm. "I suppose. But don't think I mind any. I can use the rest, and you're sure easy on the eyes."

"Why, Miss LaFlamme, I do believe you're flirting with me," Hank teased.

"I'd do more than that if I thought it'd do any good. But shoot, I know you ain't interested in the likes of me."

"Well, actually I am, Cat. I'm afraid it's not the kind of interest you're hoping for, but still, it's interest. I'm here about your visit the other day with Miss O'Shea."

Cat cocked her head at a sidelong angle, quirking a sly smile at him. She looked for all the world like her namesake, a curious cat. "You sweet on her or something?"

Hank laughed, tamped the ashes off the all-but-forgotten cigar in his hand, and said, "Or something." Then, his face sobered. "Why don't you tell me what you two talked about, Cat."

Cat sat up straight, the alarmed look back on her face. "I didn't mean no harm, just up and talkin' to her like that. I know she's a decent woman an' all, and I'm just a—"

Hank reached over to her, intending to put a comforting hand on her arm. But Cat, her eyes widened in sudden terror, flinched away from his touch. Hank pulled his hand back. "Cat, don't be afraid. It's all right. I'm not angry. But even if I were, I wouldn't hit you. You have nothing to fear from me. And if you don't want to tell me about your talk with Miss O'Shea, you don't have to. In fact, Miss O'Shea would be the first to tell me that what you two ladies talked about is none of my business."

Cat relaxed a little and even smiled uncertainly. "That sounds just like her, don't it?"

"Indeed it does."

"Can I ask you something first?"

"Certainly."

"Why do you want to know?"

"Well, I think I already do know. It was about running for city council, wasn't it?"

Cat nodded. "Yeah. So why are you asking me?"

Hank admired her directness. "I just wanted to be sure. What did you tell her?"

"Why do you want to know?"

Hank laughed. "Has anyone ever told you you'd make a great lawyer?"

"I don't know nothin' about that. But I do believe I'd make a great councilman . . . woman. 'Cause if there's anybody in this town who hears it all about city affairs, it's me."

"I don't doubt it in the least. So, are you going to run on the ticket with Miss O'Shea?"

"Yeah. Me and her shook hands on it and everything."

Just as he'd suspected. Rhiannon's headlong determination to run for mayor was placing her and the other women, especially this one, directly in the path of danger. Hank took a deep drag on the cigar, exhaled the smoke, and crushed out the fire in an already full tin ashtray on the table. Trying to keep his voice casual, he asked, "What's Big John going to think about that?"

Cat took a short breath. "That's the part I ain't worked out yet."

Hank looked directly into her eyes. "Well, that's the part where I come in."

Cheryl Anne Porter

*　　*　　*

"Here comes Mrs. Hawkins now. I guess that means we're all here. Except of course for Miss LaFlamme . . . who can't be here today . . . because of . . . business."

Rhiannon caught the other women's exchange of glances. She'd have to talk fast and sweet to beat down their resistance to having a prostitute on the ballot with them. But she knew she could do that; after all, hadn't she gotten them all to come here this morning to the back of Gruenwald's Dry Goods Store for their first official strategy meeting? And who would have thought that was possible even ten days ago? Or even conceivable.

"Mrs. Hawkins. Please have a seat." She indicated the only empty chair that sat around the piece of board Freda Gruenwald had placed on top of a barrel for them to use as their table. A heavy curtain separated their meeting area from the store out front. Rhiannon decided she was nervous enough without Mr. Gruenwald poking his head in here every so often to glare and to ask when his wife'd be through. He needed her out front, he said.

"I want to thank you all for coming today," Rhiannon began, standing on the opposite side of the plank from the other women and looking at each candidate for office in front of her.

On her left was Joletta Hawkins, the large, bad-tempered woman who was known for her pies—and her rolling pin; it was her husband, on that day in the saloon that seemed so long ago, who'd first brought up the idea of running the women. Rhiannon wondered if she could control Mrs. Hawkins's outbursts and if she would be more trouble than she was worth to the campaign.

Next to Mrs. Hawkins, and leaning away from her in abject terror, was timid Susie Johnson, the town doctor's spinster daughter. The woman looked and acted like a little brown sparrow, and was known to flee at the first sight of a man. Rhiannon wondered if the bookish woman would hold up

182

under the strident opposition they were sure to face during this campaign. In her favor, though, was her father's support of them all. Perhaps he could keep his daughter buoyed up.

The Widow Calvert, new schoolteacher in Wolfe and the bane of all little boys who misbehaved in her class, sat very primly. Johnny-Cake was right—she did have a big nose, and she did look mean. But Rhiannon suspected other qualities underneath that stern exterior, qualities such as education, intellect, organization, a sense of commitment and purpose, all things any good teacher needed. And she'd asked Rhiannon to call her Emma; she'd even smiled when she said it.

And bless her heart, there was Freda Gruenwald, the stout, blond, laughing, handsome German immigrant who lived for her husband, her children, and this store, in that order. The Gruenwalds had what, to all appearances, was a happy and productive life. Rhiannon hoped that the woman's decision to run for office did not ruin all that for her. Even now, she had the first frown on her face, after her husband's latest foray back here, that Rhiannon had ever seen. And of all the women gathered here, Freda Gruenwald had the least reason to upset her life like this. For that very reason, Rhiannon wondered at Freda's decision to throw in with them.

"I suppose you all read *The Wolfe Daily* this morning?" Rhiannon asked. Then, she stopped. How many of them could read? And how could she ask them that? But seeing a few of them nod, she hurried on. "For those of you who didn't get a chance to see it, let me tell you what it said. Apparently, the incumbents, the men who now hold the offices we're seeking—"

"And will get."

"Thank you, Mrs. Hawkins. The men who now hold the offices we seek have taken it upon themselves to call for a special election to be held inside of a month, instead of waiting for the legal election day this fall."

"How can they do that, Miss O'Shea?"

"Please, Emma—and the rest of you—call me Rhiannon. We'll be working together very closely in the next few weeks, so—"

"And the next few years, when we're running this town."

"That's certainly true, Mrs. Haw . . . Joletta. I admire your . . . spirit. Now, to answer Emma's question. They can call for a special election just by citing special circumstances."

"Vhat are dey?" Freda asked in her heavily accented English.

"The impending arrival of Carry Nation and the Temperance League, of course. That's what started all this, if you'll remember."

"Are the men afraid of her?" ventured Susie, clearly showing that she was, too.

"They are, if they're smart," Joletta Hawkins cut in, sending Susie almost into Emma Calvert's lap.

"Yes," Rhiannon went on, trying to regain control. This wasn't going very well. "They want the election over with before she brings the League to town. The men say they don't want the town divided with her here."

"What they really mean," Emma said, a politician's smile lighting her face, "is they don't want the women of the Temperance League adding their voices to our campaign."

"You're probably exactly right." Rhiannon smiled, heartened by Emma Calvert's quick grasp of the situation. She'd been right in her assessment of the widow. "And what this special election means to us is we don't have the luxury of time. Today we need to list our strengths and weaknesses, assign tasks, and get our campaigns up and running. First of all, I think we need a slogan. Something that people will remember and repeat."

Hank had never seen such a big crowd of men in Gruenwald's at one time. In fact, he believed there was a quorum here if anybody cared to vote on anything. But even more perplexing than the numbers was the pall which seemed to hang over them. There was almost complete silence in the store. Had someone died? Certainly, no one was searching the many tables, shelves, or bins for needed supplies. In fact, no one was doing anything. They were all, to a man, standing around, looking very much like expectant fathers.

Stymied, Hank put his aunts' list in his shirt pocket. It amused and humbled him that, though he was 32 and the reigning head of Wolfe Enterprises International, his aunts still thought nothing of sending him to the store for their personal needs, saying they didn't wish to bother the servants. Looking around him, and reluctant to break the silence since he had no clue as to its reason, he directed a questioning look at the nearest man, who happened to be Mayor Driver.

The mayor leaned towards him and whispered, "They're back there."

Hank looked to where the mayor's pudgy finger pointed. He saw a harmless curtain. He asked the obvious question, keeping his voice low. "Who?"

"The women."

Hank had expected robbers, desperadoes, a foreign invading army, marauding Indians, something ominous to cause this much cautious attention and silence in the town's men. But women? Unless they were getting ready to come out naked. Even though he was beginning to regret starting this apparently inane conversation, Hank asked the next obvious question. "What women?"

"Miss O'Shea and the rest of them who're running for office."

Hank digested this with silent nodding of his head. "I see," he said, but he didn't really. "Mayor Driver, are you telling me that your opponents are in that back room meeting and you men are out here spying?"

The mayor's eyes bulged. "Spying? Hardly!"

Hank's voice rose a little, drawing the attention of the other men in the crowded room. "Then what do you call it?"

185

His voice apparently drew the attention of the women on the other side of the curtain, too, because the length of heavy fabric flew back on its rod, revealing the candidates.

Gruenwald's had never seen such a sudden and frenzied buying spree as the one that took place right then and there. Hank thought the scurrying men, who picked up things they couldn't use in a thousand years, had all the intensity of purpose of buyers and sellers on the floor of the New York Stock Exchange. It was hard to tell who was more dazed— him, the women, or Mr. Gruenwald.

It was Rhiannon who recovered first. She poked out her bottom lip in that stubborn way of hers that he was coming to recognize as trouble. Then, the possible mother of his child stalked right through the frenetic activity, weaving her way unerringly toward her prey. Behind her, he could see that the other women sought out their husbands or some poor unfortunate man near them. Only Susie Johnson remained by the curtain, her eyes wide and her hands to her cheeks.

Hank crossed his arms, content to let Rhiannon come to him. That was the way it would be from now on, he'd decided after their scene in his headquarters two days ago. She would have to come to him. He'd said his piece when he'd told her she was going to marry him. She'd flung it back in his face, but he could outwait her. Even if time weren't on his side, meaning she could be carrying his . . . their child.

"What are you doing here, Hank Wolfe?" she fumed, voice raised to be heard over the din, her hands at her waist.

Hank had all he could do to keep his hands from her waist. He'd been without her for three days, and they had been hell. But he wasn't about to let her know that. By way of an answer, he pulled his aunts' list out of his pocket, waved it in front of her face, smiled, and then pushed by her, searching for thread bobbins, whatever the hell those were.

But he didn't get far. He felt her hand on his arm and allowed her to turn him back to her, but not before he wiped a secret smile off his face. "Yes, Miss O'Shea?"

"Don't you 'Miss O'Shea' me, Hank Wolfe. What were you and all these"—she gestured wildly to indicate the other men in the store—"men doing out here?"

It was hard to carry on a civil conversation, not that this one was, in the midst of all this noise and confusion, but Hank tried valiantly. "I can't speak for my esteemed colleagues, but I am here on a legitimate errand." He looked at his list and then at Rhiannon. "What are thread bobbins?"

She stared at him blankly for a long few seconds. "They're over there in that bin."

"Hmph, never would have found them." He turned in the direction she'd pointed, but again, he didn't get far.

She came around him and put her sweet little body directly in front of him. "Stop that this instant."

"I beg your pardon? What am I doing?" It felt good to be infuriating for once. A dose of her own medicine wouldn't hurt her in the least.

She frowned up at him. He wanted to kiss that forehead—for starters. "You know damned good and well what I mean."

Hank feigned shock. "Such language for someone wanting to be a public figure. And about that figure, might I add—"

That did it. She looked like she'd like to kick his shins. "Were those men listening in on our meeting?"

"I couldn't really say, but they did give every appearance of doing just that. You should be flattered." Hank ran his gaze over her face, her body, her hair, all of her as he spoke. She was absolutely intoxicating.

"Flattered?" she said "I think not. We're far from flattered by the dirty campaign tactics of our opposition. And I would think that you, as the—as the . . . what are you in Wolfe?"

Hank leaned the slightest bit toward her. "I'm afraid I don't—"

"For pity's sake. Officially. What are you officially in Wolfe? What's your title?"

Cheryl Anne Porter

Hank pretended to think about this, just to prolong this meeting with the charming little dickens who was taking over his life. "Supreme ruler?" he finally offered.

Rhiannon stopped tapping her foot and put her hands to her waist again, something he would have liked to have done himself. She narrowed her eyes at him and pressed her lips together.

"No?" he said. "Well, how about benevolent dictator?"

"How about absurd jackass?" she flung at him.

"No," Hank drawled, cocking his head to one side and frowning. "I don't think that's it. I think I'd've remembered that one."

Rhiannon threw her hands up. "Fine. That's just fine, Hank Wolfe. Don't take this seriously. I shouldn't have expected anything different. You've obviously sided with the men of this town. Well, Mr. Absurd Supreme Jackass Ruler, two can play this game." With that, she stomped around him and forced her way through the crowd of men, who were now queued up in line waiting to pay, their arms ladened with all manner of disparate purchases.

Just before she stomped out of the store, she turned abruptly and called out, "Now all of you listen and hear me good. I expected a fight with you men over this election, but I did think it would be a clean one." She paused; the men had the grace to look sheepish. "But don't think for a minute that you've won. We will meet again—just the women—right here tomorrow, and we will take up just where we left off. And let me tell you one thing. If you don't wear a skirt, you're not invited!" With that, she exited the store with all the grace and flourish of the great lady she'd been trained to be. The silence that followed in her departing wake was broken by the sound of shuffling feet and packages.

Hank huffed out a breath. Dammit. He was as bad as the rest of these men. Hell, he'd just been teasing her, but she was right. His teasing had been demeaning. With a sigh, he admitted to himself that he owed her an apology for being flippant. Turning on his heel, he followed after her. The men, their eyes averted sheepishly, nevertheless parted for Mr. Wolfe.

Once on the boardwalk outside the dry goods store, Hank made a sweep of the street, looking for Rhiannon. He didn't see her right off as he'd expected he would. Now where could she have disappeared to so quickly? Then his gaze lit on a familiar-looking boy of about 15 or 16. It took him a moment to realize who the boy was, but then it finally came to him. It was Eddie O'Shea, Rhiannon's sandy-haired, blue-eyed brother, and he looked fit to be tied as he strode purposefully past Gruenwald's, his eyes forward, a hard frown on his face to match his balled-up fists at his sides.

A frown came over Hank's face. What could a boy of 15 have to look so fierce about? Almost everything, if memory served. Still, Hank stepped off the boardwalk and turned in the direction Eddie was walking. Aha, there she was. Rhiannon. She was half in, half out of the doorway of the offices of *The Wolfe Daily*. She had her back to Eddie and Hank, and appeared to be having quite an animated conversation with a pretty black-haired girl who was still young enough for the schoolroom. Whatever Rhiannon was saying to her, the girl was vigorously agreeing. Hank shook his head in amusement; Rhiannon wouldn't be happy until she'd converted and enlisted every woman in town, from whores to housewives, from schoolgirls to schoolteachers.

With Rhiannon finally in his sights, Hank gave a defeated sigh and started for her, no longer thinking too much about Eddie's reason for being angry. That is, until Eddie got to Rhiannon before him. Hank was too far away to stop the boy, but was close enough to see and to hear him. Hank's face hardened and his step quickened when Eddie spun his sister around sharply. Almost a man, tall and leanly muscled, Eddie nearly sent a much smaller Rhiannon to the ground.

The black-haired girl gasped out in startled alarm, instinctively stepping back. Reporter Jimmy Pickens immediately appeared in the doorway, his face a mask of concern as his eyes cut from the brother to the sister and back. Then, his eyes widened in genuine fright when he saw Hank Wolfe loping up the street in their direction.

"Get away from her, Rhiannon," Eddie said. "Leave her alone. I don't want her having anything to do with your foolish ideas. Haven't you done enough, embarrassing the whole family by running all over town, playing politics, and talking to whores, without ruining Emily, too? How many fights do I have to get into, because folks make fun of you, before you'll stop?"

Hank heard the raw emotion in the boy's speech, but it only barely registered, because all he could see was Rhiannon's stricken face. His heart tore at its moorings in his chest and rage exploded in him. Gaining the boardwalk in one smooth leap, Hank grabbed the boy by his shirt collar—by God, no one, not even her own family, would lay a hand on her—and hauled him backwards to face him.

Black eyes sparking fire, Hank looked straight into Eddie's stunned eyes and snarled, in a low growl, "Don't you ever lay a hand on your sister again, do you understand me? Because if you do, you'll answer to me. You're almost a man now, boy, so act like it. Men don't take care of their private business out in the street; and they sure as hell don't bully their women—or anyone else's. You got me, son?"

Despite his terrible anger, Hank almost admired the boy's unflinching regard of him. Instead of cowering and whining, which was the usual reaction, in Hank's military experience, of most untried boys of Eddie's age when faced down by a much stronger and more experienced man, Eddie surprised Hank by looking him right in the eye unflinchingly and saying, "I got you."

Their gazes remained locked for a tense moment. Then, Hank eased his grip on Eddie. No longer wanting to destroy the young man once he'd made his point, Hank let go of him, stepped back, and said, "Apologize to your sister and then see to the young lady."

"Yes, sir." He turned to Rhiannon, who had stared wide-eyed at this whole exchange as she held Emily's hands in hers. "I'm sorry, Rhiannon. I had no call to yell at you"— he cut his eyes over at Hank, and then looked back at his sister—"in public. I didn't mean to hurt you. But I can only take so much."

Rhiannon put her hand out tentatively, but then pulled it back, as if sensing the emerging man before her, who would not appreciate any mushy display of emotion. But still, she couldn't stop the wet brightness that came to her eyes. "Oh, Eddie, I'm so sorry. I never meant to cause you any hurt or embarrassment. I love you."

On hearing Rhiannon's last words, words he would have given his life to hear her say to him, Hank swallowed just as hard as Eddie did, and decided he'd thrash the boy right there if he didn't make some loving gesture toward his sister. But Eddie didn't move; he stayed put, rigidly staring at his sister. Hank's heart went out to Rhiannon when she visibly sagged in dejection. There were some things that just couldn't be made right, no matter how much you wanted it.

After a tense moment, Eddie turned to the young girl with the thick, black hair, pale skin, and luminous gray eyes. "And Emily, if you can forgive me for such a scene, I'd like to see you home."

Hank watched as Emily looked anxiously from Eddie to Rhiannon. He knew her dilemma—how to leave with Eddie, which was clearly what her face said she wanted to do, without appearing to abandon her will, not to mention Rhiannon, a woman whom she obviously worshipped. And that, Hank thought, could mean no end of trouble for young Mr. O'Shea.

191

For Hank knew firsthand the power Rhiannon had.

When Rhiannon let go of Emily's hands and nodded, almost imperceptibly, for her to go with Eddie, Hank wanted to applaud her. Rhiannon was growing in maturity and astuteness on a daily basis. But instead of applause, he watched with her in silence as Eddie put a possessive arm around Emily's slim waist and led her off in the direction of the eastern outskirts of town to the working-class section of plain, clapboard homes.

After a moment, Hank turned to Rhiannon, catching her unguarded expression of deep pain. He wanted very much to reach out to her and make the sort of loving gesture he thought Eddie should have made. But they were still out in public, and they still weren't alone. Jimmy Pickens hadn't moved from his vantage point in the doorway.

Hank caught the cub reporter's eye. "If I read one word of this, Pickens, just one word, in the newspaper, I'll—"

"Oh, no, sir. Don't worry," Pickens rushed to say. "I wasn't thinking anything along the lines of news. I was just making sure Miss O'Shea and Miss Washburn weren't being accosted. You can count on me to keep private matters private, sir."

A terse "Good" was all Jimmy got for his sincere speech. Knowing when to leave, the reporter stepped back inside the office and closed the door. Hank turned to Rhiannon, putting a hand on her arm. "Are you all right?"

She looked up at him, the sad smile on her face plainly belying her affirmative nod. This was the first time he'd ever seen her at a loss for words. And he didn't like it. But not as much as he didn't like her next words.

She turned away from him, went the few steps to the edge of the boardwalk, crossed her arms under her breasts, and said, "I'm not going to run for mayor. Not if it hurts and embarrasses my family. Their feelings mean more to me than some childish venture of mine that's only meant to stir up trouble and keep me from being bored."

Hank moved to stand beside her and join her in looking out over the street scene before them. He hooked his thumbs in the waistband of his denims. "Is that what this race is all about—a childish venture to stave off boredom?"

He felt her eyes on him. He turned his head to look down at her. "No. It's much more than that, Hank."

"But you're just going to give it up." He couldn't believe he was trying to talk her back into what he still thought of as a foolhardy scheme.

"I should."

"Why?"

"Because I'm hurting so many people who care about me."

Hank wondered if she counted him in that group. "Think how many you'll hurt if you don't run, Rhiannon. Not to mention yourself. It's been my experience that dreams die hard."

She looked wistful and far away for a moment. Then, she said, "Do you mean when you had to leave the cavalry? Wasn't that your dream?"

"Yes. It was."

She looked down and fiddled with her fingers. "I'm sorry you had to give it up, Hank."

He was glad she wasn't looking at him right now, because he was positive that for that moment, his love for her was plainly visible on his face. "It's not so bad, Rhiannon. At least I lived it for a while. Besides, I've found a better dream to take its place."

She looked at him, a quizzical frown on her face. "You mean here in Wolfe? I'm glad, Hank." Then: "Hank, I'm sorry about the things I said Saturday."

Hank let her think his dream was Wolfe, when it was really her. "Don't be, you meant them. Look, running for mayor is what you need to do, whether you realize it or not. If you don't, you'll always wonder, Rhiannon, if you could have done it. Yes, if you give it up now, you'll make everyone happy. But not yourself."

Rhiannon stared at him a moment. "I'm just like that wolf with his foot in the trap, aren't I? If I don't free myself, I'll certainly die, and if I do free myself, I just might die anyway."

"Damned if you do, damned if you don't," Hank offered.

Chapter Fourteen

"O'Shea will seize the day!" It was a fine slogan she'd come up with once she'd decided, in Hank's words, to be damned if she did. And she'd worked at a feverish pace since then, only three days ago, to bring the women, still without Cat since she couldn't get away from Big John, together on a platform of issues pertinent to them and to Wolfe—the town, not the man. Not directly, anyway.

Rhiannon hated the fact that her dream of independence, of really living, was carrying her further away from Hank and from being the wife he wanted her to be, even if it was only because he thought she was carrying his child, which she wasn't. She'd have to find a moment to tell him. He would probably be as relieved as she was . . . or was supposed to be. Or would be if only she could get the images out of her head of all the things they'd done together in his bed, and if only she could stop shivering every time she thought about being in his arms. And how much she wanted to be again.

Well, he was the one who'd encouraged her, on more than one occasion, to pursue her freedom. Why would he do that if he were so opposed to the idea? Why did he act like it was as important to him that she be happy in her dream as it was to her? Not that there was anything he could do to stop her. Actually, there was. With his power and influence in this town, he could have squelched this campaign with one word. But he hadn't. Well, maybe it was just because he really didn't care that much what she did. No, she knew better than that; she'd seen his heart in his eyes too many times when he looked at her. So maybe if he could be happy for her to live her dream, maybe they weren't so far apart in their thinking as she felt them to be at this point. Maybe her slogan was really for Hank, too.

And the slogan didn't deserve to be shredded and left on the streets. Rhiannon would never have thought it of the people of Wolfe, whom she'd known all her life. But here was the evidence—along with the advertisements for the Temperance League and Carry A. Nation, inviting the town to a meeting on the outskirts of town. Someone had torn down those and the women candidates' posters. Someone. As if she didn't know who. It was certainly suspicious that the posters for the men were intact on this fine late afternoon.

Rhiannon looked up and down the dusty side street, her lips pursed in anger. The few people about merely looked over in her direction and passed by, not even curious about the mess. As if nothing were wrong. She then exchanged a look with Susie Johnson, who held another batch of hand-lettered signs in her thin arms. Suddenly angry at the injustice of it all, Rhiannon threw down the torn poster and said, "Give me another one, Susie."

Susie promptly handed one over. Rhiannon nailed it right back up where the previous one had been. "Do you think we should be doing this, Miss O'Shea? I don't think the men will—"

"Oh, hang the men, Susie. And call me Rhiannon, please. Now, don't look so stricken. We have every bit of a right to campaign as the incumbents do." Her task completed, she resettled her jaunty straw hat trimmed with pink ribbon.

"Do you think they did this?" Susie looked all around her on the ground at the torn bits of paper.

Rhiannon put the hammer back in her reticule. Today it also carried nails—and nothing feminine. This was war. "Why, of course I do. Who else?"

"I don't know. I just hate to think that people we've known all our lives would do something like this. Daddy says he doesn't think the men did it."

Rhiannon looked at the little brown face that was almost completely obscured by the deep hood of a homespun sun-bonnet. "I believe your father is right, Susie. I don't think all the men did this, either—just a few of them in particular."

Susie was breathless. "That's what Daddy says. He says it . . . it could be those strangers in town."

Rhiannon almost laughed at Susie's hushed tone, as if "strangers" was a dirty word not to be repeated in daylight. With a shake of her head, she started walking around the corner, intending to step up onto the boardwalk at the front of Gruenwald's. With her eyes on Susie, she said, "Forever more, Susie, sometimes I think—"

And then she ran smack into Big John Savage. The huge mountain of a man took advantage of her surprise and momentary disorientation to grab her by her arms. "No, Miss O'Shea. I don't even think you think sometimes. I don't think you think at all."

Shaken but recovering, her nostrils full of his stale body odor and cigar stench, Rhiannon fought down a gag and said, more evenly than she would have thought possible, "Take your hands off me . . . this instant."

"Not until I'm good and ready, Miss O'Shea. So you just hear me out. And you too, Miss Johnson, so there's no mistaking what I say."

Rhiannon chanced a look at Susie; she couldn't see her face because of the bonnet. But Susie's knuckles were rigid and white as she clutched the posters to her thin bosom. To Rhiannon's endless surprise, she heard Susie say, "You'd best let go of Miss O'Shea, Mr. Savage. Because if you don't, Mr. Wolfe will . . . will throttle you, for sure."

"I ain't scared of no Mr. Wolfe. He ain't got nothing over me."

Susie's attempt at bravery was evidently just a flash in the pan, for his last words sent her scurrying behind Rhiannon. Wishing that Joletta Hawkins and her rolling pin were here instead of Susie Johnson and her spinsterish timidity, Rhiannon returned her full attention to the cruel man who held her arms in a painful, vise-like grip. If only she could get to the hammer in her reticule; she'd like to put an extra hole in this horrid man's head. But she couldn't, so she was forced to listen—and to pray that he let her go unharmed.

"I seen all them posters all over town, touting all you women for office. But I'd best not see any of them on my establishment. I just ran off them two littlest brothers of yours."

Rhiannon's heart leaped, and she bucked in Big John's grip. "If you hurt them in any way, I swear Mr. Wolfe will be the least of your worries!"

"I didn't hurt no kids. I just told them to scat."

"Oh, that's a surprise. So you draw the line at children, do you? But not at women. Women you'll beat. Don't think I don't know, Mr. Savage!"

"Uh, Miss O'Shea, perhaps now isn't the time to—"

"Hush, Susie," she called over her shoulder. She then looked at the very ominous expression on Big John's huge, bearded face. But she didn't heed the danger. "I've seen the bruises on Cat. And worse, I've seen you with my own eyes throw her around like she was nothing."

"She is nothing. She's low-down whoring scum. And that's another thing. You better stay away from my establishment—and my whores. I seen you talking to Cat more than once, putting fancy notions in her head about a better life. And Scarlet, too. Making them think the folks of this town would welcome them. Hell, there ain't nobody in Wolfe who'd welcome those two into their fancy parlors, least of all you. So you hear me good. You stay away from my saloon and my whores. And if you don't, you're going to look like them signs on the ground, Miss O'Shea." He held her back away from him and looked her up and down. "And that would be a mighty shame, a woman like you."

Rhiannon's breath left her in a gust; Susie made the same sound behind her. "I think you're threatening me, Mr. Savage," Rhiannon said.

"Well now, I take back what I said earlier." He let go of her arms and stepped back. "You do think right sometimes." With that, he turned his bulk around and went back the way he'd come, back towards the Fancy Lady, which was across the street and at an angle from Gruenwald's.

Rhiannon leaned her back against the wooden building behind her, one arm slung over her eyes, her other one hanging loosely at her side. Her reticule slid from her nerveless grasp and hit the ground with a dull thunk. She felt a light patting on her shoulder and opened her eyes.

Susie was patting her, but seemed almost to be unaware of what her hand was doing. For her head was turned to watch Big John's retreating figure. Rhiannon looked down; Susie had dropped the campaign posters, and they lay in a fanned-out heap in the dirt. Ironic, Rhiannon thought; in the dirt, just like the campaign itself had been from the word go. She caught Susie's bony fingers in her grasp, drawing the woman's gaze. Her eyes glittered at Rhiannon from the shadowy depths of the bonnet.

"I'm fine, Susie. Really. Are you? You're not crying, are you?" Rhiannon pushed away from the wall to stand up straight. She let go of Susie's hand and smoothed her pink and lavender gingham dress. She then bent over to pick up her reticule.

Susie ignored Rhiannon's questions and stated, "We have to tell someone, Miss—Rhiannon. We have to tell. That man will kill you for sure."

Rhiannon was impressed. Susie wasn't crying, she'd called her Rhiannon, she wasn't whining to quit, and she didn't sound scared. Susie Johnson was full of surprises. But Rhiannon couldn't let her tell anyone what had happened.

"No, Susie. We can't tell—not even the other women. They'd all want to quit. And that would just prove the men right when they say we can't do anything without them."

Susie looked down and fiddled with her fingers for a moment. To Rhiannon's infinite relief, she then pushed the bonnet off her face and to the back of her head. That pinched, angular face showed more conviction on it than Rhiannon believed she'd ever seen there before. "Then we have to get . . . Cat to quit the campaign. Maybe if she's not in with us, Mr. Savage will leave you alone."

Rhiannon's heart sank. For a moment there, she'd thought Susie was coming around. She rubbed her sore arms and looked at Susie. "No, Susie. We can't do that. I . . . I made a promise to her. To help her. She wants out of the life she has now—and so does Scarlet. Did you know that Scarlet is only sixteen years old? I can't walk away from Cat and Scarlet, Susie. I can't."

"Not even if it means you'll get hurt?" Susie looked at her from a sidelong gaze.

"No. Not even if it means I get myself hurt." Rhiannon held her breath. Could the ticket be falling apart already, beginning right here with Susie? Would she be the first defector? The race had been plagued with one false start after another, Rhiannon realized, and mostly from her own indecision. But now she was firmly committed to this course. No more changing her mind, no more ducking her tail at the first sign of trouble. And she knew it was essential that the women all stay united. If one broke, they all would.

"Well, then," Susie began, "I suppose we have to do something about getting Cat and Scarlet out of that saloon and into someplace safe, so Mr. Savage doesn't take his anger out on them."

Rhiannon wanted to hug the older woman—and did. "Oh, thank you, Susie. You're so brave and wonderful."

"No, I'm not—not in the least. Well, only when I'm with you. And Daddy says that some day you'll probably get me shot. Wouldn't that be just dandy?" Her chirruping voice told Rhiannon that Susie thought the idea of being shot in the line of action to be wildly romantic.

Rhiannon laughed out loud, in spite of herself. Getting them all shot could be closer to the truth than she cared to admit to Susie. Wisely, she didn't share that observation with her. Instead, she said, "Come on, Candidate Johnson. Let's pick up these posters and call it a day."

The two women did just that, and then walked off together in the lengthening shadows of evening, their heads together conspiratorially. "Now then, Susie, we need a plan to get Cat and Scarlet out."

"Yes, we must do it quickly, too. Mr. Savage was awfully angry. We'll need to take them to a place that's safe for them, but also safe for the people they stay with. Someplace where Mr. Savage wouldn't dare make trouble."

"Why, Susie, I hadn't thought about that. Now, hmmm, where could we take them that fills that bill?"

Rhiannon's hand shook the least little bit as she raised it to the brass wolf-head knocker on the Wolfe mansion's front doors. The setting sun behind her bathed the mansion in shades of rose. This errand, really a mission of mercy, had seemed much simpler last evening when she and Susie had come up with it. But not this evening with her actually here on Hank's doorstep. What would he say? Was he even home?

The door opened. The butler, Watson, to his stiff and starchy credit, did not drop his mouth open wide and stare in shock. At least, not for more than a fraction of a minute.

For pity's sake, he acted as if he'd never seen a woman in man's clothing before. Eddie would be livid if he knew she'd borrowed the clothing without asking. But her costume was part of the plan—even if her being dressed like this was against the law. Now wouldn't Effie Parsons just love to have her sheriff husband arrest her for being out like this?

"Good evening . . . madam?" Watson looked beyond her to the horse tethered at the brass hitching ring back by the sweep of the circular drive. He brought his gaze back to her.

"Good evening, Watson. May I come in?"

He actually hesitated, but then relented. Stepping aside to allow her entrance, he felt compelled to ask, "Is the master expecting you? Or the Misses Penland?"

Rhiannon's boots, "borrowed" from Paddy—Eddie's feet were much larger than hers—sounded on the marble entryway tiles as she walked across them to the central table with the huge bouquet of fresh flowers. She toyed with a flower while she spoke, avoiding Watson's steady gaze. "Uh, no, not exactly."

"I see," Watson said, but he didn't. She could tell.

"Are . . . they home?" She hated to just come right out and ask for Hank without even inquiring about his aunts.

"I'm afraid not."

Rhiannon's heart sank. Now what?

"At least, the Misses Penlands are not" Watson said. "Mr. Wolfe is upstairs preparing to leave for town, but the Misses Penland have already gone to the evening's festivities . . . which I believe are in your honor."

Relief swept over her; Hank was here. But she still had to get past the butler, who was acting like she owed him an explanation as to why she wasn't in town for the picnic supper and barn dance being given for all the candidates, male and female, by the Ladies Aid Society. Rhiannon had been as shocked as anyone by this virtual sanctioning of the female candidates by such a formidable social institution in Wolfe. Especially since her own mother, the presiding officer, professed to be so against her daughter's candidacy; at least around her husband she did. Which was another reason

Rhiannon didn't have much time—her presence would be quickly missed by her mother and duly noted by the voters.

Frustrated with Watson's continued delaying tactics while he obviously struggled with whether or not Mr. Wolfe should be disturbed, Rhiannon drew herself up and used her best finishing-school haughty, disdainful voice. "All the more reason for me to see Mr. Wolfe immediately. Please inform him that I am here."

It was pretty hard to sound regal and confident while dressed in one's brother's clothes, she discovered. But still, it was enough for Watson.

"Certainly . . . madam." He turned, indicating she should follow him into the morning room. He left her standing by the fireplace as he closed the doors.

As soon as he did, Rhiannon ran across the room and placed her ear to the door. Yes, Watson was going upstairs; she could hear his footfalls. She stepped back into the room, pacing back and forth and rehearsing what she was going to say. She put a hand to her chest, as if that could still the wild thudding of her heart. Hank is going to kill me, Hank is going to kill me, Hank is going to kill me—this was her litany. When the door to the room opened, she jerked her head up and stared wide-eyed at Hank framed in the doorway. Now her heart thudded furiously, out of fear of his reaction, certainly, but also out of sheer physical response to his overpowering male presence.

"Good God." He looked at her and then down at himself, as if verifying they were dressed very similarly in denims, cotton shirt, and boots. But his fit him.

"I can explain." She hoped.

He stepped into the room and closed the door. "This I've got to hear." He sat down rather heavily on the delicate settee behind him.

Rhiannon rushed to join him, hoping to turn his momentary shock at seeing her in men's clothing to her advantage. "You see, yesterday afternoon when Susie Johnson and I were hanging campaign posters in town—there were several pairs of women all over town, hanging posters. Susie was my partner—Big John threatened me, and—"

"He what?!" Hank's bellow of rage should have rattled the windows and ruffled the curtains.

"Not now, Hank. Anyway, he grabbed me and threatened me and told me to stay away from Cat and Scarlet, because if I didn't he'd make me look like the torn-up posters and—"

Hank had heard enough, obviously, for he jumped up. "I'll kill that no-good son of a bitch. I'll crush him under my boot heel. I'll rip out his goddamned heart and feed it to him!" His anger carried him to the door, which he jerked open with such force that it slammed back against the wall.

"No, Hank, wait! You don't have to. It's not going to be necessary." She scrambled to catch up with him.

He turned around so suddenly that she nearly ran into him. "Why? Did you already kill him?" His voice was now murderously calm.

"No, I—"

"Then it's still necessary."

He turned back around and walked straight to the curving stairs, ignoring Watson's stunned presence at the foot of the elegant, polished staircase, and started a pounding ascent. Rhiannon, after shrugging her shoulders helplessly at the butler, followed Hank and his continuing string of epithets right up the graceful stairs. She fully expected Hank's vocabulary to peel the paint right off the walls.

Just as she fully expected Hank's murderous rage to be turned on her, instead of Big John Savage, when he heard the rest of her story. "No, Hank, wait! You have to listen to me. There isn't much time." She pulled on his arm with both hands to slow him down, but she had all the effectiveness of an ant pulling on a lion.

Giving up and winded by the time Hank's anger and long-legged stride had carried them to the third floor to his bedroom, Rhiannon let go of him and stood in the doorway to catch her breath. She then lost it again when Hank yanked open a drawer and pulled out a vicious-looking Colt revolver that was holstered in a gunbelt bearing the stamp of the U.S. Army. "Hank, what are you going to do?"

He looked up at her, apparently somewhat startled to see her there, as he strapped the belt low down on his hip. "Something I should have done a long time ago." He tied the leather thong at the end of the holster around his denim-covered and tensed muscular thigh, and then pulled the long-barreled pistol out of the holster to load it with bullets from the gunbelt.

"Hank, you can't shoot him." She stayed where she was in the doorway, realizing that she was genuinely afraid of him right now and of what she had unleashed in him.

"Why the hell can't I?" He reholstered the gun and settled the worn leather belt on his lean hips. He next grabbed up his black Stetson from his dresser and made ready to put it on.

"Because . . . because . . ."

He settled the Stetson on his head, down low on his forehead. His black eyes flashed out a warning at her. "Spit it out, Rhiannon."

She looked at his chiseled, handsome features and knew the time had come for the truth. "Because Susie and I stole Cat and Scarlet out of the Fancy Lady, after we talked them into quitting. And they're on their way here right now. I told them they can stay with you and you'd protect them from Big John and he wouldn't dare hurt them while they were here, and oh, Hank, you just have to help us. Big John would kill them for sure if they stayed there another day, because Cat told him she wouldn't quit the campaign and that he didn't have to like it and . . . and . . ."

She took a deep breath and went on in the stunned, pregnant silence of the room. "And I dressed in my brother's clothes, so nobody would recognize me right off, and went into the Fancy Lady, after almost everybody had gone to the picnic, to get Cat and Scarlet, even though they didn't want to come at first, until I told them where I was taking them—here, of course; and Susie—she's in her father's clothes so no one will know it's her—waited out back of the saloon with the wagon for them, so they could lay down in the back of it under some canvas to make their getaway without being seen . . . and I rode out here ahead of them to tell you."

She stopped, drew another breath, and bit at her lower lip. Hank said nothing; Hank moved nothing; Hank didn't even blink. Rhiannon felt compelled to add, "They should be here anytime now, barring any trouble."

"Barring any trouble," Hank repeated flatly, as if she'd asked him to.

"Yes. Barring any trouble."

Hank stared at her for a long, long time. Rhiannon didn't dare speak . . . or move. But when he brought his hand up, she tensed, sure he meant to shoot her; instead, he just squeezed his eyes shut and pinched the bridge of his nose with his thumb and forefinger. When he opened his eyes and brought his hand down, he looked at her, blinking rapidly several times as if trying to figure out exactly who she was. Then, he hooked his thumbs in his gunbelt. "Rhiannon, I'm beginning to understand Eddie."

"Eddie?"

"Yes . . . Eddie. Your brother who's always having to fight everybody in town because of you? That Eddie."

Rhiannon looked at him and wet her lips. "Does that mean you'll help us?"

Chapter Fifteen

Does that mean you'll help us? Hank couldn't believe it. Yes, he could, as he looked over at Rhiannon riding so desultorily along beside him. Susie trailed behind in her father's clothes and driving her father's wagon. What choice had he, since Watson had knocked on his bedroom door right then to tell him there was a wagonload of . . . ladies to see him? And now those ladies were ensconced in two of the guest bedrooms at his house, with more maids and hot water and clean beds and good food than they'd ever seen.

And some fatalistic instinct told him that his aunts' reaction to having two . . . soiled doves in their home would fit right in with the rest of this bizarre turn of events. Joy. They would react with joy. They loved company. Hank could just see it all now. His aunts having high tea with Cat and Scarlet in the morning room. For crying out loud. What the hell was he going to do with them—all of them?

And what the hell was he going to do about Big John? His reaction to his fancy ladies being gone, with the revenue he made off their labors, would be far from joy. Far from it. Hank wished he'd left his gun on, but second thoughts had caused him to take it off. He didn't normally wear one, and the sight of him with one on could only cause rampant rumors that trouble was brewing.

Speaking of trouble, Hank looked over at Rhiannon. He could wring her beautiful little neck. After he finished kissing it for the next thousand years. How in the hell had he gotten mixed up with her? But try as he might, he just couldn't seem to remember a time in his life when she hadn't been in it, or in his thoughts, or in his blood. If only there were some way to get her back in his bed... as his wife.

Finally, Rhiannon broke the silence. "What are we going to do now?"

The question surprised him, but it shouldn't have. "We? You mean you hadn't thought this grand scheme of yours through, past getting Cat and Scarlet to the protection of my house?"

Hank looked back at Susie Johnson when Rhiannon did. Her expression under her father's hat gave her the appearance of a startled bird. She was clearly going to be of no help to Rhiannon right now. Hank fought back a grin and turned a questioning gaze on Rhiannon.

"No," Rhiannon said.

A heavy sigh escaped him. He didn't think that he'd ever sighed in his entire life until this summer. "Well, let's see what we have. At this point, the only safe ones in this whole scheme are Cat and Scarlet, and that's only until Savage discovers them missing. Which he may not do for a while." Then, a thought struck him. "I assume that he was at the barn dance when you raided his establishment?"

Seeing her nod, he continued. "Good. Then he may not know yet. We won't know until we get to town. The first thing we have to do is get you two back to your homes undetected and changed and at the festivities. And think up some excuse as to where you've been, because even though I suspect Miss Johnson's absence could conceivably

Thrill to the most sensual, adventure-filled Historical Romances on the market today...

FROM LEISURE BOOKS

As a home subscriber to the Leisure Romance Book Club, you'll enjoy the best in today's BRAND-NEW Historical Romance fiction. For over twenty years, Leisure Books has brought you the award-winning, high-quality authors you know and love to read. Each Leisure Historical Romance will sweep you away to a world of high adventure...and intimate romance. Discover for yourself all the passion and excitement millions of readers thrill to each and every month.

Save $5.00 Each Time You Buy!

Six times a year, the Leisure Romance Book Club brings you four brand-new titles from Leisure Books, America's foremost publisher of Historical Romances. EACH PACKAGE WILL SAVE YOU $5.00 FROM THE BOOKSTORE PRICE! And you'll never miss a new title with our convenient home delivery service.

Here's how we do it. Each package will carry a FREE 10-DAY EXAMINATION privilege. At the end of that time, if you decide to keep your books, simply pay the low invoice price of $14.96, no shipping or handling charges added. HOME DELIVERY IS ALWAYS FREE. With today's top Historical Romance novels selling for $4.99 and higher, our price SAVES YOU $5.00 with each shipment.

AND YOUR FIRST FOUR-BOOK SHIPMENT IS TOTALLY FREE!

IT'S A BARGAIN YOU CAN'T BEAT! A Super $19.96 Value!

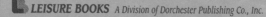

LEISURE BOOKS *A Division of Dorchester Publishing Co., Inc.*

GET YOUR 4 FREE BOOKS
NOW—A $19.96 Value!

*Mail the Free Book
Certificate
Today!*

Get Four Books Totally FREE— A $19.96 Value!

▼ Tear Here and Mail Your FREE Book Card Today! ▼

PLEASE RUSH
MY FOUR FREE
BOOKS TO ME
RIGHT AWAY!

Leisure Romance Book Club
65 Commerce Road
Stamford CT 06902-4563

AFFIX
STAMP
HERE

go unnoticed for some time, I seriously doubt that yours will be for more than a few minutes."

Hank was glad to see she had the good grace to look down and not to look offended. Still, he hated seeing her look so contrite. He had the insane urge to ruffle her feathers some just to see that crusading spirit light up her eyes. He loved her best when she was on a tear, he realized. "Of course, there is a ready solution to all this that could forestall any trouble at all with Big John."

Her head popped up and huge ginger eyes looked hopefully over at him. "Yes?"

"We could just make an even swap."

"Swap?"

"Yes. You and Miss Johnson for Cat and Scarlet. I'm sure Big John would be more than satisfied." Hank did a slow count, seeing how many seconds it took for that to sink in. Three, four, five—

"What?!" Rhiannon shrieked, reining her little mare so sharply that Hank's paint stallion was a few paces ahead before he could get the big horse stopped. A small dust storm swept by him and Rhiannon as Susie fought to bring her startled team to a stop, which she did with only an inch to spare.

"You don't like that idea, I take it?" His chuckling laugh did nothing to endear him with her, he saw.

She glared over at him, every bit as rigid as her mare's stance. "Damn you, Hank Wolfe! You're lucky you left that gun of yours behind, or I'd use it on you. Why, the very idea! I can't believe you'd suggest such a thing, and not even knowing yet if I'm carrying your child!"

Hank appraised her for a moment and then cut his eyes over at Susie, who was trying valiantly to appear as if she hadn't just heard what she'd just heard. "Well, don't leave me and Miss Johnson in suspense, Miss O'Shea. Are you?"

Rhiannon's eyes widened in guilty shock; a telling red stain crept up her face. Her lips worked angrily before she spat out, "No, I'm not! There! Are you satisfied?"

"Actually, no. I suppose we'll just have to try again." Hank felt his body's quickening response to just the mere suggestion of bedding Rhiannon again.

Their gazes locked, and the silence stretched out interminably, only to be broken by Susie's timid little voice. "If you'll excuse me, I'll go on ahead . . . and leave you two alone. We may not draw as much notice if we go our separate ways."

She didn't wait for a response, which was good because she didn't get one. She clucked to her team and pulled them around the frozen statues of Hank and Rhiannon. She was some distance away in the dusty flatness of western Kansas before the spell was broken by the impatient stamping of the horses under the lovers.

"We're wasting time sitting here," Hank remarked evenly, being deliberately vague. Let her draw her own conclusions about whether he meant joining the festivities in town or . . . trying again.

"You're right," she said just as evenly, just as vaguely. She dug her heels into her mare's sides.

After that, they rode on in silence until they reached Rhiannon's home, having skirted the main streets of Wolfe and come in by a back road. Hank followed Rhiannon's lead as she directed them to the back of the house, where she dismounted and then appeared surprised to see Hank doing the same thing.

"What are you doing?"

"I'm coming in with you."

"Why? Why don't you just go on to the barn dance? Do you think it's wise for us to appear there together?"

"We don't have to appear there together. But I'm coming in now with you while you change."

"Why?"

"Because we don't know if Big John knows yet, that's why." He looked toward the quiet house and then back at her. "It doesn't look like anyone's here; probably not even

Ella. I've been to enough of these town get-togethers in the past six months to know that if your mother's involved, Ella's involved. So, do you want to be alone here if Big John shows up?"

Her forehead wrinkled; she vigorously shook her head no.

"I didn't think so. Come on." He took her elbow and moved her toward the back door.

Hank had been right, Rhiannon mused. Ella wasn't here, either. In fact, Rhiannon and Hank were alone in the house. She'd left him alone downstairs sitting in the long shadows of the parlor since he didn't want to draw attention by lighting a lamp. And she was upstairs trying to change çlothes in the same dusky light. Undoing her brother's shirt with fumbling fingers, she attributed her clumsiness and the high heat in her cheeks to the anticipation of the dance. But her woman's body knew differently; her symptoms were directly attributable to a heightened awareness of Hank's presence with her in the otherwise empty house.

The light knocking on her bedroom door stilled her fingers on the buttons and sent her heart racing. She swallowed hard and looked at the door with an intensity of effort that should have allowed her to see right through it. "Yes?"

"Rhiannon?"

"Yes?" she breathed on the end of a whisper. His deep, smooth voice saying her name had awakened and moistened her female place.

"I'm coming in."

She was silent for a moment. A thousand reasons why he shouldn't went through her mind. But what she said was: "I know."

The door opened without protest at his touch. Just like me, she thought. And then he was in the room and closing the door behind him. He turned the key in the lock, a gesture that seemed necessary even though they were alone. Her room was not very large; and especially not with him in it. Only one step brought him to her. He looked down at her with black eyes burning with an animal intensity. Rhiannon was lost, drowning. Had breathing not been automatic, she would have died right there.

While his eyes held her soul, his hands, with slow, sure movements, undid the remaining buttons. Never releasing her gaze, he slipped the overly large shirt off her shoulders; it fell unheeded to the floor. And then he was undoing the laces of her summer camisole; the gooseflesh belied the heat of his fingers as they touched the bare skin of her chest.

Rhiannon's eyes fluttered closed, and she rocked back on her heels. Hank caught her at the front of her denims by the waistband and began opening them. Other than his one hand holding her steady, he did not touch her. Rhiannon breathed shallowly in the thin air that was their slow, burning desire. She again felt his touch; this time it was his fingers on her belly. She heard a low moan and realized it was her. She would die if he didn't soon kiss her, didn't soon take her, didn't soon love her.

The pleasurable sensations were greatly heightened with her eyes closed. It was as if he were a shadowy presence in a dream, one she could not control but could only submit to, one who could touch her where he wished, one who could control her responses by never letting her know where next he might touch her. And so it was that she nearly collapsed when his warm, moist lips found the tender spot on her neck where it met her shoulder. As he nuzzled there with infinite tenderness, she felt a flooding of desire warm her abdomen. She couldn't wait much longer, but this slowness, in the growing darkness of the room, in the complete darkness of her closed eyes, was too delicious to rush.

"Tell me, Rhiannon. Tell me. What is it you want?" His words were breathed into the shell of her ear; the warmth of his breath, as well as the heat of his words, fanned the baby hairs on her neck.

She opened her eyes as much as she could against the drooping heaviness of her lids. She saw his eyes glittering down at her; his high cheekbones slanted in a line, drawing her gaze to his mouth. "Oh, God, Hank. You. Only you. Nothing more but you. I love you. Please, I can't wait any longer. Don't make me beg."

A wolfish grin formed on his wide, firm mouth. "You're mine," he growled in a low voice. It was then, and only then, that he took her in his arms for a hard, intimate kiss that rocked Rhiannon's world. When it ended, they both were breathing raggedly and helping each other to undress.

Rhiannon was naked first, totally unashamed to be bare in front of him. It seemed like the most natural thing in the world to have him rubbing his hands over her, smoothing and warming her young, firm body. Countless mirrors had told her that her body was exceptionally formed, that it was slender and curving, yet possessed of a fullness that shouted her womanhood. And now Hank's hands and eyes and lips were confirming her desirability.

No longer content to be only on the receiving end of these delicious sensations, she stilled his hands and reached out for him. Seeing his acquiescence, she nearly tore his clothes off him before she could get him naked in her sight. The sheer magnificence of his male body, so different from hers, so tantalizingly different from hers, so rough yet smooth, so rock-hard yet warm, made her forget she was a lady. Tomorrow he would bear the marks of her nails everywhere she had raked them lovingly over his arms, his chest, and his abdomen. She could not get enough of the feel of him, of the shuddering responses he had to her touch, of the absolute power she had over this wonderful, intoxicating male.

When she took his shaft into her hand for the very first time, he grabbed her shoulders, his grip almost painful. One ragged word was torn from him. "Rhiannon." Watching his face, his eyes closed in ecstasy, her other hand on the wall of his chest, she stroked the pulsing length lightly, slowly until it sprang to a new and heightened life.

Before she'd even realized he'd moved and had taken her with him, she found herself on her bed with Hank over her, nudging her knees apart with one of his. The slow torture was over; in its place was an overwhelming urgency, a sense of now, now, now. Rhiannon brought her bent knees up and locked them around Hank's lean hips. He surprised her, and taught her something new about lovemaking, by pulling her up off the bed to him, putting her arms around his neck, and settling her on him, slowly bringing her down until she completely ensheathed him in her tightness; so slowly that she was completely wild with wanting him.

Almost instantly, an instinct as old as the rhythm of the universe, and as new as the love she'd just discovered in her heart for Hank, put her hips into motion. Hank cupped her bottom in his hands and suckled each of her nipples in turn as Rhiannon rocked them, setting a driving tempo that quickly, deliciously, painfully took them to a place of purely physical pleasure, a place that didn't allow for thought, for the outside world, for the differences that separated them. It allowed only feeling; only pulsing, rippling, heated . . . explosive release that rung cries from both of them. A release that took them over the edge into a spiraling blackness that had nothing to do with the night, nothing to do with their eyes being closed, nothing to do with anything except their own creation.

When it was over, when the last pulsing spasm had died, they stayed as they were, content in the love-slickened patina and slipperiness of each other's embrace. Content to just be holding each other.

Minutes later, when Rhiannon was capable of thought again, she realized she had her mouth on Hank's shoulder, that she'd actually bitten him. Curious, and not appalled in the least as a corner of her mind told her she should be, she ran her fingers over the spot; they registered only the faintest impression of her small teeth. She'd marked him as hers, as surely as this coupling had marked them as one.

"I bit you," she confessed, looking into his face, memorizing each detail.

"I know," he answered, intent on nuzzling her jaw.

"Did it hurt?" She traced the shell of his ear with one finger.

"Yes." He kissed the point of her chin.

"I'm sorry." She flicked at the corded muscles of his neck with the tip on her tongue.

"Are you?" He raised her slightly on him so he could reach the hard bud of her breast.

"No." She shuddered as his mouth closed over the sensitive area. She entangled her hands in his hair. "Hank, I think—"

"I know." He maneuvered them, without separating them, to lie stretched out on the bed, Rhiannon under him.

She couldn't believe it. He was hard again inside her.

"The saints preserve us, here she is! Where on earth have you been, Rhiannon? I've had the Devil's own time making excuses for you!" Patience O'Shea railed at her daughter. She kept her voice deliberately low and hid her agitation with a tight smile, for the benefit of the milling crowd that moved around them over by the long wooden tables that practically bowed under the weight of the many delicious foods that had been made for the picnic.

Ella stood just behind and to one side of her employer, wiping her hands on her apron and eyeing Rhiannon archly. Patience had immediately pulled her errant daughter over to her, looking her up and down to be sure she was dressed properly. She pulled and tugged on Rhiannon's calico skirt and loose white blouse until she was satisfied.

"I'm sorry, Mother, I couldn't help it . . . truly. There was a problem with the campaign and something that needed my personal attention. I came as soon as I could." Well, it wasn't a lie. Cat was involved in the campaign. And her personal attention? That part was for Hank. Certainly, this second . . . interlude had only entangled their lives even more. They'd parted with nothing settled between them, except the shared knowledge and indulgence of their fierce attraction to each other. But she knew it went much deeper than that. And that was the tangle. What to do about it?

"Campaign problem?" Patience said, stepping back. "Oh, dear God, what now? Will there be no end to this?"

"Nothing for you to worry about, Mother. It's over. I handled it." Until Big John finds out. A thrill of fear skirted through her at the prospect of having to see him this evening—before and after he found out.

"And thass ex-act-ly what worries me," Ella cut in, crossing her arms under her bosom.

Rhiannon felt the color come to her cheeks. Having Ella see her in Hank's arms had been about the worst thing that could have happened. If she only knew. "Thank you for your vote of confidence, Ella."

Ella snorted and turned away to set out more food, stir this, open that. She muttered to herself as she went down the line of tables. Rhiannon watched her for a moment and then turned back to her mother, forcing a lightness she did not feel. "Well, the problem is past, and I'm here now." She looked around at all the festive banners and the obvious pains her mother's organization had gone through to make this event a successful one. If only Rhiannon could harness all these organizational skills for her campaign. But she knew that this event was probably about the only level on which her mother and her friends would be willing to be involved. "My compliments to the Ladies Aid Society. Everything is wonderful—all this food! Why, look at all the lights and the banners. I'm impressed, Mother."

Patience O'Shea preened under her daughter's rare compliment of her endeavors. "Why, it was nothing. Just twist an arm here, call in a favor there, and it's done." Then she looked up at her eldest child. "But I guess you're finding that out on your own now, aren't you?" Her voice broke. "My girl is a grown woman now. Sometimes I just can't realize. . . ."

She took out a lace hanky and put it to her nose.

Moved and surprised, Rhiannon took her mother into her embrace for a warm hug. Patience felt warm, soft, and the least bit fragile in her smallness. "Now, Mother, I'll always be your little girl. You know that."

"And now what have you done to make your mother cry?"

Rhiannon looked up to see her father standing on the other side of the serving table. "It appears I've grown up, Father."

"And that made her cry?" He wandered off with his full plate, shaking his head. "Thank God the rest of them was boys."

Rhiannon held her mother away from her, loving the familiar tiny age lines of her face, her thin straight nose, and full little cheeks. "Are you all right now, Mother? I love you, you know."

That brought a fresh rash of tears, onlookers be damned. Still, Patience fluttered her wet hanky at Rhiannon. "Of course, I'm all right. Just being a silly woman. I love you, too, darling. Now, go on, go on. See to your campaign. That's what this is all about. And I'd best go see to your brothers. No telling what trouble they'll find."

Rhiannon parted with her mother, but felt somehow that they were closer than they'd been in years. It was a good feeling. As she worked her way through the gaily chattering crowd, keeping an anxious eye out for Big John, she spotted Susie and nodded to her. Susie, dressed now in her own plain clothes, traded a conspiratorial nod and smile with her. Rhiannon was pleasantly surprised to see her new friend standing in a knot of people and actually chatting, instead of hanging back on the fringes of life. Well, drawing Susie out was one good thing this campaign had done.

Rhiannon spent the evening working her way through the crowd, assuming the roll of politician, shaking hands, chatting, joking, even exchanging barbs, mostly good-natured, with the men who were running against her and the other women. The night, a warm, dry night just like a thousand others in this summer of drought and tension, held the promise of a new unity, perhaps even a healing that they all desperately needed. Rhiannon certainly hoped it lasted.

Before the night was over, she'd eaten more than she should, danced more than she should, talked more than she should, shooed her baby brother, Johnny-Cake, and Charlie Driver, the mayor's son, away from the jars of home brew in the barn at least three times, spent time with her running mates, made political speeches and debated the issues, assured Aunt Penelope and Aunt Tillie that there really was no need to go ahead with wedding plans at this point, and just generally had a wonderful time.

Except for three things. One, Big John seemed to be everywhere she was, and she certainly did not like the looks he and his mean-looking cronies sent her way. But they hadn't done anything but look, so she wasn't too concerned. He'd have done much more than that if he'd already discovered Cat and Scarlet's defection.

Two, no one seemed to be able to find Eddie, her oldest brother. She'd seen her parents searching for him on more than one occasion, but Rhiannon was sure he had sneaked off to be with an equally absent Emily. She completely understood their desire to be alone. The younger couple made her think of her own relationship with Hank. A decision would have to be made there—and soon, before the Misses Penland sent out wedding invitations. MacGregor, Hank's valet, had stayed in Wolfe with the sisters and would see them home. He'd added his disapproving stare to the conversation when it had come around to the sisters' not understanding how the scene they'd witnessed hadn't led to an immediate marriage. At least, Penelope hadn't understood; Tillie had just wanted more pie.

And three, Hank wasn't there. He'd made a brief appearance at the festivities, coming in from the opposite direction as she had earlier, eaten, visited some, and left. And of course she knew why. He needed to be home with Cat and Scarlet to settle them in and get ready for Big John's reaction when he discovered them gone. Hank had told her before he left that he felt she was relatively safe here in Wolfe since the entire town was in the streets. Even if Big John discovered his loss before the night was over, he wouldn't do anything with so many witnesses. She knew Hank was right.

But if her stomach lurched now thinking about his face and his parting words, "We have to talk—about us," it was because she knew she had to tell him they could never again be intimate. It was too complicated and too chancy. She did not want to get pregnant, and therefore have to get married. So why had she cried when she'd gotten her monthly flow last week?

"Fire! Fire!" The shouted word, so feared, but especially in this time of drought, broke into Rhiannon's thoughts as she sat by the barn door fanning her hot face after the latest dance. Her own mouth suddenly dry, she jumped to her feet, as did everyone around her, to look in the direction two young boys were pointing. Sure enough, thick smoke and an occasional lick of red flame shot up over the rooftops. It appeared to be two streets over.

The fiddle music stopped on a discordant note as the news spread rapidly through the assembled people. The men broke through the crowd and began running toward the heat and the light, calling out to each other to form brigades and to get buckets; women grabbed for or called out frantically for missing children; babies cried; horses, smelling smoke and sensing fear, bucked and neighed.

Rhiannon looked all around her; she had to do something. She just couldn't stand here and huddle with these women, wringing her hands. Every hand would be needed at the fire scene. Making up her mind, she turned to the remaining women, some of whom were crying, some of whom appeared

219

to be in shock. Putting her hands up for attention, she called out, "Listen to me! Listen!"

Hushing sounds went through the women. When she had their attention, Rhiannon spoke. "We've got to help. Some of the women are already there. We have to go, too. If you will, some of you stay here with the children. But the rest of us need to go help. We don't know what's on fire! It could be any of your homes or businesses! Every hand will be needed there—we can't afford to hang back now. The men need us to work the buckets while they search out water!"

"So, let's go!" It was big, bossy Joletta Hawkins, bless her. And she was herding the women forward as she spoke. Rhiannon could have kissed her. "You heard the lady. Let's go help the men! Ya'll know they can't do nothing without us telling them how, anyway!"

Her words drew a laugh from the women and started their feet moving forward. As they left, some of them pushed their children toward other women who had babies in their arms and so would be staying behind; Effie Parsons, herself so very pregnant, seemed to be in charge of the women watching over the little ones. Rhiannon smiled at Effie and got a shy smile in return. She then turned and, sure of the women's support, picked up her calico skirt and began running toward the trouble. Typical, a corner of her mind noted.

They slowed down their pace as they approached the fire; the smoke was thick and choking this close to its source. It was Gruenwald's. The dry-goods store was burning. The women stopped in shock at the scene that greeted them. A serpentine line of men was passing full, sloshing buckets of precious water on up toward the store. Other men were running to and fro, hoarsely yelling for more buckets, more water. Some men, overcome by heat and exhaustion, were being dragged back a safe distance. Doc Johnson was bent over one man, administering help.

"Daddy!" Susie Johnson yelled, grabbing two other women to go with her to help her father treat the fallen.

The women fanned out, appearing to sense where they were needed, each according to her own strengths. Rhiannon, like several of the women, broke into the line and quickly picked up the cadence of the passing buckets. It was a mind-numbing job, passing heavy bucket after heavy bucket. She looked down the line; each bucket was being dumped into a huge water barrel in the bed of a wagon. In turn, that water was then pumped, by two men working the pumping unit, through a hose forcefully onto the blaze. She looked at the store; most of the fire seemed to be at the back of the wooden building where she and the women had been having their meetings. They'd have to find another place to meet now, but that was really the least of her concerns. By craning her neck she could see the fire hadn't spread yet to the building next to it, the barbershop. That was one piece of luck.

She could tell they were having an effect on the fire, because of the hissing sound and the thick grayish-white smoke that was billowing out of the building. Choked, her throat and eyes stinging, her lungs full, just like the men around her, Rhiannon turned her head to cough. And spied Big John and his cronies sitting casually on the front porch of the Fancy Lady. The bastards. They even had drinks in their hands as they all sat with their feet propped up on the hitching rail. Some of them were even smiling. They wouldn't even lift a hand to help their neighbors, the same men who would have come running if it had been the saloon that were on fire. The same men who bought their drinks at that very saloon. Rhiannon hoped, prayed, the men would notice. And she began to look forward to Carry Nation's visit. Maybe a little temperance was needed around here.

Rhiannon brought her attention back to her task. Her arms felt like lead weights, and her back was protesting the twisting and turning she did to pass the precious buckets. She was so afraid she would drop one. Gritting her teeth, she concentrated all that much more fiercely, ignoring the tendrils of her hair that fell into her face, ignoring the painful splinters of wood that worked their way into her palms from the rough buckets, ignoring the urge to cry out of sheer exhaustion.

But like the men and women around her, she worked silently, conserving her oxygen and her energy for the never-ending buckets. She tried desperately to numb her mind, to suspend her thoughts; somehow that made it easier not to notice how blazing hot the air was, how alive it was with flying sparks of burned matter that floated on the smoke and fell onto people's hair and clothing. Every now and then someone would bat at himself or his neighbor, trying to put out the embers. And so Rhiannon was not surprised when it was her turn to feel someone hitting at her back. She didn't even spare this kind person a glance because she had to deal with another bucket.

But she was surprised when strong arms reached over her and took the bucket in her stead and passed it down the line. She looked back and up. It was Hank, and he was looking down at her, tender and grim at the same time. She wanted to melt into him and give in to tears, but she was too tired to move and too dried out from the heat and smoke to do either, so she just stood there. Until he used a pause in the line of buckets to move her behind him and to step into her place in the line. "Go sit down and get some water," he ordered.

But she didn't. She couldn't. Her arms and legs were as heavy as wet sand. Frozen in place, she numbly watched the play of muscles under Hank's shirt, which quickly became sweat-stained right down his spine; she registered that he was standing with his booted feet planted apart, his long muscular legs easily supporting his weight; she could see his black hair curling over his collar; she saw his large hands easily handling the buckets. She could see him, watch him, register details about him, and love him, but she couldn't move. She couldn't sit down, she couldn't fall down. Until the world began spinning and then went black.

Chapter Sixteen

When she awoke, it was to a sensation of floating on air, as if her body wafted effortlessly through a liquid night. A familiar man-scent filled her nostrils, bringing a contented smile to her lips. She curved into the wall she was nestled against; it felt warm and solid, even slightly yielding. Then, memory returned. The fire! Her body jerked in response to the scare; steel bands tightened around her back and under her legs. Her eyes popped open wide.

"It's okay, Rhiannon. I've got you. Hold still. You fainted, but you're all right. I'm taking you home." It was Hank, and he was carrying her home.

She sank back against the warm protection of his chest, feeling weak and sick, her hand gripping his wet shirt, not even minding the smell of smoke and sweat that mingled with the Hank-smell that she loved. As her head cleared, she could hear the fading sounds of people calling out and horses neighing. She also became aware that there were other people around them, and they too were walking away from the business part of Wolfe.

"Is the fire out?" she asked, surprised at how low and raspy her voice was. And at how much it hurt to talk.

"Yes," Hank answered easily. "I think you're going to have to find another place for your campaign headquarters."

"Is it all gone?"

"Yes, it's all gone. The whole store burned."

"Was anybody hurt?"

"You mean besides you?" There was a hint of amusement in his voice. "No, no one was hurt. Thank God."

She looked up at his soot-smudged, tired, handsome face. "I'm not hurt. You can put me down."

He stopped and looked down into her face. "Okay." He put her down; her knees immediately buckled. He caught her and picked her up again, shaking his head.

Rhiannon put her arms around his neck. She could see in the moonlit night that they were nearly to her house. "How did you know about the fire?"

"I was riding back into town when I saw the smoke and flames."

"Why?"

"Why what?"

"Why were you riding back into town?"

He chuckled and the vibrations in his chest rumbled through her, too. She liked that feeling. "Because I knew I couldn't leave you alone for very long before you'd get yourself into trouble."

It's hard to argue with someone who's carrying you, but she tried anyway. "I do not. And I do not need a champion."

"If you say so."

"Quit grinning."

"I'm not."

"You are so."

"Here we are."

"What?"

"Here we are at your house."

Rhiannon looked around her, and her disappointment grew.

Yes, here was her house, and there were lights on inside. She didn't want her ride to be over. She looked up at him. He was grinning again. "What is so funny?" she asked.

"Nothing."

"Is my hair mussed or something?"

He laughed out loud at that, and her frustration with him grew. "More like it's singed."

"Put me down."

"We already tried that."

"I will not be carried into my house only to scare the life out of my parents."

"Well, then, should I just leave you in a heap here at the gate? You can't walk, Rhiannon. You're exhausted, most likely from the heat and the smoke in your lungs. Now, cooperate for once in your life and unlatch the damned gate."

Feeling small for being petty and ungrateful after all he'd done for her, Rhiannon bit back her retort and reached out to unlatch the gate. Just as he walked through the opening, she said, "I'm sorry."

He stopped dead in his tracks, kicking the gate closed behind him with his boot. "What did you say?"

"I said I'm sorry. Is that so hard to accept?"

"No. It just surprised me, coming from you."

"Now what does that mean?"

"It means you don't usually apologize, or even seem to realize you need to. You just tackle everything and everybody all hell-bent for leather and leave the strewn bodies in your wake, that's all."

"I do not."

He looked into her eyes, his brow arched in a challenge. "I do?"

"Yes, you do."

She looked into his eyes. "You don't like me very much, do you?"

He slumped the slightest bit, but still maintained his grip

on her. "Goddammit, Rhiannon. Very much? No, I don't like you very much. I like you too damned very much."

She felt a thrill of triumph ride the crest of her nerves. "Then why does that make you mad?"

"Because," he exploded, "if I had any goddamned sense, I'd toss you right into that scraggly west Kansas bush right over there and walk away and get the hell out of Wolfe for good."

In the silence that followed his outburst, the front door to her home flew open. Patience O'Shea came running out in her nightclothes, closely followed by Ella and all three O'Shea brothers. "Oh, my God, what's happened? Rhiannon, what's wrong? It was that fire, wasn't it? Oh, my poor baby! I just knew I shouldn't have left so early in the evening!" She whipped around to face the boys. "This is all your fault—eating too much, running around and carrying on until I had to bring all three of you home! Now look what's happened!" All three boys' eyes popped open wide; they got no sympathy from Ella, either. She crossed her arms and voiced her disapproval. After glaring at her sons for emphasis, Patience turned back to Hank and Rhiannon. "Your father came home to tell me that the store was on fire, and then he left again to go see to the poor Gruenwalds. Where is she hurt, Mr. Wolfe?" She reached for her daughter, as if to check her for injuries, but was cut off by Eddie's strident voice.

"For crying out loud, Mother, let the man speak!"

"Well, Eddie, I'm just concerned about your sister. Now hush and let Mr. Wolfe talk." She relented some towards the boys, and put an arm around Johnny-Cake's shoulder as he clung to her legs. Paddy stood at her other side, his hands at his waist.

Rhiannon was surprised to hear Eddie talking like that to their mother, but was more surprised by the note of respect in his voice for Hank. Usually, Eddie didn't like anybody who was an adult; it was a stage he was going through. Rhiannon remembered it only too well—she'd only gotten out of it in the past month herself.

She looked up at Hank, who was grinning at Eddie. "She's all right; she's just exhausted from working the fire."

"Working the fire? Rhiannon?" It was Eddie and he was plainly incredulous.

"She was in the relay line for the buckets. From what I hear, she's responsible for getting all the women involved in helping out. A true hero—who's getting heavy."

Rhiannon shot him an outraged look. Heavy?

"My goodness, where are my manners? Bring her this way, Mr. Wolfe. Get out of the way, boys, Ella. Let Mr. Wolfe through."

But Hank couldn't get by Patience O'Shea. She was the one blocking the walk up to the house. Finally, she realized it and scooted on ahead of him, shooing the two younger boys ahead of her. Ella went next, but Eddie followed at a more manly pace behind his mother and ahead of Hank.

Once inside, Ella finally stated her opinion, shaking her head and muttering, with a rising and falling pitch, "Uhm-uhm-uhm-uhm-uhm. Ain't nobody done asked me what I think. So I sure ain't going to say nothing."

Hank ignored her, and then surprised them all by announcing, "I'll just take her on up to her bedroom." And then he proceeded to do just that. From her vantage point in his arms, Rhiannon could see all the little black O's that were her family's mouths. She wanted to shrink into the wallpaper of the stairwell.

When Hank laid her on her bed and straightened up, the memory of this afternoon, the two of them right here in her bed and the things they'd done together, was in his eyes.

Rhiannon felt it, too. They'd made love in his bed and now in her bed. And that was just the thing she needed to talk to him about. "Hank?"

"Yes?" he breathed, leaning over her, resting his fisted hands on the bedspread and to either side of her.

Cheryl Anne Porter

"When you get back downstairs, would you please explain to my family exactly how it was that you knew which bedroom was mine?"

As Hank shaved the next morning, he kept nicking his neck every time he pictured himself carrying Rhiannon unerringly and without directions right into her bedroom. If he didn't quit laughing, he was going to cut his own damned throat. Talk about a pregnant silence when he'd come back down. Ouch, goddammit; he put his finger to the latest cut. And just his luck, Edwin O'Shea, Senior, had arrived home and had joined his family at the foot of the stairs when Hank finally came back down. They'd all just stood there and stared at him, and had silently parted for him to walk through their midst and out of the house. He'd felt their eyes on his back, too. Hank knew for a fact that his red face was what had lit his way back to his horse in town. That was the first time he'd blushed since he'd been out of the nursery, he was sure.

With a sigh, a newly formed habit of his, Hank completed his shaving. Drying his face off, he decided he wouldn't be surprised if he had a call today from Mr. O'Shea demanding that Hank marry his daughter. As if he hadn't tried.

There was a knock on his door. "Come in."

MacGregor entered, his face carefully blank. "There's a Mr. O'Shea to see you, sir."

Hank muttered a long string of foul epithets.

MacGregor bowed. "Indeed, sir. I'll send him your regards and inform him you'll be right down." He then very stiffly left the room. And that was the way it had been between him and MacGregor since he'd walked in on his master and Rhiannon in bed and there hadn't been a wedding yet.

Looking at the closed door, Hank used every foul word that he knew as he pulled on his shirt and tucked it into his pants. His vocabulary was sufficiently large enough to see him into his boots and with his hair combed. He was making up combinations as he loped down the two staircases that would take him downstairs and into the morning room.

When he opened the door, a very formally pressed, starched, and dressed Edwin O'Shea, Senior, was standing in front of the marble fireplace, his hat in his hands and obviously very ill at ease at being here. Hank felt sorry for him. The opulence of this damned place was pretty overwhelming. But he knew that it wasn't the house that was upsetting the man; it was the owner.

"Edwin," he said by way of greeting, offering his hand.

Edwin shook it readily enough, but just bobbed his head without speaking. He kept looking everywhere but at Hank.

"Cigar? Coffee? Breakfast?" Hank urged, trying to be a good host and to put Edwin O'Shea at ease.

Edwin shook his head no.

Hank hated to rush the man, but he truly had one hell of a mountain of work to take care of today. And since he believed he knew the nature of the man's errand, and since he knew for a fact that it was useless, given Rhiannon's prior refusal to marry him, he took the helm. "Please, sit down, Edwin."

Finally, he did. Hank sat, too. "Let me make this easy for you," Hank began. "I believe I know why you're here. And I don't blame you."

"You don't?"

Hank hated like hell that he'd put Edwin O'Shea in such a difficult predicament—how do you demand that your employer do the proper thing by marrying your daughter, with whom he was already intimate and so had ruined her honor, without losing your livelihood in the bargain? Edwin O'Shea was one hell of a banker, a friend, and a good man. Hank felt the first tiny tendrils of guilt and shame for his actions that he'd felt in recent years.

"It's about Rhiannon, Mr. Wolfe." His Irish accent could have crushed a horse it was so heavy.

"Please call me Hank—under the circumstances."

Edwin looked ready to bolt at that. But he didn't. "It's come to me attention that me own daughter and yourself are . . . are . . ."

"Yes, we are," Hank urged. He could tell that Edwin had a little speech all prepared, and there would be no hurrying him through it.

"Well, now, you admit it then?"

"Yes."

Edwin stood up, angry now, not humble, not afraid. Hank wanted to cheer him for having a backbone. He knew it was a hard thing to do, to stand up to a Wolfe in this house. After all, hadn't that been what he'd had to do himself his whole young life? He knew firsthand what it was like to try to face down someone you felt held your entire future in his hands.

"Mr. Wolfe, you've ruined me girl's reputation and her virtue. Me entire family is very distraught over this matter. And I'm here, as the girl's father, to tell you that you will be marrying her." He nodded his head once for final emphasis. There, he'd said his speech.

Hank stood up and looked Edwin right in the eye. "I would love to marry your daughter."

"Ye would?" Edwin sat down rather heavily on the dainty chair behind him.

"Yes, I would. In fact, I've already asked her."

"Ye have?" Edwin stood back up.

"I have. Only she said no."

"She did?" Edwin sat back down.

"She did. Over a week ago."

"A week ago?" This time he stayed seated.

"She wants nothing to do with marriage, Edwin. She wants her freedom."

"Her freedom?" Edwin hopped back up. And this time his anger wasn't directed at Hank. "Her blasted freedom, is it? Do ye have any idea how many times I've heard that same blarney from the girl? Do ye? And what if there's a babe growing in her? What about freedom then?"

"She agreed she would marry me if there is a baby. But she already told me there isn't."

The import of that statement—that the two had been intimate long enough for Rhiannon to have had a flow—pinned Edwin to his seat. "I thought, Hank, we'd done a better job of raising the girl."

Despite Edwin's finally calling him by his first name, Hank felt his anger rising. There was nothing wrong with Rhiannon. "You've done a great job of raising her, Edwin. She's independent, headstrong—"

"And that's just what's wrong!"

"No, that's just what's right. She is beautiful, spirited, exciting, intelligent. . . ." Hank's voice trailed off under the older man's scrutiny.

"Ye really care about me own girl then, don't ye?"

Hank sat down, for the first time feeling like the suitor asking the father for the girl's hand. "Yes, I do. Very much. Only she won't have me."

"And why is that, Hank?"

He sighed and sat back on the sofa. "Because she wants to be mayor first."

"Great God in Heaven." He said it with all due respect and reverence, for it was a prayer.

"Indeed, as my valet says," Hank drawled.

Just then the door opened and in trooped Aunt Penelope, Aunt Tillie, Cat LaFlamme, and Scarlet Calico. Cat and Scarlet were particularly impressive in various and sundry pieces of the Misses Penlands' wardrobes.

"Let me tell you, Hank, this here little lady"—Cat had an arm around Aunt Tillie—"can really pack away the grub for such a tiny little thing. I thought for sure me and Scarlet was back at the Fancy Lady at mealtime."

Aunt Tillie looked especially pleased to have found a friend who appreciated her particular talent. But Aunt Penelope, her hands clasped at her waist, had a pinched look on her face.

She kept cutting her eyes over at Scarlet, who was copying every gesture of hers and practicing each graceful movement several times until she felt comfortable with it.

With a sinking feeling in the pit of his stomach, Hank cut his own eyes over at Edwin O'Shea. Just as he'd expected; had the older man's horse come in to tell him he was ready to go and was tired of waiting, Edwin could not have looked more stunned.

"Would you like a whiskey, Edwin?" Hank asked, a droll, defeated inflection in his voice.

With his eyes on the parade of ladies, as they nodded their greetings and proceeded out through the French doors and into the small garden, Edwin said blankly, "Please."

As Hank got up to go to the whiskey bottles off to one side of the room, he thought he knew what the next question would be.

"Does Rhiannon know that those . . . ladies are out here?"

Hank kept pouring. It was early but, hell, Edwin was going to need this. "Yes, she does. As a matter of fact, she brought them out here."

Silence followed. Then: "Make that a double."

Hank turned around with the drinks in his hands. "Already done."

Rhiannon figured she probably shouldn't venture out today, seeing as how her lungs still ached and her throat was raspy, and seeing as how Big John had to know by now, nearly lunchtime, that Cat and Scarlet were gone. But caution had never been her strong suit, so here she was in the buckboard wagon on her way to the Gruenwalds' with Ella; the bundled-up clothing and dishes of food that Ella and her mother had prepared for the unfortunate family bumped along in the back. Patience O'Shea had left a note telling Rhiannon that she was to accompany Ella to the Gruenwalds', while Patience took the boys to the schoolhouse for some summer instruction from Mrs. Calvert, their teacher. She'd concluded that she would be along later with the boys to ride home with Ella in the wagon.

Rhiannon was secretly glad that her family had not been at home when she got up. She still didn't know how she was going to explain, to anyone's satisfaction, how Hank had known which bedroom was hers. The truth was too . . . evident. Luckily, Ella hadn't seen fit, not yet at least, to give her the benefit of her thinking. She'd just looked over at her favorite child, as she called each one of the O'Shea offspring, and muttered, "Uhm-uhm-uhm."

Rhiannon, trying to ignore Ella and to forestall the inevitable lecture, turned her thoughts to the upcoming meeting with her running mates; she figured most, if not all of them, except for Emma Calvert, the schoolteacher, and Cat, would be at Freda Gruenwald's doing the same thing she was— seeing how she could help. If and while they were there, she was going to try to corner them to decide on a new neutral meeting place . . . and to tell them that Cat LaFlamme would soon be available to campaign with them.

Thinking of Cat, Rhiannon tried not to smirk as they rode by the drawn windows and closed doors of the Fancy Lady. Nothing looked out of the ordinary on the outside; the saloon didn't normally open until later in the afternoon, anyway. But inside? Whoo, she bet there were fireworks.

She really wasn't all that worried about Big John; he couldn't know she'd had anything to do with the girls' disappearance. She and Susie had been too cautious. Oh, he'd probably suspect her, but that would be all he could do. And she would have all she could do not to flaunt it in his face if he confronted her. Well, rash she might be, but she wasn't stupid. He wouldn't hear a confession from her.

In fact, the more she thought about it, the only confessing that needed to be going on was Big John's about the fire at the dry-goods store. She had more than a sneaking hunch that he was responsible or knew who was. It was awfully suspicious that the fire had started at the back of the store—

where the women met. Well, if it had occurred to her, it had probably occurred to other people as well, like Sheriff Parsons, Effie's husband.

Pulling the wagon to a halt in front of the burned-out hulk of the store, Rhiannon smiled, not the least bit surprised to see half the town there, men and women. They looked like worker ants industriously going over the burned-out hulk of the store, sorting through, carrying off, salvaging, crying out every now and then that they'd found something worth keeping.

Rhiannon and Ella got down from the wagon, somewhat surprised to see her mother, brothers, and Emma Calvert standing to one side, all with long expressions on their faces. Somehow—maybe it was the way they were all looking at her—she knew their expressions had nothing to do with the fire. She exchanged a look with Ella.

"Well, you ain't goin' to find nothin' out standin' here starin' at me." Ella waved her away and went around back of the wagon to start unloading. Several people came over to help her; she bossed them around as much as she did the O'Sheas.

Rhiannon hurried over to her mother, smoothing her simple cotton skirt down with a brushing motion of her hand. The day was scorching, without a hint of rain in the clear blue sky. It had just been one dry, beautiful day after another since anyone could remember. She had on as few articles of light-colored clothing as she could decently be seen in public in, but still, moisture trickled down her back and between her breasts. She held her heavy hair up off her neck and fanned under it as she walked.

"What are you doing here? Did you finish your lessons so soon?" she asked, a smile on her face, but dread in her heart. Something was definitely wrong. She looked from one to the other of them. They all seemed hesitant to tell her.

Johnny-Cake broke the silence. "We ain't got no school no more." He looked like he didn't know if he was supposed to be happy or sad over that bit of news.

Then, Eddie took a breath and told her, "Mrs. Calvert here got fired from her job. It seems the school board has decided that she isn't fit to be a teacher. They said she was neglecting her duties while she ran for office. And she'd have to decide which one she wanted to be—schoolteacher or politician."

Rhiannon was flabbergasted. "Neglecting her duties? Why, it's summertime. There is no school right now!"

Emma Calvert looked scared and defiant. "It's no use, Rhiannon. I told them all that—your momma told them all that. It's the men. They don't want to make this campaign easy. I told them I'd quit my teaching job."

"And, Rhiannon," her mother cut in, "what is Mrs. Calvert going to do? She has no place else to go. She lived behind the school building."

Rhiannon mulled all this over, trying not to see the accusing looks on all their faces. Somehow this was all her fault. Then, she had an idea. "Mother, what did Father say? He's on the school board. Surely he didn't side with the other men— most of whom are city councilmen, I might add."

Now it was her mother's turn to look uncomfortable. "I haven't exactly talked to your father about this yet."

"Well, let's go talk to him now," Rhiannon ordered, already turning and holding her skirt up slightly.

"Uh, dear, we can't. He's not at the bank right now."

Rhiannon turned back to her mother. "Not at the bank? Well, he's not at home, and he's not here. Where is he?"

Rhiannon had never seen her mother look sheepish about anything before in her life, so it took her a moment to recognize the emotion on her face. And when she did, she knew a horrible sense of dread in the pit of her stomach. "What, Mother? Where is he?"

All heads turned toward Patience O'Shea. She cracked under the pressure. "Why, if you must know, young lady, he's out at the Wolfe mansion demanding that Mr. Wolfe marry you."

Rhiannon gasped; in fact, several gasps were heard, and not all of them came from the little knot formed by the O'Sheas and Mrs. Calvert. There was a decided slowdown in the working pace of the people nearest to them.

"Tell me you're joking, Mother."

Patience O'Shea, her face red, her lips pursed, finally said, "I'll do no such thing. You left us no other choice."

Rhiannon stared blankly at the people in front of her, as if she wasn't sure who they were. Then, she exhaled an "Oh, my God," and turned and ran for the wagon.

Patience, the boys, and Mrs. Calvert ran after her. As Rhiannon bolted up into the driver's seat, she saw her family—including a dumbfounded Ella, whom Eddie hauled up with him without so much as a word of explanation—and then Emma Calvert all pile into the now-empty bed of the wagon. Rhiannon was too angry and too desperate to get to Hank's to argue with them about whether or not they were going. She knew why they thought they had to go, too. With the exception of Emma Calvert, who had nowhere else to go anyway, the O'Sheas and Ella had seen Rhiannon like this too many times to allow her to go off on her own. They knew what she was capable of.

Rhiannon wasn't even shocked to see her mother, all sense of decorum obviously left in the dust, clambering over the buckboard seat to sit by her.

"Not one word, Mother," Rhiannon warned as she backed the team up and turned them towards the outskirts of Wolfe. Knowing exactly what her daughter meant, Patience didn't criticize Rhiannon's handling of the team for once. Indeed, at the pace her daughter was setting for the heavy horses, all she could do was hold onto the seat and her hat.

The ride out to the Wolfe mansion was achieved in record time and in record silence. Sure enough, her father's chaise was out front. Her heart in her throat, Rhiannon braked the wagon, almost setting the horses on their haunches, and jumped down, oblivious as to whether or not her family and Emma were following her. By the loud crunching of the gravel behind her, though, she knew her retinue was close on her heels.

Apparently it was decorum and manners be damned, because Rhiannon didn't wait for anyone to answer the door before she went in. Indeed, how could they, when she hadn't even knocked? Watson appeared from the narrow hallway that went back to Hank's office and eventually the kitchen, took one look at the assemblage in the foyer, and merely pointed to the closed door of the morning room. The man knew his limits.

When Rhiannon turned towards the room, so did everyone else, as if they were a swarm of bees. Just like the front door, she didn't knock on this one, either; she just barged in. . . .

And found her father having tea and a high old time with Hank, the Misses Penland, Cat LaFlamme, and Scarlet Calico.

Greetings flew around the room: "Rhiannon!" "Patience!" "Father!" "Edwin, what on earth?" "Well, howdy, Miss Rhiannon!" "Who're those ladies, Momma?" "Hank!" "Oh, dear, have the girl bring more cakes!" "I'll have more cakes." "Not you, Tillie!" "Lookit our new clothes, Miss Rhiannon!" "Edwin!" "Patience, what are you doing here with the boys?" "Look, Cat, it's Little Eddie!" "Don't nobody ask me nothin'. I'm just along for the ride."

And then, silence reigned. And reigned. Until Hank stood up from his careless sprawl on the sofa and suggested, "Aunt Penelope, why don't you show our guests the gardens and the gazebo while I speak with Miss O'Shea and her parents?"

"Why, that's a lovely idea, Henry. We have so much to celebrate. Such a good-news day. And all this company!"

"Henry? Who's that?" It was Cat.

"I told you before. That's what she calls Hank. Makes him damned mad, too," Tillie fussed.

"But we already seen the gardens," Scarlet pouted.

"Well, you're gettin' ready to see 'em again, girl. Come

on, let's go." Cat stood up, taking charge and herding everyone out, linking her arm with a very red-faced Eddie Junior. "Now, Little Eddie," she was heard to say as the crowd trooped out the door ahead of her, "tell me why you ain't been around to see me and Scarlet lately. Is it because of that little Emily gal you was tellin' us about?"

As the door closed behind Cat and Little Eddie, Rhiannon's parents exchanged a very stunned look, much as if small forest fires were springing up all around them and they didn't know which one to put out first. Rhiannon looked at Hank, and despite everything, had to bite back an oh-no grin, just like he was doing; that sudden coughing fit of his didn't fool her in the least. She put her hands to her waist, tapping her foot and refusing to be sidetracked.

Hank recovered and didn't even try to hide his grin. "Well, Rhiannon, your father and I have had a most interesting conversation."

"I don't doubt it in the least." She shot her father a withering glare, but he only pulled himself up straighter and put his arm around his wife's waist. "Dare I ask what the outcome of it was?" Rhiannon said.

"Well, darling," Hank replied, "it seems we're to be married after all. And damned soon."

Chapter Seventeen

Just as she'd suspected. "I see. And it doesn't matter in the least what my feelings are on the subject?"

Edwin extricated himself from his wife. "As a matter of fact, we did discuss your feelings, daughter."

Rhiannon turned to him. "Oh, did you?"

"Dear, you keep a civil tongue in your head when you're talking to your father."

Rhiannon ignored her mother and kept her eyes on her father. She didn't dare look at Hank, standing there looking all male and relaxed and desirable. Over her initial anger now, having expended it on the ride out here, she was now more susceptible to Hank's considerable physical charm, no matter how much he might make her want to strangle him on this one point of marriage. She concentrated on her father, who was talking to her.

"—and it seems to me, and to Hank, that you have . . . demonstrated your feelings for him quite . . . adequately. At any rate, the deed is done, and now you have to . . . to . . ."

"Get married," Hank finished for him, grinning widely.

And he was the only one grinning. Edwin looked a little flushed and dazed, just like Rhiannon felt, and her mother had started to sob quietly. This was ridiculous and she was just the person to put an end to it.

"There will be no marriage without my consent. And I don't give it." She crossed her arms under her bosom and tried very hard not to poke out her bottom lip, her childhood sign of impending stubbornness.

Edwin O'Shea left his wife's side, where he'd been patting her shoulder, and strode over to his errant daughter. His attitude, one of anger, brought Rhiannon's arms down to her sides and moved her back a step. Over her father's shoulder, she saw Hank tense and that look of wolf-like possessiveness steal over his features. An image of him jerking Eddie up short when he'd laid a hand on her flashed through her consciousness. Her father wasn't a big man, but he was her father, which made him intimidating . . . sometimes.

He stopped in front of her and put his hands on his waist. When he leaned toward her slightly in his agitation, Rhiannon was surprised to smell liquor on his breath. "Now, see here, young lady. You've got the whole town in an uproar over this mayor thing of yours; you've got the nice Misses Penland planning a wedding that you say is not going to happen; you have as much as kidnapped Miss LaFlamme and Miss Calico right out from under one dangerous man's nose; you've got your mother crying, your brothers asking questions I can't answer, and . . . and the Good Lord knows what else—"

"And Gruenwald's burned down, and Emma Calvert fired," Rhiannon added for him, completing his list and making the case against herself even worse. Too late, she saw Hank's eyes narrow even more; he turned his head slightly, listening interestedly, but not interfering . . . not yet.

"What?" her father asked stupidly.

"It's true, Edwin," Patience corroborated, drying her tears. "Talk in Wolfe is that the fire was set. It did start in the back where Rhiannon holds the campaign meetings. And people are saying that John Savage is behind it all."

Edwin turned to Hank; the two men exchanged a look that told Rhiannon she was about to gain a tremendous amount of protection, whether she wanted it or not.

"Now see here—" Rhiannon began.

"Tell me about Mrs. Calvert," Hank ordered, cutting her off. His face brooked no argument.

"The school board fired her," Rhiannon said, making it sound almost like a challenge. She heard her father's gasp, an honest reaction that bespoke his innocence.

"On what grounds?"

"Various ones, but mostly because she's running for office, and with the exception of you, Father, so are all the other members of the board. I think it's pretty dirty."

"I knew nothing about this," Edwin O'Shea protested.

"We know that, dear. But now poor Emma has nowhere to live and no money," Patience said.

All eyes went to Hank. He stared back at each of them in turn, and sighed in defeat. "Of course she can stay here."

Bright smiles from Rhiannon and her mother were his reward.

"On one condition."

The smiles vanished.

"That you, Rhiannon, agree to go nowhere alone, and preferably with an armed escort, which I will provide, until this campaign is over."

Rhiannon could have kissed him. She'd thought he was going to use Emma Calvert's plight as leverage to force her into marriage. But he hadn't; and while she loved him all the more for respecting her freedom and her dream of truly making a difference in the world, she had to admit to the slightest niggling of disappointment that he hadn't pressed his advantage. Irrational, she knew, but . . . there it was. "Agreed," she sighed.

Her father clapped his hands together and began, "Well, good. At least that's one thing—"

241

"On one condition," Rhiannon broke in. Two could play this game.

"And it is?" Hank asked, shooting her a suspicious look.

"That we hold our meetings out here."

"Out here?"

"Out here. Cat and Emma will be staying here; I can't go anywhere in town without armed protection; and Freda Gruenwald has no more store for us to meet in—thank heavens she and her family didn't live there."

"Or they'd now be living out here, too." Hank's voice held a note of amusement.

"Of course," Rhiannon agreed, and then went on. "What's more, I don't believe anyone else will want to lend us space for our meetings. So, your home is perfect. You have the room, and certainly no one would think to harm us here. All I would have to do would be to collect Joletta Hawkins and Susie Johnson and Freda—"

"Stop." Hank held up his hand.

Rhiannon did as she was told for once, looking from Hank to her parents and back to him.

"You can meet here. But on one condition."

"For the love of Mike . . ." It was Edwin. Patience patted his arm soothingly, the look on her face one of complete absorption in the wheeling and dealing going on between her daughter and the high and mighty Mr. Wolfe.

"And the condition is?" Rhiannon asked, using his earlier words.

"That you stay here, too. Until the campaign is over."

"And all without the benefit of marriage?" Edwin boomed, as if remembering his original purpose in coming here today.

"Hush, Edwin. Do go on, Mr. Wolfe," Patience encouraged.

"Thank you, Mrs. O'Shea," Hank responded, nodding his head in respect. He then turned back to Rhiannon. "I've thought better of my previous condition. There's no way I can protect you all the time with you in Wolfe, trying to make the trip back and forth with two other women. It's too risky. And you could be putting your family in jeopardy by staying at home. The simplest thing to do is to install you out here, too, right along with Cat and Mrs. Calvert." He then turned back to Edwin. "I should think they would satisfy any requirement of yours for chaperonage?"

Edwin grumbled and mumbled under his breath for a moment, but finally got a poke in his ribs from his wife. "Oh, I suppose you're right," he blurted out, not the least bit happy. "It is only for a few weeks."

"Perhaps," Hank commented, his voice low and his eyes boring into Rhiannon. "Do you agree, Rhiannon?"

To what? To stay here? Or that it would only be for a few weeks? She swallowed hard, afraid to acknowledge the excitment that was building in her at the thought that with her out here, he might not leave. But just as exciting, just as knee-weakening, was the prospect of being with Hank day . . . and night. "Agreed," she said, letting out a deep breath.

And so it was that, about 30 minutes later, Rhiannon found herself on the wide front steps of the Wolfe mansion with Hank, Cat, Scarlet, Emma, Penelope, and Tillie, waving good-bye to her parents, her brothers, and Ella.

When the O'Shea wagon and chaise were well on their way, Tillie turned back to go inside. "When's lunch?" she grumped.

"Dear, what do you think about roses?"

Rhiannon looked up distractedly from the papers spread out before her all over the long table in the library of the Wolfe mansion, the new campaign headquarters, to see Miss Penelope Penland smiling and holding out for her inspection several cuttings of different types and colors of roses. It took Rhiannon a moment to switch mental gears from campaign strategist to judger of roses. "Why, I love roses, Miss Penland. All sorts." She added that last statement to forestall a discussion on exactly what sort of roses.

Penelope looked very distraught at that. "Oh, dear."

Rhiannon sighed and gave in. The room might be a beehive of activity and noise; there might be close to 30 women in this room alone, working singly or in small groups on some aspect of the six women's campaigns, not to mention those who'd spilled out into the foyer or those upstairs in the ballroom; there might be total chaos surrounding her and 20 decisions to be made in the next five minutes, but Rhiannon was going to have to make time for Miss Penland.

Seeing the old woman standing there, looking down and sadly fingering the different cuttings, Rhiannon felt her heart go out to her. "But I do believe I especially like the ones you grafted yourself a few years back—the yellow ones with the pinkish tips on the petals. They are the most beautiful, Miss Penland."

Penelope perked up immediately. "I told Sister you would like those. I just knew it! And you must call me Aunt Penelope. After all, I'll soon be related to you by marriage, dear."

Rhiannon put a finger up to countermand that notion, for the hundredth time since she'd moved in a few days ago, but never got the chance. For one thing, Penelope moved away, totally happy again and humming a sweet tune. And for another, Rhiannon was mobbed by women with problems, questions, and squabbles.

Much later, when the crowd of volunteers had thinned out considerably, and the remaining workers were putting away their day's labors, Rhiannon sensed another presence and looked up to see Hank standing across the room from her in the doorway. Her heart performed an impossible leap in her chest. She'd scarcely seen him since she'd move in and he'd brought her the clothes that Patience had bundled for him. She had to wonder if his distancing himself was on purpose, much as if he were disinclined to breach the boundaries of etiquette that being her host forced on him. Not once had the door between their bedrooms (he'd had her put in the one that adjoined his) been opened from either side. She wondered if he were waiting for her to make the first move.

But now, he was here, and was leaning a shoulder against the doorjamb, his arms crossed over his broad chest; a warm, indulgent smile extended to his eyes. To Rhiannon, he looked especially handsome, dressed as he was in a black suit and stiff white shirt. She knew he'd been in Wolfe all day, going about the business of running his vast holdings. She'd had no idea before now that it absorbed so much of his time.

For some reason she couldn't fathom, Rhiannon felt suddenly shy in his presence. Perhaps it was his eyes on her. Perhaps it was the other women's eyes on him and her, and the knowing smiles they exchanged with one another. Perhaps it was their hasty clearing out, and their quickly murmured farewells. Perhaps it was their giggling as they went out the front door, held open by a long-suffering Watson, a particular target of Cat LaFlamme's less than coy flirtations.

When they were alone, Hank looked long and deep into Rhiannon's eyes, causing her to forget when it was she'd breathed last. She longed so very much to be able to go to him, to have him put his arms around her and ease her tiredness, and to discuss the events of her day with him, and to listen to his day, but she couldn't. He couldn't. That intimacy was a sweet privilege reserved for husband and wife. So she stayed on her side of the room, and he stayed on his side.

"So, Madam Candidate, how goes it?" He looked around the cluttered room that had once been his orderly library.

"About like you can see." Rhiannon laughed. "I never realized. . . ." She let her voice trail off, gesturing to the amount of paper spread around the room.

"Somewhat daunting, isn't it?"

"Yes," she was only too glad to admit, feeling suddenly weary.

Hank straightened up and put his hands in his front pockets. "Where's the rest of the household?"

Just like a father asking where the children were. This tender travesty of a domestic scene was almost too much for Rhiannon's control. "I don't know. I suppose they're about. I believe your aunts took Cat and Scarlet out back to the gardens. Something about a secret the old dears have that they wanted to show them. And I believe Emma is—"

"It doesn't matter. I don't really care, Rhiannon. As long as we're alone."

"Oh." She didn't know what else to say, so she looked down and picked up a stack of papers, needlessly straightening them. She gasped when his hand reached out from across the table to still her actions. She hadn't even heard him approach her. She looked at his hand on hers; it was so much bigger than hers that her hand was virtually lost in his. When he raised her hand to his lips, her eyes followed.

"Sweet Rhiannon with the ginger eyes." He kissed each fingertip in turn. Rhiannon's blood raced crazily through her veins.

"Hank . . ."

"Yes?" He was kissing her palm and beginning a trail up her wrist and arm.

"I . . ."

"You what?" He was slowly pushing her sleeve further up her arm to her elbow, kissing each bit of skin on her inner arm as it was exposed.

"I don't . . . I can't . . ."

He reached out his hand and stilled her words with his fingertips pressed to her lips. "Shhhh. I want you to come to my room tonight. Will you?"

She could only look at him, her heart in her eyes.

"Say yes." His eyes, black and glittering and liquid, like India ink, willed her to give in. He took his fingers away from her lips.

"Yes," she heard herself say.

"I'll be waiting." He raked her up and down with a look rich in sexual promise, one he, as well as she, knew he would keep. Then, he turned and walked away.

Rhiannon's knees buckled. She grabbed the table edges for support and stared at the open doorway long after he'd disappeared around the corner.

Dinner that night was especially excruciating for Rhiannon. Would this evening never end? She'd bathed from the washstand and changed into a simple muslin dress of mint green before coming down. She'd left her hair down, allowing it to wave around her face and down her back. Hank had changed, too, and was dressed more casually. But there was nothing casual about the electric charge in the air between them. Rhiannon had to keep from yelling, "Eat, dammit!" each time the meal lagged.

Until this evening, the easy camaraderie of the odd assortment of people, from virtually all social and economic backgrounds, as they sat at one end of the long, long table in the dining room, each in his or her own tacitly claimed seat, had warmed Rhiannon's heart. She'd thought of them all, herself included, over the past few nights as some sort of ragtag family of misfits who somehow, crazily, fit together. But tonight she wanted to feed, bathe, and put to bed all these "children," so she could be alone with Papa. And that scoundrel wasn't making it any easier. He pretended—she was sure of it—profound interest in the sparkling if disjointed conversation that made the rounds of the assemblage. What were they going on about now? Rhiannon forced herself to listen, and was glad she did.

"Well now, Hank, how're things at the Fancy Lady?" Cat ventured, heaping potatoes onto Tillie's plate. Tillie immediately dug in; she always sat right by Cat now.

Hank put down his wine goblet and shot Rhiannon a look before he answered her. "Let's just say I'm glad you three are out here where I know you're safe."

Rhiannon exchanged a look with Cat and Scarlet. For once, Scarlet dropped her imitation of every gesture of Penelope's. "I bet he's fit to be tied!" She leaned forward as she spoke, pulling a lace shawl she'd borrowed from Penelope up around her thin shoulders. Her high-necked lace dress was Penelope's, too. She looked like a little girl playing dress-up in her grandmother's clothes.

Hank smiled. "You could say that. You don't have to look so scared, Scarlet. Nothing will happen to you."

"Maybe not while I'm out here. But I can't stay here forever." She sat back with her hands in her lap and looked down at them. Penelope patted her awkwardly on her shoulder. She was beginning to accept Scarlet's imitation of her as the tribute it was.

"Well, you're not leaving any time soon, so don't worry."

Rhiannon really hated him for making her love him all that much more with his tenderness and concern for the poor, scared child that Scarlet was.

"Has . . . has there been any word from the school board, Mr. Wolfe? I certainly don't want to impose on your generous hospitality." Emma hardly ever said anything, so all heads swung to her proud, narrow face with its big nose.

Hank looked at Rhiannon again, as much as if to say, what's going on here tonight? "No, Mrs. Calvert, nothing yet. Although Mr. O'Shea is stridently opposing their decision, I'm afraid he's outnumbered. And you're far from imposing on me. Why, I've heard from MacGregor that you're teaching some of my employees to read. That is a valuable service for which I should be paying you."

Rhiannon was surprised. She hadn't realized Emma was doing that. She looked at Hank and gave a slight shake of her head and a shrug of her shoulders.

"Oh, no, Mr. Wolfe. I couldn't take pay for that. It's my pleasure. They're good students."

"I'm certain they're an improvement over my brothers," Rhiannon teased, trying to lighten the somber mood.

Cat did her part, too. "Well, I don't know about that. Little Eddie proved to be quite the good student, if you get my meaning. Ain't that right, Scarlet?"

"That's right, Cat."

Rhiannon had a sudden coughing fit into her linen napkin. Hank, seated at the head of the table with Rhiannon to his right, laughed out loud and patted her back with enthusiasm.

A moment later, Penelope said, "Henry, dear, Rhiannon has chosen the yellow rose with the pink-tipped petals."

Rhiannon looked at her across the table. Chosen?

"Indeed? Good choice, sweetheart." He winked at Rhiannon, who frowned at him.

"When's dessert?" This, of course, from Tillie, who ate like a lumberjack and looked like a tiny little gnome.

"Aunt Tillie, if you don't slow down, you're not going to fit in the dining room," Hank teased.

"So I'll eat in bed."

Hank put his bent elbow on the table and rested the side of his face in his cupped hand. He laughed in defeat. "I don't doubt that you would." Then he put his hands, palm down, on the table and prepared to stand up. "If you ladies will excuse me, there are some things I must attend to in my office, some men I have to meet with. But please, don't let me interrupt your dessert and your conversation. I'll say good evening now."

With that he arose and nodded to each of the women in turn, all of whom wished him a good evening. His eyes rested the longest on Rhiannon, changing from cordial to heated. So burning was his gaze that Rhiannon knew she would not be surprised to find she'd melted into the fabric of the chair on which she sat.

She melted a little bit more, once Hank had left the room, when Cat hooted, "Whooee, if a man like that looked at me like that, Rhiannon, I'd've cleared this room and this table and would've had him right then and there."

Over Penelope's and Emma's gasps, Scarlet's snicker, and Tillie's loud belch, Rhiannon could only fan herself with her napkin and try to pretend she wasn't aware in the least what Cat was referring to, no more than she was aware that her face had to be as red as Cat's, Scarlet's, and her own hair—all put together.

Leaning back in his chair behind his desk, Hank listened to the knot of men in front of him, all army veterans whom he'd served with or commanded, and whom he now employed, as they filed their reports on the investigations he had ordered. Tired, Hank closed his eyes and rested his elbow on the chair arm, using his fingers to rub his forehead. He didn't like what he was hearing at all. But it was no more than he'd suspected.

Opening his eyes so he could look at Jim Gaines, his Vice President in Charge of Operations, this time covert operations, whom he had introduced to Rhiannon in town at his office a few weeks ago, he asked, "And is the big son of a bitch still making threats?"

"Afraid so, Major. Dire ones. Against both of the ... women who worked for him, and against Miss O'Shea. Hell, even Mrs. Carry Nation herself."

"That's what I've heard, sir."

"Same here, Major."

Hank, accustomed to being addressed by these men as Major, his former rank, didn't notice their use of it now. As long as they didn't say it in town; that would raise too many questions. Even his own father hadn't known that he was involved in intelligence, or spying, in his military days. He put both elbows on the chair arms now, tented his fingertips, and brought them to his lips while he thought. "Any talk of him making a move against them?"

Gaines spoke up again. "No, leastways not with them all out here. He ranted around a while, not too pleased with talk of him having been skunked by a bunch of women, but that's all he's done, seeing as how they're out here."

"Damned good thing, too," Hank spat, narrowing his gaze. "Does he know yet exactly how it happened that Cat and Scarlet are out here?"

"I think he's about got the story pieced together. You know, with all the women coming and going, someone was bound to talk."

"Don't I know it. Still, I can't be here all the time, so I want you to continue to keep some of the men out here . . . just in case."

"Yes, sir."

"How many are around?"

Gaines flipped a few pages on his notepad until he found the one he wanted. Reading from it, he reported, "Uh, six in in all. Two as gardeners, two in the stables, and two as handymen so they can be inside the house or close to it."

"Good. What else you got?"

Gaines jerked a thumb at one of the men standing behind him. "Smith here picked up some talk to do with the fire at Gruenwald's."

"Let's hear it." Hank was already pretty sure he knew what Smith, a nondescript man of about 30, the perfect sort for blending in and hearing things, was going to say.

"Well, talk at the Fancy Lady is that those toughs hanging out there and putting their heads together with Savage are friends of his from over Kentucky way. They're doing some powerful strong hinting that they was responsible. And they're acting like the cats what got the cream."

Hank shook his head and pursed his lips. Not enough to take to Sheriff Parsons. Innuendo and rumor wouldn't hold up. "Damn them. People could have been killed."

"Speaking of that . . ." It was Gaines again.

"Yes?"

"You'd better hear what Simington has to say."

Hank signaled to the man to step forward. Simington, a tough, wiry man with a mean look to him, stepped up to the desk, his military bearing still intact. "Major, I played drunk the other night at the Fancy Lady, acting like I was passed out at a table close to where Savage and his men sit. From what I overheard, they're planning some pretty mean

251

Cheryl Anne Porter

fun when Carry Nation gets here . . . and, uh . . ."

Hank didn't like the man's hesitation. It wasn't like Simington. Dread formed a hard ball in Hank's stomach. "Go on, Simington."

"Yes, sir. I couldn't hear everything, but I did hear Miss O'Shea's name come up."

Hank's gut tightened, but he gave no outward sign of the icy rage that surrounded his heart. "Go on."

"Well, you'd best know that if they get their hands on her . . . death would be a kindness. They got it into their heads that she's somehow the cause of Carry Nation coming to town, and Savage especially seems to have something powerful against that woman. I heard him say he wasn't running no more."

Hank frowned, not able to make much sense out of that. How could Big John Savage hold Rhiannon responsible for Carry Nation's visit? That had been announced weeks before Rhiannon ever came home from Baltimore. And who or what was Savage through running from? And why was he running? "That sure as hell doesn't make much sense, does it?"

"No, sir, Major," Simington agreed. "But I'll keep my ears open."

"That's all I can ask." He turned to Gaines. "Anything else?" He was suddenly impatient to be done with this meeting, so he could go find Rhiannon, just to assure himself that she was indeed safe.

Gaines looked at each man, drawing negative shakes of their heads. "No, sir, I guess not."

Hank stood up, shaking each man's hand. "I thank you for your work. When I gave you civilian jobs, I never figured I'd have to ask you to use your military training again."

The men gave tentative if not hesitant smiles, but Gaines spoke for them. "That's all right, Major. This'll keep us from getting rusty. Besides, there's not much we wouldn't do for you, sir. The way we all figure it, we wouldn't any of us be alive right now if it hadn't been for you."

252

"I didn't do anything that any one of you didn't do for me," Hank said gravely and sincerely. Such words of loyalty and gratitude were rare from men such as these, and Hank was touched. Flashes of the past ten years they'd all spent together out West, flashes of countless life-threatening encounters they'd faced together and had survived because of a reliance on each other, kaleidoscoped through Hank's mind.

Amid embarrassed coughs and sniffs, he came around from his desk to escort the men out. As they passed the open doors of the morning room, they drew several sets of feminine eyes their way. They acknowledged the ladies, nodding and making comments such as "Evening" and "Ma'am" as they filed out the front door. Watson looked particularly pleased to be performing his duties for men once more.

Once the door was closed behind the men, Hank went into the morning room. He surprised himself with the fiercely tender and protective surge he felt toward all the women present in this room. Yes, they were a disruption in his life, and yes, they were an inconvenience in his home. And never before had he seen so much hot water being lugged upstairs; never before had he heard so much feminine conversation and giggling all in one place, except for the fancy brothels in San Francisco. And never before had he been so involved in the lives of the people of Wolfe.

And he had one sweet little redhead with big ginger eyes to thank for this old monstrosity of a mansion seeing so much life. He, like his father before him, had always kept apart from the town named after them, feeling as if he could never be an accepted part of town life, due to the deference always paid him. Being part of the founding family had always set him apart as a youth. But not anymore, by God. Now he was right in the thick of things. And, he realized with an emotional start, never had he been happier. He'd actually caught himself humming this morning while he'd shaved, something he would not have admitted to out loud, even under the threat of torture.

Feeling all these tender emotions well up in him, and throwing in the thought that he was sorry his father had never let the good people of Wolfe into his heart and his home, despite his love for his wife, Hank's mother, Hank expressed his emotions in a teasing manner, one sure to get a rise out of Rhiannon. It was only fair; after all, she always got a rise out of him—and all he had to do was think about her.

"Now, Aunt Penelope, tell me how the plans for my wedding to Miss O'Shea are coming along."

Chapter Eighteen

Rhiannon bit at her thumbnail and frowned at the light that shone from under the door between the two bedrooms. She must have reached for that crystal doorknob a hundred times in the past ten minutes, only to pull her hand back as if the knob were a rattlesnake all set to strike. What in the world was so hard about opening a door, she chastised herself. As if she didn't know. It wasn't the door; it was what was on the other side of it. Or who, more exactly.

Chickening out one more time, she scurried back to the high four-poster bed and jumped up on it ungracefully. She sat in the middle of it Indian-style and stared at the closed door. This wasn't going to work. She just couldn't, despite not being a virginal maid any longer—she rolled her eyes— just couldn't brazenly open the door and announce, "Hello, Hank. Well, here I am. Let's make love."

A squeal of embarrassed laughter nearly escaped her; she covered her open mouth with both hands. Why in the world had she said she would come to him tonight? Was she a woman or a timid little child? Both, she decided after a moment's thought. The woman had put on the sheerest nightgown she owned, the one with the tucked front and boat neckline fastened with a length of ribbon—and left off the underthings; but the child had scrambled away from the door and up onto the bed.

In the bottom of her heart, Rhiannon knew what was wrong. She hadn't been the initiator in either one of her and Hank's past two . . . encounters. Both times, he had opened the doors that separated them. And now he wanted her to perform that task; he wanted her to make the gesture that would show him she was committed to this act between them, to this beautiful sharing of two souls and two hearts, as much as two bodies. But the commitment was much more than to the act they would do together.

It was to the relationship, pure and simple. When—if!— she went through that door, there could be no more talk of not marrying, no more talk of freedom, no more talk of taking on the world to prove her education, her intelligence. Her very passion for life was so much greater than could ever be contained within the narrow restrictions placed on her, and every other girl, to be simply and foremost a lady, a wife, and a mother.

But had Hank ever said she couldn't be all those things and not pursue her political career? Well, yes, at first. But no, she thought dazedly, sitting up straighter. He'd given up that notion early on, and had even persuaded her to continue with her campaign when she was ready to quit. Why, he believed in her! He'd truly believed in her and in what she could accomplish, even when she hadn't believed it herself. She thought back to that day in his office in Wolfe when they'd had that terrible fight and she'd pushed away his declaration of marriage and his love. Had he even given up on her then? No! No, he hadn't.

Rhiannon scooted off the bed. She had to talk to him. Perhaps there was a way to work all this out. It—he—was certainly worth the try. Excited, Rhiannon practically skipped to the door and opened it boldly. She was well into the room and on her way to his bed, where he lay bare-chested, his lower body hidden by the covers, and reclining against the pillows, a thick sheaf of papers in his hands, before she remembered the supposed consequences of her coming in there. She came to a skittering stop at the foot of the bed.

Hank looked up at her entrance, a slight smile curving his lips. He put the papers down nonchalantly, and said, "Yes, Rhiannon?"

Rhiannon's nerve fled, as did all thought of what she wanted to talk to him about. Nervously fingering his bedding, she asked, "What are you reading?"

He chuckled, a throaty, husky sound. "A review of my financial assets for the past quarter. It's pretty dry reading, but I'd be happy to lend it to you if you'd care to look at it."

"No." She drew out the word, striving desperately for the same nonchalance he was displaying. "It's really none of my business."

Hank quirked an eyebrow. "I assure you it is, Miss O'Shea."

"How do you mean?" Was this another allusion to marriage? That was what she wanted to talk to him about, she now remembered.

"How do I mean? Well, the entire financial health of the town of Wolfe depends, directly or indirectly, on my financial health, as sole heir of the assets of the Wolfe estate, which includes liens on or outright ownership of almost everything in Wolfe, the town."

She hadn't thought about that. "Oh."

"Rhiannon," he said, sounding tremendously patient, "did you come in here for a lesson on economics?"

"No." She didn't know where to look. Certainly, she couldn't keep staring at his broad, bare, tanned, muscled chest that was covered with dark, crisply-curling hair.

"Then, what?" His voice dropped to a husky growl as he threw the covers back, a wolf on the scent.

Rhiannon couldn't help herself; she had to look. Thank the stars, he wasn't naked. He was barefooted, of course, but he still had on the buff-colored pants he'd worn this evening. And here he was getting up—the washboard ridges of his stomach moving in and out with each breath he took—and advancing on her. She'd seen that look before, that first day she'd come out here to meet with his aunts. The wolf was back. But now he wasn't scary; he was thrilling. He was mouth-watering. But he wasn't scary.

So why was she backing up? Why was she breathing funny and clutching handfuls of her sheer gown? How was it that she could feel her heart pulsing in different parts of her body, including . . . down there? She had to do something, say something to break his powerful spell on her. "Hank," she stammered out, "we need to talk."

Taking her wrist in his hand, he said, "Later." And with that one word, she was swept up into his arms and deposited gently on the bed. Lying there, propped up on her elbows, she watched Hank take his pants off. Her mouth went dry, and her teeth pulled at her lower lip. With him standing there naked before her, proud and muscled, young and virile, Rhiannon could only stare and remind herself to breathe. That he wanted her, a provincial little miss, despite her schooling in Baltimore, struck wonder in Rhiannon's heart. What had she done to win this magnificent male's heart? And what was she going to do with it now that he belonged to her?

Time for thinking was ended abruptly when Hank came to her on the bed. He didn't climb onto the bed, as she had expected. He stood beside it and slowly raked his eyes up and down her body, much as if he were a starving man peering at a banquet laid out for him. He hadn't touched her yet, but it didn't matter, for Rhiannon felt his hands all over her; and she felt her womanhood moistening, opening.

"God, Rhiannon, you are so beautiful," he said, bringing his gaze to her face. "Living chastely under the same roof with you has been pure torture. I can't tell you how many times I've wanted to open that door between us. . . ."

There were things Rhiannon wanted to say to him, too, words of love and of longing, but somehow the midnight blackness of his eyes quieted her voice and kept her arms at her sides. More than anything else she wanted to entwine him in her embrace and make him take her right then and there. But that was not to be; he wanted no part of hurrying, she could tell. And she could also tell that his keeping his hands off her was taking a great act of will. Indeed, his hands, too, now gripped handfuls of the sheet.

"I want you so badly I'm afraid I'll hurt you. Can you understand that?" Not waiting for an answer, he finally reached out to her with one hand and rubbed his fingers across her body, slowly stroking her skin through her bedclothes from her stomach to the beginning of the triangle of reddish-brown curls at the vee of her thighs.

Rhiannon felt herself actually rippling under his easy touch; she had to close her eyes and turn her head, her mouth slightly open so she could get the air she so desperately needed. "Oh, please, Hank, don't make me beg," she whimpered.

"My sweet, Rhiannon," he whispered, finally climbing onto his bed with her and helping her off with her gown. "I'd never make you beg. Never."

When Rhiannon reached up to encircle his neck with her arms, Hank took hold of her hands and pulled them above her head. Her eyes widened, but he held her hands as he leaned over her to take her mouth in a scorching kiss that mimicked the love act, that brought to her mind vivid images of what his mouth and tongue had done that first time . . . to her womanhood. And she wanted that again . . . craved that again . . . needed it. But she didn't know how to ask for it.

Finally, Hank let go of her hands and her mouth as he turned his attention to her neck. With a groan of pleasure, Rhiannon gripped his shoulders with both hands, drawing him down, down to where she wanted his mouth. Hank obliged, moving his body down hers, allowing his erect manhood to stroke her belly and then her thighs as he went. But first he stopped at each breast, laving the nipple with his tongue, drawing it into his mouth, suckling the bud. Keeping his hands molded to her sides as he moved over her, Hank stopped again at her navel, poking the tip of his tongue into the tiny bowl-like indention. Rhiannon's womb rippled and spasmed with this new sensation.

She groaned out loud and tried to turn over, away from the pleasure-pain he was giving her. But Hank would not release her. Far from it. In one swift move, he had her thighs opened and over his shoulders. Cupping her buttocks and lifting her to receive the homage he was intent on paying her, Hank breathed in deeply, as if memorizing the musk that was the essence of her femininity. A low groan escaped him, and he took her into his mouth. Rhiannon's legs tightened across his back; her toes curled; her head tossed on the pillows. He knew exactly where her bud was, for he found it unerringly.

With sensual coaxing, and tongue-flicking teasing, he brought the bud out from its hooded hiding place and teased it into full bloom. Rhiannon was beyond coherency; she heard her own moans, but could do nothing to stop them. Nor did she want to end this wildfire of sensations that overwhelmed her nerve endings.

And all the time, the pressure was building to a climax, building to thought-numbing intensity, building until this moment was the only one in her life that mattered . . . until the pulsating spasms exploded and spred outward, much as if a rock had been thrown into a calm pool. The exquisite flooding of nerve endings centered in her belly, but traveled outward to encompass every part of her body, from her thrown-back head to her arched back, from her jutting nipples to her curled toes.

When it was over, when she'd cried out from the very depths of her throat, Hank released her. He moved up and over her again, making growling, guttural noises. When he was fully over her and on his knees, much like a wild wolf covering its mate, Rhiannon raised her head, put her arms around his back, and pulled him to her enough so that she could lay scorching kisses on his nipples.

Hank groaned and rolled off her and onto his side, facing her, but with his eyes closed. Rhiannon watched the play of emotions over his face as she ran her hand through the curling black hair on his chest. His erection fairly danced at her touch; it jutted out as if searching for her warmth. But Rhiannon was in no hurry to claim that final victory as her own. Instead, she wanted to take her time, too, to explore this man's body that was at once so familiar to her and yet so foreign. Where she was soft, he was rock-hard; where she was smooth, he was rough. But all of him was tantalizing, from his broad shoulders and muscled chest, to his trim waist, and on down to his flat abdomen. And here she stopped, urging him onto his back. Then, with a fire and a brazenness she hadn't known she possessed, she found his erection and took him into her mouth.

Hank nearly jerked off the bed; Rhiannon felt triumphant. The swirling motion of her tongue over and around the swollen head, the laving of the steely shaft had to have all been instinctual, because she'd never even dreamed this pleasure before. She could feel the rippling tearing through Hank at her kiss, and she reveled at the power she had to make him respond just as strongly to her as she did to him. She became merciless in her ministrations.

But finally, Hank could stand no more. He pulled her up and turned her over onto her stomach. Tugging her up to her knees, he mounted her from behind. Shocked at first, she tried to move away, but Hank soothed and smoothed her, while all the time rubbing her opening with his manhood. Within moments, the tenseness went out of Rhiannon, and she moved backwards toward Hank's belly. Up on his knees and holding onto her waist, Hank prodded gently at her opening. Rhiannon held one of Hank's pillows tightly in her hands and bit down on it as he entered her. If she'd been expecting this to hurt, she was wrong . . . so very wrong.

When Hank slid into her until he was fully sheathed in her wet velvet folds, Rhiannon made a muffled sound into the pillow. This was even better than before; Hank's hand stole around her front to find her secret bud, which he stroked in time with his thrusts into her deepest realm. She hugged the pillow for all she was worth and rocked back and forth in time with Hank's driving pace, which could have gone on all night for all she cared. But had it, she knew she would have lost her mind, so intensely pleasurable was his body to hers.

Yet she was unprepared for the intensity of her release when it came. She could do nothing but let her body react of its own accord, as it clenched and pulsed around Hank and drew from him a hoarse, shuddering cry as he went rigid, lost in his own paroxysm of pleasure that her body afforded him. And they remained like that for a few moments, locked in their oneness, lost in their reverie of this physical act that consummated the spiritual coupling of two souls.

Indeed, when Hank withdrew from her and lay down on his side, drawing Rhiannon to him, her back to his chest, his arm around her and cupping a breast, she felt a sense of well-being and, strangely enough, melancholy. After a few moments of reflection, she knew why. It was time to talk.

"Hank?"

"Yes?" His voice was low, relaxed, indulgent.

"We can't go on doing . . . this."

He tensed the slightest bit and stirred somewhat behind her. "Why?"

"Because it's not right."

Hank kissed the back of her head and pulled her even more closely to him. "I assume you mean on some other level than the physical one, because it certainly seems right to me . . . if memory serves."

She kicked a foot back to hit his shin. "Quit teasing me. This is serious."

A low chuckle escaped him. He was so damned sure of himself, Rhiannon fumed. "You know what I mean. We can't just keep . . . doing this."

Hank didn't say anything for a moment; then he shifted position and turned Rhiannon on her back to face him. He covered her thighs with his leg, and rested his head in his hand, his elbow bent. His other hand rested on her shoulder nearest to him. "Tell me why we can't, Rhiannon."

"You don't know?" Now she was stalling, letting her gaze take in the shadow of his beard that had only moments before rasped sweetly over her entire body.

"Of course, I know," he said with a laugh. "I just want to hear your reasons why. See if they're the same as mine."

"Oh. Well, for one thing, we're not married. And only married people are supposed to—"

"Make love?" he cut in.

"Yes. And of course, the more times we . . . make love, the more chances there are that I will—"

"Carry a child?"

"Yes. And think of the scandal that would cause."

"You mean it could ruin your political career?"

There it was, what she wanted to talk to him about. "Yes. No. What I mean is, I truly believe there are things I can do in this town that will really make a difference, Hank. But I have to be the mayor to do them."

"And you can't do them if you're married and a mother?"

"No. Yes . . . could I?"

"Who'd stop you?"

Rhiannon hadn't thought about that. She'd always considered marriage and child-rearing as the end of any aspirations she might have as a person, an obligation she'd assume once she'd done everything else in her life she hoped to accomplish. And too, looking at other people's marriages had made the entire institution seem rather dull and boring. But would it be if Hank were her husband? Somehow she knew it wouldn't be anything even remotely resembling boring.

But there were other considerations: Would any strides forward she made in Wolfe be the result of her husband's influence? How could she truly know if her accomplishments were simply because of her last name—as opposed to her own efforts? Would the town merely indulge her out of fear of her husband's reprisal?

Hank's voice brought the present back into focus. "The little wheels are going round and round in there, Rhiannon. Tell me what you're thinking." He smoothed away a loose strand of her hair and twined it loosely around his finger.

Rhiannon stroked his forearm and frowned. "This is all very confusing, Hank."

"Why don't you tell me about it, and maybe we can sort it out together."

"Okay." Impulsively, and completely oblivious to her nakedness, Rhiannon sat up Indian-style on the bed, pulling the curl from his fingers. "Here goes. We can't make love anymore because we're not married, and I don't want to have a baby."

"Okay. We won't."

Rhiannon stared at him blankly. "We won't?"

"No. Not if that's what you want."

She looked at him askance. Was he teasing her? She'd expected a fight, a declaration of love, of marriage, but certainly not simple acquiescence. Did she mean nothing to him? Left with no other choice, she said, "It's what I want."

"There, that wasn't so hard, was it?"

She looked at his smiling face for long seconds. "Hank Wolfe, you go to hell." She slapped his face and scooted off the bed, scooping up her discarded nightgown as she passed it.

"Rhiannon!"

His voice stopped her. Maybe . . . "Yes?"

"Be sure to close the door on your way out."

Burning up with anger and embarrassment, Rhiannon stomped to the open door, not even caring if her nakedness gave him an enticing picture, crossed the threshold, and slammed it with all her strength, not even caring if it awakened the entire household and alerted them to the goings-on in the master's suite.

But the closed door still didn't drown out the sound of his laughter.

After that night, an uneasy truce existed between Rhiannon and Hank. The door between their bedrooms remained closed. But other than that, Hank still treated Rhiannon with all the deference due her; he still left his home open to the campaigning women; he still was a congenial host in the evenings to the women he was harboring. And he didn't even complain when his maids and cook got involved in the campaign. So what if meals weren't always on time, and the mansion wasn't always all clean at the same time? He just shook his head and sighed. But other than that, he stayed away during the day, preferring his office in town to his private study in his home.

Rhiannon's heart ached for his nearness. Why had she said they couldn't make love? Why hadn't she told him instead what was in her heart? Why hadn't she told him that she loved him? But she knew why. To say those words would put an end to everything she hoped to accomplish on her own. And, of course, there was Hank's desire to leave Wolfe. She would not stand in the way of his pursuing his dreams; who was she to keep him tied down?

Too, she was sure he'd realized the irony of their situation—it was just like that of Hank's father, who'd fallen in love with a local girl and stayed. Not that Hank was in love with her—she suspected he was, but he'd never said it. Still, she felt she knew enough about how Hank's mind worked to know he would rebel at the very idea of his life in any way being modeled after his father's. There was just no hope for them. And that thought made Rhiannon deeply sad. She just wished that if he were going to leave, he'd do it soon, before she found herself more in love with him—and carrying his child. Her chin quivered the slightest bit at the thought of living life without Hank Wolfe. But she never got to explore that reaction, because at that moment . . .

"Rhiannon! Rhiannon! You're not going to believe this. You're just not going to believe this!" A smiling Joletta Hawkins came into the library-office at a dead run, an impressive sight given her size. Watson could be seen still staggering backwards from the shove Joletta must have given him when he answered the door and was in her way. She held aloft a copy of *The Wolfe Daily,* and was followed by Freda Gruenwald and Susie Johnson, who also looked excited.

Rhiannon, along with Cat LaFlamme, Emma Calvert, and the dozen or so campaign workers present, a sizable number of them household servants of Hank Wolfe's, including MacGregor, looked up from their work. Rhiannon, for one, was happy for the distraction. She would be willing to bet she'd read the same paragraph of her campaign speech 20 times without comprehending it.

"What's got you so all-fired heated up?" Cat asked. Cat was now an accepted and acknowledged equal on the slate. Joletta had taken an instant liking to Cat's sassy tongue and was now Cat's champion. If you didn't like Cat or want her around, you kept that notion to yourself, or you'd face Joletta and her rolling pin.

"It's the newspaper! The newspaper!"

The three women at the table exchanged glances; they could see that much themselves. But they knew they had no choice but to wait for Joletta to tell them what had her and Freda and Susie all smiling.

"That danged editor telegraphed a story about us all over the country, and now it seems we're big news. A bunch of reporters from back East and from out West are on their way to Wolfe, just to cover our election and see what happens when Carry A. Nation gets here. Can you believe it?"

"Come on, Emma, let's go read that paper. I aim to show you I been listenin' to your lessons. I can read as good as anyone now," Cat crowed, dragging Emma over to Joletta.

Rhiannon sat stunned in her chair. Yes, she decided, she could believe it. Jim Sullivan, "that danged editor," like him or not, knew exactly what he was about. She smiled. National publicity wouldn't hurt their campaign or Jim Sullivan's reputation. And having droves of reporters descend on Wolfe would put dollars in everyone's pockets. After all, they'd have to eat and sleep somewhere. Very good, Jim Sullivan, she acknowledged silently.

Joletta wrestled the newspaper from the other women and plopped it down in front of Rhiannon, sending her own papers flying. She pointed to a specific paragraph. "Look there, it says the first reporters can be expected today or tomorrow. You think things have died down in town enough to allow for all six of us to go there?"

The women all looked at Cat, whose wide-eyed look belied the raising of her chin a brave notch or two. Rhiannon smiled at Cat; she looked much better these days. The ugly red dye was slowly wearing out of her blondish hair, and she dressed more conventionally in clothes given to her by different women from town. And there were no more bruises marring her face or body. "Don't say no on my account," Cat said levelly. "I ain't . . . I'm not"—she cut her eyes over at Emma as she corrected her own grammar—"afraid of Big John. Never was."

Rhiannon put a hand on Cat's arm. "I know you're not, Cat. But still, we have to be careful. I suspect Mr. Savage is capable of much more than we've seen." Then, turning to MacGregor: "MacGregor, do you suppose you could get word to Hank . . . Mr. Wolfe that we wish to have an escort into town tomorrow? He'd probably need to arrange for that during the day today."

MacGregor put down the pile of placards he'd been sorting through with several of the kitchen maids and straightened up. Rhiannon had to smile at the deference with which he treated her, as if she were the lady of the manor. "Certainly, madam. I'll see to it right away."

He left the room, signaling to one of the handymen who'd volunteered his free time to the campaign to follow him. As the men left the room, Rhiannon reflected that she wasn't sure what she thought of that man; she didn't even know his name, but she'd caught him staring at her several times. No matter where she went on the grounds of the mansion, now that she thought about it, it seemed there was a man not too far from her and always watching her.

Not that there was anything sinister about their mission. She just figured the sudden growth in the number of male employees at the Wolfe mansion could be explained by Hank's notion to protect her and Cat and Emma. And she wasn't stupid enough to countermand Hank's order that the three of them not leave the grounds without a sizable escort, just in case. Bravery was one thing; imprudence was another. Besides, the memory of her two encounters, for lack of a better word, with Big John were still pretty vivid in her mind, and could produce a shiver of dread every time she recalled them. Like now.

No, her anger at Hank's refusal to be upset because they were no longer going to be intimate did not cloud her judgment when it came to her safety, and that of the other women. Rushing off by themselves just to prove that he couldn't tell her what to do would definitely have been something she would have done as recently as a month ago, when she'd been a stubborn girl, she had to admit. But now, she was a woman, thanks to Hank Wolfe and this campaign, and she no longer had the luxury of being impetuous.

While the women all gathered in groups to discuss this bit of news—the candidates were going into Wolfe united as one after being virtually isolated out here since the day after the fire!—Rhiannon made her way over to Freda Gruenwald. She got Freda's attention by putting her hand on the woman's stout arm and signaling with her head, much as MacGregor had done to the handyman, for her to step away from the crowd. Off to the side, Rhiannon smiled at Freda and said, "I'm surprised to see you here, Freda. Does this mean things are getting back to normal for you now?"

"Yah, dey are. Herr Volfe has been zo kind. He brought in men to do za vork vit him und my Hans to rebuild our schtore. Und he even has your brudder, Eddie, vorking. Herr Volfe zaid not to vorry about loan payments for now, but yust get back on our feet. Und he is paying for everysing for za store to zell, alzo. Is zat not vunderbar?"

"That is very wonderful, indeed!" Rhiannon felt a warmth in her heart for Hank's quiet benevolence. He'd never said a word about his part in the Gruenwalds' recovery. And certainly he'd never mentioned that he was helping with the actual rebuilding. And on top of that, he had Eddie working with him? She could only shake her head. And wonder what he'd say about her request for an escort into town.

She didn't have long to wait. Within 30 minutes, Hank rode up with the handyman MacGregor had sent into town, a cloud of dust and sandy dirt marking the horses' path from Wolfe. Rhiannon had been upstairs in the ballroom checking on the progress of the volunteers, who consisted of Hank's maids and Scarlet and the Misses Penland, with the blue and white campaign ribbons. Every now and then she had to check up on Scarlet to forestall her from relating the spicier details of her past profession to her very agog but quite innocent audience, including Hank's aunts.

Rhiannon happened to look out one of the open French doors and saw Hank's impending arrival. Knowing she'd better be immediately available when he hit the front door, she hurried out of the room, and was just to the top of the stairs when Watson, this time seeing another agitated presence approaching the front door, pulled it open and was much quicker about getting out of the way.

Hank stormed into the house without looking left, right, or up, and went immediately toward the library, calling for her at the top of his lungs. "Dammit, Rhiannon, what the hell do you think you're doing?"

Chapter Nineteen

Rhiannon couldn't get down the stairs quickly enough. He'd scare the life out of the gentlewomen in that room, all except Cat, of course. Sure enough, when she hurried across the foyer to the library and looked in, she could see the women were frozen into place, their eyes looking like those of startled, frightened does. Even Cat. That did it—he must have that ferocious wolf look on his face.

"Hank, I'm right here—"

He turned around so quickly that Rhiannon pulled up short and took a step backwards. His face was a mask of terrible anger—and something else . . . fear? Protectiveness? Without a word, Hank took her arm, spun her around, and escorted her trippingly down the narrow hall that led to his private office. Not a sound followed them from the library. Hank shoved the door closed behind them and turned her to him. His black eyes snapped and glittered, like stars on a clear night. "Explain yourself," he ordered.

"How dare you haul me out of the library like that, like I'm some kind of a . . . of a naughty child. And exactly why are you so angry? You told me to let you know when we wished to go into town, so you could provide us an escort. Isn't that exactly what I did? We could have just gone on without saying a word, you know." Rhiannon felt the heat of her anger color her face. "Let go of me this instant."

He did, abruptly. And just as abruptly, his anger faded, his posture slumped; he spoke softly. "I'm sorry."

Rhiannon wanted to be sure about this. "For what?"

He looked at her, his eyes burning with a light she'd not seen before. "For embarrassing you, for hauling you in here like this, for handling you like that." His words were apologetic, but his voice was wary, finally ending on a soft note. "For caring."

Rhiannon's heart flip-flopped. Only now did she notice things about him that would have been obvious to her under less strained circumstances. Indeed, just as Freda had said, he was in work clothes, denims, cotton shirt, and boots, and they were dirty and sweat-streaked. He even had bits of sawdust in his hair. But that wasn't what bothered her. He looked tired; tension lines were apparent on his face, especially around his eyes and his mouth. He actually had circles under his eyes; and had he lost weight? Suddenly concerned for him, Rhiannon put a hand on his arm, wanting to ask him what was wrong.

"Don't do that." It was an order. He turned away from her and ran a hand through his unkempt hair.

Rhiannon didn't know what she was supposed to do, to think, even to say. But she did know that whatever was wrong with him, it was her fault, or at least it was because of her. She tried again. "Hank, what's wrong?"

He spun back to face her. So fierce was his expression that Rhiannon's hand went to her heart; her other hand clutched at the back of the sofa for support.

"What's wrong, Rhiannon? You ask what's wrong? Well, what the hell is right? That's what I want to know. What the hell is right?"

"I don't understand." She felt as if her throat were closing, so her voice was no more than a loud whisper.

"You don't? Well, let me tell you. Is it right that I have to endure the torture of having you so close to me, and yet so far away, day in and day out, without being able to touch you? Is that right, Rhiannon? Is it right that I'm completely insane inside with wanting you? Is it right that I can actually feel you and smell you when you're nowhere around? Is it right that I'm going out of my damned mind with love for you, and you don't even want it? Is it right that I'd go to hell and back for you and you don't even care?"

The raw anguish in his voice distressed her more than his anger had, filling her with self-loathing. How many times had she thought it before—that she was the only one capable of destroying this proud man? And it seemed she was doing just that. But it didn't have to be this way; she did love him! And she had to tell him, hang the consequences. What was a political campaign in the face of her love for this man? "Hank, please. Don't say anymore. I—"

But his raised hand, palm toward her in a "stop" gesture, stilled her voice. When he spoke, the anguish and pain were gone; only defeat and sadness remained. "You made your decision about us. No lovemaking, no future, no children. I acted as if I didn't care, as if it didn't matter. But God help me, it does, Rhiannon. I love you so damned much it hurts. And when Evert rode into town to tell me you wanted to go into Wolfe tomorrow and place yourself purposely in danger, I'm afraid I snapped. Again, I'm sorry. You've never lied about your feelings or your intentions. You've always said exactly what your plans are, what your dreams are. And not once have you included me in them, so I had no right to say or to do any of these things today. Can you forgive me?"

Rhiannon closed her eyes; tears streamed down her face. Gone were the great, racking sobs of her childhood when she didn't get her way. In their place was the silent anguish of the tortured soul of a woman. "Oh, Hank, I'm so sorry," she sobbed out finally.

"Don't be," he said gently, putting a hand on her shoulder. "You can't help what I feel."

"But you don't understand," she cried. "I do owe you an apology. You see, I . . . I love you, too. I just didn't tell you before . . ."

"Oh, God, Rhiannon, don't do this. Not out of pity."

"Pity?! Hank, I love you. I do. I love you. But I couldn't tell you. I . . . I couldn't keep you here with me when you long to be someplace else. You hate it here; you've always said that. You've always said you didn't want your father's life. Well, that's exactly what you would have had if I'd become pregnant. And how long after that would it have been before you hated me? You want your freedom as much as I want mine, Hank, don't you see? Marriage would never work for us.

"And . . . and those crates in your office in town. I saw the men packing those. You want to leave; I've been hoping you'd hurry up and do it before I was so in love with you that I'd die when you rode away. But Hank, it's too late; I already love you that much. I do." She opened her soul to him, letting the truth shine in her eyes. "What am I going to do when you're gone?"

She didn't get a chance to go on like she wanted to, for Hank went down on one knee and circled her waist fiercely in his embrace; he pulled her tightly against him and pressed his head to her chest. Rhiannon looked down at him, the strong man whom she'd brought to his knees, and wrapped her arms around his proud, dark head, cradling him to her bosom.

She knew in her heart that she'd never love him more than she did at this moment, when he'd humbled himself at her very feet, when he'd admitted in the most vulnerable way possible that he needed her, when he'd let her see into his soul.

After one tender, frozen moment in time, Rhiannon whispered, "Oh, Hank, what are we going to do?"

Hank roused himself and stood up to enfold her in his embrace. It was his turn to cradle her head to his chest. "We're going to cherish our love, Rhiannon. That's all we can do right now. But there's one thing I want you to know: The only way I'd ever leave Wolfe now is if I couldn't have your love, Rhiannon. I haven't wanted to leave since the night of your parents' dinner party. And those packing crates? I'm having some of my father's old reports and papers boxed and stored, so we'll have more room for current paperwork. All this time, you've worried about nothing. I'm so sorry, sweetheart."

"Then you're not leaving?" Rhiannon's voice broke on a hiccupping sob.

"No. And my offer still stands. I love you, and I want to marry you. I want to have children with you, Rhiannon. And I want you to know that I no longer hold any grudges against my father. I understand him better now, for I know if he loved my mother even one tenth as much as I love you, then his life here truly had to be a heaven.

"I see now that he did what he had to do, given the circumstances he found himself in, a young widower with vast holdings to oversee during and after a war. I don't know what else I would have done differently. And I have you to thank for that insight. I only hope that one day I can claim that promise of heaven you told me about in my gazebo."

"That seems so long ago," Rhiannon murmured against his shirt. Even with him dirt-streaked and sweaty, she loved the smell of him. He had a Hank-smell to him that was to her what nectar was to bees.

"But it wasn't. Only a matter of a few weeks. And look how things have changed. Just think how they'll be different in a few more weeks. Anything is possible."

She looked up at him. "Can we hang onto that, Hank? Can we wait a few more weeks to see what happens?"

275

He looked down at her. "Only if you won't keep me away from your body. I can't eat; I can't sleep. I'd probably have already pined away over you if it weren't for working myself senseless on Gruenwald's store. You didn't know that's what I've been doing, did you? See? You've reduced me to working by the sweat of my brow, a common laborer."

Rhiannon smiled at his jest, but it was laced with deep affection. "Yes, I know. Freda told me today."

"Well, I'm glad someone finds it amusing. I'm shot to hell, and you're looking like a rose in full bloom. Now, is that fair?"

"No," she chirped. "What are you going to do about it?" There was no mistaking her teasing manner, or her rubbing herself suggestively against his crotch. Her efforts were rewarded almost instantly by the feel of his manhood springing to life rigidly.

"Damn you," Hank whispered, lowering his head and taking her mouth in a hungry kiss. Guttural murmurings issued from him as he devoured her mouth, her neck, her upper bosom. "I have to have you right now." His voice was absolutely ragged. "But I'm dirty." He looked down at himself and then at her.

Rhiannon raised an eyebrow and gave him a look as old as Jezebel. "So am I."

Hank sucked in a breath, released her, and went to the door, turning the key in the lock. He turned back to her. "Get your clothes off."

And she did. And he did. And the leather sofa got its initiation in the wonders of loving lust. This coupling was neither tender nor brutal, but it was primitive in its simplicity and its intensity. Hank laid Rhiannon on the sofa and mounted her straight off; she was ready for him. There was a flurry of arms and legs, of scratching nails, of questing mouths that tasted salt and roses, of whispered words that promised forbidden deeds and loving things, of grunts and moans, of rutting and of lovemaking. And their mutual climax was overpowering, wrenching from both of them a primordial sound that rent the air around them. When it was over, they and the sofa were sweat-slickened and slippery.

After a brief respite to regain their breath, they moved, and sent themselves sliding to the floor. Awkward little gasps escaped them, but still they didn't let go of each other. Hank was able to roll and thereby save Rhiannon from his crushing weight, though. In the process, he slipped out of her.

"Nooo," Rhiannon fussed. So in the heap on the floor, when Rhiannon found herself on top of him, she said, "Now it's my turn."

She sat up and rocked her hips back and forth, allowing her moistness to cover and to coax his manhood to respond. She didn't have long to wait. With an arch grin on her face as old as womanhood, she looked into his black eyes, feeling every bit the victor in this loving battle. She leaned forward over Hank's chest, allowing her breasts to rub tantalizingly over the muscled hairiness of his chest, and put her hands on the floor to either side of his head. Kissing his mouth with all the abandon she felt, she moved herself slowly down Hank's chest, kissing his neck and his chest until he made the sounds she wanted to hear from him. Then, and only then, did she brace her hands on his chest and scoot down to his pelvis and begin the slow, delicious slide that would impale her with his flesh. She adjusted her position to give him full access to her . . . and she took him in, reveling in the silky, smooth hardness of him.

Sitting up on him, her knees bent, her arms stretched out with her hands on his ribs, she allowed him to put his hands on her hips and to help her with the rocking-horse motion that would carry them to the edge of splendor. When it happened, when her bud tightened, when his manhood was turgid, when sensation bordered on pain, the world exploded, splintering down into spirals that threatened to pull them into the vortex.

Rhiannon collapsed on Hank's chest, her face in the crook of his neck, her hair soaked and covering her face and his neck. Neither one of them could speak for a long time. Indeed, breathing was a feat worthy of a medal right then.

Then, there was a timid knocking on the door. Rhiannon and Hank exchanged startled glances, disentangled as quickly as they had entangled, and began throwing their clothes on.

"Henry, dear, is everything all right in there? I heard . . . sounds."

"Good God, not again. It's Aunt Penelope," Hank whispered, looking comical as he hopped around on one leg trying to get his pants on.

But Rhiannon didn't laugh, for she was turning round and round in circles trying to fasten her dress in back. Then she remembered—it fastened in the front. With a muttered curse, she whipped her arms out of the dress arms, tugged the dress around to its proper place and thrust her arms back in. "For heaven's sake, answer her," she hissed.

"Nothing to worry about, Aunt Penelope. We—I'll be right out," Hank called out. He got his pants on and fastened, and then went on a hunt for his shirt. "Have you seen my shirt?" he whispered to Rhiannon.

"No, but here're your boots," she whispered, holding them up.

"Are you sure you're all right, Henry dear? You're not sick, are you?"

"Dammit," Hank spat in a low voice; then he called out, "Aunt Penelope, why don't you go see to Aunt Tillie. I'm sure she needs you."

"No, I don't," Aunt Tillie's cranky little voice said. "I'm right here."

"What's going on?" That was Scarlet. Evidently quite a crowd was gathering on the other side of the door.

"Oh, dear, I think Henry's sick, but he won't let me in. I've tried the door, but it's locked."

Rhiannon froze in place, as did Hank; they stared at each other in shocked astonishment. She'd tried the door? When?

"Here, let me try. I'm good at picking locks. Give me one of your hairpins," Scarlet ordered.

Before Hank could say anything, another voice was heard. "May I help you, madam?" MacGregor!

Rhiannon, her bloomers in her hand, knew she should be concentrating on getting her clothes on, but she was mesmerized by the goings-on on the other side of the door. Hank appeared to have the same problem, as his gaze was riveted on the door's lock. And he had yet to find his shirt. His socks were in his hand.

"Henr—Hank's in there, and Miss Penland here says he's sick. I'm going to pick the lock."

"I see."

"I heard noises, MacGregor."

"Indeed, madam, what type of noises?"

Bad question. Immediately came the sound of sweet, innocent, maidenly, spinster Aunt Penelope mimicking the calls of lovemaking that had erupted out of Hank and Rhiannon just minutes before. A heavy silence followed her rendition.

"Here's your hairpin back, Miss Penelope. He ain't sick. In fact, I'd say he's feeling pretty good about now."

"As would I, madam."

"Well, what the hell's going on?" That was Tillie.

"Well, if you're sure, MacGregor, Scarlet. I suppose he's fine."

"Trust me, madam. He's fine."

"I said what the hell's going on."

"Never you mind, Miss Tillie," Scarlet coaxed. "Now why don't you two come show me the pattern you've picked out for Miss O'Shea's wedding gown."

"An excellent idea, Miss Calico," MacGregor chimed in. "I do believe a wedding is becoming a more and more imminent necessity."

And with that, the last bit meant purposely for Hank's and Rhiannon's hearing, the crowd moved away. Rhiannon slumped onto the sofa, her arm covering her eyes. She heard

Hank pull his desk chair out. After several moments of relieved silence, Hank's voice brought her arm down and her head up. She saw his head down on his desk and supported by his folded arms. His voice was muffled because he didn't raise it to speak. "Miss O'Shea, you've got to marry me and make an honest man out of me. I can't take much more of this."

Rhiannon giggled, realizing it sounded the least bit hysterical, but still unable to stop herself. "Perhaps I will, Mr. Wolfe. Perhaps I will."

The next day, the three candidates from the Wolfe mansion, Scarlet, and their volunteers from among Hank's staff set out in two carriages and a wagon for town for the huge rally quickly called to coincide with the arrival of the big-city newspaper reporters. Escorting them were six fully armed, mean-looking, silent men whose presence added a note of seriousness to the women's high spirits. Scarlet had spoken for all of them when she'd said, after seeing the men, that she was sure glad they were on her side.

Still, there was a sense of this trip being the culmination of all they'd worked for the past month or so. The six female candidates would face the six male incumbents, speeches would be given, issues would be discussed, and worthiness for office would be decided. The election was only several days away, and that would be quickly followed by the arrival of Carry A. Nation and her Temperance League. So, no matter the outcome of this election, the victors would have little time to rest or to celebrate before facing that challenge.

But the first challenge would be their reception in town. Reports had filtered back to the Wolfe mansion that Big John and his cronies were still sore at the loss of Cat and Scarlet and could possibly make trouble; indeed, Hank was already in town with a small contingent of men to monitor that situation.

And that wasn't all. Only a handful of women had come around, despite Joletta's, Susie's, and Freda's best efforts, to help with the campaign or even to state their support. Without a doubt, the fire at Gruenwald's had spooked the townfolk and kept some of them away. As a result, most of the volunteers had been Hank's staff at the mansion and some of Emma Calvert's older students. But they had been tireless workers without whom there would be no banners, no ribbons, no placards.

Still, Rhiannon felt a little hurt that her mother hadn't come out to support her and brought along the leading lights of Wolfe social society, the wealthy matrons who comprised the membership of the Ladies Aid Society. As they went, so went Wolfe. But Rhiannon had been heartened by the arrival of Emily Washburn, her brother Eddie's girlfriend, who'd come when she could get away from her job as a hotel maid. She'd kept Rhiannon filled in on the goings-on in Wolfe, and even in her own family.

Rhiannon looked at the other women in the carriage with her and felt an overwhelming sense of pride. Who would have thought that a drunken joke in a saloon would have led to an entire town being changed, as well as these women, and perhaps even history? Despite all the problems, heartache, and complications this campaign had caused in her, it was well worth it, she decided. Just look how the six women had grown. They'd gone from raising children and raising hell to raising money for a political campaign; they'd gone from obscurity to front-page headlines; they'd gone from managing homes and families to managing budgets and campaign volunteers. Even if they lost, things would never be the same in Wolfe, Kansas.

"I wonder what it will be like in Wolfe," Cat said to no one in particular. Thanks to the skilled seamstresses in Hank's employ, she looked resplendent in a blue-and-white-striped gingham skirt and fitted bodice; her hair was upswept in the latest style, on top of which sat a wonderful straw hat trimmed in blue and white, their campaign colors.

"I was just thinking the same thing," Rhiannon answered, herself a modern vision in a summer wool gown with puffed sleeves and a lavender, black, and creamy-white striped bordered skirt. Perched on her hair was a wide-brimmed straw hat trimmed with lavender ribbon and pink blossoms.

"Well, one of two things will happen," Emma Calvert chimed in, her practical teacher's mind presenting the possibilities. "There'll either be a huge crowd, lots of noise, and probably trouble, or there won't be a soul about."

"Well, give me the crowd, the noise, and the trouble. I can stand that much better than I could just being ignored by the whole town," Cat huffed.

"Same here, Cat," Rhiannon agreed. "We've been ignored long enough. If things are too quiet, perhaps we can stir them up a little bit; what do you say?"

"Count me in," Emma said, smoothing her silk patterned skirt over her lap. She'd never worn silk before, she'd told Rhiannon, and so was still awed by the smooth feel of it.

"Me too," Cat said. "I ain't—I'm not no—I'm not a stranger to noise and trouble. Won't bother me none—any."

Rhiannon swallowed an amused grin; she admired Cat's real struggle with her grammar too much to give in to the humor of it all, what with Cat cutting her eyes over at Emma's stern face every time she uttered a sentence.

"Well, I only hope that Big John don't do nothing to hurt any of us," Scarlet said, rubbing her arms as if a chill had taken her on this sweltering summer day. Her scared-girl's face tugged at Rhiannon's heart. If not for that sweet face, Scarlet would have looked silly in one of Penelope's high-necked, long-sleeved, rose-colored gowns.

Scarlet loved everything that was Penelope's. The two even had some secret or other that only they and Tillie knew about, and it involved frequent trips to a little-traveled area of Hank's property. They were quite furtive in their efforts not to be noticed as they crept toward their hidden place, which was all the more amusing because they were so obvious. Still, no one begrudged them their harmless pastime, whatever it might be, for Scarlet was as good for the old dears as they were for her; in fact, they'd taken over the young girl's mothering.

"You just stay with us, Scarlet, and Big John won't even be able to get close to you," Rhiannon reassured her. "Why, just look around you at these big, ferocious men. Who'd even dare get close?" She made a comical face as she leaned across the carriage towards Scarlet. Her efforts were rewarded with a trilling laugh from Scarlet, her first since they'd left the safety of the Wolfe estate.

As their little caravan approached Wolfe, the women found that Emma's first assumption was the correct one—there was a huge crowd, lots of noise, and trouble already, for gunshots and bands could be heard; men, women, and children could be seen running hither and yon; the buildings were draped in banners, some lauding the male candidates, some praising the female candidates (Rhiannon silently thanked her little band of volunteers who'd seen that the women's banners and ribbons were passed out, since she herself had not been able to do it); and every citizen seemed to be supporting the candidate of his or her sex, as declared by campaign ribbons, shouted slogans, and bobbing placards.

The cacophony only worsened when Rhiannon and her entourage pulled into town. The noise became deafening as people flocked to the incoming carriages and the wagon, running alongside to either cheer or jeer. The drivers were barely able to creep along to the location designated by Hank as their meeting point, the partially reconstructed dry-goods store. He would have the other three women with him. Indeed, had it not been for the escort of men he'd provided, they'd never have made it past the edge of town. As it was, the armed men had to call out and threaten the citizenry to get the candidates through the aroused throng.

Fearful as the sight was, it was like music to Rhiannon. She felt her blood fairly singing with triumph. This reception was as good as a victory; it meant the concerns and the issues she and the other women had been raising would be heard by practically every voter in the town. Looking around her, she could see that stores were closed, even the bank and the post office. Only the Fancy Lady Saloon and the town's only hotel, aptly named the Wolfe Hotel, remained open. And strangers abounded; these men with the striped or checked or plaid suits, each one sporting a bowler hat and holding a pad and pencil, had to be the reporters. At least, their shouted questions to her, Cat, and Emma seemed to indicate their profession. Well, she hoped they enjoyed the show being put on partially for their benefit.

Finally, they reached Gruenwald's. And there was Hank. And her entire family, all sporting huge grins and blue and white ribbons. Rhiannon nearly burst into tears seeing them all there for her. And of course, Susie and Freda and Joletta, each one as perfectly dressed as the women in the carriage, awaited her. Keeping her eyes on Hank's tall, handsome presence, Rhiannon smiled despite her concerns for the day and despite the fearsome noise and milling presence of the crowd.

For to her, Hank was like an island of calm in a swirling sea. She had only to look at him to know that everything would be all right. He took her hand and helped her from the carriage; a melting warmth spread over her as he looked into her eyes and mouthed, for her eyes only, "I love you."

Rhiannon could only stare at him, so handsome in his finely cut and tailored gray suit and striped silk vest. She loved him all the more for having on a blue and white ribbon that declared his support of the women. It was such a small gesture in actuality, but such a tremendous one in import that all she could do was look from the ribbon to his eyes in astonishment. He didn't say anything at first, but only winked at her, a devastating grin lighting up his clean-shaven face.

Finally, he said, "Did you ever doubt?"

Rhiannon laughed. "No, I don't suppose I did."

While the armed men helped the other women from the carriages, including Penelope and Tillie Penland from the second carriage, Hank escorted Rhiannon the few steps to the makeshift dais that was the boardwalk in front of Gruenwald's. With his arm around her waist pulling her close to him, it was hard for her to miss the hard bulge at his hip that could only be a gun concealed under his long coat. She prayed it wouldn't be necessary. But looking across the way, she could see the hard stares being sent her way, and Cat's, from Big John Savage and his gang, who were also armed. Seeing her look at him, the big bartender spat onto the ground and went inside his saloon, followed by his men.

Rhiannon pushed his upsetting gesture from her mind when she was joined by the five women running with her; they all shook hands with the incumbents, headed by Mayor Driver and Ed Hanson. A great cheer went up from the crowd; the debates were on. And it was all being recorded by big-city reporters. If this didn't put the small town of Wolfe on the map, then Carry Nation's visit certainly would!

Chapter Twenty

For once, Rhiannon was glad for the remoteness and the security of the Wolfe estate. Still in her morning clothes and holding a cup of coffee, she looked out her bedroom window, grateful for the sight of the armed men who were patrolling the perimeters of the place. If not for them, she probably would be swamped by reporters, supporters, and detractors, who even now could be seen trying to talk their way past the guards, but to no avail. She only hoped her family and the candidates who lived in town weren't being unduly harassed for quotes, interviews, and stories. She knew her turn would come later today at a scheduled interview in Wolfe, set up by the Ladies Aid Society, bless them.

She could just imagine the conclusions the reporters were drawing from her and Cat and Emma being holed up out here. Well, that would give them some fodder for a great story, she thought, making a face. She had to admit to the sense of disappointment that had accompanied her reading of today's copy of *The Wolfe Daily,* which had been placed on her breakfast tray and brought to her room. That damned Sullivan had gone for the cheap stories, the sensational ones,

ones dealing with each woman's personality and past, more so than the issues. But his job was to sell newspapers, and apparently her job was to create news.

She sighed. But for now, the day after The Great Debate, as the headlines of *The Wolfe Daily* screamed, she needed quiet and rest. Yesterday was already one big blur in her mind, a blur of sounds and sensations. She just knew she'd talked too much, shaken too many hands, smiled too much, yelled over the crowd too much, stood too much, had too much sun . . . and on and on, everything to excess yesterday. That was why she'd been surprised to awaken today to find nearly half the morning gone. And a tray sent to her room? She had always joined everyone else for breakfast downstairs. But the little maid who'd carried it in said Mr. Wolfe left orders that Miss O'Shea was not to be disturbed.

Rhiannon smiled at that, and then had to wonder who was daring to disobey that order when a knock sounded at her door. Her first impulse was to turn toward the door which connected her room to Hank's. But the knock came again, turning her toward the other door, the one to the hallway. Pushing down a sense of disappointment that it wasn't Hank, she called out, "Come in," and walked over to her tray to set down her coffee cup. When she looked up, MacGregor stood in the open doorway, rigidly formal except for his darting eyes. His entire demeanor said volumes about how uncomfortable he was to be in her room; so why was he here? Certainly, she hadn't sent for him.

"Why, MacGregor, what a pleasant surprise," she said by way of a greeting, hoping her smile would put him at ease. "Won't you come in?"

"Thank you, madam," MacGregor replied, closing the door behind him. And then he just stood there, looking at her in a funny sort of way, like he was sorry he'd knocked.

Rhiannon became somewhat alarmed. He was acting most peculiarly. "What is it, MacGregor? Is something wrong?"

"I'm afraid so, madam."

A sense of dread filled Rhiannon. She envisioned illnesses, injuries, accidents, shootings, fires, all happening to someone or other that she loved. And in all the scenes, there was Big John . . . and Hank. With a shaking hand to her throat, she willed the quaver out of her voice. "What is it?"

"I'm afraid it's the Misses Penland, madam."

"Oh, dear God, what's happened?" Rhiannon clutched at the small table in front of her, a tight feeling in her chest making her knees weak. Where was Hank? Was he with them? Had one of them—no!

"Nothing, madam."

Rhiannon inclined her head toward the valet, sure she hadn't heard him correctly. "I . . . I don't understand."

"Indeed, madam. Neither do I."

Rhiannon stared at him blankly for a moment or so. Was the man being purposely obtuse? "For God's sake, MacGregor!"

Now he came into the room—and he was actually wringing his hands, looking everywhere but at her. "I am so sorry, madam; I don't mean to be difficult. But events have taken such a turn that I find I can no longer stave off the inevitable."

"What are you talking about?" Rhiannon was nearly yelling by now.

"Your . . . ahem . . . wedding, madam."

"My ahem wedding?" she repeated stupefied.

"Yes, madam."

"What about it?—I mean, what wedding?"

Now MacGregor looked slightly green. "To . . . uh, Mr. Wolfe, madam."

Rhiannon stared at him again, not able to make any sense out of this—or of his part in any of this. "MacGregor, sit down." She pulled out the chair that was on the opposite side of the small table from her. She sat down in her own.

MacGregor hesitated. Rhiannon pointed pointedly to the chair. MacGregor rushed to obey her. He sat completely upright in the delicate cherrywood upholstered chair, his hands folded in his lap, and stared ahead, but not exactly at Rhiannon.

Rhiannon leaned in the direction he was staring until she caught his eye; she then slowly straightened back up, drawing his gaze with her. "Now then. Tell me what all this is about. You nearly scared the life out of me, you know."

"Indeed, madam. I'm most sorry. But, you see, I find I don't quite know how to handle this situation with the Misses Penland."

"Well, why don't you tell me exactly what 'this situation' is with them, and maybe I can help. That is why you're here, isn't it?"

"Indeed, madam." And here he hesitated, as if gathering his thoughts. "You see, I made a deathbed promise to Mr. Ezra Wolfe that I would stay in America with the young Mr. Wolfe until he was . . . ahem . . . married. And then I would be free to return to my beloved Scotland."

"I see," Rhiannon commented when he took a breath. But she didn't; at least, she didn't see how all this pertained to Hank's aunt.

"Indeed, madam. Well, the Misses Penland, bless them, have decided that you're to be the next Mrs. Wolfe and the mother of the future heirs, despite your or Mr. Wolfe's wishes or plans."

Aha, now she saw. "I've noticed," Rhiannon said with a laugh, thinking of the sisters' constant references to the wedding plans they were supposedly making. Neither she nor anyone else of whom she was aware paid them the least bit of attention or even tried to dissuade them. It was generally thought of, both by the occupants and the staff of the Wolfe mansion, as something harmless to occupy them.

"How could you not, madam? Well, I'm afraid things have taken a serious turn."

Rhiannon sat forward. "How?"

Cheryl Anne Porter

"Well, madam, I'm sure you're not aware—indeed, no reason why you should be—but today is my birthday, and—"

"Why, MacGregor, happy birthday! What wonderful news! We'll have to plan a celebration!"

"Uh . . . no need, madam. I've had so many that one more is really just a nuisance. At any rate, I've received my present from the Misses Penland."

"Indeed?" Rhiannon queried, consciously using Mac-Gregor's trademark word. "And is that what has you so concerned?"

"Yes, madam. Very astute of you. You see, this is what they gave me. And I must say I have absolutely no idea how or when they came by it. They must have enlisted the help of one of the maids." MacGregor reached into the inside breast pocket of his cutaway coat and pulled out what appeared to be a ticket. He handed it to Rhiannon.

"Oh, no," she said with a moan, not able to stop the slight laugh that accompanied it. It was a ticket—a ticket for first-class passage on a ship leaving for England in a month. "Why, MacGregor, even if you intended to use this—do you intend to use this?"

"No, madam."

"Good. Even if you intended to use this, you'd have to leave now to be in New York City by this departure date. The sweet old dears, what were they thinking?"

"It's quite obvious, madam. They're thinking you and Mr. Wolfe will soon be married. But there's more. . . ."

"Good heavens, MacGregor, this is no time for dramatic pauses! What else have they done?" She handed the ticket back to the old gentleman.

He put it back in his pocket. "Indeed, madam." He sighed. "Apparently, the old dears have sent for a seamstress, who is here now, mind you, to fit you for a wedding gown, and—"

"And?! And?! There's more?" Rhiannon's emotion hauled her to her feet. A seamstress?! Here?! Apparently, Hank's blockade of armed men was not totally impregnable.

MacGregor looked up at her with an apologetic smile on his face. "Afraid so, madam. You see, they've sent wedding invitations to the printer, and—"

"Wedding invitations?!" It was a most unladylike shriek.

"My reaction exactly, madam. And, to make things worse—"

"Oh, please, by all means, make things worse."

"And, to make things worse, the printer the Misses Penland use is the one at *The Wolfe Daily.*"

"Noooo!!!" Rhiannon was pulling at her hair. Sullivan would have a field day with this. And he was enough of a bastard to publish a story, true or not, on her impending wedding to Mr. Henry Penland Wolfe, doing all he could to use this tidbit to disrupt her campaign. She knew he would do anything to scoop the city reporters.

MacGregor hopped up, his eyes widened in alarm. "Are you quite all right, madam?"

Rhiannon had almost forgotten he was in the room, so flooded was her mind with strategies to stem this avalanche. "What?! Am I quite all right?" She was gesturing wildly as she spoke. "I was quite all right before you came in when all I had to worry about was a campaign, an election, Carry Nation, John Savage, my reputation, and whether or not I'm already carrying the Wolfe heir. But now?! No, MacGregor, I am not quite all right! I may never be again!" She was in a profuse sweat, her hair sticking to her hot face, with her hands balled up in fists at her sides before she finished.

The Scottish valet and the candidate for mayor stared at each other. And stared.

Then, Rhiannon took a deep breath, the first one she could remember taking in several minutes. She willed herself to calm down. "Don't worry, MacGregor, I won't kill the messenger."

"For which I'm eternally grateful, madam." His very seriousness made him comical all of a sudden.

Rhiannon laughed. And laughed, until she was quite afraid she'd snapped. She couldn't stop laughing, and MacGregor's terrified face didn't help. She had to get ahold of herself—before she started to cry. She put a hand firmly over her mouth and nose until her lungs hurt. Now she could be serious. Taking in a great breath, with a hand to her chest, she said, "Let me think. There's got to be something we can do."

"I'm afraid I can't think what, though, madam. And I didn't see how I could go to Mr. Wolfe . . ."

"Why not?" Rhiannon's head snapped up. Of course, that would have been logical—for MacGregor to go to Hank, not her, with all this. Suspicion coiled in her belly.

Now MacGregor was truly hesitant. And Rhiannon thought she knew why. In all his life, he'd probably never uttered a word of doubt or suspicion about his employer, who was really more like a son to him than an employer. Finally, his mind made up to trust her, if his change in expression could be read correctly, he firmed his lips and said, "Two reasons, actually, Miss O'Shea. One, Mr. Wolfe signs all the Misses Penlands' bills from town. So—"

"So he'd have to know about the ticket . . . and—and the invitations. The bastard!"

"Hardly, madam. I can attest otherwise."

"I didn't mean 'bastard' literally, MacGregor."

"I know, madam. That was a bit of levity."

"Oh." Rhiannon looked at him askance, almost forgetting to smile at his . . . levity. It wasn't like MacGregor to joke, or even to call her Miss O'Shea. She'd been "madam" from day one. Not daring to think on the implications of Hank's duplicity in all this, actually paying for a wedding he knew was not going to take place, Rhiannon rushed on. "So what's the other thing? You said there were two reasons. . . ."

"You may not like hearing this, madam."

"MacGregor, my dear man," Rhiannon purred drolly, "I have not liked hearing most of what you've had to say since you came into my room. So, please . . . go ahead."

"Well, Miss O'Shea, there's the seamstress."

Rhiannon had forgotten about her. "Yes?"

"The only people allowed onto the property are those who have been approved personally by Mr. Wolfe."

"I see. Isn't she the Misses Penlands' seamstress?"

"No, madam, she's not. If you'll remember, they have their own here on the premises."

"That's right. Then, I don't get it. Why didn't they just send *her* to me to measure this . . . this wedding gown?"

"Well, madam, the old dears deemed her too busy with the campaign wardrobe to be bothered. So they sent for Mrs. LeFleur. Apparently, her French name appealed to their sense of high fashion."

"Indeed." She absently bit at her thumbnail while she stared at MacGregor. This was indeed a tangle. But the biggest mystery of all was why MacGregor had divulged any of this to her, beyond announcing that the seamstress was here. She then could have found out all this for herself, albeit not as quickly or as succinctly . . . and not without a tremendous amount of embarrassment, both on her part and Mrs. LeFleur's.

She gave the valet a very arch look and put her hand to her waist. "MacGregor, why are you telling me all this?"

For the first time, MacGregor turned away from her. At first, Rhiannon thought he was going to head for the door. But he didn't; he stopped only a few steps away from her. "Because . . . because Hank loves you so very much, so I didn't want you to hear any of this from anyone else. I couldn't take a chance on your not understanding his reasons and maybe leaving here . . . before things were settled."

MacGregor had called him Hank. He was unmasked, no longer the valet but the loving, if surrogate, parent protecting his child. That and his words of Hank's love for her turned her legs liquid. She quickly sat down, putting her elbow on the table and resting her forehead in her hand, her eyes closed. She was afraid she was going to cry. "I don't understand." She didn't know MacGregor had come back over to her, or that he had sat down, too, until she felt him take her hand resting on the table. She opened her eyes and looked at him, waiting.

"You are the one, miss. Whether he knows it fully, or you know it at all. You are the one. Now, I don't know how deep your feelings are for Hank . . . but I assume you feel something." His arch look told her her was thinking about walking in on them in bed. Rhiannon's face heated. "Just as I thought. And so I'll not allow silly promises or coincidences or seeming duplicities to keep you two at odds and not being about the business of resolving this . . . affair."

The tears that had been blurring her vision spilled over and ran unchecked down her cheeks. "Oh, MacGregor, I don't know what to do."

"Yes, you do, lass. You listen to your heart, and you do what it says." His soft Scottish burr was very soothing, as was his tender concern for her feelings, even had they been at odds with how Hank felt about her. He made her think of the pastor in town, the Reverend Philpott, who could always make her feel good and bad all at the same time when she'd gone to him with her childhood misdeeds.

Rhiannon put her other hand on top of MacGregor's. "Will you tell me one thing more, MacGregor? Why did Hank allow these things to happen—I mean paying for your ticket and allowing the seamstress to come here today. I just don't get it. It seems so . . . calculating."

"Ach, you did not hear me, lass. I spoke of a silly promise, did I not? You don't remember? Well, it explains everything. Before I tell you, I want you to promise me one thing—there now, dry your eyes—promise me you'll not get mad."

Rhiannon dried her eyes on the lace hanky she had in her pocket. She felt her spirit coming back, and so spoke to MacGregor with a watery smile on her face. "MacGregor, it's been my experience that when someone first makes me promise not to get mad before they tell me something, what they have to tell me is going to make me mad."

For the first time ever, Rhiannon saw a smile light up MacGregor's stony Scottish face. He was really quite the handsome older gentleman, now that she really looked at him. "Your experience is going to prove you right again, lass. You see, Hank had no choice but to allow invitations to go to the printer, just as he had no choice but to let his aunts proceed with wedding plans for the two of you, or to allow the seamstress to come here today. He knew her visit would most certainly bring things to a head between the two of you, but what could he do?"

"Why, MacGregor. I want to know why he didn't have a choice. And what silly promise are you talking about?"

"The one he made to your father."

"My fath—?" Rhiannon started to rise from her chair, just as her temper started to rise. MacGregor's hand stayed her. She sat back down heavily and stared at him, narrowing her eyes the slightest bit and pressing her lips together. "Where is Hank? I want to see him."

"He's not here; he's gone into Wolfe on business, after leaving a list with the men outside of who is to visit today. Otherwise, I would not have risked coming to you like this."

"I do not recall when I've ever been this angry before."

"You promised, lass."

"No, I didn't."

He thought about that. "You're right, you didn't. But here's the heart of the matter: Your father, thinking only of your reputation and your well-being, wouldn't allow you to stay out here during your campaign unless he had proof from Hank that he truly intended to marry you . . . given your . . . ahem . . . intimacies already."

"Why, that—"

"He's a loving father who's only looking out for his daughter. And as for Hank, he's a man who loves you and was scared for your safety. So he had no other choice."

That stopped her. She closed her eyes and shook her head in several quick little movements, as if trying to clear it. "When did they agree to all this?"

"The same day you and your family followed your father out here, the day you moved in. That's what Hank and your father were discussing over tea; the Misses Penland, Miss LaFlamme, and Miss Calico were essentially witnesses."

"I feel like such a fool; all this going on around me, and me not even aware. But I just cannot comprehend Hank Wolfe's hand being forced like this. Can you explain that to me, MacGregor?"

"Because he out and out wanted it, lass. There's no forcing a Wolfe to do anything he doesn't want to do. He would never have agreed to this, much less going behind your back, if he didn't love you . . . and if he didn't hope the wedding would eventually take place. You know him well enough to know he'd have sent any other father packing had he even mentioned such a thing. But not yours. Because it's you he wants. It's you he loves."

Rhiannon looked down. "I know. I love him, too."

"That's good. That's good." MacGregor sounded tremendously relieved.

"But there's more to it." She looked up at him now, eager to have him understand her. "I have to run for mayor. I have to. It's very important to me. I don't think I knew just how important until yesterday when I faced the voters and debated the issues, when I saw firsthand the power that goes with the office. And I mean the power to do something lasting, something good in the world. I can make a difference here, MacGregor; I can. And I want to do it on my own; I want to know the achievements are mine—and not because my last name might happen to be Wolfe. And Hank understands that; he told me he did. He is the one encouraging me to run for office. He wants to see me succeed—on my own. And to do that, I must have my freedom."

MacGregor smiled at her when she finished. A Mona Lisa smile, completely enigmatic. He stood up and patted her shoulder. "Aye, lass, ye've got some more growin' ta do, I can see that now. I only hope you come to understand that yer never freer than when ye have love ta back ye up."

Rhiannon had never heard his Scottish accent so thick. She had a feeling he was using it on purpose. She gave him a curious look, her head to one side; what did he mean?

But he wasn't about to be forthcoming. For right before her eyes, MacGregor the confessor, the mediator, the father, turned into MacGregor the valet, starchily stiff and formal. "Shall I send the seamstress up now, madam?"

Well, here she was again—damned if she did, damned if she didn't. If she allowed the woman up, she would have to have a scene with Hank, for it would mean she knew that his aunts' wedding plans for them were genuine and not just an indulgence of his aunts on everyone's part. But if she turned Mrs. LeFleur away, she'd have to have a scene with the seamstress and Hank and Penelope and Tillie. Opting for the lesser of the two damneds, she said, "Send her up."

"Very good, madam."

Rhiannon looked up sharply at the valet. Was his reply just simple acknowledgment of her order? Or was it a statement of support for her decision? She'd never know because MacGregor bowed slightly right then, turned away, and walked out of the room. Rhiannon felt the trap closing more and more tightly over her foot.

The seamstress, the fittings, the armed escort into town, the heat, the interview with the newsmen, the continuous questions, the yelling, the jostling, the smiling, the promises, the long ride there and back, had all combined to give Rhiannon sore feet, a tired back, and a bad headache. She always felt uplifted when she was in the middle of the fray, so to speak, but coming back home, meaning Hank's home for now, always left her feeling drained, empty, alone. Was this what MacGregor had meant earlier today, about having love to back you up? About having someone there to hold you when the crowds were gone?

Rhiannon lifted the cool cloth from her eyes and put it on the table beside her bed. The long shadows of afternoon stretched cat-like across the floor to her bed, which she was lying across, still clothed in the forest-green and dusky-rose gabardine shirtwaist she'd worn to Wolfe. She'd removed only her shoes and hat before flopping onto the bed and calling for a wet cloth. Pretty soon she'd have to get up to change for supper, but for now, lying here was all she wanted to do.

"Rhiannon? Are you asleep?"

She jerked at the sound of Hank's low voice and turned her head toward the door that joined their rooms. Hank stood half in and half out of the room in the open doorway.

"No. Come in." She sat up and swung her legs over the side of the high bed. Feeling her heart go thump-thump, she ran her hand quickly through her mussed hair and pulled down on her bodice. Her gaze met his, making her forget she was supposed to be mad at him for the things she'd learned this morning from MacGregor.

At her words, Hank came fully into the room and approached her bed, stopping only when he was about an arm's length away. He didn't say anything; he just looked at her, his hands in the pockets of his lean-fitting, buff-colored pants. The pants were a light contrast to his highly polished, knee-high black boots and the dark loose-fitting shirt, which apparently he'd been unbuttoning when he decided to open the door, because the shirt was open to halfway down his tanned and powerful chest.

Rhiannon tore her gaze away from the sight of his bare flesh and looked into his eyes. His intense gaze, so full of an unnamed emotion, seemed to tug at her, to caress her. She swallowed hard. Why didn't he say something? Why didn't he come to her? She so desperately needed him to hold her, but she knew she had no one to blame but herself if he didn't. She was, after all, the one holding him there at arm's length, even without raising a hand.

"They were pretty rough on you today in town," he finally said, a smile slowly coming to his face.

"Yes," Rhiannon allowed, feeling the quickening low in her belly that was her body's response to Hank's nearness. She wet her lips. "I didn't see you there."

"I was there." Tiny dust motes, floating on the thin shafts of sunlight in the room, found Hank and danced around his dark head, giving a luminescence to his cheek and jaw that was all the more staggering for not being intentional.

"Oh," she said, nodding her head slowly.

"You handled yourself pretty well."

"I suppose."

He cocked his head to one side, throwing the light off his face. "Are you all right?"

Was she all right? No. She wanted to yell; she wanted to burst into tears; she wanted to throw herself into his arms; she wanted to beg him to hold her, to tell her she'd made the right decision and that he would be there when all this was over. "Of course. Why wouldn't I be?"

"No reason. I understand Mrs. LeFleur was here today."

"Yes." Rhiannon had a sudden image of herself standing in this very room this morning, half-naked and surrounded by Hank's aunts, Cat, Scarlet, and two or three maids, Mrs. LeFleur, and yards of satin and lace. Listening to their oohs and aahs had been excruciating. Apparently she and Hank were the only ones, aside from MacGregor, who knew the tenuous nature of the wedding preparations.

"The announcement will be in the paper tomorrow." His voice held a hint of fatalism. "I never intended for this to get this far out of hand, Rhiannon. You have to believe me."

"I do."

Finally, a laugh from Hank. "Now, there're two words I certainly hope to hear from you under very different circumstances."

Rhiannon smiled self-consciously, despite herself. "I know everything, Hank. And it's okay. You did what you thought you had to do, under the circumstances."

He looked at her for a moment without commenting. Then, he shifted his weight, and said, "MacGregor told me he'd been in to see you. I half expected you to throw something at me or to shoot me when I stuck my head in just now."

"This morning, I would have. But I've had time to think, believe it or not, given everything else that's gone on today."

"And?"

"And I'm very embarrassed that my father put you in this position. I mean, paying for all these extravagances, Hank, like the dress, the food, the flowers . . . the invitations. And all just so you could keep me safe from Big John. Which is all the more unnecessary since he seems to have just vanished from town. I . . . I suppose I could just go home, now that there's no danger from him."

"No," Hank said quickly, emphatically. "You're staying. It's much more dangerous for you and Cat and Scarlet with us not knowing where he is. And I don't think he's gone far, because even with the Fancy Lady closed down, the men are still getting liquor from somewhere. I believe he's just laying low and supplying liquor to the town's men."

"I hadn't thought about that. Hank, are you sure you're safe? I'd die if something happened to you because of me."

"Nothing is going to happen to me, Rhiannon. Just like nothing is going to happen to you, not if I can help it, not if I can keep you here."

She looked down, touched at the depth of his caring for her. Still, she had to absolve him from any responsibility to her or to these cockeyed wedding plans being made for them by his aunts. She had to offer him his freedom, yet again. Still looking down, she said, "Hank, when this is all over—I mean the election, any threats from Big John—you don't have to marry me. You know that. The plans your aunts are making are in no way binding on you, despite what my father made you promise."

Her words were met with silence. Then: "I know that."

Rhiannon looked up, hoping to lighten their mood. "I mean, it's all so silly when you think about it. Here's this grand wedding in the planning stages; a dress being made; invitations being mailed; an announcement in the paper. And you and I . . . we . . . there's been no proposal or anything—"

"Then, I've been remiss." He came over to her bed and took her hand, holding it in both of his and next to his chest. She could feel his heart thudding under her fingers. "Rhiannon Pauline O'Shea, will you marry me?"

Chapter Twenty-one

Rhiannon said nothing at first; she just removed her hand from his and looked down at it in her lap, stung by his proposal, which to her way of thinking was offered under duress, but also moved to the depths of her soul by his asking. She would have sworn that a jolt passed through her body when he touched her just now. "That's not funny," she whispered, not trusting herself to look up.

Hank's hand came into her line of vision. He cupped his forefinger under her chin and raised her eyes to meet his. "It wasn't meant as a joke, Rhiannon. You know how I feel."

Rhiannon found it hard to look away from the intense darkness of his gaze. "But you're only asking because you have to."

"Rhiannon, the only thing I have to do is make you understand that I love you and that no one is forcing me to do anything I don't already want to do."

"But I can't marry you, Hank—not now. You know that. You know why, too."

He let go of her chin and dropped his hands to his sides. His face changed from tender to angry. "Yes, I know. Your damned freedom. Your desire to live, to make this grand difference in the world before you have to give up your precious independence by getting married and becoming a dull matron who's merely an appendage to her boorish husband."

His words were even more acerbic than his voice, and it hurt. She thought he understood what was driving her. But apparently he didn't. Truth to be told, she wasn't sure what it was anymore, either. Still, she heard herself say, "I'm sorry, Hank, I have to turn down your offer."

"Don't bother," he said acidly. "It's withdrawn." Then he pulled a small box out of his shirt pocket and held it out to her. "Here, wear this anyway so you don't have to answer a host of ridiculous questions when our wedding announcement comes out in the paper tomorrow. And don't worry—I'll know that it doesn't mean anything. And isn't that what's important—that you and I know the whole affair is a sham?"

He set the box roughly in her hand and said, "It belonged to my mother. You can give it back when things have settled down in Wolfe." With that, he turned on his heel and strode angrily from the room, slamming the door behind him.

Rhiannon simply stared at the closed door and willed the tears back. Why was she always throwing his love and his proposals right back at him? When would she learn that there might not be a next time? She then looked down at the small jewelry box in her hand. Not knowing what else to do about Hank right now, she gave in to her curiosity and opened it.

And gasped. Nestled in the satin folds was a wide, heavy gold band on which was set the largest emerald-cut diamond she'd ever seen. She immediately looked back up at the closed door, and stared for the longest minute. Then, with trembling fingers, she lifted the ring from its satiny bed and turned it this way and that, allowing the filtering rays of the sun to capture its facets and play off the walls and the ceiling in a rainbow of sparkling color. A wondering smile lit up her face as she placed the ring on the third finger of her left hand. It fit perfectly.

Rhiannon was proving to be a boon to newspapers across the country; and she was quickly becoming the darling of the press. If the reporters who'd descended on Wolfe to get the story of the female mayoral candidate and her all-woman city council had thought they were covering the story of the year, it was nothing as compared to their glee over her and Susie's kidnapping of two whores from the town's saloon, which had in effect closed it down because the owner had fled. But that was nothing—now the lady who wanted to be mayor was going to marry one of the richest men in America. And there was still more—if she won, she was going to face down Carry Nation and the Temperance League. It just couldn't be any better than this for newspapers or reporters.

And no one was more aware of that than the lady in question out at the Wolfe estate. As if the mansion didn't already resemble a beehive on top of an anthill, what with the female occupation and its designation as campaign headquarters, the wedding announcement in *The Wolfe Daily,* reprinted in all the newspapers across the nation within the week, elevated it to repository of well-wishers and their gifts.

Rhiannon was astounded by the sheer volume of telegrams and gifts and visits she . . . they received. But she was absolutely overwhelmed in the next few days when gifts arrived from the White House, from the governor of Kansas, from heads of state of foreign countries, from an army general or two, as well as from heads of industry. She'd known that Hank was rich, and probably therefore powerful, but she'd really had no idea! How in the devil would she bow gracefully out of this now? It simply wouldn't suffice to say, "Oh, never mind. It was all just a joke." Why hadn't Hank warned her what to expect? Indeed, why hadn't Hank warned her to clear out the ballroom to store gifts?

But through it all, he was by her side, holding her close, playing the happy groom-to-be in public. His nearness was so bittersweet for Rhiannon that she almost began to believe that the wedding would take place. Hank joked with the men, called her dazed parents and her brothers his family now, kissed his lovely bride-to-be to the swooning delight of the town's women, and fended off the more difficult questions and comments about their romance.

He even forestalled the inevitable round of parties, parties that in reality would never happen, by begging off for now because of the campaign, the impending elections, and Carry Nation's visit. He said it was all too much for his lovely fiancee; why, couldn't they see how pale she was? He assured everyone that there would be plenty of time later on for their wedding celebration. Plenty of time.

It was only when his black eyes met hers in a quiet moment that she could see the truth of his emotions. The looks he gave her were stark and wintry, full of raw pain and Wolfe pride. She would have given anything to be able to throw everything and everyone aside and declare unequivocally to Hank that she truly loved him and wanted to marry him. But nothing was ever that simple, was it? She was set on her course, and she had to see it through to its natural end, good or bad, happy or sad.

"Well, hog-tie me and toss me on a manure pile. Will you just look at what's coming up the drive."

Rhiannon blinked back to the present and at the blank sheet of paper in front of her when Cat LaFlamme spoke out so eloquently. Well, so much for speechwriting, and the election only a week away. "What is it, Cat?"

"I said come look. I don't think I can describe it to do it justice." A guffawing snort escaped her as she kept her eyes riveted on the scene outside the long window in the library. Every volunteer in the room, all essentially Hank's employees, hurried over to the long windows and jockeyed for position. Several gasps and oaths escaped them.

305

"Let me see!" squealed Scarlet. She jumped up from her new favorite pastime of sorting through the latest arrival of wedding gifts and ran over to the window, peering over Cat's shoulder. Her face took on a look of awe. "My lands. Make room for me on the manure. You just ain't goin' to believe this, Miss Rhiannon."

Rhiannon exchanged a glance with Emma Calvert, who sat across from her, and stood up, pushed her chair back, and went over to the window. "Well, what in the world's gotten you all so—oh, my God. What is that?"

"Well, near as I can tell, it's every woman and child in Wolfe. Them . . . those guards Hank set out must have just about given up on keeping everyone out, because now everyone's in, wouldn't you say?"

"I most certainly would. What can be going on?"

"Well, either they came to help us or they came to hang us, I'd say," Cat quipped.

Rhiannon looked at her and then at Emma, who was now looking over Rhiannon's shoulder. "Let's go find out which, shall we?"

With that, she set off for the foyer, and was intercepted by Watson, who still insisted on performing his duties as butler, at least until he could devise a method to make the front door simply open by itself what with all the comings and goings out here lately.

Behind Watson was the open door of the morning room, through which Rhiannon saw Penelope and Tillie with their sweet old heads together, no doubt working on their secret project or her wedding. She called out to them. "Aunt Penelope, Aunt Tillie"—they insisted she call them that, now that they were to be family—"come see who's here."

The sisters exchanged glances that Rhiannon could not interpret, and then gathered up the precious papers on which they were constantly writing or drawing. "Oh, dear, I do hope it's not . . . our order from town. It's a secret, you know," Penelope sang out as she arose from her chair and pulled

Tillie up. "Come, sister, we must go see."

"Why?" Tillie huffed. "I was just getting the recipe—"

"Hush, dear, remember it's a secret now," Penelope fussed brightly, literally dragging Tillie behind her as she came over to the foyer.

Watson opened the door, and once again was rewarded by being shoved out of the way; he was knocked into Cat's waiting arms by Patience O'Shea, who ran to her daughter, her arms out; she grabbed her in a bear hug and exclaimed, "Look, Rhiannon! Can you believe it? We've all come to help you; why, you simply must be swamped what with the elections coming up and the wedding gifts and letters arriving daily. They've all been asking me how they could help, so I just brought them all. It seems, dear, that you have quite a bit of support from the women of Wolfe, even if they haven't been speaking up for you before now. Isn't that wonderful? Now, how can we help?"

Rhiannon blinked. Help? She looked past her mother. There had to be over 50 women and their children present, along with her own three brothers. Among the women she saw Ella; Eddie's girlfriend, Emily Washburn; the other three women candidates—Joletta, Freda, and Susie; Effie Parsons and a few other of her childhood friends; the entire membership of the Ladies Aid Society; and dozens of women whose names she could not have called because she didn't know them.

And they were here to help her? Had they suddenly decided to join her because of the wedding announcement in the paper? She felt a sting of guilt stab her at that thought. Too, she wondered if her being an engaged woman made her somehow, in their minds, more like them and less of a threat to what their lives stood for, meaning home and family.

"Well, Rhiannon, don't keep us waiting. What do you want us to do?" her mother urged.

Rhiannon was overwhelmed; her hands went to her mouth for a moment. "You mean you all are here to support us in this campaign, and not just because of my . . . engagement?"

A resounding yes answered her wondering question.

"Even despite what your husbands might think or say?" She had to know the depth of their commitment.

Another chorus of yesses and nods answered her question.

"Well, then, let's get to work!"

A sound of hurrahs went up from the women. Rhiannon spent the next few hours delegating responsibilities and duties, when Ella and her mother would allow it; she then freed Hank's maids and his cook to return to their paying jobs, telling them their help had been invaluable to her and that she would always be grateful; next, when things were running rather smoothly and the children were out roaming through the gardens under Scarlet's and Effie Parson's watchful eyes, she gathered together the other women candidates for a much-needed strategy meeting.

Finding no other quiet corner, she led them to Hank's private office, where they closeted themselves, heads together over his huge cherrywood desk. Susie Johnson was just about to make a point on the number of women voters registered when the door burst open and Hank rushed in, a look of near-panic on his face.

This was the first time in many days that Rhiannon had seen him during the day; he usually left after breakfast and went to work in the relative peace and quiet of his office in town, not returning until supper time. After that meal, he usually retreated from the all-female company to the sanctuary that was this room, in essence avoiding Rhiannon whenever he could, except for those times when he had to play the besotted fiancé. If his behavior was strange to the women who lived here now, they didn't comment on it; they just exchanged glances and looked at Rhiannon. But his behavior was beginning to tell on Rhiannon's face and her nerves. She didn't know how much longer they both could keep up this happy pretense for her father's sake.

Rhiannon and the other women jumped and gasped at his sudden entrance. But Rhiannon knew that wasn't the only reason for her heart pounding. It always pounded when Hank was near. She jumped up before the other women could. Thinking he was angry because she had now invaded his private den, she spoke rapidly. "Oh, Hank, I'm so sorry. I guess I didn't realize the time. I hope you don't mind. I—"

Forgetting himself in front of company, Hank cut her off. "You moved the whole damned female and child population of Wolfe to my house? Tell me you didn't, Rhiannon! My God, where will we put everyone?"

Rhiannon stared at him unblinkingly for a few moments. Then she burst out laughing, thinking how it must have looked to him to ride in on such a scene—horses and wagons in rows out in the drive, bewildered guards, children running and playing all around outside, women busily working in every room on the first two floors, maids hurrying to and fro with food and drink, his butler being used as a messenger between the rooms and the floors, and his valet overseeing the entire production. The poor man. What a shock.

But what was so funny, and so endearing, was his acceptance of the situation, as if to say that whatever she did on this crusade of hers to elevate the status of women in Wolfe, Kansas, was fine with him, but where was he going to put everyone? That if she said they were to live here, then so be it—even if it wasn't her place to open his home to the citizenry. Rhiannon wanted to run to him and kiss him. He'd as much as said that he didn't care who he had to put up with as long as she was here. And she'd never loved him more than she did at this moment . . . but she couldn't tell him that, because of the obstacles she'd put in her own way.

"What in the hell is so funny?" he demanded, his hands at his waist. "Just how long do you think it's going to be before their husbands and fathers show up? Then what, Rhiannon? And of course they'll be followed by the reporters. Oh, this is just great." He took his Stetson off and rapped it against his denim-clad thigh, raising a small cloud of dust. Susie sneezed delicately.

Denims? Dust? Where had he been? She'd thought he was in Wolfe at his office. But he was dressed like a cowpuncher. Ignoring all of his questions and concerns, Rhiannon asked him, "Where've you been?"

He looked at her blankly, and then at the other women in the room, as if they could tell him what she meant. They said not a word; he was clearly on his own. "What?"

"Where've you been, dressed like that? You don't wear your denims to the office." Even to her own ears, she sounded like a wife.

"Well, if you must know, Miss O'Shea"—he emphasized her status as a miss—"I've been participating in the branding of my cattle. Recently, I've felt the strangest need for dangerous physical activity."

Rhiannon's hand followed his eyes to her throat. She cut her eyes down at the other women, who were proving to be a very rapt audience; even Joletta Hawkins was strangely quiet. "I see. And what are you doing home so early?"

"If you mean how did I know about the crowd, one of my men whose unenviable task it is to protect you rode out to find me to tell me that you've now made his job almost impossible. He said anyone could slip in among this crowd and—"

"I get your point. Well, then, let me put your mind at ease, Mr. Wolfe. None of these women, nor their children, is staying. They've all just volunteered to come out during the day for this last week of the campaign. And I should think you'd want to thank them all, for their presence here has freed your cook and maids to return to their respective jobs in your home."

Hank looked at her and then the other women, a look of contrition slowly replacing the panic and the anger. "Oh. I see. Well, that's different, of course. And you're right." He began backing out of the room. "That's very good. I'll just go . . . clean up before dinner. I'm sure I can use a bath. . . ." The door closed behind him.

Rhiannon stared at it for a moment, and then turned a sickly smile on her fellow candidates.

"I do believe we will all be glad when this election is over. I'm afraid it's wearing on all our nerves," she offered by way of an apology for the preceding scene.

"Naw, that ain't what's wrong with him," Joletta Hawkins said. "He's just got a case of the male jitters before the wedding. My own Henry was like that—a regular stud waitin' to get at his filly. You should have seen him."

"Gott in himmel," Freda breathed. The looks that went around the desk said plainly enough that no one wanted to go to her grave with that particular image implanted on her brain, so everyone began talking at once, lest Joletta feel compelled to relate that story in detail.

"About the voters—" Susie began.

"Yes, please do go on," Emma encouraged, almost frantically.

"Now where was that paper with them . . . those numbers, Joletta?" Cat muttered, frowning with a vengeance as she sorted around on the desk.

Having successfully derailed Joletta's train of thought, the women worked on for another several minutes, compiling stacks of paper covered with names, addresses, and businesses. They were all concentrating on the task at hand, except for Rhiannon. She was suffering from guilt pangs that had various origins. Guilt about taking over Hank's home; guilt about having already had that wedding night Joletta had referred to; guilt over keeping Hank so tied up in emotional knots; guilt over the sham that was their engagement; and guilt over the beautiful diamond that flashed every time she moved her left hand, a diamond that had belonged to his mother, a woman worthy of the Wolfe name, and which did not belong on the finger of a woman who was one big lie after another.

Her thoughts crowding in on her, Rhiannon abruptly stood up, scraping her chair on the wooden floor and startling the women. "If you'll excuse me, I have to go . . . to go talk to . . ."

"Oh, go on, Rhiannon. I would have been gone a long time ago myself." It was Cat, and she had a warm, understanding smile on her face. Rhiannon clasped her hand in a sisterly squeeze of thanks.

"Yes, we can handle things here. Go to him." It was Emma Calvert; she had a hint of moisture in her eyes. "I'd give anything if I still had my husband to go to. Don't let anyone or anything come between you two, Rhiannon. Love is what gives meaning to life."

Freda put an arm around Emma and hugged her, while Joletta patted a moved and sobbing Susie. But Rhiannon just stared at the gathered circle of women; they had all known what she was going through inside. But did they know just how much each of them had come to mean to her? Rhiannon gained a sudden insight into the women gathered here because of her arm-twisting after the fateful article in *The Wolfe Daily* so many weeks and so many lifetimes ago. They were sisters now, on a level beyond that of the bonds of flesh and blood; sisters of a shared experience, a shared awakening.

For the first time, Rhiannon began to understand what she'd set into motion in tiny Wolfe, Kansas. She'd drawn every man, woman, and child into her web of politics and intrigue. She'd disrupted all their lives, set the entire town, indeed the nation now, abuzz with her ambitions and her antics. They were now all her responsibility, for none of their lives would ever be the same after this summer. And they'd all have her to thank or to curse for that.

"Thank you," Rhiannon said in a low voice, barely able to get the words past the lump of emotion in her throat.

"You're wasting time, girl. Get!" Cat teased, smacking at Rhiannon's rump. The other women laughed, glad for the relief from the intensely emotional moment that had just passed.

With a grin of determination, Rhiannon bounced out of Hank's office and weaved her way through the maze of rooms, stairs, and volunteers that cluttered her way to the third-floor bedrooms. It took her a full ten minutes to navigate the course that would take her to Hank. With her mind so distracted by the endless demands on her for answers and decisions as she'd come up, she thought only of the peace and quiet of the sanctuary that was Hank's bedroom, and so did not knock or otherwise announce her presence out in the hall.

Indeed, she merely burst into Hank's room much as he'd burst into his office downstairs about 30 minutes ago. But at least he'd been dressed then. Whereas now he wasn't. It was then that she remembered the bath he'd said he was going to take. And he was obviously just now stepping out of the adjoining modern bathroom that was connected to his room. She had one just like it joined to her bedroom. Rhiannon's hand froze on the doorknob, and her feet grew roots into the wooden floor. "Ohmigod, I'm sorry. I should have knocked! I forgot about your bath. I—"

"Rhiannon, come in. And close the door." He'd been in the process of wrapping a towel around his waist when she'd entered. Now he completed that action and tucked a corner in at his waist. "It's not like you haven't—"

"Don't say it, Hank!"

He grinned—wickedly. "As you say, but that doesn't make it any less true."

"Please." She put a hand up to stop him.

And it did. He sobered and stared at her from across the room. He ran his hand through his wet hair and then wiped his hands on his towel by rubbing them across his buttocks. To Rhiannon, he gleamed and glistened with male vitality, with male virility, with almost animal power and grace. And all he had to do was stand there to make her woman's bud ache for his touch, for his kiss.

"If not to see me in my bath, what did you come up here for, Rhiannon?" His words were teasing, but his voice wasn't.

But all she could do was look around at the floor and twist her hands together as she cast about for the reason for her presence here. She didn't know; well, she decided, she did know . . . only she didn't know how to put it in words. When she finally looked up at Hank, seeing him across his bed, she saw he had crossed his arms over his magnificent chest and had arched an eyebrow at her. Damn him; he was going to make her come to him—again.

"I'm waiting, Rhiannon."

"I know, I know," she practically wailed. Not liking that desperate voice, she brought herself up short and took in a deep breath, which she blew out noisily. If only he wouldn't stand there looking like some avenging savage god who was going to behead her at any moment. "Do you have to stand there like that?"

That brought his hands down to his sides. He looked down at himself and then back up at her. "Well, how should I stand? I only know one way."

"I don't know. Just do something different." As she spoke, Rhiannon fluttered her hands in the air in front of her to punctuate her words.

"Son of a . . . Like what?"

"I don't know. Get dressed or something."

Hank looked at her archly. "Are you sure?"

"Well, of course I am. Why in the—" Off came the towel. Hank's glorious nakedness was exposed for her viewing. "Hank Wolfe, you put that towel back on this instant!"

No." He started walking toward her, his manhood rising the closer he got to her.

Of course, she could have turned and fled at any point in his stalking advance on her, but somehow that never occurred to her. With her mouth dry and her throat closing, and with other parts of her moistening and opening, Rhiannon made a small noise at the back of her throat when Hank stopped right in front of her, close enough for her to see his nipples harden, just as hers had. She pulled her gaze away from the curling hair on his chest to look up into his black, glittering eyes when he spoke.

"Tell my why you're here, Rhiannon. Tell me what you want."

The sheer animal magnetism of the powerfully built male in front of her drew her closer to him. She reached out to him and put her hands on his chest, splaying her fingers and rubbing them through the black curling hair she found there. He kept his arms at his sides, but she could see that his hands were now fists. "I want. . . ." She swallowed and tried again. "I want there to be no distance between us, Hank. No lies. No hurt. I can't—"

He grabbed her to him, crushing her mouth in a bruising kiss that left her gasping for more. "Tell me more, Rhiannon. What else do you want?" He was undressing her as he whispered the magic of his love words into her ear, her neck, her shoulder, her breast. He went down on one knee in front of her; her hands clutched at his hair. "What else do you want?" He had her shirtwaist and her camisole off her and hanging from her skirt's waistband. "Tell me." With the tip of his tongue he was drawing lazy moist circles around the aureole of her breast, while his hands cupped her buttocks. "Tell me."

"I . . . I can't, Hank. I can't think. I can only . . . aghhh . . . please." The sounds escaped her when Hank took the nipple of the breast he'd been teasing into his mouth.

While he suckled at her breast, he completed her disrobing until her clothes were in a swirled heap at her feet. Then Hank found her navel and thrust his pointed tongue into its depth. Rhiannon was lost; the gentle undulations of her womb sent liquid wildfire through her legs. Hank went lower . . . lower, until he found the tangle of ginger curls at the vee of her thighs; he nipped and pulled at them gently with his lips. Rhiannon clutched his head, taking handfuls of his hair into her hands. But Hank was relentless. Using his tongue to part her velvet folds, he found the bud he sought, flicking it until Rhiannon cried out with the shuddering spasms that rocked her and nearly bent her over him.

Ony then did Hank stand up. He lifted her up under her arms, freeing her from the tangle of her clothes. He put her arms around his neck and her legs around his waist. She moaned and whispered little nonsense syllables into his ear. They seemed to excite him all the more, for his powerful legs carried them across the room to the wall. He put her back against it. She opened her eyes against the heaviness of arousal and let her brow form the question she couldn't ask.

"Trust me," he whispered. "If you don't like it, I'll stop." With that, he pulled Rhiannon's hips away from his slightly and began her on the slow, torturous, decadent downward slide of her life to ensheath him in her slippery wetness.

Rhiannon gasped at the burst of bundled nerves that had centered in her woman's place. Her body was actually greedily grasping for him, taking him in, surrounding him, making him one with her. In the throes of agony-ecstasy, she braced her hands on his shoulders and her back against the wall, with her legs still wrapped around him, and pushed down, thereby completing the union of his body with hers.

"Awww, Rhiannon, I love you," Hank whispered, his lips against hers, his hips beginning the powerful thrusts that arched Rhiannon's back and offered up a nipple to his mouth.

"I love you, too," she groaned out as she rocked her hips in time with his thrusts, loving the feel of him inside her, loving the feel of his hands gripping her waist and hips, loving the feel of the hard wall at her back. He was so damned . . .

But the thought was never finished, for right then the coiled tightness in her belly sprung, sending heated pools of honeyed spasms through her, drying the back of her throat and curling her toes. She clutched spasmodically at Hank as he reached his climax with her; she carried on the rocking motion he was no longer capable of sustaining, frozen as he was in the throes of her body's celebration of him. Only when he cried out and grasped her to him, as much to stop her torture of him as to hold her close to him, did she relax and slump against him. Hank slide them both gently to the thickly carpeted floor in this part of his room.

He withdrew from her, turned on his side, and drew her into his embrace, kissing her temple and stroking her hair as she lay on her back, not saying anything until their breathing had returned to a semblance of normalcy. "You never told me to stop," he teased a few minutes later.

"I didn't have to unless I didn't like it, remember?"

Hank pretended to think about that. "Ohh, now I remember." Then, he turned serious. "You're going to make an old man out of me, Rhiannon Pauline O'Shea."

She frowned up at him as he leaned over her; she was using his forearm under her head as a pillow. "What do you mean?"

Hank looked into her eyes and smiled. She loved how his smile formed little laugh lines to either side of his mouth. She reached out with a finger and traced those very lines. Hank caught the tip of her finger in his mouth and drew it in to suckle it. Fascinated, Rhiannon could only watch, could only let him do whatever he wanted to with her. Releasing her finger, he took her hand in his and kissed her knuckles, stopping at the finger which bore his ring. He pointed her hand back at her, showing her the ring. "What do I mean? I mean you play me like a fiddle, girl. You pull on heartstrings I didn't even know I had. I give you everything I've got . . . everything. And it's not enough somehow. You have something eating at you, something I

317

understand. I've felt it myself before; hell, I lived it for years, always searching, always hungering. Then I found you, and I knew what it was I was searching for. But it's not like that for you; I know that. Not yet anyway. And I also know that you've got to face it on your own."

Rhiannon was beginning to get scared. "What are you saying?"

"I've decided to leave for a while, Rhiannon. I'm going on the cattle drive next month to Salina."

Chapter Twenty-two

"But . . . but how long will you be gone?" She couldn't believe this; she'd come up here to tell him she didn't want any distance between them, that she wanted to marry him, that she . . . but what good would it do her now? He wouldn't believe her now if she told him.

"That won't take but a couple months at the most. I'm interested in seeing the refrigerated cars for shipping the meat from there to back East."

"Oh." She was sitting here naked in front of him, and he was interested in seeing cattle cars? It was over.

"Then I think I'll head East myself to check on my holdings there. It's hard as hell to keep up with business from this far away. That could take a while."

Rhiannon's heart sank. She was losing him. And there wasn't a damned thing she could do. Yes, there was. She sat up quickly, oblivious of her nakedness. "Hank, I'll drop out of the race. I will. Don't go. Please don't go." She didn't even care if she begged, if she groveled. She had no pride anymore, only love for Hank.

"Rhiannon, don't do this." He sat up too. "You can't drop

out of the race now. You've fought too long and too hard to get to this point. Besides, this isn't even about politics or campaigns or anything like that."

"Then what is it, Hank? Tell me what it is, and I'll do it—or stop doing it. I swear I will. I love you! Please don't leave." She bowed her head, wanting to hide her tears from him.

He stroked her hair, pulling her face up to his. "It's about being sure, Rhiannon. It's about knowing who you are and what you're about. You don't know any of that yet. It's just like you've said all along—you need to live some first. You'd never be happy with me, or anyone else, if you don't grow some on your own first."

Or anyone else? Her blood had chilled at those words. Or anyone else? What was he saying? Had he changed his mind about her? Did he love her only when he was loving her? "Do you want your ring back now?" She was barely able to get the words past the razor-sharp pricking in her throat. All she could think was she'd barely had time to get used to the ring's weight on her finger before she had to give it up.

"Hell, no. It's yours; I gave it to you. Do you think I do that lightly? Just go around giving women rings? I know I told you before you can give it back to me when things settle down, but I don't think I ever want it back . . . no matter what happens in the next few months."

He was pulling away from her; she could feel it. "And if I'm carrying our child? What do I do then if you're gone? And the wedding invitations? What about those? And the presents, the announcements, your aunts' arrangements for our wedding?"

Hank stared at her, long and hard. His eyes still glittered and gleamed a tender black. "We'll know before I leave if you're carrying our child. If you are, we'll get married. As for the other things, everything can be cancelled and sent back. Things like this happen all the time."

Rhiannon looked at him, hurt to the depths of her soul. "But not to me they don't, Hank. Not to me." She stood up in one fluid motion, and began gathering her clothes.

"Rhiannon," Hank called out, reaching for her. She moved out of his range. "I don't think you understand what I'm saying to you. I'm not saying I don't want you or I don't love you. I'm just—"

"Please! Don't say anything more. You've said enough already."

The next week flew by for Rhiannon. She kept his ring on; it was just easier than answering a lot of questions right now. She remained at Hank's home; how could she leave? The only thing that had changed was her relationship with him. His home was still her campaign headquarters, and she was still under danger of retaliation from Big John Savage. And there'd been scattered reports of him being in the area and making threats against her personally. Some said he was holed up in an old cabin outside of town, but Hank's men had gone to investigate two or three times, and he hadn't been there. So, other than her heart being broken, nothing had changed. And if she and Hank behaved distantly toward each other, it could be explained away as the pressures of the election.

She did her best to hide it, even going so far as to slip off from everybody to be by herself so she could foolishly cry her eyes out when her monthly flow came. She hated herself for crying over something like that, when only a few weeks ago she would have been crying if she hadn't gotten her flow. Had she hoped to hold Hank and trap him into a marriage with an innocent baby? How low would she go? But now she knew that answer—to any depth to keep him. But no, that was wrong, too. She wouldn't lie to him and tell him she hadn't gotten her flow. So, she did have some pride left.

After that, she picked herself up and carried on, campaigning with a zeal that had been missing for a while. She marched, she spoke, she went door-to-door, she handed out leaflets, she spoke to various organizations in the town, she made known the issues that needed to be brought out, and she and the other women debated the issues with the men.

In essence, she kept herself exhausted, so she couldn't think about Hank leaving next month. August. It was only a few days away, just as was the election. But he hadn't said when in August he was leaving. Maybe she had more time than she realized to change his mind, to prove to him that she knew who she was and what she was about . . . whatever that meant.

Finally, the day arrived. Election Day. And it wasn't a day too soon. Everyone in town was absolutely ragged from the campaign. The men were tired of fighting with the women about the issues and about the amount of time they spent at Hank Wolfe's every day. The women were tired of the men trying to tell them what they could and couldn't do. They were voters, too; they had a voice, and they intended to use it. Rhiannon, Emma, Cat, Susie, Joletta, and Freda were tired of trying to keep it all together. They wanted to cast their votes and be done with it. They were tired of the implied threats against them from Big John's men, who rode through town whooping it up and generally scaring everyone. One month of campaigning had proven to be about two weeks too long.

Still, it was with nervous anticipation that the women walked the new floor at Gruenwald's late this afternoon. They'd already voted at the polling place, Hank's office in Wolfe, as had everyone in town, but the polls were still open for ten minutes. So nothing would be counted until closing time. Rules were rules. Hank's office had been decided on as the voting place because of the measure of safety he could provide with his name and with his men present. No one dared intervene with a Wolfe.

Still, there was a big crowd here at Gruenwald's waiting with the women candidates, their female supporters, and the out-of-town reporters. Notably present were Hank, her parents, Jim Sullivan—editor of *The Wolfe Daily,* his reporter Jimmy Pickens, Joletta's husband Henry, Freda's husband Hans, Susie's father Doc Johnson, and a shakily sober Ole Jed—the town drunk who'd nominated Rhiannon in the first place. And beyond them, there were quite a few of the town's men who had no connection to the women. It heartened Rhiannon to think she'd won over some of the men and that this election wasn't really just a man-versus-woman contest.

She just wished they'd hurry up about getting the votes counted; she was going to have her nails bitten off to her elbows by the time the votes were tallied. She looked down at herself, checking her blue-and-white-striped silk dress for the hundredth time. If she won, she wanted to look her best. But she was also looking down to avoid Hank's eyes, which kept boring into her own every time she looked at him across the room, where he was so negligently leaning a hip against one of the new tables, looking so cool and relaxed. Damn him.

Why was it always like this? She couldn't be in the same room with him and not feel his magnetism. That would never change, she just knew it. He might leave, he might never come back, he might come back with a wife from the East, she might see him every day of her life, but his tug on her would never change. It might grow stronger, but it would never diminish. Damn him.

"You look lovely, Rhiannon."

"Damn you." It was out before she could stop it. She'd just been thinking it, and then there he was at her side. As if she'd called him over to her.

He looked at her, a frown marring the width of his forehead. "I see. All right, you look beautiful."

For two cents, she would slap his smug face. He knew the effect he had on her. "That's not what I meant," she said.

"So I gathered." He was standing right in front of her, effectively blocking her, and his face, from the rest of the room. "How long are you going to stay angry, Rhiannon? How long are you going to keep that dresser in front of our mutual door?"

She'd felt the least bit foolish about having had some of the maids help her to move that incredibly heavy piece of furniture over to block that door; indeed, their looks had been beyond curious, but they hadn't questioned her. Now she felt the tiniest twinge of triumph knowing he had tried the door, only to find it blocked to him. "So you tried the door."

"No, I didn't, as a matter of fact. I opened your door from the hallway to check on you, like I do every night before I go to bed, and saw it there. Do you really think that would stop me if I chose to come to you?"

He checked on her every night? How sweet. Stop it! "No, I don't. I put it there to make a statement. Besides, I think I know you well enough to know that you wouldn't come to me if I didn't want you to. You're much too civilized for such brutish behavior."

His face changed perceptibly, from civilized man to predatory beast. He leaned toward her and whispered, "Don't be too sure, madam."

As he walked away from her, leaving her with a thudding heart and weak legs, Jim Sullivan came over to her. "Well, Miss O'Shea, here it is, Election Day."

"Yes, it would seem so, Mr. Sullivan."

"Nervous?"

"Yes. Who wouldn't be?"

"That's true. That's true. Still, I think you've got it sewn up. I'm not so sure about some of the other candidates, though." He let his gaze slide from hers.

"You mean Cat LaFlamme, of course."

He looked at her again. "Right again. Although I have to say she's made a pretty good showing of herself, no pun intended. So what'll you do if she loses? Abdicate?"

"Mr. Sullivan, I suppose it's your editorial nature to ask the most compelling questions at the most inopportune times, but still I have to say 'no comment.' "

"Oh, we were off the record, Miss O'Shea."

"Undoubtedly."

He laughed and moved away after doffing his bowler hat to her.

Rhiannon huffed out a breath or two before she calmed down. Trying to avoid Hank's eyes, she looked around the room and caught sight of Old Jed. Poor dear, he actually looked pale and sickly when he was sober. Not that he'd had any urge to quit drinking. But with the saloon closed down, what choice did he have? That, and the fact that he couldn't vote if he smelled of liquor. She wondered what he and Emma were talking about. Emma certainly looked stern, whatever the topic was. Rhiannon smiled; Emma always looked stern, even when she was happy.

Right then, Eddie came running in, calling out as he came, "Rhiannon, Rhiannon, the votes have been counted! You and the other women are to come to the Wolfe Enterprises International building right away."

The room was instantly quiet, expectant. Her heart in her throat, she grabbed her brother's arm. "Eddie, do you know who won? Do you know?"

"No, Rhiannon. They wouldn't tell me. You have to come now!"

Rhiannon looked around the room, looking first at Hank. He winked at her and gave her an encouraging smile, a silent show of support. She blinked and acknowledged him with a weak, tight smile. A little to his left were her parents, who were gripping each other's hands and staring at her, their pride obvious in their faces. Then, slowly the other women made their way to her.

Silently, they joined hands and looked at each other. If Rhiannon had expected cheering and calling out, she would have been wrong. If she'd expected a mad, unladylike dash, she would have been wrong. Instead, the women proceeded with all decorum to exit the store and form a line behind

325

which all their supporters gathered and marched with them. It was an impressive show of unity that brought tears to Rhiannon's eyes. She looked over her shoulder to see Hank right behind her. Not for the first time, she was grateful for his presence and his strength. She might need both in just a few minutes.

And from the other side of the street came the men with their supporters, a considerably larger crowd than the women's. They'd been waiting at City Hall, surrounding themselves with all the legitimacy of their offices. The two factions met in the middle of the street. Mayor Driver put his hand out to Rhiannon, which she took. "Miss O'Shea, I have to shake your hand. You've put up a good, clean fight. I can't say when I last enjoyed such a lively campaign. May the best man—or woman—win."

"Mayor Driver, I thank you for your kind words. I would just like to say publicly that if you were chosen by the people again to be mayor you have my full support. I hope that the same will be true of you if I am the new mayor."

"Madam, I can't think of anyone whom I'd rather support than you."

Cheering broke out from both parties. The candidates, male and female, walked side by side to Wolfe Enterprises to hear the verdict of the people. The members of the election board came out almost immediately upon spying the crowd. They held their hands up for silence and got it.

The Reverend Philpott was given the tally sheet and the honor of announcing the new mayor and the city council. With all eyes on him and a much more attentive audience than he was used to on a Sunday morning, the young preacher felt a sermon coming on. "Ladies and gentlemen, brethren, sisters, my flock, I have been given the distinct honor tonight of announcing the winners in this, our special election. Will you please bow your heads for a moment of silent prayer as we give thanks to the Lord for the many blessings in our lives."

One or two murderous glances were sent the young man's way, but in the end the men took their hats off, a collective sigh went up from the crowd, heads were bowed, and a moment of silence was observed.

The reverend's raised voice startled everyone back to attention. "Tonight we have the opportunity to come together as a city, as a loving flock that cares for even the least of these, my lost sheep. We have the unique opportunity to love one another and to cherish each other in the hope for a better future. This is a time of new beginnings in Wolfe, a time for forgiveness, a time for a—"

"Lynching of a holy man if you don't get on with it!" That was yelled from the back of the crowd, which was in real danger of turning into a mob by now.

Everyone froze, except for the one or two who had the audacity to snicker. Rhiannon kicked her foot back and hit Hank in the shin; she was sure one of those snickers had come from him. He disguised his yelp of pain with a sudden coughing attack. Rhiannon kept her eyes wide and innocent and straight ahead at the good reverend. At least she did until someone right behind her pinched her bottom hard right through her skirts! Gurgling sounds came from her at the same time that her eyes filled with tears.

The reverend's face went a bright red. "Oh . . . well . . . I see. Ahem, let me see what we have here." He looked the paper over, and up and down, and around, front and back, for so long that Rhiannon was terrified that someone would shoot him. Finally, he cleared his throat, consulted with one or two election board members who flanked him, nodded a couple dozen times, and said, "Well, that's simple enough, I suppose. Heh-heh-heh. Dear heavens, yes, here it is. Are you ready?"

Only the adamant front line of candidates, women and men, hands linked, kept the crowd from trouncing the preacher. "Good heavens," he pronounced. "We'd best proceed." He looked nearsightedly at the paper again. "Well, that's simple enough. The women have won all the seats, including the mayor's."

A half second of stunned silence ensued, and then a roar went up from the crowd. The new mayor and her city council were congratulated nearly to death. The riotous celebration took on the overtones of a cattle stampede what with the reporters, who sensed history being made, vying for the women's attention; the ousted men shaking the women's hands; the crowd, no matter whom they had supported, hugging and cavorting in the streets; the shouting going up and down the streets and sending even more citizens into the melee; and the stunned women themselves trying to take it all in, trying to shake everyone's hand, trying to survive the crushing throng of well-wishers, and trying to congratulate each other all at the same time.

But when Rhiannon was nearly shoved to the ground, in the exuberance of the crowd, Hank stepped in. Staggered, Rhiannon had no idea who had a hold on her arm, for she couldn't turn to see who was behind her now. All she knew was that the armed men who had been guarding the polling place were now working their way through the crowd, long rifles up and very visible, as they shouted for a path to be cleared. They stopped in front of Rhiannon and formed a human wall to either side of her, giving her clear access to the raised boardwalk in front of Hank's office building.

Rhiannon knew of only one person who was capable of that sort of command. She twisted around as best she could and saw Hank's grim face peering straight ahead; he was using his facial gestures and his other hand to signal silent orders to his men. He looked down at her, signaling with a nod of his head that she was to precede him up to the boardwalk. So, to repeated shouts of *"O'Shea will seize the day!"* Rhiannon approached the boardwalk and stepped up onto it. Hank signaled that the other women should also come up there.

When they had joined Rhiannon, he raised his hand for

quiet—and got it. He addressed the crowd. "I believe a few words are in order from our new mayor and the city council. What do you say?"

Loud cheering and thunderous clapping followed; even Mayor Driver and his city council joined in, looking genuinely pleased.

Rhiannon was overcome. She put a hand to her heart and looked up at Hank. He winked down at her and put his arm around her waist. Over the din of the crowd, but for her ears only, he said, "Go ahead, Lady Mayor. Address your constituents."

For a moment, Rhiannon could only look at him, lost as she was in her love for him. How could she ever let him leave? But she'd have to worry about that later. For now, she had voters to thank. She raised her hand for silence. Feeling a sense of accomplishment beyond anything she'd ever achieved in her short life, she stood up a little straighter and spoke up in a little bit stronger voice. "Would any of you believe me if I said I am at a loss for words?"

Laughing, cheering, and hooting met her words. When it began to die down, she smiled and went on. "I thought not. Let me begin by saying that I believe we, and I mean each of these women up here with me, faced very worthy opponents, men who've brought Wolfe, Kansas, to where it is today, men who've given everything they had and have done the best they could for all of us. For that, they have our thanks."

The sounds of clapping and hurrahs went through the assembled citizens. "And beyond that, I want to thank each and every one of you, women and men alike, for your time and your helping hands when we thought we'd have to go it alone; for your support when we wanted to quit; for your strength in our moments of weakness; and most of all, for your belief in us even when we ourselves didn't believe. You've placed your faith and your trust in us as your elected officials. I want you to know that we will do everything in our power to carry out the duties of our offices with all the fairness and all the wisdom of our predecessors. Thank you, Wolfe, Kansas." She raised her hand and waved to the crowd. The other women joined her, clasping their hands together and raising them with Rhiannon's, a sign of victory and of unity.

Hank looked down with pride at the new mayor of Wolfe and smiled, shaking his head. The little political zealot was curled up next to him on the seat of the carriage, sound asleep, with her head resting on his chest, her drawn-up thighs resting on his near thigh. Her arms were around his waist. And his arm was around the little ball she made on the seat. Miss Hellfire and Damnation was exhausted, he mused, quirking his mouth in amusement.

Hank looked up at the back of his driver. This midnight ride back to his estate seemed particularly long tonight, probably because their armed escort made the pace necessarily slower. It had been quite a celebration, he had to admit, even without all the drinking that the men would have engaged in had the saloon been open. Still, he'd seen the jars of homemade liquor being passed around among the men. Hank wasn't surprised that it hadn't taken them long to find a source, or to get a still of their own up and running somewhere close by. Hank laughed to himself; he felt sorry for the poor bastard who owned the still when Carry Nation got here.

He smoothed a curl back from Rhiannon's face, allowing his more tender emotions toward her to surface. He felt the power of his love for her wash over him. He'd never experienced this strong an emotion before in his life. It threatened to sweep him away, and it scared the hell out of him. He'd always thought that loving a woman like he did Rhiannon would make him weak somehow, more vulnerable. But he had surprised himself with how vital, how alive he felt when he was with her. And how bereft he felt at any thought of being away from her. God, he couldn't believe he was following in his father's footsteps, to fall in love with a local girl who was hell-bent on staying right here.

Fall in love. It had a strange ring to Hank's thinking. But he knew why he'd always hidden from love before; hadn't he, as a young boy, seen the horrible anguish his father had suffered when his beloved wife had died? Hadn't he, as a young boy, suffered from the same grief, the death of his mother, only to have it doubled when his father withdrew from him and stayed away so much? Then, he too had died. After that, Hank had made a vow that he would never marry, never leave himself open again to the depth of hurt that the loss of a loved one inflicted on your soul.

Well, Hank snorted, tucking Rhiannon closer against his side, so much for that vow. Here he was wrapped up neatly right around this woman's little finger. She could command him with the ease of a puppeteer, if she only knew it. She didn't need to know it, either. He knew it, and that was scary enough. He looked down at her in the dark. She moved her hand in her sleep, bringing it, her left one, up to rest on his chest, right over his heart. The huge diamond he'd given her glinted in the moonlight. The irony and the symbolism of her unconscious gesture were not lost on Hank. She wore his ring, but not his name. She held his heart in her hand, and she wasn't even aware of it. And he couldn't stay here if she didn't want his heart and his name.

Which was why he'd decided to go on this next cattle drive and then on back East to New York City for a while. He expected that by the time the herd was ready for market in about a month, the threat that was Big John Savage would be resolved . . . one way or another. If he saw the bastard again, he'd kill him. It was that simple. Then, Rhiannon could return to her parents' home in Wolfe and do some of that living she was always talking about, experience some of that freedom.

Another month. Another month of sleepless nights, of burning for her closeness, for the sweet pleasures of her woman's body, for the sound of her laughter, or even her anger. Another month of not . . . possessing her, dammit. He had all the possessions in the world, but he'd give them up in a heartbeat if it meant he could have her. But she'd turned him down twice already. And he'd sworn he wouldn't ask her again. But another month. That might be enough time to convince Rhiannon to marry him. Or . . . it might not.

Chapter Twenty-three

The next morning dawned in a blaze of bright promise. The six women would be sworn in today at City Hall. Consequently, the Wolfe mansion was ablaze with the soft swishing of silks and satins as the women readied themselves for their big day. Maids rushed hither and yon readying the nervous elected officials and the Misses Penland. There was much slamming of doors to be heard, a bit of swearing that had nothing to do with ceremonies, and much exchanging of brushes, hairpins, and powders to be done. Glimpses into the half-opened bedroom doors revealed such sights as half-dressed women, harried maids, a coiffure in the making, and a final tug on this bodice or that skirt. Only in the master's bedroom was the pace tranquil.

Standing in front of the full-length mirror in his room, Hank submitted quietly to MacGregor's ministrations as his valet straightened the lustrous black broadcloth suit coat over his shoulders. Hank tugged down on his gray brocade vest and ran a finger around the tight collar of his snowy shirt. He shook his head and made a self-deprecating sound.

"Is something wrong, sir? Perhaps the fit of the cloth?" MacGregor was quick to ask.

"No, nothing like that," Hank assured him. MacGregor was especially sensitive to any suggestion that his master's tailor-made clothes were not perfect, since he himself oversaw the measurements and picked out the fabrics.

"Then, may I ask what, sir? If I may say so, you're much more . . . cooperative than usual."

Hank laughed. "Am I now?"

"Yes, sir, indeed. Would your, uh, cooperation have anything to do with Miss O'Shea's announcement that she wishes to return to her parents' home straightaway?"

Hank looked in the mirror, but not at himself. He found his valet's reflection at his left elbow and met his gaze. "Partly."

"I see, sir. It's really none of my business. I shouldn't have—"

"Dammit, MacGregor, she can't go home yet. Savage is probably waiting for something like that to happen before he makes his move, the bastard. If Rhiannon leaves, then Cat and Scarlet and Emma will feel they have to leave, too. And where will they go? Who will protect any of them? I don't think Rhiannon has thought this thing through."

"Indeed, sir. So it would seem. But what's to be done? The lady is most adamant. She's asked the maids to begin packing her belongings today."

Hank stiffened. So soon? She'd given no indication until this morning at breakfast that she felt any urge to leave the haven that was Hank's home. "Well, you tell them for me that they are not to begin any such thing. I will have a talk with that particular young lady."

Hank caught the barely suppressed grin on his valet's face, but decided to ignore it. He knew that MacGregor, as well as every other person on his staff, was in love with Rhiannon and wanted her to stay on as the mistress of the estate. Well, so did he. And he intended to press his suit with her just as soon as this swearing-in was over.

"When, sir?"

Distracted in his thoughts, Hank asked, "When what?"

"When will you speak with Miss O'Shea?"

The baldness of the question, coming from someone as reticent and reserved as MacGregor normally was, drew a sidelong glance from Hank. He turned from the mirror, giving a final tug to his lapels. "Do you think I'm dragging my feet where Miss O'Shea is concerned, MacGregor?"

With a glance at his master's bed, MacGregor said, "Hardly, sir. But I'm sure I couldn't say."

"Oh, you say quite eloquently enough. But perhaps I haven't been quite eloquent enough with the lady in question." He looked at the closed door that linked his room to Rhiannon's. His gaze swung back to MacGregor. "Well, there's no time like the present."

"As I always say, sir."

Hank gave a curt nod as a reply and stalked over to the door. Just as his hand gripped the doorknob, he remembered that damned piece of furniture Rhiannon had placed in front of this door on her side. "Dammit!"

Feeling somewhat sheepish, and wondering if to his household staff he was a defiler of innocent young women who had to bar their doors against him, Hank turned on his heel and strode angrily to the other door, which opened onto the hallway. When he reached MacGregor and stormed past him, he said, "Not one word, MacGregor. Not one word."

"No, sir," MacGregor promised.

"That was two words, MacGregor." He opened the door and stalked through it.

"Yes, sir."

"That was two more." He turned to his immediate right, went the few paces in the hall that took him to Rhiannon's door, and jerked it open abruptly.

The door opened inward, so Hank was three steps into the room before he realized what he was witnessing. Not that it would stop him . . . well, not for more than a few moments, anyway. He stood frozen with his mouth open and his hand raised, his right index finger poised to stab at the air as he made his points.

But Hank was no more frozen than were the room's occupants, namely Rhiannon and two of Hank's maids. At least he assumed the one in the middle who was having a dress drawn over her head by the two maids was Rhiannon. All he could see of her were her feet, pantalets, petticoats, and upraised arms above the dress. The two maids stared back at Hank, their hands not moving from their positions on the dress sleeves and skirt.

"What is it? What's wrong?" came the muffled voice under the rose-and-cream-colored silk dress.

The maids, as one, looked at the covered head and then back at their employer. He signaled with his thumb for them to leave. They grinned and fairly skipped out, but took great care not to be heard. Hank shook his head as he quietly closed the door behind them. Apparently, the entire damned house was determined to see him wed this headless, arms-waggling apparition in front of him. Because certainly the grins on those maids' faces had been the first ones he'd seen today following Rhiannon's announcement that she intended to return home in the next day or so. And they'd been staring at him all morning as if he were the cat who'd eaten the canary. He'd never in his wildest dreams ever thought that he'd marry to appease his household staff. But . . . here he was.

"Hello? Is anyone there? What's going on? Who came in? I can't breathe!" came the voice from somewhere inside the folds of the dress. The headless vision twisted this way and that as if trying to locate the maids.

"Here," Hank said, freezing the dress's occupant in place. "Allow me."

There was a moment of heavy silence, which Hank took advantage of to walk up to her.

"Hank Wolfe, is that you? Get me out of this damned

thing! Where did Sally and Daisy go?" She didn't sound happy at all.

"Uh, they had to leave suddenly."

"I bet."

Hank pulled down on the dress.

"Ouch! Watch out for my hair!"

"Sorry," he said, frowning. How in the hell did this thing work? He gave it another tug; a tuft of ginger-colored hair appeared. "There we go!"

"Hardly," came Rhiannon's sarcastic retort. The dress was now down far enough to reveal her eyes—and they were snapping.

"I see your point, madam," Hank conceded, ineptly tugging and pulling until the dress—he hoped—was in proper place on Rhiannon's body. At least, all the parts of her he thought should be exposed were exposed. Except that the bodice was showing too much of her—

"Stop that!" Rhiannon, her sweet face flushed and sweating, slapped his hands away from her bosom.

"I hardly think you need expose that much flesh to your constituents, Mayor. I merely—"

"You merely mauled me and ruined my hair, is what you did, Hank Wolfe."

He looked at her hair. He honestly didn't see anything wrong or out of place . . . well, there were several curls sticking out or down at odd angles. But not sure that wasn't the intent, he wisely kept silent. For a moment. "How can you tell?"

She balled her fist up and punched ineffectually at his chest. "That does it! What are you doing in here? I have to get ready, Hank! I hardly think being late for my own swearing-in sets the proper tone for my administration, do you?"

"And that brings me to my point, madam."

She narrowed her eyes at him and put her hands to her

waist, shrugging to settle her dress. "I'm about to get a lecture."

"I beg your pardon. I do not lecture."

"Yes, you do. Every time you call me 'madam,' I get a lecture."

Hank looked at her, and wanted to kiss her angry little face. But he didn't dare. For if he did, he would be lost. And he had important things to say . . . first. "Here, turn around; I'll do up your buttons. . . . all right, don't. But you're the one who doesn't want to be late. I have all the time in the world." He only wished that were true.

With a huff of defeat, Rhiannon jerked around, presenting him her slim back. "Oh, very well then. What choice do I have?"

"None. None at all." Hank's fingers worked deftly upward on the seeming thousands of tiny round buttons that secured her dress. "And that's what I came in here to tell you. You have no choices left."

She started to turn back around—to protest, he was sure. He put his hands on her rounded shoulders and firmly kept her in place. When she calmed down, he continued with the buttons. "I've thought this through, Rhiannon. You're not leaving my home. Uh-uh, be still. Hear me out. Until now we've put everything else ahead of our love for each other. Your ambition, my restlessness. Your need to test the bounds of freedom; my need to shrug off the responsibilities of my inheritance. Your need to prove yourself to the people of Wolfe; my need to free myself of the responsibility for the people of Wolfe. All that, Rhiannon, we've put ahead of our happiness. But no more."

He was finished with her buttons. With his hands on her shoulders, he turned her to face him. He could see he had her attention. Her precious peaches-and-cream face looked all soft and yielding; he felt encouraged. "And so, I've decided you're not leaving my home to return to your parents; you're not placing yourself in danger; and you're not going to bear the name of O'Shea for much longer; and you are going to bear the name of Wolfe soon. Why? Because I love you, Rhiannon Pauline O'Shea; because I love you more than my own life. Because I want to have children with you. Because I want to hold you even when you're ninety and still teasing me about stuffing food in Aunt Tillie's pockets. Because I can't live without you, dammit, and because my staff would sooner see me leave than you."

Hank watched her face carefully as several emotions played over it. What was she thinking? Had he made another mistake? Had he pushed her even further away?

"Your staff?"

Well, he hadn't expected that. "Yes. Haven't you noticed they treat me like a leper if they think the least little thing is wrong with you and that it might even remotely be my fault?"

A huge grin spread over her face. "They do?"

"Oh, stop it. You're enjoying this entirely too much. I should never have told you. Now you'll be unbearable."

Then, her face changed; she looked young, insecure. "I have been unbearable, haven't I, Hank?"

"No," he rushed in, "that's not what I said. I was—"

"I know what you meant. But I have been. I know it. And all those things you said? You're right. But they are important things, Hank, things that could tear us apart if we're not really sure that this is what we want. I'm scared, Hank."

He finally took her into his arms. She melted into him as if she couldn't get close enough to him. Relieved, Hank took what he felt was his first deep breath in days. He just knew that everything would be all right if she was in his arms. "I know you are, sweetheart. But think about this: If we didn't love each other—you do love me, don't you?"

"Of course, silly."

"Say it."

"I love you."

"There, that wasn't so hard, was it? Now, if we didn't love each other, then the problems I've stated would be insurmountable. They would tear us apart. But we do love each other, Rhiannon. And I've never loved anyone in my entire life like I love you. I'd die for you; I'd—"

"Don't say that! I couldn't bear it! Please don't say that!"

"All right, I won't. But it's true. I will say this, though: Rhiannon O'Shea, will you marry me?"

This time, there was no hesitation. "Yes."

Rhiannon stared numbly at the charred remains of City Hall and leaned heavily against Hank, whose arm around her shoulders steadied her. Then, she looked up at him, so glad for his quiet strength during the turbulent events of this past month. She could see that his jaw was set in a determined line and his eyes were flint-like. She had a feeling that there would be no words to keep him from going after John Savage this time. That thought caused a knot to coil in her stomach. No one had to tell her she lived in a violent time when gunplay solved more problems than words.

She sighed. What a morning this had been. She and Hank had spread the word at the mansion that the wedding was definitely and seriously on. The general reaction had been one of wildly cheerful relief, much like the reaction to the news of a cease-fire in a war. Then their happy little troupe had been met in Wolfe by the long faces of the citizens. John Savage had struck again, and escaped again. But by the grace of God, no one had been injured in this fire, either. Still, everyone knew it was only a matter of time before either Savage or one of his gang did hurt or kill someone.

Despite all that, Rhiannon had insisted that the swearing-in take place in front of the ruined City Hall. So, flanked by Hank, his aunts, and her family, she had solemnly taken the oath of office that bound her to uphold the duties of mayor to the best of her ability. Then, she had silently and proudly watched her city council being sworn in. Despite everything, the moment had been triumphant, if somewhat poignant. These women had come a long way with her, and she was proud of them.

What broke her heart, though, was that Cat thought all this trouble in town was on account of her. So, now that the crowd had pretty much thinned out with everyone, including Rhiannon's family, having gone home, exhausted after a night of celebration following the election results and then their fire fighting, Rhiannon wanted to talk to Cat. She looked around; only a few curious onlookers and one or two reporters were about.

She looked up at Hank's closed face. She could tell that violent emotions were seething under his seemingly calm exterior; he looked positively frightening. "Hank, I want to talk to Cat."

He nodded without looking at her. "Do that, but stay close to my men."

"Where are you going?" She was really scared for him.

He looked at her now; his face was remote, set. "There'll be no more of this, Rhiannon. No more. That bastard's not going to keep you and a whole town hostage. I'm going to do what I should have done a long time ago."

He took his arm from her shoulders and turned to one of his men. He made a gesture, and the man tossed him a gunbelt. Rhiannon recognized it as the one he'd strapped on that day she'd told him about Big John accosting her in town.

"Hank, please don't!" She was terrified now.

He gave her a look that stopped her cold; as he spoke, he put on his weapon. "Rhiannon, stay out of this. There's just some things you can't take care of with words. The time for talking is over. You take care of Cat and this mess here. I'll take care of Savage."

With that, he kissed her hard and then set her aside,

striding toward a horse, whose reins were held by one of his men. He took the reins and mounted the prancing animal. Then, giving terse orders to the men, he sent them out in small groups in every direction away from town; several were ordered to stay with Rhiannon, and they grouped around her.

Before he rode out with a small squad, he reined his horse and looked long and hard at her. She felt a lump form in her throat. Would she ever see him again? Had they just now found their way free to love, only to have it snuffed out in the smoke of a gun battle? It didn't bear thinking about. When Hank spurred his mount and set it on a course that would take him out of town and in the direction of the abandoned line shack a few miles away, Rhiannon turned abruptly away from what she prayed was not her last sight of the only man she would ever love.

"Where to, ma'am?"

She jerked her head around. She'd almost forgotten the men who were dogging her steps closely. She had to agree with Hank on one thing: She was definitely tired of living like a hostage, of having to travel with armed escorts no matter where she went, and of having guards surrounding Hank's mansion, watching her every move. She knew it was for her own protection, but still it grated. This was freedom? The irony was too much—she'd set herself on this political course in a search for her personal freedom. Look where it had gotten her.

She'd been looking up and down the street while she thought these things and contemplating where Cat might have gone. Spying Cat over by the saloon, she turned to the big man who'd spoken, pointed down the street, and said, "Over there."

He balked. "Over there, ma'am? I don't think that's wise. Savage could be in there, for all we know."

Rhiannon looked up at him. It was hard to see his eyes under the low brim of his hat. He was large and brawny and had a crooked nose, and he certainly didn't look like anyone a smart man would cross. But then, she wasn't a smart man, was she? "Well, suit yourself. But I'm going to the saloon."

He looked at her and then at the other men with him. A look passed among them; they shrugged their shoulders and fell into step behind her, looking like a pack of bristly dogs following a tiny kitten. When Rhiannon and her armed entourage reached Cat, who had the first tears Rhiannon had ever seen her shed streaming down her pink cheeks as she stared sightlessly at the closed and barred entrance of the Fancy Lady, Rhiannon turned to the big man with the crooked nose. "What's your name?"

"Greyson, ma'am."

"Well, Greyson, I'd like to talk to my friend here privately for a few moments. If I promise not to get myself kidnapped or shot, do you think you and your men could maybe nose around the saloon a bit?"

He looked like he didn't like that idea at all; he silently consulted the other men with them. Again, the shrugs from them. He turned back to Rhiannon. "I suppose we could do that, ma'am. But I'm going to leave Suttle here with you ladies, just in case."

Rhiannon hoped the man did indeed prove to be subtle. "That's fine," she allowed, giving in.

When the men moved off and Suttle had taken up a position on the boardwalk in front of the saloon, his long rifle braced against his thigh as he rested a foot on the hitching rail, Rhiannon turned to Cat and put her hand on her friend's arm. "Cat," she said softly.

Cat stared straight ahead, but said, no longer mindful of her new grammar, "You know, Rhiannon, there ain't been much in my life that's been able to make me cry. I've stood some hard times and some hard knocks, and I've made it through. But this . . . this is the worst thing ever. For the first time in my life, folks have accepted me and cared about me and took me in as one of their own. And how are they repaid? With fires and threats and—"

Rhiannon shook her friend gently and kept her voice low and pleading. "Stop it, Cat! You've done nothing wrong, do you hear me? None of this is your doing."

Cat finally looked at her. The flatness in her blue eyes scared Rhiannon. "Yes, it is. Had I just stayed in my place—"

"Your place, Cat? Your place? Do you hear yourself? It's not anybody's place to stay where they're being beaten and used and hurt like you and Scarlet were!" Rhiannon was nearly beside herself with emotion.

Cat finally blinked and seemed to rouse a little. "You ain't going to like this, Rhiannon, but I got to tell you anyway. You know what? Me and Scarlet didn't mind our life in the Fancy Lady at all—except for the beatings, I mean. Until Big John started beating on us, things wasn't so bad."

Rhiannon was aghast. "Do you hear yourself, Cat? I can't believe I'm hearing this! You practically begged me to get you out. You said you had money, and you wanted a new life. Or am I mistaken?"

Cat looked down and twisted her fingers together. Suddenly she looked very uncomfortable in her new and decent finery, like someone had put store-bought silks on a homemade doll. "No, you ain't wrong. I said them things, and I meant them. I'm right proud to be on the city council, and I still want to do that. But can you understand, Rhiannon, that my life in that saloon was, and still is, the only life I know? I mean, if Big John was gone, and I had some money, I'd take over this place and run it. It could be my home, something of my own. I ain't never had nothing of my own."

The poignancy of Cat's words pierced Rhiannon's heart. She felt tears clog her throat. "Cat, have you been so unhappy at Hank's?"

Now Cat put a plump hand on Rhiannon's arm. "Oh, no, don't think that for a minute! I'm very grateful for everything you done for me and Scarlet, I truly am. But . . . but I've come to realize that's not my life out there. That's your life. Can you see what I mean?"

Rhiannon thought she did, but still she felt desperate to convince Cat to stay. "But what about Aunt Tillie? She adores you! She'll be heartbroken if you leave."

Cat smiled for the first time. "I love that little old lady, too. And I ain't gone yet. Ain't nothing settled." She put a hand to her forehead and rubbed it, as if it hurt. "I guess I'm just upset and scared about what's been happening, all the burnings and folks being scared. I swear, I wish I'd never heard of Carry Nation!"

"Now, what in the world does Carry Nation have to do with this—besides, of course, getting us nominated for office?" Rhiannon managed a tremulous grin.

Cat returned it briefly; then, she sobered. "Well, Big John didn't ever beat on us until he heard that Carry Nation was coming to town. He'd hit us and yell about her taking his business and as how he'd never let that happen again."

Rhiannon stared long and hard at Cat. It was as if she'd heard only one word of Cat's last statement. "Again?"

Cat looked over at her. "What?"

"Cat, you said 'again.' You said Big John yelled that Carry Nation wasn't going to take his business again."

Cat looked at Rhiannon; her eyes got wider and wider. "I did, didn't I?" she said, her voice full of dawning realization. "Well, I'll be damned."

"There's obviously a connection between Carry Nation and Big John's suddenly showing his meaner side, Cat. What do you know about him? Has he ever said anything about his past?"

Cat put her hands to her head, as if that would help her think. "Well, he said once or twice something about Kentucky. About being from there, and there being some trouble and all. Do you think Carry Nation had anything to do with it?"

Rhiannon drummed at her lips with her fingers as she

thought. Suddenly, she moved them away and shook her index finger at Cat, using it to gesture. "That just has to be it, Cat. That just has to be it."

Cat didn't look totally convinced. "Well, that's all well and good. But that don't explain these fires and him threatening you."

Now Rhiannon was eager to press her case. "Yes, it does—in a twisted sort of way. You see, Big John hears Carry Nation is coming to town—a woman he's had a run-in with in the past; then the next thing he knows, women are running for political office because of her Temperance League's visit here; then I, a woman, threaten him because of the way he's treating you and Scarlet—and he's beating you because of his anger at Carry Nation—and then I steal you right out from under his nose. And then the whole town turns against him after he wouldn't help put out the fire at Gruenwald's, and the men stop showing up at his place, so he has to close down his business. Then, he has to get out of town because of suspicion about him setting the fire. Don't you see, Cat? It's perfect! In his sick mind, all his troubles are because of women, and especially me and Carry Nation!"

Cat looked at her as if she'd lost her mind. "Well, I wouldn't sound so happy about it if I was you."

Rhiannon laughed, drawing Suttle's attention. He straightened up and brought his leg down from the hitching post. "Everything all right, ma'am?" he called out.

Rhiannon had practically forgotten about him. "Yes, Suttle, it is. In fact, I do believe things are going to be just fine. Round up the men; we're going to find Hank."

Suttle nearly dropped his rifle once he'd absorbed her words. "Do what?" he cried. "There ain't no way we're chasing after Mr. Wolfe with you along. No sirree, ma'am."

Rhiannon narrowed her eyes at him. "Fine, Suttle. I'll go by myself. Do you think that would please Mr. Wolfe more?"

Suttle gave her a very pained look. His head cocked to one

side, he assessed her, as if trying to decide if she really would ride out after his boss by herself. He must have decided she would do just that, because he muttered an epithet, and called out, "Wait right here, ma'am. I'll get Greyson and the others."

Within minutes, Rhiannon and Cat were seated in the carriage in which they'd ridden to town earlier that morning. It was the only one left here, since Aunt Penelope and Aunt Tillie had gone home right after the ceremony, taking with them all the maids, the cook, Scarlet, and Emma. The men, all silent and grim and resigned, with one acting as the women's driver, formed a loose circle around their boss's woman and began a slow, cadenced walk on the path out of town.

But they didn't even get to the bend in the road out of Wolfe before they were approached by a thundering herd of men on horseback, coming up on them quickly and raising a cloud of dust in their wake. The men with Rhiannon and Cat reined in and waited, rifles at the ready. For all her bravery and determination, Rhiannon clutched at Cat's hands; and Cat seemed eager, too, to hold onto her.

Everyone in and around the carriage let his or her breath out when it became apparent that the riders were Hank Wolfe and the contingent of men he'd taken with him. Rhiannon said a silent prayer for his safety as he reined his lathered horse to a stop. The men with him did likewise, sending a flurry of dust up into the still air. Hank looked right at Rhiannon. "Just where the hell do you think you're going? Are you trying to make yourself an easy target for John Savage?"

There was a mighty coughing and clearing of throats coming from the men with her. They were looking awfully sheepish all of a sudden.

Rhiannon heard them, but just knew Hank wouldn't be angry when he heard what she had to say. "I was coming to find you, Hank. They didn't want to, mind you, but I told them I would go without them. So, here we are. But listen! You're not going to believe this! I—"

"Oh, I believe it completely. Only you could talk these men, who know better, into chasing after me with no thought to the danger you're all in from Savage and his men—"

"Don't interrupt me! It's about Carry Nation!"

"Oh? Would that be the same Carry Nation who is at this moment setting up her tents about a half mile from here?"

Chapter Twenty-four

A stunned silence met Hank's words. The men shifted in their saddles, sniffed loudly, and looked from one to the other. But they didn't say anything. Rhiannon looked at Cat, whose eyes were widened as wide as they'd go.

"Oh, shi—" Cat began.

"Exactly," Hank said, cutting her off and drawing the gazes of both women. He leaned over his pommel toward his fiancee. "Now, my love, what was your news?"

Rhiannon tried to look everywhere but at Hank as she spoke. "It's about Big John," she said in a small voice.

"Yes?"

Rhiannon huffed out her breath. "He's from Kentucky, and he's had trouble before with Carry Nation."

She'd expected him to be shocked or surprised or grateful for the information . . . or something along those lines. But instead, he just said, "I know that."

Rhiannon couldn't believe it. "What? How did you know that?"

Hank exchanged a look and an unreadable grin with some of his men. "I have my ways."

Rhiannon conceded defeat. "Well, at least we now know where we can probably find Big John in the next few days."

"Who's this 'we,' sweetheart?" Hank asked, grinning at her now. Some of the men chuckled.

Damned superior-acting man. "Me and my city council, that's who." Angry and embarrassed at his condescending treatment of her, Rhiannon was making it up as she went along. "We're going to pay an official visit on Mrs. Nation and—"

"We are?" It was an incredulous Cat LaFlamme.

Rhiannon pursed her lips at her friend, and then went on. "We are, and we're going to welcome her to Wolfe, Kansas, and caution her about Big John Savage." There, she'd had her say. Let him stew in that.

Her speech was followed by a profoundly deep and layered silence, with every man, except Hank, suddenly intently interested in anything on the horizon or in the galaxy that didn't have anything to do with the spitfire in the carriage.

"No, you're not," Hank said levelly, his words heavy with command.

Rhiannon cocked her head at him in an out and out challenge. "It seems to me, Mr. Wolfe, that we've had this conversation before—when you told me I couldn't run for mayor. I said it then, and I'll repeat it now: How do you intend to stop me?"

"Damn you, Hank Wolfe, you let me out of here now! You can't keep me in here forever, you . . . you . . . you animal!" Rhiannon screamed at the top of her lungs, beating on the locked door of her bedroom at the Wolfe mansion. "I'm the Mayor of Wolfe, and you will let me out this instant!" She waited, listening intently for the sound of a key in the lock. Nothing. In a red rage, she kicked at the door and then beat on it with both fists. "Let me out! If you don't let me out, I'll . . . I'll—"

"You'll what, Rhiannon?"

Rhiannon froze at the sound of Hank's voice. The stinking toad was right on the other side of the door, probably leaning negligently against it and grinning that horrid, superior grin of his. What ever had made her think she loved him? She hated him. Still, a change in tactics was due. "Hank?" she called out sweetly.

"Yes, darling?" came his equally sweet reply.

"If you'll let me out, I'll do that thing you like when we're in bed—"

"That's enough! I should tell you I'm not alone out here."

He was lying, trying to embarrass her. He was alone. Please, God. Another change in tactics. "All right, then, you wart-faced son of a donkey, if you don't let me out, I'll destroy this room and then hurt myself. I'll climb right out that window—"

"Very mature, Mayor. But perhaps I should remind you that you're on the third floor, my love."

Damn. Defeated, Rhiannon sat down in a most unladylike sprawl with her back against the door, her legs straight out in front of her. She leaned her head back so it too touched the door. "All right, Hank, you win. Point taken. You can stop me. Now, will you let me out?"

Her words, a white flag of surrender, were met with silence. Rhiannon's eyes darted this way and that as she strained to hear any sound at all from the other side of the door. She looked across the room to where the heavy dresser was still against the door that joined her room and Hank's. She'd had plenty of help tugging it over there, and knew she couldn't get out that way. She could strain for a week and not budge the darned thing. It must have grown roots.

"How do I know I can trust you?"

Rhiannon jumped up at the sound of his voice. He was beginning to give in. "I give you my word! Please, Hank!" With her palms pressed flat against the door, she placed her ear to it also.

A scoffing sound erupted from the other side and nothing

else. Apparently that was his response.

Rhiannon jerked away from the door, putting her hands to her waist. She poked out her bottom lip, a dangerous sign. "And just what is that supposed to mean, Mr. Wolfe?" she snapped.

"Uh, perhaps, Mr. Wolfe, sir, we should consider madam's word as sufficient?"

MacGregor! Rhiannon's first response on hearing the valet's voice was physical—a red-hot flush crept up her neck and cheeks; Hank hadn't been lying—he wasn't alone. And she'd said that thing about bed! A hand went to her mouth to cover it in embarrassed shock. But this was no time to be undone by weakness. She began to plead in earnest. "MacGregor, make him listen! Make him let me out! Please! It's against the law to hold someone against her will! Tell him I'll listen to him. Tell him I'll let him know all my movements in town. Tell him I'll be careful! Tell him—"

The key scraped in the lock, cutting off her words and drawing her gaze to it. She stepped back a few cautious feet as the door swung inward. She looked up to see Hank standing in the open doorway, his arms crossed over his chest. A worried-looking MacGregor peered from behind Hank's tall, muscular frame. "That's all I wanted to hear from you, Rhiannon. Just that you'd be careful and that you'd let me know where you are at all times. Now, how hard was that to promise?"

"Not hard at all," she said, striving for a nonchalance she didn't feel. She hadn't promised any such thing; she'd simply instructed MacGregor to tell him those things, not promise them. She kept that defiant little thought to herself, though. She was learning that girls might blurt out everything they were thinking, but women kept their own counsel.

"Well, that's more like it," Hank said, that stupid grin of his saying he'd won this round.

Rhiannon fought her natural inclination to narrow her

eyes at such a challenge. Besides, she hadn't lost; she'd merely . . . changed her mind. Raising her head regally and using her best haughty and cultured voice, she inquired, "I suppose I'm free to go now, and that I'm no longer to be held prisoner?"

Hank turned slightly to exchange an enigmatic look with his valet. "What do you think, MacGregor? Do you think she'll behave?"

Rhiannon's gaze shifted quickly, pleadingly, to MacGregor. His hesitation to vouch for her was making her nervous.

"I believe we can trust madam, sir."

Rhiannon blew a relieved breath out. She advanced on the open door, skirting Hank, intending to brush by him in a classic gesture meant to freeze him out as an insignificant presence. His hand snaked out and took hold of her arm. "Promise me."

The sneaky—! She pursed her lips; his grip tightened. "All right, very well, you skunk. I promise. There; are you happy now?"

"No. What are you promising?"

"I promise you one thing, Hank Wolfe. This little incident of snatching me bodily out of a carriage right in public, in front of your men, and hauling me onto your horse and then up the stairs over your shoulder, right in front of your servants, and then locking me in my room and then talking to me as if I were a child will never happen again as long as I live. I will not submit to such rough treatment of my person or my dignity."

MacGregor's eyes widened; Hank's narrowed. "Behave like a woman, and I'll treat you like one." Hank's voice dripped with icicles.

She slapped his face. The harsh sound echoed in the stunned silence that followed. MacGregor reeled back three steps, as if clearing the area for an impending boxing match.

Hank's face colored, but not to as deep a red as the stain of her handprint on his cheek. His black eyes were glacial, his mouth a straight line. The seconds ticked by. Rhiannon was afraid to breath; she hadn't even known she was going to slap him until she did. Hank let go of her arm as if he'd just had a hold on a particularly vile serpent.

"I've changed my mind, madam. You are free to come and go as you please. You need not inform me or my men of your wanderings. I sense that our protective presence is grating on your precious freedom. Therefore, exercise it."

Rhiannon's heart plummeted. She'd gone too far. "Does that mean I can leave your home and return to mine?"

His mouth worked as his eyes bored a hole in her. "Please yourself in that, as in all things you do, Miss O'Shea."

He turned his back on an already regretful Rhiannon; MacGregor scampered out of his way and shot Rhiannon a what-are-we-going-to-do-now look; he then followed his master out of the room, closing the door behind them.

Rhiannon stood there, lost in her sudden independence, which only left her feeling bereft of Hank's loving support. Freedom and independence were indeed lofty goals, but they were also lonely feelings, she was coming to realize. She slowly turned away from the door and stood still, letting her gaze rove her room. And there it was. Her room. Her home.

"Do you think we ought to be doing this, Rhiannon? I mean, we ain't got no men now to ride with us. And Mr. Wolfe acts like he don't hardly care what we do, even if you are wearing his ring and living in his house. I mean, ain't you afraid Big John might pop up at any minute?" Joletta asked, her brows knit in the first gesture of uncertainty Rhiannon had ever seen the feisty woman display.

But Rhiannon said nothing; she just kept walking toward the lit-up tent and the milling crowd as the people left after the night's lecture and rally. She didn't particularly care to be reminded of her decision to stay at Hank's, even if it was for reasons of expediency only.

"I have to agree with Joletta," Emma fussed. For the tenth time. "I'm not so sure this is a good idea. It's as if our presence at this Temperance League revival, or meeting or whatever you choose to call it, gives official sanction to Carry Nation's presence here."

Rhiannon dodged a few running children, and made way for another wagonload of people going home after hearing Carry Nation's message of temperance on the issue of alcohol. She noted that the people's moods ranged from jubilant to somber, probably depending on the amount they drank each day.

"Emma, your sudden reluctance wouldn't have nothing to do with your being sweet on Ole Jed, now would it?" Cat teased.

Emma huffed out her denial. "It's 'anything,' not 'nothing,' Cat; and I most certainly am not sweet on Jedidiah or anyone else."

"Jedidiah?" the other five women said in unison.

Emma stopped short; the mayor and the remaining city council members did likewise. "Yes, Jedidiah Wanamaker, if you must know. If any of you took the time to talk to him, you'd know that was his name."

Chagrined, the five women looked down. Not-so-timid Susie Johnson spoke for them; her voice was soft and gentle. "You have a good heart, Emma. And we didn't mean to poke fun. But I'd think that if you . . . care for Ole—Mr. Wanamaker, you'd want to see him sober."

Emma's chin quivered just the slightest bit. The five women all reached out to her at the same time, but only Freda was close enough to actually pat her shoulder. "Dere, dere now, Emma. Ve all know vhat you are feeling."

Emma's face cleared up. "I do want to see Jedidiah sober; of course, I do. But not this way. Not the way Carry Nation is doing it—using him as an example of 'the ills of drink,' as she says. Why, those temperance women of hers have even hauled him up in front of the crowd in their tent and made a public spectacle of him. It's all so very cruel."

"I heard about that, Emma. And that's why we're here, if you'll remember," Rhiannon soothed. "You're not the only one upset about that. My family was here last night when that happened. Mother said there was no end of harsh feelings after that meeting. This morning she had Eddie take her out to Hank's to alert me to what was being said."

"But what can we do?" Cat asked. "She's been peaceable enough. No fighting or disturbing of the peace; nothing we could use to make her leave." Cat had graduated to reading the city ordinances.

"Oh, she doesn't have to leave so soon, does she?" Susie asked, a plaintive note in her voice. "Daddy and I have come to see her every night. She is so . . . passionate, so eloquent. Daddy says she has the eyes of a zealot."

"As if that's something good—whatever a zealot is," Cat scoffed.

"Emma, I've meant to ask you zomezing," Freda cut in. "Vhy vas Herr Vanamacher at za meeting?"

Emma blushed; she looked almost girlish, almost pretty. The other women laughed in a teasing, cajoling way. She batted her hand at them. "Oh, you . . . Well, since the night of the elections when he and I first spoke, we found we had something in common—the loss of a loved one. You see, he lost his wife when he was really young, and he never got over it. But now . . . well, you know."

"For heaven's sake, woman, spit it out. We got a meeting to go to." Joletta's reticence had vanished.

"Well, he thinks maybe . . . that he and I could . . . be together. And so he wants to try to quit drinking. He came to hear Carry Nation, hoping her message would give him more strength."

"Oh, that's so romantic," Susie pronounced with a heaving sigh. The other women added their congratulatory murmurs.

Except for Joletta. "Yeah, and darned near impossible for someone who's been drinking as long as Ole Jed has. Has he been drinking that moonshine liquor that's been mysteriously going around?"

Cat was seized with a sudden coughing fit; Freda pounded her back while Emma spoke loudly over the coughing. "No, as a matter of fact, he hasn't. I've been very proud of him."

"It's probably because he's too sick in bed from getting off the drink." Joletta again. "Wait until he feels better. He'll go find it first chance he gets."

"Now, listen here, Joletta Hawkins, just because your Henry bought some of that vile stuff, and you can't get him to quit—"

"That's enough!" Rhiannon said. "We came out here to talk with Carry Nation. And not to argue amongst ourselves. We'll do one thing at a time. We'll speak with the Temperance League, and then we'll speak with Sheriff Parsons about tracking down the source of the moonshine liquor. And whoever it is will pay. It wouldn't surprise me in the least if it was Big John making the stuff."

Cat whooped and bent over double. Rhiannon exchanged a bewildered, concerned look with the four women before bending over Cat herself. With a hand on her friend's back, she asked, "Are you all right? Is something wrong?"

Cat straightened up. Her face was red and flushed in the light from the tents; damp tendrils of her hair clung to her chubby face. "Nothing at all," she said in a raspy voice. "I'll be fine."

"Well, if you're sure. Come on, then. I believe we can catch Carry Nation and her followers now. The crowd seems to have thinned out considerably; don't you think?"

The city council members nodded their heads and fell into step behind Rhiannon as she pushed aside a tent flap and entered the almost empty interior of the huge canvas meeting hall. Only a few men and women were left to shake the hand of the famous Mrs. Carry A. Nation, who looked to be a plump, sweet-faced woman in her mid-forties. Looking around, Rhiannon could see the women of the Temperance

League handing out pamphlets to anyone within reaching distance.

The ladies of the League greeted and handed their tracts to the ladies of the city government. Rhiannon gave a quick smile and took one, skimming it briefly while she waited for the remaining folks to depart. She preferred to speak with Mrs. Nation alone without benefit of a curious audience. Luckily, the reporters were already gone, apparently not sensing any story here other than what they'd already been printing or sending back East or out West.

Finally, the women were alone with each other. Rhiannon stepped forward to take Mrs. Nation's hand. And saw that Doc Johnson was right—she did have the eyes of a zealot. They were piercing, electrifying, as if their very intensity were meant to cover a deeper sadness, an aching hurt that wouldn't heal. Rhiannon felt a frown coming over her face, but she quickly schooled her features into a bland exterior. What was this sudden feeling of kinship she felt with this woman, who was so unlike herself, and yet who seemed to share the same burden of independence that Rhiannon shouldered?

"Mrs. Nation, I'm Miss Rhiannon O'Shea, the—"

"Ahh, the lady mayor. I've heard so much about you in the past few nights," she said, a smile on her face.

"That's very funny, especially coming from someone as famous as you," Rhiannon quipped, trying to cover the most insane urge to tell this woman all her troubles, to unburden herself to the short, motherly woman. Such was her presence. "And these women form the city council of Wolfe, Kansas." Rhiannon performed the introductions.

Carry Nation acknowledged each of them, and then turned back to Rhiannon. "So, my dear, are you here to welcome me or to run me out of town?"

Taken aback by the woman's directness, but also admiring such a quality, Rhiannon came back with: "A little of both, I suppose."

"Now this should be most interesting. Do you mind if we sit down, Mayor O'Shea? It's been a long day." She indicated a row of wooden benches. Once they were all seated, Carry Nation asked, "Would you like a drink?"

Rhiannon nearly fell off the back of her bench. "I beg your pardon?"

"Of lemonade, of course."

"Oh, of course. No, I don't wish one, but please feel free yourself."

"Thank you, I will. Ladies?" She pointed at each of the distinguished members of the city council in turn. Uncharacteristically quiet, they all simply shook their heads in refusal. Carry Nation called out to one of her followers, and was brought a big glass of lemonade. She drank half of it. "Passionate speaking is a thirsty profession, Mayor."

"I daresay, having made a passionate speech or two myself lately. But I'll try to keep this brief, Mrs. Nation."

"Which would be a first in politics, I'm sure," the temperance leader quipped. Rhiannon was really beginning to like this woman's sense of humor.

"As am I. I said our mission is twofold, and it is. We do welcome you here, because if not for you, or more accurately, if not for the men of this town feeling threatened by your visit here, we would not be the mayor and the city council. And, too, we feel your message of temperance is a valid one, one which bears repeating, if the crowds night after night are any indication."

"And they are. It's the same every place the Temperance League goes. It seems there's more fussing and fighting before we get to a town than there is once we actually get there. We really are a peaceful lot."

The women with Rhiannon laughed a little too self-consciously. And Rhiannon herself felt the least bit uncomfortable at this point. It was one thing to say you were going to chastise a famous, or infamous person, but it was quite another to actually face him or her and do it. But still, she

Cheryl Anne Porter

was an elected official of the people, and she had a job to do. The citizens would be here long after Mrs. Nation left. "I felt sure you were, Mrs. Nation. But still I felt compelled to come out here tonight regarding an incident that seems to have raised the anger of several of Wolfe's citizens."

"And which incident is that, Miss O'Shea?"

"The one concerning Ole Jed, or I should say Mr. Wanamaker." Rhiannon looked quickly at Emma Calvert, who sat stoically stiff.

"Ahh, yes. Your town drunk."

Several gasps came from the city council, five to be exact. Six, counting Rhiannon's. "Mrs. Nation, that's not a fair thing to say."

"Isn't it? Every town has one." The zealot's fervor shined from the kindly woman's eyes. "My hometown in Kentucky had one. It was my husband. He drank himself to death, Miss O'Shea. That is not a very pretty picture to carry in your heart and mind for the rest of your days. In fact, it is so ugly that I do everything in my power to see that not another human suffers what he did and what I did for years. The fight against the demon of drink is a righteous one, Mayor, one I will fight all my life. Your town drunk came to me to hear my message. I did not seek him out."

"I understand that," Rhiannon stated quickly, cutting her off before she got too far into her speech. "But you have to understand that the good citizens of Wolfe hold a very tender spot in their hearts for Ole Jed."

"So tender that they'll allow him to wallow in the muck of his own drunkenness, Miss O'Shea? I would be interested to hear how that is kind or loving. To me, allowing him to drink himself slowly to death with spirits is much more cruel than any embarrassment I could have caused him or the good citizens of Wolfe by bringing him before the crowd as an example of what liquor can do to a good person. I did nothing different than a preacher would with a reformed sinner."

Rhiannon felt the shock and outrage that Mrs. Nation's

360

words were meant to evoke. She also felt the shame, and sensed the same in the stiff quiet of her five friends. "I'm so sorry for the tragedy of your husband's death, Mrs. Nation. It must have been awful for you. And I understand what you're saying about Jed Wanamaker. You're right there, too. We have been indulgent and perhaps even unthinkingly cruel in allowing him to drink so much. I want you to know that Mr. Wanamaker has sworn off liquor and is even now recovering from its effects on his system."

"Praise God!" Carry Nation said, clasping her hands together and closing her eyes. She then opened them. "I hope he's not going through this alone."

"No, he's not," Emma Calvert said.

Carry Nation assessed the slender woman with the big nose and the stern countenance. "Good for you," she said.

Emma colored briefly and looked down. Rhiannon stood up, signaling an end to the meeting. The members of the city council and Carry Nation stood, too. "Well, Mrs. Nation, I assure you that you're welcome here in Wolfe to present your message to our citizens as long as there are no repeats of the scene like the one with Mr. Wanamaker. I assure you we have no other, uh, drunks in our midst. So, you should have a peaceful stay here."

"My message is of temperance and understanding, Mayor. Nothing more. I don't wish to be a destructive presence. If I can rescue a citizen or two along the way, then all the better. But I seemed to have roused the anger of at least one of your citizens, who, quite frankly, scared me pretty badly."

Rhiannon went cold and hot. "What do you mean?"

"I mean a very large man with a red beard and a fierce group of followers."

The women of Wolfe exchanged looks with one another. "That was Big John Savage, as sure as I'm standing here," Joletta exclaimed angrily. "He can be pretty mean."

Carry Nation smiled pointedly. "I don't scare easily, madam."

"Where did you see him, Mrs. Nation?"

"He came to this tent late last night, Mayor, apparently to tell me I had better get out of town right then or something bad, as he said it, would happen to me."

"And it just might, too. He's meaner than any rattlesnake I ever did run across." Joletta was breathing fire.

"You must be very careful, ma'am," Susie Johnson added in her soft voice.

"I assure you I always am, miss," Carry Nation replied.

"Well, we can do better than that," Rhiannon added. "You should know that your visitor was John Savage, owner and bartender at the Fancy Lady Saloon. He's a particularly violent man where women are concerned, and we suspect he set two fires in town, but we haven't been able to catch him yet. He had to shut down his saloon when the men refused to do business with him after the first fire, so now he's hiding out—we suspect somewhere close by. He is a very angry, very dangerous man. I will speak with Sheriff Parsons about setting up some protection for you and the League while you're here."

"I thank you for that. But there is something else about him that bothers me. It almost seems that I know him. He looks familiar, but then again his name isn't. Still, I may have run into him before in another town. It just seemed to me that he harbored too much anger toward me personally to be a stranger. I hope I'm wrong."

"For your sake, so do I," Emma said.

"Ja, dat is true. You must be very careful, Frau Nation." Freda solemnly shook her blond head.

Rhiannon ended the visit with: "Thank you for your time and your cooperation, Mrs. Nation. We'll leave now. I know you're very tired."

The women all exchanged farewells and left the tent, heading for the Wolfe carriage. Lantern light spilling from the huge tent behind them lighted their path. It also illuminated Hans Gruenwald, Henry Hawkins, and Doc Johnson standing by the carriage and waiting for their wives and daughter. Their concern for their loved ones heightened Rhiannon's sense of being alone now that Hank had withdrawn his armed support from her comings and goings. Riding out here in daylight hadn't been so bad, but the dark was another matter. Not that these three older, unarmed men really were a threat to Big John, but their mere presence had to be a comfort to their women.

When they reached the men, Joletta began to fuss. "Now I don't like it one bit that you three are riding out to the Wolfe mansion by yourselves. Why, anything could happen. Leastwise we got our menfolk here to walk us home."

Rhiannon had her mouth open to protest that they would be fine, a sentiment she really didn't believe, when a deep voice came out of the darkness from the other side of the carriage. "They have their menfolk here, too, Mrs. Hawkins."

Everyone jumped and spun around. "Jesus, Hank, you scared ten years of growth right out of me! What in the world are you doing? I didn't even hear you come up!" Doc Johnson railed, a hand to his heart.

Rhiannon's heart had leapt into her throat at the sound of his voice. It was back in place in her chest, but beating a steady tattoo against her ribs as she drank in the sight of Hank as he walked into the timid light offered by the lanterns from Carry Nation's tents. He was dressed in dark clothing and was heavily armed, as were about ten men behind him. He looked straight at Rhiannon while he answered Doc. "I'm sorry. We didn't mean to scare you."

"Well, you sure as shooting did. How did you get here without us hearing you?"

Now Hank looked at him, but he pulled Rhiannon close to his side and kept his hand on her elbow. She wanted to melt into him, to kiss him and tell him she was sorry, but all she could do was stand there. "Our horses are over by the Fancy Lady. We decided that Savage just might be hiding out inside since we can't find him anywhere outside of town."

"Well, did you find anything?" It was Henry Hawkins; he rubbed his stubbly chin as he talked.

"Yes, we did. I believe the bastard—excuse me, ladies—has been in there all along." He looked down at Rhiannon with a heated gaze that she felt even under her skirt.

"Well, that would explain him getting away so fast after the last fire, the one at City Hall. Nobody heard any horses or wagons or such leaving town after that, come to think on it," Doc said, nodding his head thoughtfully.

"That's what made me think he might be closer than we think. And the saloon is big enough to sleep his gang, too. But of course they aren't there now. No such luck."

"Now you know vhere to look, though, Herr Volfe," Hans Gruenwald commented, ducking his head in respect.

"Yes, and that's something. I'm going to leave some men there to watch the saloon—"

"Hank." Rhiannon interrupted him. "Big John went to Carry Nation's tent last night and threatened her."

The knot of men tensed. "That doesn't surprise me in the least. Okay, I'll have Gaines post a couple men over there for tonight just to be safe."

"And tomorrow I'll talk to Sheriff Parsons about leaving some men at her tents for as long as she's here," Rhiannon added.

"Good idea, Mayor." He smiled down at her, the first smile she'd seen from him in days. Relief swept through her—and another emotion she recognized as desire for him, pure and simple. She'd been too long without the comfort and the pleasure of his loving. Appearing to sense something more in her upturned face than was visible to the others, who were discussing among themselves the threat that was Big John, he breathed in heavily, catching her scent on the wind. As if wanting to assure himself he was reading her right, he quirked a look at her. She ran the tip of her tongue over her lips—subtly, but on purpose.

Hank's eyes widened appreciably at her obvious tease. His

hand tightened on her elbow; she moved her arm forward, rubbing his fingers along the soft outer edge of her full breast. Hank fairly gasped, and then startled the assembled folk by pronouncing, "Dammit, we have to go home now."

Chapter Twenty-five

Clothes were everywhere. Sheets and the quilted counterpane were thrown back and over the end of the huge bed. The dresser that had blocked the door between their bedrooms had been pushed roughly out of the way by a galvanized Hank while a giggling Rhiannon had looked on. With a growl of triumph, lust, and soul-searing need, he'd flung open the door, scooped her up in his arms, and carried her across the threshold into his room, much like an anxious bridegroom.

And now he had her where he wanted her—naked in his sight and in his bed. Never again would she deny him entry into her room, for when they were married, he was moving her into his room. That damned adjoining room could be converted to a nursery—because, by God, they were going to need one. With her under him and moaning and tossing her head while she raked his back and urged him on faster, Hank was shaken by the intensity of his sheer need for this ginger-eyed woman. He'd die if he didn't have her; it was that simple. The depth of his love for her was outweighed only by his fear of ever losing her. He'd kill any son of a bitch who ever even looked cross-eyed at her.

Hank's physical sensations shut down his thoughts. There was no room for anything now but the feel of her warm, smooth, soft, slick body; for the guttural sound she made in the back of her throat when her climactic tremors began; for the way she curved her back, arching her most secret place more fully into his driving thrusts; for the clinging of her arms to his back as he suddenly spasmed and held himself rigid over her, allowing his life force to flow into her warm, waiting womb. He heard his own cry forced past the tension of the cords in his neck. And then it was over—for now. Hank eased himself off her and collapsed on the bed beside her. He drew her into his embrace and planted warm, tiny kisses on her face as he smoothed her hair with one hand.

"My God, Rhiannon, it scares me how much I love you," he said in a low voice. "The things I want to do to you in this bed scare me, too."

"Like what?" she teased, wriggling herself up against him and rubbing her breasts against his muscled chest.

He sucked in his breath and felt the first faint stirrings of resurging desire. So soon? He laughed huskily. "Stop that, Mayor, or you'll find out. And I warn you, some of the things could probably get us thrown in jail."

"Oooh, I hope it's in the same cell," she cooed seductively.

"That does it!" Hank growled into her neck, drawing a delighted squeal from her. He then proceeded to show her and to teach her the most unlawful things a man and a woman could do with each other in bed. . . .

Rhiannon couldn't believe that a delegation of the town's fathers could show up so early in the morning—especially this morning when her body still rang with the wonderfully wanton things Hank had shown her and had done to her. She'd be surprised if she could walk down the grand, sweeping stairway without a limp, that devil. Still, she supposed it wasn't all that early—ten-thirty. Fortunately, she'd had time for a long, leisurely soak in the tub . . . with Hank. The most lustful grin she was sure she'd ever formed rode her face as she thought about the pleasures of the tub when two loving persons are wet and slippery. Damn him! He was all she could think about.

Well, enough of that. She'd best get that grin and those thoughts safely tucked away before she was completely down the stairs and into the morning room. She'd hate to shock the town fathers . . . a naughty giggle escaped her. She stopped on the stairs and clapped her hand over her mouth, forcing herself to assume the decorous demeanor worthy of Wolfe's leading citizen. She prissily straightened her sky-blue muslin dress about her. She must attend to the business at hand.

And serious business it must be to warrant a special trip out to the Wolfe mansion. After all, she'd told the men she would be in town today. They could have met at City Hall—no, they couldn't have. It was burned to the ground. The problems in Wolfe, Kansas, came flooding into her light mood, drowning it in the pressures of governance. With a heavy sigh, she proceeded down the stairs and made a sweeping entrance through the opened doors of the morning room, only to stop short. Hank faced her, but the delegation, consisting of former Mayor Sam Driver, former City Councilman Ed Hanson, Sheriff Parsons, former City Councilman Tom Haskell, and several businessmen, including her own father, all had their backs to her. She knew Hank saw her, but he never gave away her presence. She couldn't believe what she was hearing.

"—and we don't want this to be taken the wrong way, Mr. Wolfe. We all think Miss O'Shea is a lovely girl, a very capable girl—why, we understand she is to be your wife. And a lovely one she'll make, too. It's just that we got ourselves a right serious situation in Wolfe, one we think calls for a more, uhm, forceful presence than our elected mayor, if you will. Now, two fires have already—"

"Why, Mr. Driver, are you still making campaign speeches?" Rhiannon interrupted, angry inside but controlled on the outside. She was sure the sparks she felt in her eyes would ignite this . . . this delegation and cause a third fire in Wolfe.

The men all stood up and turned as one at the sound of her voice. But only Hank was grinning; he remained seated, pulled the humidor over to him, selected a thin cigar, lit it, and sat back in the comfort of his winged Queen Anne chair, as if to watch a coming entertainment.

Rhiannon could have kissed him. He was saying, plainer than any words, that he was deferring to her, allowing her to do her job. She advanced slowly, with measured steps, into the beautiful, airy, tense room. The men actually took a step back. She was sure the barely stifled guffaw she heard came from Hank. It had to—no one else looked in the mood to laugh.

"Now, Rhiannon, me dear, we're only thinking of—"

"Yourselves, Father," Rhiannon said, cutting him off. "Might I remind you esteemed gentlemen that I am the elected mayor, not Mr. Wolfe?"

They turned and looked at Hank. He removed the cigar from his lips, blew out the smoke, and smiled, saying not a word. Their gazes turned back to their mayor. She took the control she'd really had all along.

"Now, if you'll be so good as to be seated, we'll discuss what's on your minds so early this morning." She made a sweeping gesture with her hand, indicating the men's vacated chairs. She seated herself at one end of the damask-covered settee. Her father was the only delegate brave enough to join her there. He squeezed her hand, and she reciprocated, as she arranged her skirt artfully and turned a serene, queenly, tight smile on the men. "I believe you were discussing the fires?"

There was much shifting and settling on the chairs, much clearing of throats and sniffing, much darting of their gazes from one to the other, and from Rhiannon to Hank. Rhiannon waited with a tenseness she dared not show. For her term as mayor to be successful, these very men had to respect her and to trust her decisions. She'd done everything she could to earn that respect and trust, and this was the first test of her mayoralty. If they still insisted on turning to Hank and not her, then she would be undone as an elected official. This whole month's efforts would be for naught, not to mention her dream of making a difference in her hometown.

"Well, Mayor, it seems to us we got to do something."

Rhiannon almost wilted in relief. Tom Haskell had taken the reins and had consulted her—not Hank. She was officially the mayor of Wolfe, Kansas, as of this minute—and not as of her swearing-in. She knew it—and they knew it. "Go on," she encouraged, willing the quaver out of her voice.

"Thank you kindly. It's not just Carry Nation being here. We all know that. We had problems—big ones—before that and—"

"And way before my daughter was mayor, was home even, Tom," her father said. Apparently, he'd come along to take her side. Moved, Rhiannon sat up straighter, fighting tears. This was no time to succumb to emotion.

"Well, I know that, Edwin. No one is saying otherwise. But still, it seems things are beginning to pile up one on top of the other."

"I'm aware of that, Mr. Haskell," Rhiannon said evenly. "I assure you that I and your city council are looking into each and every problem."

Now the questions came at her almost all at the same time. "Like John Savage?"

"And the fighting between husbands and wives going on over the temperance meetings?"

"How about rebuilding City Hall? Who's going to pay for that?"

"We got men out there drunk every night. With the saloon shut down, where're they getting the liquor?"

"And them damned reporters snooping around everywhere. Everybody's getting edgy. People are at each other's throats, Mayor."

"And if that ain't enough, now the Fancy Lady's been busted up. Folks are saying it was Carry Nation that did it out of vengeance over Big John's threatening her."

Rhiannon was shocked. Yet another wanton act of destruction? She immediately eyed Sheriff Jack Parsons, Effie's big, kind, intelligent husband. "That's right, ma'am," he said. "It happened last night."

"But how? There were men posted there to watch over it," Rhiannon cried.

Jack Parsons looked at her and then at Hank. Rhiannon's gaze followed his to Hank. He'd tensed visibly, and his jaw was working. He leaned forward to put his cigar out in the pewter ashtray on the coffee table. He spoke up, now that this directly concerned men under his orders. "There's more. What is it?"

"Well, you're not going to like this," the sheriff said. "Those men were, uh, knocked out and dragged off out back. Then the place was cut up with axes. The mirrors were broken; bottles were smashed; furniture—even the piano— was busted up good."

"And no one heard a thing?" Rhiannon was incredulous.

"Oh, yes, apparently they did. When the townfolk came running, they found Carry Nation and the Temperance League inside, the axes in their hands."

Rhiannon found herself standing, and couldn't remember doing so. "What? Are you suggesting that those women sneaked up on armed men, knocked them out, dragged them to bushes, and then destroyed the Fancy Lady—a saloon already closed and not offering the drink they find so repulsive?"

The men squirmed uncomfortably. Sam Driver spoke up. "Well, what else are we to think, Mayor? They were standing there with the axes when folks came running."

Cheryl Anne Porter

"This is the most ridiculous—!" She sputtered trying to come up with appropriate epithets—and an alternate explanation. She refused to believe that Carry Nation was capable of any such heinous act as the willful destruction of another's property, even if the owner of it had threatened her. And dear God, she'd been the one to tell Carry Nation who owned the saloon.

"Where are the temperance women now?" Rhiannon asked, almost afraid to hear the answer.

"They spent the night in the jail," Sheriff Parsons said. "I had no choice, under the circumstances, ma'am."

She sat down heavily and blew out a breath, looking from one to the other of the men. "How are the men who were knocked out?"

"They're okay enough. Doc Johnson took a look at them, and we put them up at the hotel."

Rhiannon nodded and looked at Hank. He was positively grim. She looked back at the sheriff. "Jack, what did Mrs. Nation and her followers say happened?"

Here Jack fiddled with his hat that was perched on his knee. "They said they heard noises and came out of their sleeping tents, only to find Mr. Wolfe's men gone. Then they ran over to the saloon to see what was going on. And found it all busted up, but no one was there."

"That's because they did it, I tell you! And you got to run them out of town for sure now, Mayor; because if you don't, there's going to be an out-and-out war." It was skinny Ed Hanson; his large Adam's apple bobbed up and down as he spoke. Silence followed his angry words.

Hank ignored Ed and spoke to the sheriff. "Jack, Mrs. Nation's story sounds more like the truth than what the worked-up citizens came up with."

"I thought the same thing, Hank, but if I hadn't put those women in jail, I tell you I would have had to arrest the entire town—at least, the men. The women are all siding with Mrs. Nation. And we all got hell to pay at home, too."

Rhiannon supposed they did. Under any other circumstances that would have been funny, but not today. She just didn't see how things could get worse. Until Aunt Penelope, Aunt Tillie, Cat, Emma, and Scarlet joined them. Spying them in the doorway and wondering how long they'd been there, she put her elbow on the upholstered arm of the settee and rested her aching temple in her outspread fingers. Her staring at the door and then putting her head in her hand caused the men to turn to look at the door as well.

"We heard everything, dear, and I have a suggestion," Aunt Penelope offered, a sweet smile on her elegant if lined face. Frozen, everyone merely waited, knowing that God alone knew what would issue from her mouth.

"Yes, she does. And it involves food," Tillie said, clearly pleased with her sister's idea.

Cat jumped into the breach. "I know what she's going to say, Rhiannon. And it just might work; ain't—isn't that right, Emma?"

Emma nodded enthusiastically. "I love it, Rhiannon. It's certainly worth a try. And it just might draw out John Savage."

Now the women in the doorway had everyone in the room's attention. Still, they deferred to their mayor.

"By all means, Aunt Penelope, let's hear it," Rhiannon encouraged, feeling truly heartened. If Cat and Emma liked it, it just might be plausible.

"Well, I was thinking that everyone is so bothered and upset with all the goings-on in town, why don't you have a great big party to enliven everyone's spirits? And the entire town will be invited! Isn't that just a marvelous idea?" She clasped her hands together excitedly over her thin bosom.

So quiet was the room that you could have heard crickets chirp. A party? In the middle of all this trouble? A party? With everyone at each other's throats? A party? And invite the entire town? Wait a minute. Rhiannon's mind was working furiously. She unconsciously put a fingernail in her mouth and chewed on it while she thought. She didn't have to be told that every eye was on her. Even with her sight turned inward, she could feel them. A party! That's exactly what they needed!

She jumped up and rushed at Aunt Penelope, much to the gasps and astonishment of the men, all except Hank, who just shook his head and looked up at the ceiling, as if asking the Almighty to look down at what he had to deal with here in Wolfe, Kansas. Rhiannon captured the older woman in a fierce hug and planted a smacking kiss on her lined cheek. Aunt Penelope returned the embrace.

"Why, Miss Penland, you are brilliant!" Rhiannon crowed, holding onto Penelope's thin arms. "Absolutely brilliant!"

"Why, thank you, dear. I've always thought so. But still, it's nice to have one's genius recognized."

Rhiannon laughed, and was joined by the other women. The men withheld their mirth. Rhiannon turned to them with an animated sweep of her skirt; she paced and spoke with her hands as she enumerated the plan. "Don't you see? It's brilliant! We have a huge get-together, invite the whole town—I mean everyone, including Carry Nation and her followers, and the reporters; make it a big celebration of some sort, like a holiday, and feed everyone, get them to feeling good, maybe even have a dance; have it in the afternoon, say. And then when we're all together, we get everything out into the open. We discuss our problems face-to-face; we do it in an organized but informal and less threatening way than some official town meeting would be. That word 'official' just sets people off, so we'll make it a holiday. What do you say?"

She stopped her pacing, and felt the seconds tick off the clock as the men stared at her, hopefully assessing and absorbing the plan's merits. Her eyes lit on Hank, who continued to sprawl in his chair, one ankle over the opposite knee. He raised his right hand to his brow, giving her a tiny salute of support, if his grin was any indication. She felt a tiny tremor of joy warm her stomach. She would never forget this day and Hank's unqualified support of her—and she would never stop loving him. Not ever.

The silence was all the more remarkable for the cacophony that followed it when the men all began talking at once and all over each other.

"Of course, and we can post guards to watch out for John Savage and his men. He won't be able to stay away. Hank, about your men—"

"No problem."

"Good. Now, we'll need to have some sort of a raised platform for being seen when Mayor O'Shea addresses everyone."

"We can get Smith to provide the lumber for it. He always said if we—"

"Great. That's settled. Now, about a date for this event—it needs to be soon."

"Definitely soon—the sooner the better, before the whole place blows to kingdom come."

"And we need a reason for it, like Miss Penland said. Some sort of celebration. Think."

"How about to celebrate Mayor O'Shea's engagement to me?" Hank offered in a totally innocent voice.

Everyone looked at him. Paused. And then went on.

"That's perfect. Okay—it's the celebration of the O'Shea-Wolfe alliance. Everyone will love that. They wouldn't miss that for the world. That's perfect."

And so the men went on and on, warming to the idea and dredging up all the details. For her part, Rhiannon stood with the other women in the doorway, her arms crossed under her bosom, watching them. While the men raised issues, the women quietly solved them.

"Make it Saturday, Rhiannon; that's four days away," Cat suggested. Rhiannon nodded.

"Yes, plenty of time, I'd say. I believe Jed will be up by then and could attend," Emma remarked. Rhiannon nodded.

"Where you going to have a party that big, Rhiannon?" Scarlet asked, her young, pretty face just that once more— young and pretty. Rhiannon shrugged her shoulders and shook her head.

"Why, right here, of course, dear. We have plenty of room on the front lawn," Penelope offered. Rhiannon nodded.

"And food. We need plenty of food." That, of course, was Aunt Tillie. Rhiannon nodded and patted the old woman's shoulder. Everyone invited could bring a dish so there was no burden on anyone—especially Hank's cook.

"And we must have something to drink. I believe Tillie and I can provide the liquid refreshments," Penelope generously offered.

Before Rhiannon could nod her assent, stunned as she was by Hank's so casual suggestion that this party be to celebrate their engagement, Cat and Scarlet both jumped in, their very vehemence rousing Rhiannon out of her stupor.

"Uh, no, Miss Penland! No! I don't think that's a good idea at all, Rhiannon!"

"Me, neither. Not with Carry Nation being there and all."

Rhiannon looked at them in turn. "What are you talking about? What does Carry Nation have to do with Aunt Penelope providing refreshments?"

"Nothing, if it's lemonade and punch and such as that," Cat admonished, her eyes widened, her head nodding.

Rhiannon narrowed her eyes in confusion and looked at Aunt Penelope, who sighed dramatically and said, "Oh, very well. Lemonade and punch it is."

"Straight lemonade and punch, Miss Penland," Cat said in a voice meant to draw a promise out.

Penelope huffed. "Oh, very well. You really are no fun anymore, Miss LaFlamme."

"Well, I'm not half as much fun as that party would be if you and Miss Tillie provided the—never mind."

Emma and Rhiannon exchanged looks. Emma shrugged her shoulders helplessly. Rhiannon was about to question

Cat, Scarlet, and the Misses Penland about this very strange conversation, when she was drawn into the men's conversation by Hank calling them all over to the sitting area to merge their thoughts, problems, and solutions.

Once the women had joined them, the men gave up their seats and went across the wide foyer and, with the help of Watson, the butler, brought in several chairs from the library. Refreshments were ordered; tablets and pens were brought in. Rhiannon presided, and committees were formed; Freda, Susie, and Joletta were sent for; Sheriff Parsons went back to Wolfe to keep an eye on things; Rhiannon sent a boy to fetch her three brothers—they could go house to house to tell people; another boy was sent to fetch the reporters out to the Wolfe mansion . . . and so the morning and afternoon went.

Only when every detail was worked out to the mayor's satisfaction—and she was demanding—did she adjourn the meeting in Hank's morning room, now lit by tendrils of late afternoon sunshine. She walked with Hank to the front doors and said her good-byes to the committees. Cat, Scarlet, and Hank's aunts had gone upstairs to plan . . . what?

When had they left? Rhiannon wondered idly, not really giving it too much thought. She was with Hank, and his arm was around her waist, just as hers was around his. And it now appeared, for the first time in a long time, that all was going to be right with the world. Hank closed the door after Edwin O'Shea turned to leave; he had kissed his daughter's cheek and, with tears in his eyes, had nodded his head, as if to say how fine a job she'd done and how proud he was. That meant more to Rhiannon than any vote of confidence from the public for her as mayor would have meant.

Then, they were alone in the foyer. Hank looked down at her; Rhiannon smiled up at him, feeling very tired, very mellow, very secure, very hopeful. . . .

"Tell me, Mayor O'Shea, just how long an engagement is proper when one is affianced to an elected public official?"

Hank turned her towards the stairs as he spoke. They'd climbed a few before Rhiannon chose to answer. "Oh, I'm not sure, sir. I imagine it depends on whether or not said elected official is carrying a child."

Chapter Twenty-six

Rhiannon couldn't have said if she was relieved or apprehensive about the arrival of Saturday in Wolfe, Kansas. Certainly, it had been a whirlwind four days of mind-numbing proportions. Not only did she have to help in the planning of what on the surface of things was a simple engagement celebration—there was nothing simple about it, she snorted; but she'd also had to orchestrate, in private, the arrangements for security, and write a speech capable of restoring order in this small western Kansas town that now looked to her to lead it.

She quit nibbling on the end of her pen and looked over her speech for the hundredth time. One thing was clear—she hated writing; the words just wouldn't seem to come. And not only that, even the most exciting, the most inspirational words looked flat on paper. There was only one way, she decided, to make the people of Wolfe understand what was at stake, and that was to show them—she had to make the best, the most impassioned speech she'd ever given, a speech far beyond the political ones she'd delivered in the past month. A sermon, actually, she realized. She groaned, thinking of the crowd's reaction to Reverend Philpott on the night of the election. She replaced the pen in its holder on the table beside her, recapped the ink, and pushed aside her papers, deciding to just allow her emotions to carry the moment.

Which was just as well, because right now she needed to get dressed. She uncurled herself from the middle of Hank's bed, where she'd been sitting in her nightclothes since her bath. She ran her fingers through her hair; it was almost dry now. She grinned, hearing Hank in the bathroom; he was singing a bawdy tune while he finished shaving. She shook her head, a cat-like grin on her face, as she slid off the side of his bed. He hadn't let her out of his sight—and just barely out of his bed—since Tuesday's strategy session with the delegation of men. He seemed determined to get her with their child, and at the earliest possible moment. He'd decided she didn't intend to marry him unless she became pregnant. And that wasn't true—she most definitely was going to marry him, baby or no . . . but he didn't need to know that right away—the chase was too much fun.

"Hank," she called out as she padded toward the open doorway joining their rooms. The man was irascible—the door was gone. Only the doorjamb's wooden framework remained. He'd made his point—no more barriers between them.

"Yes?" he answered, closer than she'd thought. She turned back to see him standing just inside his bedroom, a towel around his midsection, his muscular body shiny with the damp of his bath. As always, she could only stare at the sheer masculine sculpture of his form; she'd never get over the sense that he was a statue of a Greek god come to life. He certainly brought everything in her to life.

"I'm going to get dressed now." That was another thing— she had to tell him every move she made . . . just like an old married couple. But she loved it that he cared.

"That's a shame," he teased. "I like you just like you are now."

She made a face at him. "I'm sure you do, but I certainly don't think this outfit will garner the respect I need today from my constituents."

"It would the male half."

"But not in the way I want it."

"Touché, Madam Mayor."

She acknowledged her victory in this verbal joust with a prettily executed curtsy. Hank whipped his towel off and flipped it at her derriere as she squealed and ran for the brutalized doorway. The wooden floor just inside her bedroom still bore the angry scrape marks from Hank's fevered removal of the offending dresser earlier this week. Once she was sure Hank wasn't going to follow her, she turned her attention to her bulging wardrobe. Her shoulders slumped; she didn't have a thing to wear. . . .

Rhiannon smoothed the pink-and-rose-striped silk of her skirt and tugged at the fitted bodice, trying in vain to pull more fabric up over her exposed bosom. Hank had commented, when she came down, that she'd been better covered this morning when all she'd had on was the soapy bubbles of her bath. His face had worn a look of disapproval—he sure as hell didn't want any man seeing that much of his intended—but his eyes had twinkled appreciatively. She gave up; there was no more give to the fabric. Still, it wouldn't have surprised her if Hank had stuffed a linen napkin down and across her bosom to restore her modesty.

Right then, her last free moment of introspection for the day was ended with the arrival of yet another wagonload of guests. She felt like half of them had been involved in the planning of this event, but that really wasn't true. There weren't 20 people, not counting the men in Hank's employ, who knew the true reasons for this gathering.

She took in a breath on a ragged sigh; fear that Big John would show up, fear that he wouldn't and his reign of terror would continue, fear that the "guests" would end up in one big brawl, and excitement over being the center of attention, as far as the "engagement" was concerned, coupled with excitement that she would be the center of the town's focus as their mayor, all combined to render her stomach queasy and to make her head feel light.

She hoped things in Wolfe settled down soon, because she'd felt this same illness for several mornings now. The pressures of the past month had even affected her monthly flow—it had been almost non-existent this last time; not that she missed the cursed thing. But still . . . events were beginning to take a physical toll on her; hadn't she been so very tired that she'd slept late every morning? Her face flushed in remembered pleasures; of course, Hank Wolfe had kept her up late many a night.

Arms took hold of her from behind, shaking her out of her musings, and a pleasantly warm kiss was placed on her bare shoulder. She smiled and brought her hand up to cup Hank's face. He turned her around, looked her up and down sternly, and then grinned hugely. "Shall we, Mayor?"

She took his offered arm, saying, "We shall, Mr. Wolfe."

Hank nodded to Watson, who opened the front doors with a grand flourish. Hank and Rhiannon left the mansion to the enthusiastic applause of the assembled guests. The Misses Penland were at one side of the double doors on the wide sweep of the front steps, and the O'Sheas and Ella stood at the other side, all of them resplendent in their finery and in their obvious happiness at this event. Hank and Rhiannon hugged their respective kin, and then crossed to greet each other's families. It was like a fairy-tale dream to Rhiannon.

Then, united as one family, they faced the citizenry of Wolfe, the reporters, the Temperance League, and their still-thunderous ovation. Rhiannon was amazed, for the front lawns of the mansion had taken on the look and the atmosphere of a carnival. Children ran hither and yon; women with small babies reposed on blankets on the lawn, men had gathered in cliques to talk and to smoke, and the Ladies

Aid Society presided over the tables. It could have been the Fourth of July.

Right in front of the happy couple were the colorful congratulatory banners that hung from the new wooden platform that would serve as a dais and a bandstand; Mr. Smith had built and erected it right where it now stood. Looking around, Rhiannon was delighted to see numerous tables, some meant for sitting at when the meal began, some laden with food, others with punch bowls and lemonade pitchers, and still others with engagement gifts for the happy couple. The tables were scattered about the roped-off confines meant to delineate the party's boundaries and, unknown to them yet, contain the guests within the area that Hank's men discreetly patrolled. They'd left nothing to chance where Big John's skulking ways were concerned.

Hank turned Rhiannon over to the squealing knot of young women, chief among them an extremely pregnant Effie Parsons, who claimed her attention first. It seemed they all had to inspect Rhiannon's engagement ring. She was so very happy for this one moment to be the carefree girl she'd been only a month ago and to share this most female of moments with her friends. She'd expected maybe more of the same jealousy or aloofness she'd experienced since she'd been home. But apparently she was "forgiven" and accepted now that she was to be married. But to her infinite suprise, there was more to her friend's comments than just the usual sentiments about a new engagement; they congratulated her and hugged her and kissed her cheek for striking a blow for womanhood, as they saw it, with her successful run for office. For about a half hour she was able to forget she had the weight of the town on her shoulders.

But then she was reminded. Cries of "Speech! Speech!" went up at different points throughout the crowd; she knew it wasn't spontaneous. This too had been orchestrated by the committee to gain everyone's attention for Rhiannon's words. She broke away from her friends, shaking hands and hugging several people as she advanced toward Mr. Smith's wooden platform. The moment had arrived. Rhiannon's heart beat in her throat, while her stomach dropped to her feet. Please, God, she prayed silently . . . all the while keeping a brilliant, carefree smile on her face.

The women who formed Wolfe's new city council also approached the dais and took up their places behind Rhiannon, seating themselves on the benches placed to either side of the podium she was to use for her speech. It was a good thing she'd decided to go with the emotion of the moment, because she'd completely forgotten her speech up in Hank's bedroom. And that reminded her—she missed Hank's presence. She wished he were by her side, but he'd told her he thought it best if she commanded the moment on her own with only her city council flanking her. She understood why, but still, she missed his reassuring presence at her side.

The crowd quieted, as much as was possible for a gathering of this size on such a hot afternoon under clear blue skies in August. Women fanned themselves; men wiped their brows. She knew she wouldn't have long to gain and hold their attention. She took a deep breath, looked back and to either side at her city council, and faced the crowd.

"My friends, my family, my fellow citizens of Wolfe, I welcome you to this wonderful gathering of folk who all care deeply for one another. Now, it may not have always seemed so in the past month. Heaven knows we've had more than our share of troubles this hot summer. And we all know that most of them were stirred up by me." There was a cheerful rumbling throughout the crowd. With a grin on her face, Rhiannon waited for it to die out before continuing. "Just like in the schoolroom: Since I started it, I have to end it. I stand before you today as your mayor, as your daughter, as your friend, as your fellow citizen, to ask you . . . to beseech you . . . to plead with you to put aside the differences that threaten to tear us apart. To put a stop to the fighting and feuding that divides us into distinct little groups, whether you're a woman or a man, a drinker or a teetotaler, a churchgoer or a sinner, and no matter your politics. We can't afford to let our differences destroy us. We have to allow our—"

Shots rang out from the outer perimeters of the crowd and bullets zinged within inches of Rhiannon's head. She hadn't even had time to blink before she was knocked to the platform floor and was covered by Hank's body. Stunned, she lay there looking up at the sky and at his drawn Colt revolver as he lay over her; his wolfish, gleaming eyes scanned the area for the shooters. Terrified, she turned her head to see a jumble of bodies lying all around her as apparently the other women were covered by men with drawn weapons, too. Where had they come from?

She heard the screaming of women and children, the hoarse yells of men, and more and more sharp cracks of gunfire. The sights and sounds were hellish, numbing, as the gunfire seemed to go on and on. Dear God, people were being killed; her worst nightmare was realized. The day of peace had been given over to a nightmare of violence. She didn't even realize she was crying until she felt a wetness trickle into her hair at her temples. She knew it was tears and not blood, for Hank was shushing her gently, telling her not to cry, it was all right.

"What is it, Hank? Who's shooting?" she cried hoarsely, so scared she couldn't think straight.

He looked at her fiercely, as if assuring himself she had not been hit by a bullet, and then turned his eyes back toward the sound of gunfire, which was, thank God, beginning to slow to a stop. "John Savage and his men, sweetheart. We got them. Now lay still."

A tremor shook Rhiannon as she clung to Hank's arm and his shirtfront. John Savage had been a threat, both open and hidden, for what seemed like years. His presence and then his threats, just like the smoke from the fires, had been a pall that hung over the town for more than a month. She didn't dare hope his season of terror was over.

But apparently it was; at least the gunfire had stopped and men could be heard, from a distance, saying it was okay, it was all over, that people could get up now. Rhiannon was afraid of what she would find—would innocent people be dead? Had their plan to trap John Savage ended the life of some unsuspecting citizens? She knew she could never forgive herself if that were true, be they men, women, or children.

People began to slowly pick themselves up. The sounds of sobbing and of parents yelling for children and of relieved cries of found relatives mingled with the called-out questions of what had happened, what was going on, who had been shooting. Hank, in one athletic movement, got up and pulled Rhiannon with him. He holstered his Colt and checked her all over, wild with anguish until he reassured himself she was indeed unharmed. The same scene was being played out over the acre or more of the front lawn in front of the Wolfe mansion. Amazingly, there wasn't much noise at this point; or else Rhiannon couldn't hear it over the roar in her ears that was fear.

Suddenly, emotional reaction set in with her. She sobbed aloud and threw herself against the expanse of Hank's chest. His arms, like steel bands, wrapped around her. His quiet voice spoke soothingly to her, while she listened to the thundering tattoo of his heartbeat against her ear.

"I love you, Hank! I will always love you!" she sobbed almost hysterically. Coming so close to death had a backlash effect—she needed to reaffirm life . . . and love.

"I love you, too, Rhiannon. I love you, too," Hank said hoarsely, planting kisses on her forehead and at her temples. "Oh, God, he almost killed you. I was almost too late. When I think—"

"No, Hank, don't say it! I'm alive. I'm fine. I love you."

And so the words and the embrace, like hundreds of others being repeated all around them, went on until a woman's scream rent the air. People clung to each other and turned to the back of the assemblage, waiting tensely, fearing the worst—a dead husband or child. Then, after a tense moment, a man's voice called out, "It's Big John! And he's dead! And so is his gang!"

No one cheered, as might have been expected. But relief did ripple through the crowd. Just then, the senior O'Sheas, with John and Patrick in tow, and followed closely by Ella, fought their way onto the platform, wild with fear until they saw their daughter alive and well. Patience O'Shea fainted in relief, causing Ella to comment, "Ain't no need for that now. The trouble's done over."

But Rhiannon could see Ella's quivering chin and the tears dancing in her eyes. She looked up at Hank; he nodded. She stepped out of his embrace and hugged Ella to her, and then went to embrace her brothers and see to her mother. Hank caught her arm, turning her to him. "I'm going to go see to Aunt Penelope and Aunt Tillie. MacGregor was with them, but I—"

She stopped him with a hand over his on her arm. "Go, Hank—please. Make sure they're fine. The poor old dears are probably terrified."

He squeezed her arm and left the dais. Assured of her family's safety, once Eddie had also found her, bringing with him the shy and beautiful Emily, Rhiannon began to walk through the crowd, calming and reassuring the more wild-eyed among the guests. She even found Carry Nation, and was relieved to see her unharmed, knowing she too was a particular target of John Savage's. The atmosphere was now like that after one of the vicious and sudden tornadoes that were so common to this area. The people were still afraid, but were picking themselves up, physically and emotionally. She knew Ella was right—the trouble was done over. She even found she was capable of a smile or two for this child or that old man.

"Rhiannon!"

She turned at the sound of Hank's voice. He was back on the platform and was indicating she should come there, too. His face wasn't grim, actually, but it was serious. She hurried to him; he gave her his hand to help her up. "What's wrong? What is it?" she asked, not even trying to keep the plaintive note out of her voice.

"While my men are clearing away the bodies, do you want me to talk to everyone? They're getting over the shock now. Maybe I can explain things and clear this up pretty quickly."

She nodded, agreeing fully that he should speak—especially since she wasn't sure herself of what exactly had happened. Hank kissed her quickly on her mouth and hugged her to him one more time. He then turned to the crowd and raised his hand. With one or two calls to the shaken crowd, he had their full attention. These people were used to the authority of a Wolfe voice and the Wolfe name. And they trusted this man. When they were quiet, Hank said, "It's all over, and everyone is fine. Everyone, that is, except for the men who were responsible for the terror and the fires and the threats of the past month. John Savage was behind it all—the fires at City Hall and at Gruenwald's. He and his men, not Carry Nation and her followers, smashed up the Fancy Lady. I know that was crazy of him, since that was his property, but there you have it—he was a madman. I believe he did it to get you to react just like you did—you turned on each other and on Mrs. Nation, who spent a night in our jail just to keep her safe from you."

He let that sink in, that they were all capable of the kind of violence they deplored in Big John, and then went on. "You also need to know more about Big John Savage. Carry Nation said all along he looked familiar to her. And he was. She was right. His real name is one Mrs. Nation will recognize—Ben Workman, and he was from Kentucky. He had a saloon there, too, and he had a hand in Mrs. Nation's first husband drinking himself to death. When she got the law after Workman for illegal activities in that state, he fled, changed his name, grew a beard, put on weight, and hid out here amongst us."

Gasps and murmurs interrupted Hank. He looked at Rhiannon, and she returned his solemn gaze. She then looked out over the crowd. Several people were patting and otherwise comforting a shaken Carry Nation.

Hank regained their attention with his raised voice. "I know all this because I've had my men—the very ones you see now at the edges of this roped-off area—investigating him, along with Sheriff Parsons' help. I don't have to tell you that the man we knew as John Savage was a cruel and vicious man, one who misused and abused the women he employed. And we're all to blame for allowing that to go on in our midst. We all share in that blame—except for your mayor. She saw what was happening, and she put an end to it, at considerable risk to her own life." He was interrupted by cheers and applause for Rhiannon. Hank pulled her to him and kissed her soundly, raising the level of noise to an approving roar.

Rhiannon was dazed, happily this time. She looked out at the crowd from the warm nest of Hank's embrace. Jimmy Pickens, whose story had started all this, called out, "Hey, Mayor! This is going to put our town on the map in a big way! Wait until these out-of-town reporters tell our story!"

As she listened to the congratulating going on around and among the townspeople, excited at the prospect of national attention, Rhiannon felt a tug on her skirt. She looked down and saw Carry Nation standing there. "May I address the crowd, Mayor O'Shea?"

"Please do, Mrs. Nation. I believe you deserve that after spending a night in our jail and after nearly being killed here today."

Carry Nation acknowledged her with a nod of her head. Cat LaFlamme and Susie Johnson stepped forward to help the temperance leader up onto the dais. Seeing her there, the crowd instantly hushed. "I want to thank Mayor O'Shea for all she's done to help insure my safety and that of my Temperance League. She hasn't always agreed with my methods—and she let me know it, too—but she has been supportive of my goal. And my goal is to get you to think about your drinking and how it can ruin not only your own life, but the lives of those around you who know and love you. I believe that has been accomplished. After all, Mr. Wanamaker—Old Jed to you—is now sober, and I understand is soon to be groom to Mrs. Emma Calvert"—cheerful calls and a smattering of applause interrupted her momentarily—"and the local drinking establishment is closed down. I'm glad you know that I had nothing to do with the Fancy Lady being broken up with axes. But I have to admit, it is a pretty effective measure—one I may give some consideration to myself in the future. But as for Wolfe, my work is done here. My Temperance League and I will be moving on. Just please don't let the evils of alcohol rob you of what is most precious—your lives and your loves."

She stepped down to thunderous applause and worked her way through the crowd, gathering her women to leave for the next town.

Then, Cat stepped forward, hesitantly at first, but then with more self-assurance as she spoke. "I . . . I just want to thank all of you in Wolfe for everything you done for me and Scarlet. You didn't have to, but you took us, and us being whores and all, into your hearts; and in Mr. Wolfe's case, his home. I . . . me and Scarlet will always be grateful for what you done.

"And . . . and I've been talking to Mr. Wolfe while I've been staying out here about the Fancy Lady. You all need to thank him, because he's going to support me and Scarlet with his money and his help to rebuild and to reopen the saloon as its new owners." Cheers, whistles, and catcalls went up from some of the men. "But with some changes!" The men quieted.

"There ain't going to be no fancy ladies no more." The

women applauded. "And there won't be anyone allowed to become a drunk. We ain't—aren't going to tolerate that. And once it's up and running, I'd like to offer it as a meeting hall in town, and also I would like to invite the women to consider it as their meeting place, too, for the Ladies Aid Society. I know you don't have no regular place to meet. I know me and Scarlet would be right proud to have you. And we'd even kick the men out and serve you punch and lemonade—or something stronger if you like." Now the women whistled and called out to Cat and Scarlet, thanking them and accepting. "And I sure hope we don't have no competition for customers with the moonshiners who've set up business since the saloon closed."

The men got very quiet. Their women looked at them, eyes narrowed. Rhiannon looked up at Hank; he shrugged, clearly at a loss. Cat poked Scarlet in the side, and they grinned knowingly at each other.

And then—*boom!* The sound of an explosion nearby set off another round of cries, gasps, and drawn guns. "It came from around there!" one of Hank's men called, pointing to the back of the mansion. Sure enough, a thin puff of smoke came wisping around the corner and lazed over the heads of the shocked crowd. Everyone seemed to turn to his or her neighbor as if asking, "What now?" They then turned to the dais for direction.

Rhiannon looked up at Hank, but her attention, and Hank's, was drawn to Cat when she said to Scarlet, "Uh-oh, I bet I know what that was."

"Me, too, but I ain't goin' to tell 'em."

"What is going on, Cat, Scarlet?" Rhiannon asked, almost at the end of her rope with all the surprises today.

"You just better go have a look-see for yourself, Rhiannon, 'cause you wouldn't believe me if I told you," Cat said, shaking her head as she spoke.

Rhiannon turned to Hank. "Lead on, Mayor. I'm right behind you," he said.

And so, headed by Rhiannon, Hank, and the members of the city council, the crowd fell into step and hurried toward the source of the boom and the puff of smoke. Guns were put away, children's hands were grabbed, and adults chatted and theorized about the boom all the way around the huge mansion, back through the gardens, and finally to a little-used back section of the grounds. And then they all stopped suddenly as if they were one body—one huge, stunned, jaw-dropped-open body.

For coming toward the good citizens of Wolfe were Aunt Penelope and Aunt Tillie, their sweet faces dirtied by soot, their hair fried. Aunt Penelope was very upset with her sister; she was holding her elegant hands at her slim waist. "I have told you repeatedly, sister, that if you don't adequately relieve the pressure on the lines, then all our work on the still will be for naught."

"So shoot me. I was eating," Tillie fussed right back, her blackened little face working furiously.

Just beyond the sisters, and behind several scorched wild shrubs, could be seen the remains of an impressive-sized still. The outhouse, no longer used since the Wolfe mansion boasted modern plumbing, that had held the still was an exploded shambles.

The silence of the crowd, twofold in nature—stunned on the part of those who hadn't known of the still's existence and guilt on the part of those who had—was broken by the outbreak of hysterical laughter and much hugging and making up, a catharsis for the tensions and hurts of this hot August in western Kansas. While the adults recovered, children scampered closer to inspect the remains of the most curious contraption.

"Right in my own backyard," Hank breathed, awe and embarrassment lacing his words. "My own sweet old aunts. Well, I'll be damned."

Cat and Scarlet rushed over to the Misses Penland, reassuring themselves that the old dears were indeed unharmed.

They patted and smoothed the ruffled feathers of the warring sisters, just as the guilty men in the crowd did with their own womenfolk.

Rhiannon shook her head. "Hank, what are we going to do with them? What rascals they are! This explains their secret project and all those trips to town for odd pieces of piping and unusual ingredients. We'll have to keep a close eye on them when our children arrive. There's no telling what the old dears will teach them."

Rhiannon's words brought Hank's undivided attention her way. His voice was positively intense . . . and hopeful. "What are you saying, Rhiannon O'Shea?"

She smiled up at him coquettishly, her hands behind her back. "I'm saying it's time we made an honest man of you."

Hank feigned surprise, but a wide grin that showed his white, even teeth gave him away. "Why, Miss O'Shea, I do believe you're proposing to me."

From the corner of her eyes, Rhiannon could see several curious heads and smiling faces turning their direction. This latest development began sweeping through the crowd. But she didn't care; she was ready to tell the world of her love and need for this man above all others. "Why, Mr. Wolfe, I do believe you're correct."

Hank stuck his thumbs in the waistband of his pants. "Let me see if I have this straight, madam."

"Hear it comes—the lecture. You called me madam."

"Don't interrupt me, sweetheart."

"So sorry."

"Thank you. Now, have you learned that freedom is hollow if it means alone, my dear?"

"I have."

"Good. Then, in the recent tradition established by my aunts and by yourself of volunteering my home as a refuge and a meeting hall, may I offer its many rooms on the second floor as a temporary City Hall and offices for you and your

393

city council until the one in Wolfe can be rebuilt?"

"We'd be most glad to accept, sir."

The heads in the crowd, all grinning crazily and poking each other and whispering rather loudly back through the ranks about what was going on, turned as one from Hank to Rhiannon, depending on who was talking.

"Good, madam. Then, finally, I suppose, would you like to also maintain your place in my home, my heart, and my life by doing me the honor of marrying me—even if you're not carrying our child . . . yet?"

A few gasping intakes of air could be heard at this most strange of proposals. But the main participants only grinned hotly at each other.

"Oh, but I suspect that I am, sir."

Hank blanched. The crowd stilled. "You are—I mean, you do. I mean—"

"I do, Hank Wolfe. I do. I do want to marry you. I love you—beyond life, beyond reason, beyond anything I've ever wanted in my whole life. I want you."

"And I want you for the rest of my life, Rhiannon O'Shea. I love you."

Almost before the words were out of his mouth, Rhiannon was in his arms and raising her face for his kiss. Oblivious to the scores of onlookers, Hank obliged her, capturing her mouth, just as he'd captured her soul.

A dramatic, romantic sigh went up from the crowd. Couples took each other's hands; young lovers, among them Eddie and his beloved Emily, looked into each other's eyes; young children made faces and groaned.

MacGregor, off to one side, and witness to the entire scene, turned his eyes heavenward. "Well, now, Ezra Wolfe, Scotland and retirement will just have to wait. There'll be wee Wolfe babes on the way, and a fine handful the little lads and lassies will be, too. The lasses will be just like their mother— great ladies. But the lads, Ezra? Someone will have to see to their becoming great gentlemen, much like their father and grandfather. And so . . . I'll be staying." A huge Scottish smile lit his face.

"Oh, dear," Aunt Penelope sighed to Cat and Scarlet. "The wedding. I'd almost forgotten. And the whole town invited. Of course, we're having the ceremony in the ballroom, and then the reception will be right here on the lovely front lawn." She turned to Aunt Tillie. "Sister, do you suppose we can get the still up and running in the next few days? If so, we can provide the refreshments."

Three captivating stories of love in another time, another place.

MADELINE BAKER
"Heart of the Hunter"

A Lakota warrior must defy the boundaries of life itself to claim the spirited beauty he has sought through time.

ANNE AVERY
"Dream Seeker"

On faraway planets, a pilot and a dreamer learn that passion can bridge the heavens, no matter how vast the distance from one heart to another.

KATHLEEN MORGAN
"The Last Gatekeeper"

To save her world, a dazzling temptress must use her powers of enchantment to open a stellar portal—and the heart of a virile but reluctant warrior.

_51974-7 *Enchanted Crossings* (three unforgettable love stories in one volume) $4.99 US/
$5.99 CAN

THE AMERICANA SERIES
Robin Lee Hatcher
Winner of the *Romantic Times* Storyteller of the Year Award!

"Warm, tender, compelling historical romance!" —Amanda Quick

Forever, Rose. Rose Townsend needs a knight in shining armor to rescue her from her drunken father and a life of drudgery. But she never expects to be forced into a shotgun wedding with Michael Rafferty. Trapped in a marriage neither of them wants, Rose can't deny her hope that one day she and Michael will forge a love as pure and passionate as the promise of her heart.

___3605-3 $4.99 US/$5.99 CAN

Where The Heart Is. Fleeing a loveless marriage, Addie Sherwood becomes the first schoolteacher in Homestead, Idaho Territory. But within days of her arrival, she receives another proposal, this time from handsome rancher Will Rider. Although Will is everything Addie has always wanted in a man, she will not accept his offer unless he believes, as she does, that home is where the heart is.

___3527-8 $4.99 US/$5.99 CAN

Wild And Wonderful Frontier Romance
By Norah Hess
Winner Of The *Romantic Times* Lifetime Achievement Award

Sage. Pursued by the man who has murdered her husband, Sage Larkin faces an uncertain future. But when she lands a job singing at the Trail's End saloon, she hopes to start anew. And though love is the last thing Sage wants, she can't resist the sweet, seductive melody of a handsome frontiersman's passionate advances.

___3591-X $4.99 US/$5.99 CAN

Kentucky Woman. Spencer Atkins wants no part of a wife and children while he can live in his pa's backwoods cabin as a bachelor. And Gretchen Ames will marry no man refusing her a home and a family. Although they are the unlikeliest couple, Spencer and Gretchen find themselves grudgingly sharing a cabin, working side by side, and fighting an attraction neither can deny.

___3518-9 $4.99 US/$5.99 CAN

Mountain Rose. Chase Donlin doesn't hesitate before agreeing to care for his dying stepsister's daughter, his niece in all but blood. But Chase never dreams that "little" Raegan will be a blooming young woman. How is he to act the part of guardian when every glimpse of her sweet-scented flesh sets off a storm of desire in his blood?

___3413-1 $4.99 US/$5.99 CAN

LEIGH GREENWOOD'S
SEVEN BRIDES *Rose*

For penniless Rose Thorton, the advertisement for a housekeeper to cook and clean for seven brothers seems like the answer to her prayers, and the incredibly handsome man who hires her like a dream come true. But when she sets her eyes on her hero's ramshackle ranch in the wilds of Texas brush country and meets his utterly impossible brothers, even George's earth-shattering kisses aren't compensation for the job ahead of her. The Randolph brothers are a wild bunch—carving an empire out of the rugged land—and they aren't about to let any female change their ways...until George lays down the law and then loses his heart to the beguiling spitfire who has turned all their lives upside down.

___3499-9 $4.99 US/$5.99 CAN

TORRID WESTERN HISTORICAL ROMANCE
HOTTER THAN THE PRAIRIE SUN.

Fire Across Texas. Married to a fire-and-brimstone preacher, Hannah Barnes has given up all hope of love and happiness. Then three gunmen kill her husband, and she fears she will lose her life as well. But in the tender embrace of the rugged ex-lawman who has sworn to save her, Hannah finally finds a blazing passion that will start her own fire across Texas.

_3640-1 $4.99 US/$5.99 CAN

Winds Across Texas. Once the captive of a great warrior, Katherine Bellamy is shunned by decent society, yet unable to return to the Indians who have accepted her as their own. Bitter over the murder of his wife and son, Slade will use anyone to get revenge. Both Katherine and Slade see in the other a means to escape misery, but as the sultry desert breezes caress their yearning bodies, neither can deny the sweet, soaring ecstasy of their unexpected love.

_3582-0 $4.99 US/$5.99 CAN

LEISURE BOOKS
ATTN: Order Department
276 5th Avenue, New York, NY 10001

Please add $1.50 for shipping and handling for the first book and $.35 for each book thereafter. PA., N.Y.S. and N.Y.C. residents, please add appropriate sales tax. No cash, stamps, or C.O.D.s. All orders shipped within 6 weeks via postal service book rate. Canadian orders require $2.00 extra postage and must be paid in U.S. dollars through a U.S. banking facility.

Name _____

Address _____

City _____ State _____ Zip _____

I have enclosed $_____ in payment for the checked book(s). Payment must accompany all orders.☐ Please send a free catalog.